I AIN'T DOUBL'IN BACK

OR

THAT ONE LAST DAY

Growing up in an Italian-American household was special. It was particularly memorable for a boy who was given way too much freedom by his grandparents, Giuseppe and Maria, who treated him like a young Italian prince. There were fun and escapades galore, many of which could have ended in jail time for the young prince and his friends had it not been for sheer luck and Grandma's influence.

Joseph L. DeMeis

Growing up in an Italian-American household was special. It was particularly memorable for a boy who was given way too much freedom by his grandparents, Giuseppe and Maria, who treated him like a young Italian prince. There were fun and escapades galore, many of which could have ended in jail time for the young prince and his friends had it not been for sheer luck and Grandma's influence. Add to the mixture, a slightly gritty, multicultural city on the banks of Lake Erie as well as the chance association with rare and eccentric people, young and old, all who teamed up to make the total experience magical. Memories of those days, long past, unfold taking the reader back to a time when ethnic families welcomed friends to Sunday meals while their kids played outside away from technology occupied instead with breaking windows, setting off incendiary devices, pelting each other with slingshots and formulating gang fights. Mangia e mille grazie!!!

I AIN'T DOUBL'IN BACK OR THAT ONE LAST DAY

Joseph L. DeMeis

BookLocker
Trenton, Georgia

Also by Joseph— From Joe's Desk: Making A School Smile, 2011, BookLocker.com, Inc.

Similar books by other authors: *And You Know You Should Be Glad, A True Story of Lifelong Friendship,* by Bob Greene; *The Life and Times of the Thunderbolt Kid,* by Bill Bryson; *Townie*, by Andre Dubus III; *Rust Belt Boy, Stories of an American Childhood*, by Paul Hertneky.

Copyright © 2023 Joseph L. DeMeis

Print ISBN: 978-1-958889-38-1
Ebook ISBN: 979-8-88531-479-4

All rights reserved. No part of this publication may be reproduced, stored in a retrieval system, or transmitted in any form or by any means, electronic, mechanical, recording or otherwise, without the prior written permission of the author.

Published by BookLocker.com, Inc., Trenton, Georgia.

Printed on acid-free paper.

BookLocker.com, Inc.
2023

First Edition

Library of Congress Cataloguing in Publication Data
DeMeis, Joseph L.
I AIN'T DOUBL'IN BACK OR THAT ONE LAST DAY by Joseph L. DeMeis
Library of Congress Control Number: 2023904466

Cover Illustration: Canstockphoto56924970.jpg
Back Cover Illustration #1: Canstockphoto15965662copy.jpg
Ending Illustration #2: Canstockphoto79732146.jpg

Dedication

This book is dedicated to all my old pals wherever they may be.

Especially to the stars, my paternal grandparents, Giuseppe and Maria, may they rest in peace. Their influence on my life has been profound. They were characters, loved by all and generous to everyone, particularly toward me. I think about them both each day. If nothing else their influence on my life lives on through my cooking especially if I do not screw up the homemade gnocchi.

This book has borrowed from experiences drawn from the author's early life including numerous changes, additions, and adornments designed to create a more interesting tale. All names of people, except a few deceased individuals, have been changed to protect their identities. Most dates and details, e.g., names of cities and chronology of events have also been altered. The reader should not consider this book anything other than a work of fiction.

Special Thanks to my friends and family, and to David, Mary Anne, Kenny, Emily, Rett, Ruben, and Debra.

Contents

Mangia, Mangia!!!

****

"You know, weight lifting will not help you lose weight," said the louder of the two women whom I could not help but overhear as they loudly chatted while rounding the bend. This was the first time I had seen the duo and their conversation could not be ignored.

"Yes, exactly, so why should I lift weights and get so tired and sweaty for such little return," her friend chimed in.

It appeared that today my ordinary state of daydreaming while rowing was being interrupted by a couple of loud millennials attempting to complete a workout. Here they were talking openly as if no one could hear them while they promenaded closer to my workout area. I could not help but notice the women approaching as the pitch of their voices became louder and louder as they neared. The two of them, voices blaring, seemed to boom beyond the breaking point of the customary din heard throughout the rather large gymnasium. Their conversation was unusually loud and clearly understood above the white noise hum of the rowing machine where I had perched myself. Here I was again, rowing at the corner of the gym, by myself, daydreaming and wishing not only the time away but hopefully also shedding a few calories. Now, it seemed, my daydreaming mind would be occasionally redirected toward the two braggadocio women, strangers to me, whose conversation would invade my established solitude each time they rounded the track.

As the two walked closer I could not stop myself from overhearing their conversation and becoming irritated with their lack of gymnasium decorum, if there is such a thing. Almost everyone else exercised quietly while gazing straight ahead, seldom making eye contact with anyone while hoping to quickly finish their session before getting on with the rest of their day. How could these two bypass the informal rule of keeping one's conversation to themselves? Ordinarily, as I rowed, I fashioned myself as an uninterested spectator at an auto race hearing the whirring sounds of engines, courtesy of the rowing machine, crescendo as I watched the silent bodies of exercisers meander around the various strength-building machines. Now, these two magpies, who possessed the need to include everyone in their conversation, were likely going to be an unwelcome intrusion into my ordinarily solitary routine.

Yes, the rowing machines had become my salvation. They were saving me from having the top of my head blown off from being forever reminded by my wife that without cardio I could die within perhaps an hour or two. As irritating as her reminders had become it was at least reassuring that she loved me enough to want me around for a long time to come. However, I hate cardio, always have, as it is so slow and boring causing one to consider whether all the trouble is worth the added longevity. To make her happy, rowing seemed the lesser of the other cardio evils so I chose it over jogging, elliptical machines, and the tailbone torture of stationary bicycles. Yucko, as the kids would say, to all the forms of cardio, so I settled on the easiest form of exercise, at least for me, that is the rowing machine.

Fortunately, the machines were located in a corner of the gym on the side of the track away from the politically correct TVs. One TV always streamed FOX and another MSNBC. They were strategically placed side by side disallowing anyone from accusing the gym of any political predisposition. The exercise club wanted to be known as an equal opportunity streamer thus enabling some to pass their time attempting to determine another person's politics by the TV they most often focused upon. The location of the rowers, off in a corner by themselves, usually offered me the convenience to think with only the glare of the sun streaming in from the ceiling glass. Today, it appeared, would be different. My ride in solitude would be interrupted by loud talkers, the heretofore mentioned female track strollers, who seemed intent on including everyone in the gym in their conversation.

The couple kept walking and talking ending their first lap. I simply rowed while shaking my head in disbelief as the image of the two became smaller with each step away from me. My rowing procedure usually included counting sequentially in my head the seconds I rowed rather than watching the built-in counter attached to the machine. Gazing at the counter was akin to waiting for water to boil making the drudgery of rowing that much more torturous. I had only counted to 100, a rather short amount of time when the booming voice of the loudest of the two women and the one with the brightest tights once again moved into earshot. This was only their second lap and their presence was already beginning to irritate me as their boisterous conversation came back into range.

****

"We just got back from a visit to see my husband's grandmother," boomed the louder one. I decided that as long as I was going to have to listen to the duo, I would assign each one a name. I settled quickly on "Hipster" for the first one with her black-rimmed, oversized glasses.

"She's in a nursing home, you know, and not doing very well; Alzheimer's or dementia, one of those things." I could not help but hear her announce.

Her buddy, who wore a fancy striped workout shirt I named "Stripes" quickly chimed in,

"Oh, so sad. I remember my grandmother went downhill pretty fast too. I never really liked her that much a n d t h a t 's, I t h i n k, b e c a u s e s h e w a s... ..,"

The pair had begun to pick up speed so I never heard the end of that last little report. I was left gazing, once again, at them rounding the bend. Their figures once more began to get smaller as they moved further down the track. As I tried to resume my counting, 119, 120, 121, my mind could not help but be lured back into its daydream. However, the loud walking talkers, my newly named workout mates, had succeeded in embedding the theme of their conversation into my otherwise sterile thoughts. Their discussion anchored my mind on my very own history, which included my grandmother, as I began thinking of a life lived long ago.

Jovy, Jovy

"Jovy, watcha tha machine, Jovy, watcha tha machine. Be-a careful. Non fa male," a familiar phrase I will never forget. The phrase was something I grew up hearing almost every day as a child. Grandma always warned me not to get hurt, "no fa male." I could always count on hearing those words in some form of Italian slang or another.

My grandmother was a worrier. She was especially nervous and anxious when it came to me but much of it was out of love. Grandma was always there for me and also for everyone in her circle and that circle was rather large. For a person who was born in another country, she knew how to make friends and friends learned to enjoy Granny.

My wife and I decided to visit Grandma during the late spring of 1985 just as we had many times before. This time, we knew, would be the last time the visit would be her own home. There was no doubt that this was her house, one of many she owned over the years and she had recently sold it. It was a duplex, one that my grandparents had built for themselves, and was situated right on the lake, that is, on the shore of Lake Erie. The house, like all past homes she and my grandfather owned would be her last at least the last where she would reign. My grandmother had always run the show and quite a show it had always been. She was the manager, the cooking and cleaning CEO who ran things no matter where she lived. In a way, this is what made life with her and Grandpa almost always exciting. As long as she lived in her own place grandma knew that she would be in charge and most people kindly moved out of her way to run things. Grandma, by the time of this last trip, seemed aware that her power was slipping. We could tell that she knew her independence was waning. My wife and I clearly understood that from the moment we arrived. My grandmother somehow figured out that changes were on the way and had little choice but to accept them. Our visit this time would be different from all those previous visits as we immediately concluded soon after entering her house.

Grandma's ordinarily happy almost overly exuberant demeanor was this time slightly subdued. From growing up under her care I could easily recognize the difference. My wife witnessed it too and we wondered what brought the changes on so quickly. How did they materialize so fast? We concluded upon arrival that something serious must have happened to hasten the process. Something, some event, must have occurred to affect her mood and why did no one mention the situation to me? Perhaps being so close others did not notice her tempered attitude. Certainly, being in the midst of a move out of her own home was stressful but it should not have altered her personality so significantly. The noticeable shift in attitude was certainly disconcerting. We hoped the stress was the cause of her difficulty and that it would soon subside after the house was sold and she resettled herself. Then maybe Grandma would return to normal as she became comfortable in her new quarters as she would be living with my father and stepmother. Could the loss of independence be too much for her to absorb or process? Conceivable, maybe, but my wife and I knew we would have to discuss her new attitude and the reasons behind them later, privately. That is if there was time.

Without saying a word, a simple glance between my wife and I communicated that these conclusions, the stress of the move, was perhaps too easy an explanation for the personality change. The move was only partially the reason, partially the cause. We would later agree that the real culprit, the real reason for her change involved more than the move itself. For starters we knew that Grandma's health, physically and mentally, was the likely culprit, serving as the impetus for her selling the home and not vice versa. She might be upset as the sale was near but there was more to it than that. After all, her possessions were readied for purchase but it was more than the loss of possessions that was weighing her down. The move was an unconscious signal to her. She must have known it was an end to her independence, and a lack of trust in everyone served as her only defense.

Yes, a noticeable lack of trust. Grandma's new attitude toward Deb and me was different, as mentioned, and we immediately felt it upon entering the house. One clue to the difference had to do with her possessions. Where she was overly generous throughout her life Grandma was quite touchy about the things she would soon be selling in preparation for her move. We had not planned for it but there would be numerous reminders of Grandma's past life scattered among the possessions she had throughout the house. Pieces of the house itself emphasized to us just how much she and her dwellings were the same. A part of her, a story was somehow connected to even inanimate objects composing her houses. Simply entering her home through the garage told a story about who she and my grandfather once were. When visiting we always entered through the garage. Entering through the garage was simple family-composed etiquette as I grew up. It never seemed strange at the time but really, who enters a house by lifting a garage door when there are other easier more acceptable ways to get inside? The duplex had doors, both front and back, but if you were a relative or regular visitor you knew you had to lift the garage door and enter through it. It did not seem to matter for most people but if you were family, a guest, or just anyone who had visited more than once, you learned to enter through the garage. While not an entirely "Italian" thing, I associated the entry technique, right or wrong, with being Italian. It was a tidy way of doing things. Entering through the garage saved wear and tear on the ordinary entry points. Rugs remained cleaner, for example. This form of entry seemed to just fit in with all the other similar behaviors and cultural things I imagined Italians did and that I found different from those of "true Americans." For instance, front doors in any of the Italian-American households where I grew up were reserved for priests, doctors, and heads of state like prime ministers and presidents should any of them decide to make a surprise visit. Ordinary people never entered our home through the front entrance. Entering through the front door was tantamount to lunacy in our neighborhood. Ringing the doorbell to enter, if you were a friend or family member, was considered a mortal sin punishable by assigning at least a few prayers, say 15 Hail Mary's and 20 Our Fathers. I only recall ringing the doorbell one time for entry into my grandparents' home. This occurred one evening when I was maybe 12 years old. I was late coming home after dark and the family was worried about me. My father was also quite angry so he decided to teach me a lesson and lock all the doors. As the door finally opened, my dad, who was reluctant to even answer my summons, was waiting for me as I entered the room. He opened the door and immediately began waving his belt in my face and swinging it at any body part within reach. He yelled that I was way past my curfew and I had to learn to never be late again. Fortunately, I was quick and agile and thus able to maneuver to my bedroom while only absorbing a mere three smacks to my extremities. This, by the way, was one of the few times I ever had to pay the price for any of my numerous transgressions, at least after my mother had already left town. Ordinarily, I was accustomed to slithering through life scot-free no matter what crime I committed. Even so, while Dad swung his belt, Grandma was busy screaming for him to leave me alone while grabbing his arm helping to interrupt his accuracy. "Loovie (Louie), no hurt-a Jovy, OOOOH,

Loovie stoppa. Pepine (my grandfather), aiuto Jovy (Joe, help Joey)." Grandma was good at running interference for me in all kinds of situations while I grew up in a crazy haphazard way.

Anyhow, entering our home through the front door was not the way we entered. As soon as Deb and I said hello to Grandma that day in 1985 we felt as if we had run head-first into a steel wall. Even the presence of our two children, ages three and one, did little to engender a smile or a hearty, "come bella," how pretty, from Grandma's lips. Instead of the usual unqualified acceptance and joy we were used to receiving, we immediately felt something heavy in the air and it was not the telltale smell of mistakenly burnt garlic bread. In place of a smile, there was a new kind of sadness, a self-protectedness and we admitted feeling a little unwelcome. We sensed that we were going to be a burden. Without a hint, we soon found that Grandma had begun considering everyone thieves and carpetbaggers and this had to do with the selling, the auctioning off, of her life's possessions. Except for only a few, she began to believe people were out to steal her chattel. Deb and I were included and categorized as being listed on the stealing team. We represented two more people who were not trusted and it hit us squarely as we had always been at the top of her spoiling list, some of the few in her closest loved ones' inner circle.

My grandmother cared for us deeply, especially me over the years, probably much more than I ever deserved. She was forever there as my protector no matter what the circumstances and I presented many while growing up under her care. This had always been the case and there was never any doubt about where I stood with her in the pecking order of our home. Growing up with granny as my surrogate mother placed me securely at the top of the hierarchy. She willingly served as my mother's replacement after my parents divorced and she spoiled me way beyond the standard acceptable grand-parenting threshold level. If there is such a thing. Grandma cooked, cleaned, and fed me first, before others, but even though I was on the top tier of her lavishness it did not end with me. No siree, her generosity included everyone within her orbit, including all her relatives, friends, neighbors, and passersby. She even treated enemies with kindness. Anyone who wandered through her garage and into the house, even those who mistakenly rang her doorbell, were fed. Feeding people, everyone, was her moniker. She never stopped working to make everyone, especially me, comfortable and welcome. That is why her noticeable change during our visit was so profound.

The trigger for this new demeanor of hers must have been pulled while we were living our lives many miles away. Something happened to rip apart the confidence and control of this woman, my grandmother who always retained command and usually had a plan for the next step. No matter how small or big the plan, the plan was hers. The move from her home, this last residence, represented something perhaps insurmountable. It was somebody else's plan and even we, thirty-somethings at the time, could figure that one out. At first, Deb and I recognized the change but could not foresee its extent as we were now facing a woman we did not recognize anymore. We would soon grow sad about what had vanished. While we did not fully predict it or realize it at the time, her lights had grown dim and they would never fully sparkle again.

My grandmother did welcome us into her home that one day but we could tell she was distant, and that her mind appeared to be on other things. Instead of offering us food and fawning over our children, she was more focused on her possessions, valuables, and the trinkets that defined her life in America. Small talk was set aside as Grandma quickly ushered us into her den to witness for ourselves what was going on. "See, you come. 'Vedi, Jovy,' see what they do."

As we made our way into the den, one of the many rooms in her home that was always vibrant, orderly, clean, and ever so neat, we were confronted by chaos and disorder resulting from an upcoming auction. Soon, 60-plus years of accumulating gizmos, gadgets, pots, pans, dishes, towels, and sheets would be up for sale to strangers who had no real idea of the history, the significance, surrounding each piece. Strangers who would not care about an item's origin, or its story, but would soon bid on an item without knowing its background. The item would soon change hands and leave its tale behind. Lost forever would be the history behind each item. Most auctions are likely that way as they are not meant to be sociological undertakings. They are cold business transactions for all but the seller. Auctions are for buyers who have no interest nor care about the history of most things unless the item was once owned by someone like Monet, Nelson Mandela, or Elvis Presley.

Laying out before us on the den floor were articles of various sorts. The articles were not only important to my grandmother but many of them had special meaning for me too. A large portion of them represented inanimate friends acquired long ago while growing up, mainly as an only child in my grandparents' home. The items personified life too as I began to understand something about my grandmother's difficulty reconciling the upcoming auction. The items may have been packed away in attic boxes or maybe stored in closets but they remained in our home and their history was still preserved. Plus, besides my grandmother, I was the one who knew the inventory best. As an only child, due to family circumstances, I devoted way too much time assessing and mingling with most of the items scheduled for sale. I sneakily logged numerous hours scouring through the house, especially those items in our attic stored away and along with us were transported to the various homes that we owned.

Let me explain. One item, for instance, immediately at my feet was a mandoline. Not to be confused with the instrument made famous by people like country musicians, Bill Monroe or Jethro Burns, but a device used to turn flattened pasta dough into individual strands of linguine. Using this device, one needed to lay the elongated flattened dough on top of the perhaps 50 wires and run a rolling pin over the top of it. The downward pressure pushed the dough down cutting it through the wires and forming them into individual strands of pasta. The pasta would fall between the wires of the mandoline and be caught by a silver mirror-like tray below. As a child, I remember discovering the strange object for the first time and figured that it was some kind of Italian instrument. I did not know its name or true function but enjoyed strumming its strings trying unsuccessfully to play, *Oh Sole Mio,* or some other recognizable tune from its metal cords. How I enjoyed snooping up in the attic all by myself hoping to find other treasures like the mysterious mandoline.

Next to the mandoline on the floor and still packed in their original boxes were what I considered the royalty of attic items, that is, the infamous family pressure cookers. Strange to think of the two pressure cookers as being famous but they represented in a kooky and bazaar way some of the irrational behaviors one learned to expect while living in our home. The pressure cookers were more a source of an argument than they ever were used for cooking. Strangely, neither cooker was ever used making the whole situation somewhat humorous. The two pressure cookers, made of thick and heavy metal, stood as the ultimate example of why gifts should be used right away rather than stored for another day. Whenever someone in our home was in the mood for an argument or if they were searching for an example to prove a relevant point then all that was needed was to refer to the noteworthy pressure cookers.

Dad: "Ma, why don't you ever use the pressure cookers we gave you for Christmas?

Grandma: "Luigi, one-a dees-a days you see, I'm-a use."

Dad: "We bought them to make cooking easier for you."

Grandma: "Ima no lazee. Whym I need-a cook easy. Ima work-a hard. You go work-a easy, no me."

Dad: "who said you were lazy? I didn't say you were lazy or didn't work hard."

Grandma: "I no need-a fancy pot to work-a harr. My pots-a good. I work-a hard-a than you and these Madigan (American) women on-a-da TV set. Ima-a work hard, right-a Joe?"

Grandpa: "Shes-a worka hard. Why you start-a the argument o da pot. Shes-a no need-a the new pot. The pressures-a pot.

Mom: "Ma, try using the cookers. They are the modern way to cook. They were presents to make you happy."

Grandma: "Mannaggia la miseria,' Ima-a no happy? I'm-a happy. No need- the pot to make-a me happy. I'm-a cooks my way, I-a know how to cook the old-a way. Itsa the best-a way ana-how. From the old country, I'm-a learn. I no need the modern way. Old-a is-a da best."

This argument and many like it were a regular part of growing up in our home. The arguments were both serious and humorous and went on for years. Most people got used to the back-and-forth blather and the ever-present chaos they mustered.

Just A Couple of Pressure Cookers

Small things, like gifts, almost anything could easily escalate into a mild battle in our house. The battles may have been often but they were meant to be forgotten after an hour or at the most a full day. This argument was over the two pressure cookers but the reason for the next argument could be over just about anything and when it occurred, which it surely would, the two unused pressure cookers were often applied as examples by someone to help bolster their concern.

The cookers, never used for cooking, were so famous that I decided to name them. After all, they had become family lore. At an early age I strangely named them, Fred and Ethel, after the famous married couple on the popular, *I Love Lucy,* TV series of the 1950s. Fred and Ethel were portrayed as arguing over small things too and that seemed to sum up the story behind our pressure cookers. While the pots were securely hidden from sight up in the attic, their presence was always just an arm's length away especially when one wished to emphasize a point. I was told the story behind the pressure cookers many times as they were the spoiled leftovers from another thwarted attempt to provide a useful gift designed to bring a coveted smile to Grandma's face.

My father and mother, before their divorce, drove to Cleveland to buy the two cookers at the now-defunct Higbee's Department Store thinking that pressure cooking, the new style sweeping the 1950s, would make cooking quicker and easier for Grandma. The gifts, of course, missed their intended goal even though my parents' intentions were honorable. The gift, the cookers, represented one of many good-hearted attempts to make Grandma happy but ended up mostly being a focal point for a misunderstanding and surely a good old-fashioned argument. My parents' failed attempt at locating the correct gift was not alone in its failure to please my grandmother. Finding a gift to make her happy was on a scale equal to locating gold in the Sierra Madras Mountains. People tried in vain over the years to discover gifts, perhaps even something practical, to please Grandma Mary but making her happy was way too elusive for the amateur gift giver. It took a professional, maybe a fortune teller, to know what would make her happy. The pressure cookers represented a basic problem that vexed many well-intentioned people over the decades. Finding something she would covet and use was near impossible. Much of the time, I concluded after considerable analysis, that failure was mainly due to misjudging Grandma's needs from the beginning. That is, most people never really understood her from the start. If they did, using the pressure cookers as an example, they would realize that she did not want cooking to be easier. People always mistakenly wanted to make Granny's life easier in some way but that is what they envisioned was her need. What she wanted for herself was something different. All she wanted, the minimum, was a little respect. Just like Aretha Franklin, she wanted some respect and acknowledgment that someone thought of her. Cooking was her life and she did not want some invention to come along to signify that she had been doing things the hard way, the wrong way. The old way of doing things, just like it was done in Italy, the old country, was the only way food or for that matter, life should be prepared. She was simply happy that someone thought of her before they visited her and ate her food.

Each birthday, Christmas, or Mother's Day people would tax their brains trying to uncover an ideal gift for Granny. The search was on for the one present in a million that would satisfy her. She needed nothing as she had all that she truly needed. Social custom, however, prescribed that she was not respected if one showed up for her birthday or a holiday event empty-handed. Therefore, she most often silently demanded and required a gift of some sort even though it would likely never be used or appreciated. It was certain that Granny's mostly Italian friends, similar women from the old world, would likely find out that their friend, Marietta, the diminutive form of Maria, was publicly embarrassed by someone who turned up empty-handed. The news of this *faux pas*, arriving without a present, would surely sweep the Italian community by storm. This is how it was in our ethnic mainly working-class little town in the 1950s and 60s. The guilty parties would not know the significance of their error, showing up empty-handed, until much later when it was already too late. Their indiscretion, with no malice intended, would likely be the topic of conversation long after they returned home ending up potentially as a story dredged up, perhaps being discussed alongside the pressure cooker story, during some future family argument.

Understanding the gift-giving situation requires explanation. The empty-handed soul, a guest, for instance, would never be directly confronted. Confrontations were not part of the culture, in most situations like this at least. No, these matters, showing up empty-handed, were handled silently, internally. Pity the poor soul who did not know all of the unwritten rules in the Italian-American household. In this case, Marietta would not let on that a major error had just been made. She would certainly, however, never forget the slight blunder. No siree, she would not let it be immediately known that a gift, some type of tangible gesture, would have been better than no gift at all. A bad gift was likely expected, but at least there was a gift. Showing up without one, however, placed the visitor into the minor league of visitors earning them a tier-one crime. The only immediate response given to an empty-handed visitor would be a smile. However, as soon as the party went home that is when the real debate began. I can almost hear it playing in my ears, that is, granny beginning to blame herself for the mistake.

Grandma: "Niente, Hanno portato niente," nothing, they brought nothing. "Maybe they no like-a my pasta. I'm-a no make-dem a happy, maybe-ah? Maybe I no give-a dem enough?"

Dad: "Don't worry about it, Ma. It's not important. You told them you don't need anything anyhow. Some people just don't know. Maybe they forgot or are too cheap. Who cares?"

Grandma: "Cheap-a skate, maybe. I'm-a no knows nothing no mo. Everybody knows to bring soma-a-ting. Maybe a cookie, cake ana-ting. How they no know?"

The conversation concerning the giftless visitor would continue to dominate as a topic for quite some time. It was easy to see that Grandma, who had the biggest heart in most instances, was also quite complicated. Her response to situations, such as this one, illustrates just how treacherous life could be for individuals who were not equipped with the rule book. Granny tended to take things personally. One needed to learn the rules.

"Maybe they no lik-a my house-a so much-a," she might add. Or worse yet if the person had any reputation for being cheap. "They poot-a evry penny in-na da banka, them cheap son a ma betcha."

Mostly, however, Grandma was perplexed and disappointed that the rules were not followed. Everyone knows the rule, don't they? How could the empty-handed people not realize that a gift, some token of appreciation, was polite, a social norm that required strict adherence? Did the visitor not know they would be treated to a four-course meal while visiting? Did they not know they would be sent home with enough food to have another dinner the next day? Nothing brought to reciprocate the hospitality? Anything less than showing up with some small token of appreciation, a small trinket of some sort to Grandma could signal the end of civilization itself. She believed everyone knew the rules or at least should know them. For her, the rules were simply universally recognized. Were these people ignorant, cheap, or what? There had to be a reason. Oh, the conjectures that would be advanced when the coast was clear. Trying to explain to her that everyone did not understand the rules did no good. Deep down I think my grandmother, and many older Italians, in those days anyway, somehow believed that this etiquette, Italian etiquette, was universally understood. If quizzed, Grandma and her pals might even believe that knowledge of the rules is genetic or at a minimum part of some United Nations resolution. Anyone who did not adhere to the rules was considered a "chooch," that is, an idiot. Everyone should know, by adulthood, how to behave when you visit, especially during a special event, and know without saying that you will be fed until your stomach explodes.

Eventually, through body language, gossip, or perhaps even acts of God, flubbed mores of this sort were usually corrected. Those who intended to repeat their visits to Grandma's house, and many did, would learn the rules of engagement sooner or later and then, without hesitation, follow them in the future. People were always accepted into my grandparentts' home, no matter what, but those who followed the rules were especially welcomed with perks. Besides, after sampling her pasta, homemade rolls, and Italian wedding soup one was addicted and had no choice but to make repeat visits. Therefore, learning the rules was in everyone's best interest. Besides, and perhaps more importantly, everyone enjoyed my grandparents' company, especially my grandmother. Even without the food and generosity, Marietta, quirks and all, was a character, a real personality to be loved. She was entertaining, engaging, and eccentric. Everyone thus wanted an ongoing relationship with Marietta.

By the way, "Marietta" was just one of her many names, some correct, others mispronounced, that people used when addressing her. No matter how bad the mispronunciation, Grandma never corrected them. Officially she was Maria Loretta but was seldom referred to as either of those two names. Most friends referred to her as whatever sounded phonetically correct to them when they were first introduced. More than likely Italians were saying Marietta when making the introduction but it sounded different to various people. Muddy-eta was one of the most common mispronunciations but there were many others. Since no one knew Marietta was the diminutive form of Maria, all kinds of mispronunciations of her name were developed. Some referred to her as Mutty-eta or Mee-etta, while others Mary-eta, and Mootietta. One person kept calling her Mary-etti while another said, Martietta. Some played it safe and simply called her Mary or Aunt Mary or even Mrs. Many of my friends referred to her, just as I did, as Grandma and that was fine with her too. Granny was a sort of earth grandmother anyhow so why not just call her Grandma too? Italian friends often referred to her as, "Coo-mahd" from the Italian "comare," one way of saying, "godmother," or an old friend. These were the days before the TV show, *The Sopranos,* made the word, a Sicilian slang word, "Goomah," unsavory given its assigned meaning, that is, a wise guy's mistress. Believe me, my grandmother was nobody's mistress.

Likewise, close Italian friends referred to my grandfather as "Goombah," or comrade. Many called him Pepino, Pepine, Zio

(Uncle) Pepine, or simply, Joe. Few referred to him as Giuseppe. Nonetheless, I got a kick out of listening to people chop up their names, especially Grandma's names. However, mispronunciations never seemed to bother her. She took whatever name she heard right in stride. Nor did she or anyone else ever step in to suggest a correction. Not once did anyone ask Grandma or anyone in the family to spell her name. I cannot prove it but I bet people in our own family did not know how to spell the correct version of her name, that is, Marietta. One thing I always knew was that whatever name a person first began calling Grandma, right or wrong, well that was the name that stuck and they used their version forever. There could have been four people all visiting at the same time with each one repeating Grandma's name differently and each would stick to their pronunciation no matter what. I enjoyed hearing all those pronunciations and miss hearing them now.

Our house was a lively place back then. Boy was it ever and I deemed it commonplace that everyone in America had daily visitors who brought things with them whenever they visited. Items like homemade Italian bread, fruit fresh from their tree, or wine fermented down their basement. These were some of the offerings enjoyed regularly and the visitor would, in turn, leave with a plate of some goody, such as the pasta du jour, Grandpa's tomatoes, or a carafe of some exotic soup. People were always dropping by, most every day. It was a natural people-watching environment and without knowing it I was being educated in the fine art of getting along with almost anyone. Grandma's house was like the stereotypical small-town barber shop or an early form of *Starbucks,* a place where people dropped by regularly to simply catch up on life and be with others. However, the main difference between our house and a modern-day coffee shop was twofold. No computers, instead people communicated usually through loud talking, and limited listening while all the while engaging in the fine art of using numerous hand gestures to get their point across. One certain thing was that people arrived with opinions and were not afraid to announce them. Conversations in our house were not for the meek. Why should they be hidden, everyone was usually talking all at once so it was unlikely that an opinion would be heard by anyone else anyhow. Secondly, at our house, a bag full of homegrown banana peppers or perhaps a large zucchini or two bought you a cup of coffee, a torrone cookie, or on a lucky day a slice of Italian lemon cream cake. My grandparents were always prepared. No matter who stopped or when they dropped in Grandma was continually prepared to not only serve up some tasty snack but also after a heated discussion, send the visitor home with some other tasty treat. Perhaps they would leave with a whole lasagna. One never knew. So, whether or not someone came equipped with something to barter no one went home hungry or empty-handed. Most people, I would wager, left our house with more than they arrived with.

Over the years this system of give and take slowly filled our house with every conceivable type of bric-a-brac or device. Everyone did not bake bread or grow zucchini. To pay back Muttietta and Pepine for their generosity, gifts of various sorts turned up at our doorstep all the time. Everything from bread boxes to scarfs to toaster ovens was offered as payback for my grandparentts' generosity. Most items landed in the attic or if it was wool, it filled our home's numerous cedar storage areas. The smell of cedar often permeated our household, depending on which cupboard was opened. Now the smell of cedar, when confronted, immediately causes me to think of my grandmother's home. Mostly, these non-food items were stored and never used right away. New articles were to be savored, put away, and saved for a rainy day. After all one never knew when another Great Depression would hit our country. My grandfather, particularly was certain that another severe economic downturn was just around the bend and he wanted to be prepared. New things, except some food, were stored, and forced to stand in line waiting for other things to wear out. My grandparents always wanted to be prepared for any contingency like an economic downturn so storing was their way of being ready. In some ways, they were early survivalists. Sometimes, however, the system backfired since stored items could be forgotten. Stored gifts could spoil or deteriorate over time as they were simply never needed. Things rotted, styles changed, or gifts simply vanished as well but overall, the attic grew fuller. Unfortunately, many of the stored items were never used and many of them were now on the floor being readied for auctioning off. I can, nonetheless, still hear my grandfather's prediction.

Grandpa: "Jovy, yu see, these-a no good sonna-ma-betcha inna Washynotona DC they gonna make a nudda depresh (Great Depression). Yu sees Ima right some-a-day soon."

Me: "Maybe Grandpa. We'll see."

Another object I discovered, in what seemed to be the vastness of my grandparentts' overstuffed attic, seemed magical to me at the time. Snooping around up in their attic in one of our homes, one located on 21st Street, I discovered what turned out to be dad's U.S. Navy seabag. My snooping in the attic must have begun around the late 1950s more than a decade after he returned from the war. I was maybe seven or eight years old when I first discovered the bag. I remember unpacking and repacking that seabag a dozen times seemingly always noticing something new each time I opened it. See, my dad enlisted in the Navy during WW II and according to Dad, Louie, he preferred dying at sea rather than being shot on land if the occasion ever came up. The war provided my father with years of experience as the U.S. Navy provided him the chance to visit exotic places throughout the world that he would not have otherwise been able to experience. Many of Dad's favorite stories, especially as he aged, were about the war and the ports where his ship docked. The war condensed years of travel experiences into his 36 months of enlistment. Dad lived into his nineties and remained most animated when reliving his days while in the Navy serving as a gunner's mate on troop transports and supply ships.

The one story that never fails to resonate with me, especially since becoming a father myself, was the day Louie tells me he left for basic training. Dad has repeated the story to me many times explaining in detail how my grandfather, Giuseppe, accompanied him to the designated bus pick-up area in front of the old post office on Main Street in our hometown. I can only imagine the masculine emotions shared as my dad describes his father's tears as he hugged his son goodbye, telling him how proud he was for enlisting and to please return home safely. It is difficult for me to imagine sending your child, in this case, an only child, off to fight in a foreign land knowing the odds were great that he would never return. While my friends and I would eventually complain about how life had dealt us some bad cards, at least none of us had to fight a war, especially one of the magnitudes of World War II.

That seabag up in the attic for some reason held my interest even though at the time I had little idea of the circumstances surrounding the war and the sacrifices people made through their enlistment. I knew Dad was in the Navy but seeing the shirts and other articles made it so much more real. As a child, all I knew was that I was enamored with the U.S. Navy shirts, a deep blue with stripes on the collar and patches on the arms. As I modeled the shirts I imagined men standing at attention as I barked out orders. The wool pants, complete with bell bottom cuffs, seemed even to a kid too scratchy for anyone to wear. After putting them on once I quickly refolded them and returned the pants to the very bottom of the bag never to be worn again. I wondered how my father or anyone else could have worn the things in a war or for that matter anywhere else.

As I searched the contents of the sea bag I was enamored by all the interesting and strange objects inside. One object was unusually different to me as it appeared as underwear but I was not exactly sure why it was so flimsy and shaped so strangely. Starring right at me was my first confrontation with a jockstrap. Being uneducated about its use I wondered why the Navy required sailors to wear such unusual kinds of underwear especially since the wool pants were so scratchy. I remember that the strap appeared so complicated that I had no idea which side was front and which side was back. This was one article of clothing from Dad's seabag that I refused to model. Dad eventually did explain the use of a jockstrap and that knowledge would eventually come in handy in junior high school. For example, all the guys in seventh and eighth-grade gym class were forced to wear a jock by our physical education teacher the notorious Mr. Zapper. Mr. Z. was pretty old by the time we entered his class at Hawthorne Junior High as my father also had him as a teacher when he was in school. The one thing I recall most about the old teacher was how he felt quite strongly about the benefits of wearing the jockstrap during physical activity. From the very first day, Mr. Z. was obsessed with making sure each of us wore one during class. He did not leave wearing one to chance either. What he did to make sure each of us was donning a strap was to individually check each guy out before every class. Mr. Z's system included having us stand in a straight line facing him. Next, he would command, "Attention," followed by, "About face." Next, the wiry Mr. Z would begin moving down the line pulling back each boy's gym shorts, checking to see who was or who was not wearing a jock, and then letting go of the elastic waistband allowing it to zap right back in place. During each class there was always some poor sucker, maybe two, who forgot their jockstrap and they would, unfortunately, have to pay the ultimate price. Guys without jocks were required to run the infamous gauntlet. That is, they would have to run or crawl through a tunnel of guys as each one of us was required to swat the jock-less fellow with our hands as they passed by. More than one guy had to fight back tears as he maneuvered his way through the human tunnel. It all seems so antithetical that he wanted us to wear a jock for protection yet when it was forgotten a kid was pommeled and put in danger of genital injury just to remember to wear the protective device the next class. I can only imagine what would happen to a teacher now who pulled back a guy's gym trunks viewing hundreds of rumps each day while searching for a missing jock let alone send a kid through the gauntlet. Crazy stuff but true.

For years I recall wearing my dad's endless supply of white, Dixie cup sailor's caps which seemed to be the only practical thing in the bag for a kid to wear in public. The only time I saw Dad wear any of his stuff from that seabag was when he retrieved one of those white caps and wore it as he painted the house. The remainder of the bag's contents, metal belt buckles, a knife, an ammunition belt, a metal cartridge box, and many pictures of guys Dad knew as he served his country, were left as memories in that old white seabag up in the attic. I imagined that the items in the bag were happy to have someone, me, rummage through giving life back to the clothing that at one time fought in a war. Stuff in that bag was just the type of thing that captured a kid's imagination during a time when WWII movies filtered through the TV screen. The seabag was one of many objects that captured a little boy's attention as he searched around in the attic. The attic was a special hiding place for me that seemed miles away from the rest of the house and the real world.

The attic, closets, and basement in my grandparents' home were filled with many unused treasures and were a living testament to my grandparents' immigration success story, let alone their generosity. Even now I daydream about all the gifts Marietta, in particular, received decades before especially when I watch my own family open their holiday or birthday presents. I can still see Grandma Mary delicately unwrapping the decorative paper making sure not to rip it as maybe it could be used again someday. Once inside she would eventually and slowly open the box as everyone waited in anticipation for her reaction. While no one said a word most were thinking, will the gift be a success with Marietta or simply satisfy the custom of giving? People would gather around her, the family matriarch, as Marietti first pretended that the gift should not have been purchased followed by her customary frown while repeating that no one needed to buy her anything since she had everything that life required. Once the gift was revealed everyone in the room silently wagered what her reaction would likely be as she gazed upon the treasure. Grandma would never immediately reveal whether or not she liked the gift Whatever the prize, there would first be a scowl met next with an angelic, "Grazie." However, her, "Grazie" would soon be followed by, "Hai sprecato soldi," you wasted your money, a stock response to almost every gift.

As explained, everyone knew that a bad gift, even one where money was wasted, was better than no gift at all. So, to my parents' credit their attempt at finding the perfect gift for my grandmother, those pressure cookers, was thoughtful and full of honest intent but as noted finding the right gift for Grandma was almost impossible. She was a difficult and tricky person to buy for so ultimately the rejection of my parents' gift of pressure cookers should have been expected. Mom and Dad tried and failed at providing, "Ma," as they called her, with a gift she would both like and find useful. Instead, I figure that their gift, since I was not as yet born when the pressure cookers were first given, received the standard, "Hai sprecato," followed a few days later with my grandfather being ordered, when no one was around, to store the cookers upstairs to their ultimate resting place, the attic. Years later with my mom safely miles away and their divorce papers finalized, I would one day uncover those two pressure cookers for the first time. To an eight-year-old, the pressure cookers were certainly not as interesting as discovering my first jockstrap but the tale of the disrespected pressure cookers would become a humorous part of family lore for years to come.

Now, as my wife and I gazed at the objects laid out on Grandma's den floor, many that began as gifts, we could only shake our heads as we understood what the objects represented. We knew some of their history and their place in Grandma's life story. Those godforsaken pressure cookers in their original boxes were the prime example. There they played a gift to my grandmother that lasted through a divorce, a remarriage, and decades of living. How could mere objects take on an existence of their own? While we all lived downstairs, those cookers listened from above, stored in the attic, confident that they would be moved from house to house within our hometown. They and most of the other items were all leftover symbols, artifacts of a life well lived, a life lived Grandma's way.

My wife and I could also foresee the obvious as we predicted what was coming next. We could see the mistake that were the future. With good intentions, those time-saving objects, designed to make life easier were considered by Grandma as making life harder for her. Now, with good intentions in mind, selling the house and moving elsewhere was similarly designed to make life easier for her as well. Both, however, would accomplish the same thing, that is the exact opposite. Life was going to get much harder for my grandmother.

Walkers

****

Hipster: “You know, the other day in school, my daughter forgot her lunch money and she got so worked up that I had to drop everything and drive over to that school to calm her down,”

I figured it must be their third lap, maybe fourth perhaps if I counted correctly. I could have possibly daydreamed too deeply thus missing one or two of their revolutions. It was obvious that the two women were quite absorbed in their conversation as it was also obvious they were not following normal track etiquette. Here they were spread out across the track, slower traffic was supposed to walk on the outside lanes, and faster walkers and joggers were forced to bunch up behind them as they neared the curve. Exasperation was visible and becoming noticeable on the faces of a few of the joggers’ faces.

Stripes: “You would think that the teacher or counselor or someone would have noticed and calmed your daughter instead of allowing her to get so upset.”

Hipster: “No one over at the school knows anything. Thank heavens my girl smuggled her cell pho ne i n t o t h e r e s t r o o m w h e r e s h e...,”

The straight-a-way finally helped the faster walkers and joggers pass the talkative twosome that was hogging up the track making it difficult for others to pass. The two socialites in tights were so absorbed in their conversation that they did not notice the traffic jam they were creating. As the track traffic soon smoothed out I returned to my thoughts. I kept focusing on that visit to my grandmother's house reliving the personal sadness that we confronted on that day. She was not the grandmother I knew. It seemed the Grandma I knew was somehow replaced by an imposter. The one I grew up with would have invited my wife and me to help ourselves to whatever we wanted from her floor before it was sold at auction. She would have said,

"Jovy, take-a what-a you want, and put away so no ones-a sees." Whether it was the best piece of meat for dinner or a $20 bill she would always give me things, the best stuff while placing her index finger up to her lips, smiling and communicating, "Shhhhhhhhhh, non dice a nessuno (don't tell anyone)!"

Instead, my wife and I got the notion that Mootietta now considered us the same as others. Opportunist is what we had become in her mind even though she had no idea of the word's meaning. Always perched on top of Grandma Mary's pedestal, I was now relegated to the same rung as everyone else or maybe worse, as a potential thief wanting to take advantage of her. I found that Deb and I were not the only ones on the list. Almost everyone in her mind was out to steal her belongings before they were placed up for sale. Never, ever was I on Grandma's suspicion list but now here I was included in a group of people she believed was out to trick her. Marietta had, we later learned, begun to imagine that her things were disappearing, worse yet, being stolen by the people she previously trusted. She was losing control and was silently becoming aware of it and her belongings were all she had left to control. It was almost as if each possession represented a piece of her power and losing each item represented a chipping away of her soul. She was once quite formidable, the matriarch of the family dominant over both family, friends, and husband. Now sadly, where trust, love, and acceptance were once the norm paranoia had ebbed in to fill the void.

Let me back up from this tale and explain that most of my grandmother's life was filled with self-assurance and much success. Until her later years, she was a satisfied woman and her happiness was simply infectious. It was, however, her kindness and generosity that most defined her. Her story, really my grandparents' story, began well before I was born during an era considered by some to be part of what has become known as, "The Greatest Generation," a term used by Tom Brokaw who coined the phrase in his book by the same name. Their story, the one I know, my grandparents' chapter per se, is the one that I enjoy recalling. If I was an imitator I would focus and concentrate on my grandparents and their life because recalling them puts me in a happy place. They would be my focal point. Their story, the one explained here, began with my grandfather.

Records indicate that he, Giuseppe, Pepine, Grandpa I mostly called him, had initially immigrated to the United States at age 17, leaving his small village, Tussio, "belonging to the municipality of Prata d'Ansidonia, in the province of L'Aquila, region Abruzzo," in Italy? He left Tussio to travel to Naples where he and many of his generation embarked on ships bound for the USA. The first time he sailed to the United States was on March 15, 1909. He left Italy to find work, as did many Italian immigrants since meaningful employment was near impossible to find anywhere on the Italian peninsula. Between 1900 and 1910 about two million Italians immigrated to the United States to escape poverty and a slumping Italian economy. Historical statistics reveal that between 1880 and 1924, more than four million Italians immigrated to the United States with half that number heading to America around the same time as my grandfather. Giuseppe and his brother, Eugenio, somehow found work as coal miners in Pennsylvania and lived and worked for years in the Monessen, PA area. How he obtained the job has been lost to history because I never asked the question or perhaps I did not pay attention to that part of his story when it was told.

My grandfather enjoyed telling anyone who would listen to him about all the hard work he performed during his early days as a miner in Pennsylvania weaving tales about the men from various European countries who worked by his side. One of his most interesting stories became a family legend and it occurred during his time in Monessen. My grandfather was rooming with his brother who emigrated with him. Working long hours in the mines and saving his money, Giuseppe hoped that one day he could return home to Italy and live comfortably or maybe remain in America to raise a family of his own. During his time in the mines, Grandpa said that one evening, after working many hours, there was a knock on his apartment door. When he answered the knock he was confronted by a local member of the "Black Hands," an Italian extortion group that sprang up in the early part of the twentieth century. It is said that one of the ways they terrorized people was to leave a black handprint, often from coal dust, on the doors of miners to indicate that a portion of a worker's payday needed to be handed over to a gang member as a form of protection. While the Black Hands extorted money from a variety of men, they concentrated most of their attention on fellow Italians. The wise guy who confronted my grandfather told him that he expected to receive a percentage of Giuseppe's pay each week so that nothing bad would happen to him.

"Giuseppe, vuoi stare al sicuro, non tu," you want to stay safe don't you.

Sharing his pay would keep my grandfather safe from any unforeseen accidents and secure his protection according to the sinister visitor. He went on to state that if Giuseppe did not pay up there would be no guarantee of his future safety, "Capisce!"

I do not remember what my grandfather's immediate response was to the crook's threat but I know he never intended to comply with the fellow's demands. My grandfather was a kind, quiet man most of the time but he could be stubborn and tough when he wanted. Some people knew that Giuseppe had a temper if pushed too far so it was not unexpected that Grandpa was not about to share any of his money with a crook. He had worked too hard to give part of his weekly check away without a fight. What Grandpa did instead of caving into the demand of Mr. Black Hands was to become prepared for the criminal's next visit. When the Black handed fellow came around to collect his first installment my grandfather showed him into his apartment. Instead of the cash, Gramps produced the barrel of a recently purchased German Luger, his "Pistola." My grandfather liked to refer to the handgun as, "La mia piccola pistola," my little pistol. Grandpa's story ended with him explaining to the thug that all he would get next time he came around was, "A bullet in the head," that is, "una pallotta in testa." Grandpa was mainly a mild-mannered fellow but I always knew that he was also not the type of guy who would take anyone's shit so I figured his story was true.

Growing up I was always on the lookout for that pistol but never located it. That was probably a good thing. Rumor has it that the Luger was safely hidden for many years, just in case it was needed again, but its whereabouts and its final resting place were never divulged. How my grandfather was able to scare off the Black Hands member without repercussions also remained a mystery. Pepino survived the threat in Monessen, PA and his tenacity paid off as he lived to fight another day.

It was soon after this incident that Giuseppe Luigi DeMeis became a citizen of the United States on November 9, 1914. This was a few years before he decided he had saved enough money to travel back to Italy to find a wife, an Italian bride who fortunately turned out to be my grandmother, Marietta. Records on his passport application do not mention his intention to find a wife and marry as a reason for returning to Italy. Instead, documentation indicates that he was departing for Tussio on September 15, 1921, to visit his parents. He was around 29 years old at the time having worked in the United States for some 12 years by then. Records further indicate that he was to remain in Italy for no longer than six months or approximately until the middle of March 1922.

There was limited mixing of cultures or religions during those times so marrying someone other than an Italian catholic gal was never really considered. He must have had it planned from the start that when the time came and after he had saved enough money to feel secure, he would marry someone just like himself, maybe someone who was also from his hometown. How he chose my grandmother is unknown but in those days marriages were not dependent solely on love as much as convenience, pragmatism, and survival. Whether it was love at first sight or arranged, no one knows. Most likely their marriage was not left to chance. Perhaps it was informally arranged first and then love was expected to follow. Their marriage lasted until my grandfather died in 1976, a total of 55 years, obviously a much longer period than my parents, whose marriage dissolved after less than seven. So, who is to judge whether love is better than convenience?

Zio Pepino was 12 years older than my grandmother when they married. Their age difference never seemed strange to me as my father was a decade older than my mother, as well, when they got hitched. What did surprise me was how well my grandparents got along seldom arguing or complaining about each other or life in general. Perhaps this was accomplished in a way, as my grandparents were a living, breathing, marital joke as my grandfather simply said yes to all my grandmother's directives and demands. That attitude worked well for them serving as a major reason for their marital success. Joe and Mary, ever since I can remember, were continually driven toward one main goal and that was making life, as simple as theirs was, comfortable for themselves and their family. That doesn't mean that they never complained or assigned blame. Like anyone, there were times when life irritated them too. Grandpa's blood boiled, for example, whenever he read about an elected official voting against some issue that he was passionate about, for instance, social security. His favorite phrase was, "They should-a be all-a fired out." Anyone in government who voted against a working-class issue should be fired, dethroned, tarred, and feathered according to the philosophy of Goombah Pepine. He read the local newspaper daily, cover to cover, often muttering to himself about government inefficiency. It was commonplace to hear Joe mumble rather loudly from his built-in desk next to the TV, calling some official or another, "That-a no good a-son-ne-ma-betcha." This was often followed by my grandmother yelling, "Pepino, chiudi la bocca, stare zito," that is, Joe, close your mouth, keep quiet. Reading the paper was soon followed by watching the nightly news on TV and shouting at the box as if the newscaster could somehow hear his complaints. "All-a crooks, alla no good." Gramps seldom had a positive thing to say about politicians.

Like most young people, I was too self-absorbed and mostly uninterested in hearing my grandparents' life stories about emigrating to America. I was unfortunately wrapped up with being a kid, then a teen, then a busy father of two little children of my own to bother listening very closely to them. It took time and maturity to appreciate what I missed and to do a little research every so often on my own into their lives. They were part of history and their achievements were somewhat heroic. As I searched the Internet for information about them I wanted to kick myself for not asking more questions about their past before they died. For instance, why did my grandfather and grandmother, newlyweds from the same hometown, travel separately back to the United States? He arrived back in the United States via the SS Aquitania on April 30, 1922, while his new bride arrived in New York on May 13, 1922, via the Minnekahda, a ship carrying 2,150 passengers. There were so many questions I could have asked but did not. Now that information is lost in time.

I have often imagined what it was like for my grandfather, still, a teen, to embark from his home in Italy and move to a new country without a secure job or command of the English language. Similarly, I wonder how my grandmother, a 17-year-old woman at the time, went about setting sail across the ocean, pregnant and by herself, to a country that would soon be her permanent home. Yes, she was pregnant, as well, with my father. Marietta must have been somewhat scared but also excited about traveling to a new country determined to make a good life for herself and her new family. Did she know that she would leave Italy and never return home again? Certainly, she must have known that her husband, Giuseppe, intended to remain in the United States since he had already become a United States citizen. As she boarded the ship in Naples did she know that she would never see her mother and sisters, in person or in photographs, ever again? She would, fortunately, see her father,

Antonio, as he would travel to our hometown in Ohio many times during the Great Depression. While saving his money my great-grandfather lived with my grandparents working long enough during each visit to make enough cash to send back home to support his family.

Fortunately, my grandmother would eventually get to know two of her younger brothers, both born close to when she emigrated to America. Rudolpho was born only a few months before she set sail, and later still, Domenico was born in Italy months after she had already settled in the United States. Sadly, Grandma would never see or speak directly to her two sisters or mother in person again. Instead, communication would be accomplished only through letters tucked securely into packages of goodies regularly sent back and forth across the Atlantic. Grandma habitually mailed blankets, sheets, and other treasures, purchased from our local JCPenney Department store, back to Italy. In return, we received a healthy supply of Italian delicacies like Torrone candies and various types of biscotti in addition to other small trinkets, such as rosaries and scarves.

Torrones were a favorite of mine and they always seemed to be available in our home particularly due to the package swaps. The candies seemed to remain edible for months, although arriving somewhat chewy after they arrived at our home. These were nougat candies mysteriously wrapped in decorative tin foil with each one tucked away in its little printed box depicting images of saints with unrecognizable Italian words written on the side. The candy's name, I found out later, is derived from a Latin word meaning "toast" as another main ingredient in the candy is toasted nuts. I marvel at their present availability at supermarkets and specialty stores almost everywhere. Once a rarity found only in Italian-American homes, I was recently surprised to see a stack of Torrones on the counter next to some Bic lighters at a local pharmacy. All I could wonder was, is nothing sacred?

I also wonder if Grandma knew early on in life that although her name, Marietta, was the diminutive form of Maria, she would succeed in becoming anything but diminutive in the eyes of the many people she would befriend in her new country. Now as an adult, I continue to marvel over so many things, such as, what did my pregnant grandmother do for those two weeks on the SS Minnekahda upon departing from Naples? Did she meet other Italian women traveling to the new land with similar goals in mind? I wonder how she traveled from Tussio to Naples and what it must have been like saying goodbye to her family. Perhaps I should have listened and asked more questions. I once had a professor in college who repeated over and over in class something like, "If should've's and could've's were raisins and nuts, every day would be Christmas." I force myself not to dwell on what I should have asked instead cherishing the memories that remain.

Without much of a formal education, my grandparents were able to achieve so much during their lifetime. They, like many immigrants, took risks to better themselves and in the process, they sacrificed much. Perhaps in so doing, they realized the importance of raising their own family and making sure that their values of hard work and achievement were transferred down the line. One of the ways they did this was to continually emphasize the importance of education. My grandfather remained quite proud that he was able to attend school long enough to complete what he indicated was the eighth grade. He said he wanted more schooling but his family situation did not allow for it. One of the cherished remains of my grandfather's life is a document dated "20, del mese di Novembre, del anno 1905" (November 20, 1905) handed out when he was 13 years old. The

"Certificato Degli Esame Complimento Dall Obligo Dell' Instuzione Elementare Inferiore," was a formal certificate listing his elementary or lower grade exam results. The report indicated that he successfully mastered all subjects, and thus he passed his lower grade experience. Giuseppe earned test scores ranging from a six out of 10 in history to a 10 of 10 in "Arithmetica." Strangely, while he was proud of his education he never showed anyone this certificate while he was alive and I did not obtain the document or know of its existence until it was given to me by my father.

Both of my grandparents appreciated the importance of education even though my grandmother may have only attended school through third grade. My father earned a high school diploma but my mother dropped out of school never obtaining a degree for herself. My family's goal was always for me to attend college, be smart, and grow up to be somebody. I never recall a time when I did not plan on attending college because it was simply embedded in my upbringing. College was an expected part of the timeline, a milestone to achieve, with the process being part of life's continuum. Education was expected, especially enrolling in college, so there was never a doubt that I would do so.

My grandparents were two hard-working people unafraid of back-breaking work. They began working the minute they stepped foot off of their respective ships and continued to work hard until the day they died. Both were stocky with my blue-eyed grandfather being 5'6' and barrel-chested and my brown-eyed grandmother similarly built and standing perhaps 5'2' while wearing her trademark unzipped black rubber boots. There was never a day that I would define as being wasted by that duo. Days were filled with work of some sort or another, not unlike the work ethic of most Italians and others who emigrated from their homeland. I never remember them

standing about wondering what to do next and complaining about being bored. I never heard them say, "There is nothing to do, we are bored." Instead, it was more likely to hear:
"Jovy, non siamo annioati. E ora di lavorare," (that is, Joey we are not bored. It is time to work).

One of my grandfather's favorite phrases, something he often heard from a fellow worker hailing from some European country was, "Gotta work hard to make-a da bread." Pepine would then chuckle as if he exposed the phrase to the world for the very first time. For him, those words always rang true.

Both of my grandparents had their passions helping to keep them active. Giuseppe had his gardening. He loved his garden and religiously wore his straw hat to shield his light skin from the sun. Grandpa could have easily been confused with the aging Don Corleone, the fictional Mafioso, who was filmed while gardening in, *Godfather* 1. I let everyone know that Grandpa wore his hat in the garden long before the film depicted the aging gangster wearing his. I never knew where he acquired the hat thinking that perhaps it was left behind by a visitor because he seldom went shopping. As long as he was supplied with a steady supply of cow manure, the real stuff, for his garden, he was happy. I can only remember one time that Grandpa went shopping and it turned into a family tale.

Grandpa and a close friend, Joe Cappello, somehow ended up in a department store called, *O'Nemos's,* which was located near their home. Joe was one of the many colorful characters who regularly dropped by our house along with his wife, Feliciana. They seemed to stop by for food, drink, and conversation almost every weekend. Joe was known for many things including producing a red wine that smelled and tasted a lot like old socks while carrying a punch akin to aged whiskey. Joe was also known by those closest to him as a harmless petty thief and my grandparents attributed this proclivity to being from Naples, Italy where many Italians, including my grandparents, believed the art of stealing was first conceived. I likened Joe to a crow. If it shined Joe would take it whether it was valuable and if he needed it or not.

Both of the "Joe's" found themselves hanging around the men's department at *Onemo's* waiting for Marietta and Feliciana to complete their shopping. After the two women finished shopping the two couples began walking out of the store. As the two guys walked through the electric door heading out to the parking lot, my grandfather noticed that his friend Joe was wearing a new hat and Grandpa wondered when Joe paid for it. Joe had never left Grandpa's side while they were in the store so how did he pay for his new head attire? My grandfather at first figured that the sale must have taken place rather quickly or perhaps Feliciana bought it for him. Then it hit my grandfather especially when he next noticed that the price tag was embarrassingly hanging out from the back of Joe's new hat as it began flapping around for all to see. Of course, the purchase of Joe's hat never transpired. Joe, a stolen fedora on his balding head, kept on walking through the parking lot to his car as if nothing different or illegal had occurred. My grandfather just about pooped his pants because stealing anything was simply so foreign to him. Grandpa was an honest man who would never break a law even if incarceration was not possible. Grandpa earned a good laugh after his experience with Joe once they were safely home. He swore that he would never go shopping with Joe Cappello again and to my knowledge he never did. Many stories included Joe and Feliciana, two wonderful people, over the years, and this colorful couple was just two of the reasons that living with my grandparents was so interesting.

Upon first hearing the stolen hat story I surmised that possibly it was Joe Cappello who supplied my grandfather with his gardening straw hat. I will never know. What I did know then, as I know now, was that as long as Grandpa, Pepine, had his tomato plants and a shovel he was content. He was in heaven as he quietly spread cow manure throughout his garden and enjoyed pulling off the suckers from his tomato plants. He could fiddle in his garden from morning until night with our fat wiener dog, Ginger the Dachshund, by his side. Ginger, by the way, was as fat as a walrus and looked like a mortadella sausage due to regularly slurping up copious amounts of leftover pasta The pasta was simply plopped in her bowl and she would scarf and slurp at it until each strand was down her throat. All that remained was the tomato sauce caking against her snout. Once finished, people would enjoy watching Ginger begin licking her chops until all the remaining sauce disappeared. She served as good entertainment especially for visitors witnessing the event for the first time. Any time that there were leftovers, and there were always leftovers, Ginger received her treat and she was known to eat anything placed in her bowl. Our chubby pet led a long and healthy life despite being extremely obese. She proved what most Italians already knew and that was that a Mediterranean diet was the way to assure health and longevity.

While Ginger the Dachshund and people like Joe Cappello were just a couple of the daily characters in my grandparents' life, my grandmother was the main character. By the time I came around, she seemed old but I guess people in midlife in the 1950s and 60s seemed much older than they do today. Grandma was a personality in every way. Before saying a word and without knowing her reputation her appearance left an indelible impression on most people she met. Starting with a full head of gray hair, always gray with tinges of white sprinkled in, the next characteristic one noticed was her matching gray plastic framed glasses. Those glasses, never fitting properly required continual readjustment as they were usually situated perched on the end of her nose. She must have spent half her day pushing the glasses back up to where they were supposed to be on her nose. While she enjoyed seeing medical doctors Grandma would never buy an expensive pair of glasses from an optical store preferring to buy whatever was on sale at the local 5 & 10 cent stores like S.S. Kresge's or later W.T. Grant Co. In addition, she kept regular appointments at her beauty parlor but she would have nothing to do with changing the natural color. She possessed a thick head of hair that was usually pulled back and held away from her eyes with a set of black bobby pins.

Like most Italian women of her generation, she was short and stout, sporting a hefty bosom all of which was supported by sturdy hips and muscular legs. If she were able to run fast enough Grandma would have made a good lineman, most likely a guard or defensive nose tackle on the local semi-pro football team. One also never found her at home without her signature torn floral dress, usually a matching shade of gray worn over an equally ripped white slip. She most often wore an apron too and one could usually tell what was on the day's menu simply by seeing what stains were on the front of that gown. Flour meant bread, tomatoes meant sauce, oil meant a fried pork chop, and others. One of the stand-out features of Granny's wardrobe, distinguishing her from almost anyone else, her friends included, was the fashionably unzipped black faux leather boots that I previously mentioned. The boots were worn without socks and this helped them to slosh about and make a familiar clomping sound as she walked almost continuously up and down her linoleumed cellar steps to the spot where all her cooking took place. Many arguments took place over her insistence on wearing those unattractive black boots. She claimed they kept her feet warm as she stood on the cold cement (that she referred to as the “la cheement”) basement floor. She went on to explain that the boots were comfortable given her numerous corns and callouses found on her seemingly oversized feet. Dad and others never stopped trying to get her to wear something else, on the pretext that the boots were unsafe and that one day she would fall and hurt herself, but I knew that day would never come. She wore those boots until her last day in her own home. When one pair of boots wore out the world would stop until another pair was located. Usually, if all else failed, a quick stop at Jacuzzi's Shoe Store downtown would supply a perfect replacement pair.

The boots were great insulators against the chill of the basement's cement floor where Grandma Mee-etta performed her daily cooking, cleaning, and clothes washing. Every Italian I ever knew did their cooking in the basement allowing only a few things like coffee or toast to be prepared upstairs on the seldom used pristinely kept stove. The upstairs stove, oven, and countertop in our home were mainly installed for display and had to be kept spotless and sanitary at all times. One never knew when someone would need a quick appendectomy or a mother would go into labor thus requiring the use of the counter for delivery. Even in Italian homes, emergency room procedures would not be relegated to the basement. They could perhaps take place upstairs in the kitchen if necessary.

The upstairs stove was almost a museum piece or an heirloom in our home as it was never intended for serious cooking. My grandparents lived in their last home for almost 30 years and the upstairs kitchen oven was never used. Not even once. She instead clomped up and down her linoleum cellar steps numerous times each day because cooking was the primary purpose in her life and one of the main reasons to face each day. Granny's whereabouts were never a

mystery as long as she wore the boots since the flapping of those clodhoppers could be heard from many yards away.
Rounding out Maryetta's appearance was her lack of teeth. Strangely, she did not look so bad without them, nothing like the skinny guy with one lower tooth that is often associated with The Rivinton's song, *Papa Oom Mow Mow.* She had at least two sets of false teeth that were seldom worn and could be easily located in a cup of water on top of her dresser that she referred to as her "Comeau." The only time she wore the teeth was when she either attended a wedding or especially a funeral which unfortunately at her age presented itself with increasing frequency.

Between members of the family, I can still hear the continual entreaties for her to dress differently and pay better attention to her appearance. My father, mother, and later stepmother, Hanna, would continually complain directly or behind her back by saying something like,

"Ma, why don't you wear your teeth? You would look so much better when they are in your mouth and not on your Comeau."

Their response would be when Grandma would say the teeth hurt her mouth,

"Well, you have to get used to them and they will feel more comfortable."

Just as she ignored their entreaties to use the pressure cookers and wear her false teeth, she ignored all their attempts to persuade her to do other things. For example, Aunt Mary simply preferred wearing old dresses, usually worn out in some way, saving the new ones for some special day.

"Ma why don't you wear a newer dress? Your closet is filled with new dresses."

Her response to their requests, if she gave more than a scowl, was to simply say something like, "Ma, sto lavorando, ill vestige si sporchera," (that is, "but I am working, the dress will get dirty").

There was no way to change her mind about her everyday appearance and herein lies another example of how people proved their lack of understanding of what made Mary tick. Most people never seemed to get it either. My family tried continually and in earnest to coerce Grandma to change into what their image of an elderly woman should be. Somehow I figured out at an early age that their attempts were futile. Their entreaties meant nothing to Granny except to irritate her and there was little chance that their ideas would ever be accepted. There was practically no way she would ever comply or slightly bend for many reasons but mostly because she thought of herself as the boss. No one was going to tell her how to dress or behave. I concluded that almost from the start likely because she and I spent so much time together. She also confided in me because I never tried to convince her to change much of anything. While there may have been many reasons she and I got along, it was likely my lack of pressuring her to change things, like that tattered old dress and especially those black boots, that kept me in good stead with her.

Saying my grandmother and I got along, that is saying it lightly. I already mentioned that I was a very spoiled kid and she was the one who protected and spoiled me the most. I could do no wrong and as a result, I got almost anything from her that I wanted. Did I take advantage of that status? You bet I did and maybe our silent agreement was for me to listen with her end of the bargain being to continue to spoil me. Given the poor relationship between my eventual stepmother and me, that agreement was easy to hold up from my end.

"Il mio vestito non e troppo strappado," my dress is not too ripped she would plead to me when no one was around.

"Sure, Grandma, your dress is fine. Don't let them bother you," I would respond whenever she was pressured to change.

Marietta would then continue to harp about the criticism leveled against her until it finally cleared her system. Usually, it took another topic to emerge before she could move on. It was not unusual for a dirtier, more torn "vestito," to be worn the next time Hanna visited as this was done just to irritate Hanna and prove who was the boss. These little mind games were commonplace in our home and even the CIA could not have created a better psychological war technique than some of those tactics employed between Hanna, Granny, and me. Grandma Marietta, in my opinion, was the local master at winning little arguments while showing no weakness to anyone, perhaps except me, the spoiled little Italian prince.

I was continually aware of being an Italian prince too, being almost beyond spoiled. My behavior was quite evident to the many visitors, friends, and relatives, who regularly visited and some were not so subtle regarding their disdain for my behavior. Somehow, I managed to either overhear their criticism or recognize from their body language just how they felt about me. I could tell that they found my grandmother's overprotective nature toward me inappropriate but most did not dare intervene. While I assumed I was being judged, the judgments had little effect on me. I continued with my demands, often whining to get my way and refusing to change. I simply ignored any noticeable direct or indirect appraisals of my actions. Oh, what a bad boy was I. As an adult, I am not proud of my spoiled ways, but you try to get as much as you can when you are a kid. If nothing else I learned to recognize people's judgments regarding my behavior and mainly migrated away from them and found a way to ignore their opinions. In this way, I was very much like my grandmother, stubborn. And while some people negatively judged my behavior others pitied the little boy who lost his mother through a divorce.

I recall a few people, mostly women, friends of the family, who overlooked my attitude and tried nurturing me, providing care that they realized an absent mother could not. I understood, sort of, their intentions but I mostly remained stoic, rejecting their kindness. I did not fully know why I behaved like that toward their help but I did. For me, it was tough to show the type of emotion their kindness should have engendered so some gave up on me while others seemed to understand and persevere. I guess I did not want to feel different and their attention was making me face that fact. These women did everything from tucking me into bed at night to taking me, perhaps with one of my friends, on outings. I did enjoy the outings as they seemed less invasive and personal. I recall going to things like swimming pools and amusement parks with them as they tried caring for me in ways they felt my grandparents were unable to perform. Maybe I kept people at a distance, including my grandmother, because I did not want anyone to feel sorry for me. Nonetheless, I was disappointed with my lack of appreciation at the time but continued to refuse to change. I was a little hard-headed type of guy living up to the Italian term often used in jest, that is, "testa dura." Yep, I was the "testa dura," the hard-headed kid, the term my grandparents kiddingly often called me.

While many adults frowned upon my behavior, most reasonable people admitted that my parents' splitting up had at least something to do with my being a little spoiled prince. Divorce in the 50s was not as common as it is today. It would be some years yet before the divorce bandwagon would begin. In a sense, I was an early pioneer in the world of kids from divorced families. Without knowing it I was becoming socially attached to the day's headlines, part of the newly divorced generation, part of the 50% statistic, that is, everyone would soon realize that half of all marriages ended in divorce. I was part of a movement, a trend. Slowly, as divorce became commonplace I would feel less guilty for being the innocent remains of a screwed-up marriage. However, that would not occur for more than a decade after my parents split, so I lived with a little guilt and shame. To this day I still remember the look on the faces of a few upper-class neighbors who communicated their superiority by quizzing me about the circumstances surrounding my family situation.

"Now Joey," one asked. "How's your mother, I haven't seen much of her these past few weeks," knowing fully well she had taken a bus with my sister to Philadelphia and never returned.

It would not be long before I disliked the phony neighbors and Philadelphia as much as W.C. Fields disliked the city. Still, many others feigned putting up with me as I became the little Italian prince protected by my grandmother. I felt I knew which side people were on and I placed them in one category or the other while I did not show it on the outside, however, inside I knew who cared for me and who did not. Maybe this is why I did a lot of people analysis as a child. Perhaps my early analysis catalyzed my eventual becoming a psychologist as an adult. The divorce was a game changer that sent my personality development in a new direction, which I felt differed from other kids my age.

I should explain what is remembered about the divorce. There were many reasons why my parents split and my grandmother served as only one contributing reason for their break up. This conclusion is dependent, of course, on who is doing the play-by-play. My mother blamed my grandmother while my grandmother and father blamed my mother. Certainly, there was more than one person or reason for their eventual split and I got over blaming people way back in my teens. For the most part, I did not suffer as much as others from my parents breaking up. Sure, I whined about it a whole bunch as a teen but when my mom left town for good, Grandma took over and gave me everything a kid could ever want. I was overindulged, I have made that clear, and if anything, I felt a little guilty for not missing my mother. That information was never revealed to anyone at the time.

What could a seven-year-old do about the situation anyway? What did I know about Mom and Dad's relationship? I knew they often argued as we traveled from Giuseppe and Maria's home to our new house a couple of miles away. Besides, I was too busy drowning out their yelling by wrestling around in the back seat of my father's 1951 green Chrysler Windsor Deluxe with my three-year-old sister, Lorena. Perhaps by wrestling with her I was trying to refocus the argument away from them to my hammerlock hold on my sister's head.

"Joey, leave your sister alone," they would scream before my father accused my mother of spending too much money and forcing our move from my grandparents' home on 21st Street into what was defined as an "expensive" new house. Didn't she realize how often he got laid off from his job at the National Tube?

"What is wrong with living with ma?" he then barked.

My mother, not to be outdone, would respond by blaming my father for not standing up to his mother's intrusive, controlling attitude.

"How is it that I am never right and you always take your mother's side" she would yell.

Mom would invariably follow up by pointing out how she was never able to cook the family meals because we were continually eating pasta dinners with my grandparents. Dad would then make things worse by sharing,

"Why you don't like to cook anyhow, you never learned."

It would not be long before one of them, out of frustration, would turn around to smack me for continuing to clamp down on the hammerlock hold on my sister's head. Parents often used corporal punishment back in the 50s. It was the thing to do and I got my share of spankings early on as a kid, especially from my mom. That all stopped after she left as my grandmother never raised a hand to me. While driving us home, even my father reached back, seemingly nightly, with his right hand as I dodged his attempts to smack me as we careened down the road toward our home on 9th Street. Years later, I would learn that there was a word in psychology for Mom and Dad's behavior toward me: displacement. They were angry with each other but took it out on me, a fellow who was three years older than Lorena.

Most likely, my parents' marriage was doomed from the very start. So why all the ruckus? It all began years earlier when my father, a handsome 27-year-old, and his equally good-looking and single cousin of approximately the same age decided to enroll in a photography school in Philadelphia. When they were not in class they frequented a small diner in the center of the city where it turned out my mother was a waitress. She was pretty and young as she was only 17. Dating and ultimately marrying a 17-year-old was Dad's first mistake with Mom. But Mom was young and perhaps did not know any better. Times were different then, or so it seemed to me, so their age difference, while a variable, should not be compared with today's standards. Besides, more important issues than age messed with their harmony.

Mom always had a winning personality so I am sure she easily attracted the attention of the two small-town guys, Dad and his cousin Teo from Ohio. Her mother, my Philadelphia grandmother, was an immigrant from Ireland and also worked at the restaurant along with her third husband, the cook, an easygoing fellow as I recall it who coincidentally had the same first name as my dad, that is, Lou. While he treated me nicely he was not so nice toward my sister. I did not find this out until adulthood. Instead, I felt negative about my Philadelphia grandmother as she seemed to always pick on me when we visited. I could never do anything right for her. Imagine what she would have done to me after I morphed into a spoiled Italian prince.

One thing led to another and one day my father and mother somehow decided to marry. Getting married the way they decided to get hitched was likely the second major error that they made in their relationship. Nonetheless, love was in the air as they eloped, marrying in a civil ceremony while in Philadelphia.

Let's stop and analyze all the reasons thus far that serve as significant reasons this marriage was not going to work. First, let us begin with what seems like the most obvious, that is, the age difference.

Back in the early 50s age differences between marriage partners were not so unusual. In their situation, however, the age difference was a mild issue due less to chronological age and more to do with developmental age. My mother, at age 17, had more energy and different needs than my father. This became much clearer soon after their marriage. Dad was more of a stay-at-home with-family kind of guy whereas Mom preferred movement, dancing, partying, and travel. If this were the only issue affecting their marriage it certainly could have survived. A greater reason for their soon to become failed marriage had to do with how a 17-year-old daughter of an Irish immigrant was going to stand up to an Italian matriarch whom she met for the first time after marrying the matriarch's only son. Surprise! My dad was a smart man so how was it that he could have believed that eloping with a 17-year-old Protestant Irish-American from the tenements of Philadelphia would be accepted back in his Catholic Italian-American enclave situated in the Midwest is beyond my comprehension. He went to his grave believing that eloping was the cheapest, most prudent thing he could have done and that the elopement did not interfere with Mom and Grandma's relationship from the beginning. But why complain? Where would I be had they not eloped that fine day in July 1950, approximately 9 months before I would be born? Yes, people counted the months between their marriage and my birth. Geez, who wouldn't? I have never had any indication that I was conceived before the elopement but what difference would it make nowadays? It certainly gave people a bit to gossip over back in 1951.

My mother did her best to make the marriage work. She moved in with my grandparents after agreeing that she and my father would save money and later buy their own home. But there were rules, unwritten ones that an Irish girl from Philly could not have possibly understood, that is until it was too late. Once they moved in with my grandparents, however, Mom and Dad became living examples of the Eagles, *Hotel California* song, you know the part where checking out is okay but you are never really going to be allowed to leave. My grandmother simply believed that every family should live under one roof to save money. It made sense to her so it should make sense to everyone else. That was Grandma's motto. My mother felt the opposite and eventually pressured my conflicted father to buy a home of their own. There was no malice or evil attached to my grandmother's desire to keep the family close and there was nothing wrong with my mother's desire to have a home of her own. To Grandma, it was simply practical to live in one house and pay one set of bills. My mother wanted her own space to be an independent parent and housewife and who could argue with that? Grandma, on the other hand, enjoyed taking care of everyone in her home and certainly in her way too. Why live separately because there was plenty of room in her house and surely more than enough food for everyone? It was practical, "Si." Plus, I came along real soon after the marriage and Muttieta wanted me close by as well. The birth of my sister Lorena three years later only strengthened Granny's resolve to keep us all under one roof where she could preside over the whole clan.

Our little family lived together with my grandparents until I was about six years old but we were not the only ones, however, living under my grandparents' roof. Various other roomers and relatives were living with us too depending on which house we were living in at the time. My grandparents were house hoppers, buying and selling homes for a variety of reasons. Almost from the very start of their life together my grandparents made ends meet by renting out rooms in their own home to boarders. Early on they rented only to family members but later non-family members could rent but only men and never to women. Serving as landlords was one of the ways my grandparents supplemented their income. With my grandfather working in the steel mill, specifically, the blast furnace, coupled with the rent garnered from boarders, they became members of the American middle class. They achieved much despite their marriage beginning right along with the start of our nation's Great Depression. Somehow, with little to no formal education, they worked hard enough to carve out a niche for themselves that more than paid the bills. I cannot remember a time that my grandparents did not rent space to someone.

Mom lived through the moving and the boarder arrangement for quite some time. She did her best working alongside my grandmother as they cleaned, ironed, slaughtered chickens, canned tomatoes, and cooked continually. My mother even learned to speak Italian which should have strengthened her relationship with everyone except for the jealous Italian-American girls who never cared to pick up the language themselves. Mom learning Italian angered the young Italian-American women as she did the unthinkable, that is learn to speak the native tongue. Mom's achievement and motivation seemed to threaten their status. How dare this outsider, an Irish person, learn the language of the homeland that even Italian-American offspring did not have the motivation to master? Mom surprised many older visitors, especially native speakers when she began fluently speaking to them in Italian as they were doubly impressed when they found out that she was not Italian at all but Irish.

My mom believed that one day her hard work, assimilating into an Italian-American household, would be rewarded. That is, she would earn her sought-after independence in the form of a new home of her own. Mom was a fighter having to be tough and forceful while growing up with little money in the tenements of her hometown. Her toughness at first helped her when dealing with my grandmother and also eventually talking Dad into buying the home on 9th Street. Mom had hopes that the new home would allow her to finally run a household of her own without interference from others. Unfortunately, the move more than likely drove the final wedge between her and my dad.

There were many arguments over family issues which took a toll on Mom. The fighting wore her down as she did not have many who sided with her. At least this is how she felt and it is likely that few outsiders wished to take sides and get involved with mom and her position on things. Years later Mom told me she got tired of arguing with my father regarding living in the new home, as well as depressed from never seemingly being accepted into the family. There were likely other issues too but the details are unimportant. So, one-day Mom packed my sister Lorena and herself into a Greyhound bus for what was to be a short trip to visit family back home in Philadelphia. No one knew her plan but she had secretively planned to never return. After finding out Mom's intention and just how unhappy she was, Dad tried to make amends but nothing seemed to be accepted by my mother. He made one valiant attempt to save the marriage driving him and me to Philadelphia just before Christmas, 1957, earnestly trying to persuade Mom to return to their home on 9th Street. All I recall was that they got into an argument that ended in a physical altercation that I witnessed and that closed the door on that. Dad and I returned home with a bounty of Christmas gifts that Mom had bought me that filled the seats of the Chrysler where she and Lorena should have been seated. Strangely, the gifts, and there were many, helped take my mind off of my missing mother and sister. I still possess the remnants of two or three of the gifts my mom bought for me that Christmas over 60 years ago. Strange, yes, I guess so. Dad eventually filed for divorce ending their marriage.

Therefore, from the age of six, Grandma Mary became my surrogate mother which began my transformation into an Italian prince. I received everything that I wanted and even though I was less than seven years old I was also granted the freedom to come and go almost as I pleased. The spoiling process blunted the effect that a family breakup should have had on the development of a young boy and while it helped me in some ways I would not recommend the same for other families facing a similar dilemma. Maybe I was always introspective but after my mother and Lorena left I began keeping track of life's experiences and that accounts for why I recall so much from my past to this day. That is also why I had so much time to snoop among the articles tucked away in the attic. Perhaps this is why I remember so vividly my grandparents, especially my grandmother, and all the colorful people surrounding me as I grew up. Therefore, I request that no one needs to feel very sorry for me, not one person. Signed, The Italian Prince.

Anton & Guido

****

Hipster: "Ya know, my son is only a second grader. What do teachers expect of kids, with all the homework and other requirements, tests, and such?"

Stripes: "You go girl." My god, just hold me back. I detest it when White people try to talk like African-Americans. "Just too much is expected of kids." she moaned. "I was also informed by the teacher over the summer that I needed to send in tissues not to mention hand sanitizer and s n a ck s e v e r y t hr ee w ee k s o r so. Y o u kn o w I' m k i n d a t i r ed o f……."

Second grade. Hipster and Stripes happened to hit on the subject of second grade and that seemed right on cue as the two walkers were keeping beat to my daydreams, my old recollections. Plus, they were helping me get through my workout. It was like the cymbal crash on the downbeat. Yes, it was second grade when Mom left Dad and me and our home on 9th Street. We were now faced with living in a house by ourselves the very house that my mother lobbied for so hard.

Mom also left my dad with another dilemma. She and Lorena left for Philadelphia and were not returning and this all occurred just before Thanksgiving. Dad had made plans through the Christmas holiday for me to attend school but he eventually realized that another plan was needed for the remainder of the school year. After all, he had to work the day shift, 7 am through 3 pm, and our schedules were not the same so what was to become of me? How was I going to get ready for school by myself? How could we continue to live in the house with him leaving for work much earlier than me attending the local elementary school just across the park? A creative solution needed to be devised because Dad needed to be at work by 7:00 a.m. but my school day did not start until 9:00. Times were different back then so a person could get away with a situation that included leaving a six-year-old home alone to fend for himself. While a plan like that would not necessarily bring the social workers knocking on the door I am sure it was stretching the law a bit even for the 1950s. National child abuse and neglect laws would not be mandated until the 1960s so who knows?

I was consulted on the new arrangement and I bravely assured everyone that I was mature enough to get myself ready and off to school on my own. I was coached to wash up, get dressed, eat breakfast, lock the door, and go off to school. Dad would be home from work right before the end of the school day and said he would pick me up in front of the school each day. That part was easy. I would simply walk out of school and look for his green Chrysler. My lunches would be no problem. We continued to eat every dinner at my grandparents' home so my grandmother would certainly pack all my lunches. In the morning I was to grab my lunch pail out of the refrigerator, the one with Roy Rogers and his horse, Trigger, emblazoned on the front, and off I would tromp to school. When Dad explained the plan and asked me again if the plan was doable I responded affirmatively. "No problem, Dad," I was a big boy, or so I thought.

I will always remember the first day that the plan was implemented. I awoke at the designated time and still remember the dim light filtering through the window of our little American four-square home located a few blocks from Lake Elementary. I was sleeping in my parents' room. Dad figured that we should sleep together, I guess, so maybe I would not be so scared in the morning. Well, it was no surprise that the plan failed right from the very start. Upon waking up, the house seemed so very quiet, so empty. It took only a few minutes for me to realize the situation was more than I could handle. That is when I lost control and found myself scared. Even at age six I felt I was tough but found myself uncontrollably scared while at the same time ashamed for being such a big baby. I convinced myself that I should be able to handle the situation but instead, panic set in. Something unexplained took over and I felt helpless.

Fortunately, I was not so helpless that I could not figure out what I should do next. I did the only thing and the first thing that came to mind. That's right, I called my grandmother. She would know what to do. And for sure she did. She sent my grandfather to the rescue. Grandpa, never having a car or driver's license, walked the two miles through the cold and over to our house. With no trouble, he got me ready and walked me to school. From November to the end of the school year my grandfather walked over each morning and saw to it that I was taken to school and then he walked back home. Crazy but that is what was done. I can still see the scowl on my grandmother's face as she stared down my father with eyes making it clear that she would be the one making the plans from then on.

So, I was able to finish the school year at Lake Elementary School just across the park and as the name suggested, within view of Lake Erie. Lake Park would be a place where many things would occur, such as the area where I would be picked up by the police a few years later for committing some petty crime. However, way before that, Lake Elementary School was where I would first run into two interesting brothers, Anton and Guido, who would soon become a couple of my best friends. And who would know that they would someday both be with me, as well, that one afternoon at Lake Park when the police arrived? That story unfolds later.

The first time I set eyes on Anton and his younger brother Guido was right after they enrolled at my school. Seeing the duo was an experience even for me, a second grader, because Lake Elementary was, for the most part, a calm environment, the kind of school that middle-class families like to send their kids to get them away from kids like Anton and Guido. Most kids who attended Lake were middle class, seldom poor, never foreign, certainly well behaved, from intact families, and surely English speaking. Certainly, I was breaking the mold as I transitioned from the intact category into a broken, divorced family type but here came Anton and Guido to the rescue focusing any unwanted negative attention away from me. Any attention I might have garnered would soon be forgotten after these two new guys enrolled. Anton and Guido came in with a bang as their presence was not easy to ignore. Both were very active, and noisy, and since they could not understand any English they appeared incapable of following most rules. New kids at Lake Elementary customarily enrolled already possessing self-control and the basic readiness to learn. That included manners, hallway decorum, and the use of inside voices. The first time I laid eyes on the two new Italian guys was when I saw them both running down the hall, principal and secretary in hot pursuit, both trying earnestly to corral the new felons and guide them into their assigned classrooms. It turned out Anton and Guido were so excited about their new school that they could hardly contain themselves and were simply in a hurry to meet their American classmates. The brothers stood out from the start as they not only disregarded the established order but also spoke a funny language that few in the school, except me, could identify with. To the other students, these two new guys were a grand experience. They provided immediate entertainment as they wound through the school like twirling dervishes.

Anton and Guido entered Lake near the end of my second-grade year, 1959. Guido was a year younger than me and was placed in first grade. Anton, the older of the two, was two years older than most second graders but he was placed in my class to help him learn English. In those days schools decided, in some cases, incorrectly of course, that the best way to deal with non-English speakers was to place them into classrooms with much younger kids to assist with their academic achievement as they learned English. I do not know why Guido was placed in grade one but poor Anton, a full head taller than the rest of us, came to our room. Anton eventually settled long enough to remain seated and spent the majority of his day looking around smiling at the rest of us as he comprehended little of what was going on.

Anton, especially, was the more active of the two. He looked different too. Besides being a head taller, he came to school wearing black and white checkered pants that were too short for his legs. In years to come, shorter pants called "high-waters" would become fashionable but in second grade they only added to what was a humorous and surprising appearance. Anton also wore a white shirt, usually reserved for church, and black leather shoes with pointy toes. No one wore shoes with pointy toes at Lake before Anton arrived. It was apparent that these two new students shopped at different stores than the rest of us did. Because his behavior was so foreign and his communication skills so limited, I had little to do with Anton. My life due to the divorce was already in turmoil. Teachers knew my family situation even though I chose to hide it so I did not need any other variables causing me to stick out.

Just as fast as Anton rumbled into my class it seemed the school year ended and summer vacation began. A few weeks later and after my mother and father were officially divorced, Dad informed me that he sold our house, Mom's dream home, and we were moving back in with Giuseppe and Marietta. Shortly after moving back in, maybe August, Dad came home from an evening out excitedly saying that he had just had dinner in the home of a new Italian family in town. I learned much later that the family had a daughter whom they were trying to match up with my newly available father. After dinner with the new Italians, my dad informed me that he began showing some family slides that he recently developed using his 3D camera. My father was, as mentioned, a licensed photographer who was quite skilled at his work but decided he could make more money working at the local steel mill. 3D slides were the "in" thing since they produced realistic picture quality when developed.

While showing the slides, one of the kids in the family said, "Lo conosco," I know him. A full summer had not yet passed since leaving Lake Elementary and I was already outed and recognized. The Italian boy informed everyone that I was in his class at Lake, the school he just finished attending as his family recently bought a new home now only a few blocks away from my grandparents. What a coincidence! Of course, the kid I am referring to was Anton. Although we were classmates for only a very short time he pegged me as he gazed at the snapshots causing my father to promise to cart me along with him the next time he visited their home.

Naturally, my father was soon invited for dinner again and sure enough, I went along, reluctantly at first but things turned out and I am glad they did. In short order, the brothers, especially Anton and I, became instant friends. Family visits were a common form of entertainment in the 50s and 60s and Italian families were no different. It was not unusual for large groups of people to converge at a different Italian household each week. Visiting usually consisted of eating, conversing, and playing soccer. In the evening young men would also play a popular Italian card game called Scopa which always incorporated much yelling and drama. Their play was animated and included discarding their cards by cracking their knuckles down hard on the tabletop. The card game was enjoyed using special Italian playing cards and as the guys played they ate paninis and drank dark red wine and beer. By the end of the evening, the bantering increased to a fever pitch, especially when the stakes grew higher. We, kids, were usually pushed to the kitchen by then where we copied the older fellows ending our card game sooner as our knuckles could not absorb as much punishment. It was during these forays into the kitchen that I also found out just how much food Anton could eat. It was not unusual for him to down four to five salami sandwiches piled high with provolone cheese and leftover salad packed between slices of freshly baked Italian bread. For a skinny kid, he sure could eat. His eating represented the real-life version of every Italian mother's dream.

It also took no time at all for the brothers and me to begin performing all sorts of mischief together as leisure was quite plentiful in those days since nothing organized or civilized was available to fill up a kid's time. We needed no calendars, our schedules were quite open. So, we spent time trying to capture squirrels and when that did not work we bought slingshots and shot up everything in sight with stones. We also were introduced to bean shooters and spent a fortune buying dried navy beans and shooting them at just about everything. Naturally, after we finished shooting the beans at inanimate objects we began aiming at each other. The three of us learned that the legumes were a natural way of growing bean stalks throughout the neighborhood as they were quite adaptable to the soil conditions in our backyards.

When we were not out scorching the environment with dried beans, one of my earliest recollections of Anton has to do with his obsession with Elvis Presley. I happened to be at Anton's home with my father during a replay of an earlier Ed Sullivan Show. It was the famous program where Elvis' hip gyrations required the camera to mainly focus on him from the waist up. This episode is now placed in the annals of American TV culture due to its sexual overtones which occurred during a particularly prudish period in our country's history. Censors thought Elvis' movements were too suggestive and too sexual for a 1950s audience to accept so the camera had to pan him from the waist up.

I was less than interested in his hip movements but Anton was mesmerized right from the start by Elvis' music. From that moment on Anton would be forever hooked as an Elvis fan. Anton loved and worshiped everything that represented Elvis. I hated Elvis then and could not understand why Anton was continually singing his songs. Something about Elvis captured Anton as he soon took up the guitar intending to be as much like Elvis as possible. Fast forward about 20 years and Anton found a way to meet his goal of being as much like Elvis as possible. Anton became one of our county's many performing Elvis impersonators. Complete with an entourage, sideburns, and bodyguards, Anton continues to play in packed houses filled with screaming women out for a fun night on the town. Anton does as many gigs as he can fit into his busy schedule and makes good money while following his life's dream.

Anton and his brother Guido were now added to my friendship circuit as I moved back in with my grandparents who lived within three blocks of their home. This was the beginning of a lifelong relationship with the brothers and the development of one of my first friendship circuits in my hometown. Although I didn't realize it at the time, my grandparents' habit of moving houses would be a catalyst for the development of a wide circle of friendships that would last a long time and be the source of so many wonderful memories growing up.

Mr. Aspin

****

Hipster: "My son, thank heavens, was placed in Annette Bergstroff's class for next year. She's the best third-grade teacher ever. Everyone raves about her. But Claire, my friend, is so pissed, her kid got Mrs. Janesco. She's been teaching since before the saber tooth tigers roamed the state."

Stripes: "You are lucky to get Bergstroff. I heard about Mrs. Janesco's reputation and she was going to retire b u t i n s t e a d s h e d e ci d ed t o r e m a i............"

Third grade, for me, was another marker year. That was all I had to hear from the circling partners. Third grade was the year my life began, my overly exciting childhood part of life, that is. At least it is how I define it. Third grade was when the real fun began. It was the year I became aware enough of my surroundings to begin building crazy and fun relationships with friends. So much happened socially that year. Adventures began, the type I would not have experienced otherwise had my parents remained married and I had not been raised by my grandparents. Without the divorce, there would have been controls placed on my behavior thus interfering with what would become way too much freedom for a kid my age. Mom may have been young when I was born but she was strict and imposed rules. The rules were sound and the type most good parents would initiate but instead, I was now being transformed into a prince and I could do whatever I wanted. With Dad working and Grandma in control, I could do whatever, whenever, and however, I pleased. Certainly, there were experiences, good ones before my parents divorced, but I was younger then, and who remembers that much before age five anyway? Yes, there were good memories and some of them need to be mentioned here. They are worth mentioning and some of those memories are quite vivid. For example, a guy named Mr. Aspin.

Mr. Aspin was not hard to forget. He was a slightly built man with a sunken chest, dark-framed glasses, a mustache, and bushy eyebrows, that made him look very much like Groucho Marx. I loved, still do, Groucho, Chico, and Harpo back then so each time I met up with Mr. Aspin I envisioned him with a cigar in his mouth and his eyebrows twitching just like I had seen Groucho perform in many of his movie appearances. Mostly, although, I remembered Mr. Aspin for another reason. that is, before my parents divorced, my mother had little to keep her occupied during the day besides Lorena and me. While Dad worked at the local steel mill, mom would often walk my sister and me downtown just for a change of pace. It was probably 1957 and I was around six and Lorena was three years old. We would pop in and out of stores, window shop, or sometimes eat cheeseburgers at a lunch spot called *Sutter's*. I could always count on there being a never-ending supply of wadded-up chewing gum stuck under the booths in *Sutter's*. I found it fun to peel the wads off and throw them on the floor when mom was not paying attention. I guess sticking chewed gum under restaurant tables and counters was all the rage during the 50s and doubled for some mild form of teenage rebellion. I can still taste the cheeseburgers, but certainly not the gum, that Mom ordered for us at *Sutter's*. I continually search for a burger that tastes as good as the ones I enjoyed while sitting in that booth with my mother and sister at that long ago downtown restaurant.

Besides having lunch, one of the establishments where my mom usually shopped was a place that sold children's clothing and furniture. The name of the store was, *Young Times.* My mother was young herself at the time and very outgoing, talkative, and attractive. She never had any trouble finding people willing to strike up a conversation with her. Each time we stopped in *Young Times* Mom would usually have a long conversation with the mustachioed owner of the store, that is, Mr. Aspin.

My mother enjoyed conversing and could talk with anyone about just about anything. Her gabbing helped her make friends easily and in no time at all was recognized by many of the shopkeepers up and down the city's main district. Later on, she would eventually talk herself into a job working at a soda fountain in a small drugstore near *Sutter's* and *Young Times* called *Muir's Pharmacy.* It turns out that this innocent job was another minor contributor to Mom and Dad's eventual divorce. Mom was being accused of working too much outside the home and not remaining home tidying up the house like other young mothers. Dad thought that having a working spouse did not portray him as able to adequately support his family. Dad's status was being questioned, he felt, in the Italian-American community as a result of Mom's employment and he began nagging her because of the job. Her working behind the soda fountain, he said, made it appear as though he was not successful enough to provide for our family. This was years before the woman's movement officially reached full steam with many people believing the nonsense regarding a woman's place in our culture, that is, remaining a housewife. Women were supposed to manage the home and men were supposed to go to work. Mom, however, seldom took direction from anyone and so she decided to ignore Dad's ego and went to work at Muir's anyhow.

As Mom shopped and spoke with Mr. Aspin, my sister Lorena, and I slid down a slide and played in a small toy house set up in the middle of the store to keep kids happy while their parents browsed. Though the play area was modest, I still remember how we looked so forward to playing in that store while mom shopped and socialized with whoever would speak to her. I even recall my sister stealing some small trinkets followed by my mother discovering the theft and making Lorena return the item to the store. Mr. Aspin met Lorena with an, "Oh, these things happen," sort of response while my sister cried hysterically while apologizing.

Visiting interesting places around town kept Mom and us busy and also immersed her slightly in the company of other adults while Dad worked. I supposed we three appeared cute to others and visually represented the American dream.

Our Aunt Moe

There are other tidbits I remember from that period particularly from the next summer, the summer of 1957. My Aunt Moe, Mom's younger sister came to spend the entire summer with us. She was young, maybe 17 when she came to visit my mother who was by now in her early twenties. Both were gorgeous and looked great in bathing suits. One reason I know this is that Dad took many great photos of them wearing their suits using his 3D camera and some of those shots are still around. We also spent every hot day at our local beach. In the 50s it had not yet become well known that the lake was officially polluted so few worried about getting cancer from swimming in its waters. I loved going to the park and swimming with my sister Lorena. The beach was only two blocks away from our home on 9th Street so we could grab our towels, blankets, and Coppertone and be on the sand in a flash. I still remember being so hungry after swimming that eating ham and ketchup sandwiches were the best thing ever. We always seemed to eat ham and ketchup sandwiches that summer even though I would not even consider eating that combination today.

Aunt Moe attracted all the guys, especially the lifeguards, who were extra nice to Lorena and me to impress our aunt. They mostly left Mom alone since she was both older and married with children. Part of Moe's attractiveness stemmed from the fact that she looked and tried to behave a lot like Patti Page, who was one of the cutest and most popular singers of the time. Patti Page became famous for singing, *The Tennessee Waltz, Old Cape Cod,* and who can ever forget the song, *How Much Is That Doggy in the Window?* Moe's looks, energy, and being exotic, that is, from Philadelphia, brought all the guys around to show off. When Aunt Moe was on the sand sunning herself, people could have drowned before some of the stargazed lifeguards would have noticed. Mom watched us swim while Aunt Moe entertained the troops as Johnny Mathis' new song, *Chances Are*, played continually from the Beach House speakers. I will always associate Johnny Mathis's songs with that summer of 1957.

Aunt Moe finished the summer with us and eventually traveled back to Philadelphia. Strange to remember so much about an aunt I would not see again until 1999 after my mom's death. It had been so long since we saw each other that when Lorena and I picked her up at the airport her first words to my sister were, "Who is this handsome guy, your boyfriend?" Memories of life events can be so interesting.

Georgio

That was the summer before the divorce. The next summer would be different. Mom had moved out with Lorena, the divorce had gone through and I was graduating from grade 2 and leaving Lake Elementary while preparing for a new school and grade 3. After a short hiatus, Dad and I were living with my grandparents once again. I must repeat that living with them was always exciting. There was usually something interesting going on and if there was not I had a new freedom to cruise the neighborhood until I found a bunch of kids to hang with. At home, if I was not watching TV I could be entertained by interacting with the numerous relatives and friends who were seemingly always popping in and out of our house as if they were part of a sitcom.

For example, when my father and I moved back in with Grandpa Pepino and Grandma Muttyetta we shared the home for a few years with their Italian nephew who had been invited to live with them while he made a little money in the states. Georgio came to America to work and learn the culture. He was in his mid-twenties and he worked as a repair technician by day and Romeo to all the local women at night. His unstated goal, I figured, was to sow his wild oats in the US before settling down to marry a good old-fashioned Italian girl back in Italy. By the time Dad and I moved back in with my grandparents, he had lived there for about two years and was amid his second engagement.

There were a few things that I remember about Georgio besides his desire to marry every woman he met. He was tall, handsome, and also quick-tempered. One of his most prominent features, one that I have never confronted with anyone else since was his foot odor.

Giorgio must have had some type of disease or foot fungus because his feet smelled terrible. Even I could smell his feet and this was before I had a rather large tumor removed from my sinus cavity midway through third grade that made it almost impossible to smell anything. I was hospitalized for 10 days in the Cleveland Clinic after the tumor removal and was placed on a diet of broth and gelatine for what seemed like an eternity. This was the only time that I can ever recall hallucinating about cheeseburgers due to being so hungry due to my bland hospital diet. I felt like the cartoon character, Wimpy from the *Popeye* cartoons that were popular when I was a kid. Like Wimpy, I would have "gladly paid Tuesday for a hamburger today." After leaving the hospital they tell me I gained 10 pounds in one week. I was a new man after the tumor extraction but the downside was I could now smell even more of Giorgio's feet even though there was a bedroom wall separating our two rooms.

Another reason I will never forget Georgio was his penchant for putting his hands down my pants. It took me some months to figure it out but Georgio pretended to wrestle with me but when no one was looking he began touching me in inappropriate ways. This behavior seemed odd to me as I at first thought it was some type of Italian game. I believed somehow that an adult putting his hand down your pants was acceptable and simply part of Italian culture. So, while I did not like what he was doing I did not wildly protest at first since I believed this was a part of life for people who grew up in Italy. Giorgio and I began to wrestle around for a while when suddenly he would pin me to the floor, and suck on my ear lobes as people laughed thinking it was cute and all in fun. But sometimes, when no one was watching he would go further by putting his hand down my pants. This went on for some time before I figured things out and realized this touching was not part of normal Italiano customs. I soon also figured that I had had enough of that nonsense. I began staying away from Georgio calling an end to his sly little wrestling games. An end to Giorgio's grappling occurred one evening when he came toward and I yelled at him to leave me alone. When he persisted in attacking me I loudly screamed using an Italian profanity, "Malladetto, stronzo," (damn you, you shit) as I aimed a crystal ashtray at his head. By the way, adults got a crazy kick out of hearing me swear in Italian when I was a kid because they figured that I did not comprehend what I was saying. They were only partially correct. The yelling alone did not thwart Giorgio's attack nor raise any eyebrows from the others sitting in the kitchen. Fortunately, the crystal ashtray accomplished what the swearing did not. Those in the kitchen may have heard me yell profanity but did not hear the ashtray land heavily on Georgio's otherwise flawless brow. That did the trick. Those in the kitchen did not see how close Georgio came to requiring stitches on the top of his handsome forehead. Giorgio came close to losing his temper but as I grabbed for a nearby table lamp he decided it was time to call a truce. He got the message. I did not have any more problems with him after that.

Harrison School & Patsy Ricco

Georgio was one of many personalities I interacted with while growing up with my grandparents. Good or bad, experiences such as those with Georgio provided me with many varied life events to learn from. Fortunately, he was the only creep who interfered with my harmonious life while living under my grandparents' roof. I have to say that I enjoyed most of the other people who regularly dropped by the house. Over the years I met all types of family friends who would provide me with an abundance of unforgettable memories. My neighborhood on 21st Street would also supply a steady stream of characters, kids of all sorts, with whom to interact. One of the largest contributors to my list of motley friends originated from the first day I entered my new school, Harrison Elementary, where an abundance of crazy stuff would occur and where amusement began to intensify.

As the first September, after my parents divorced approached and I was scheduled to start in my new school, Grandma decided it was time to take me shopping for a school wardrobe. She and I would walk downtown to shop just as my mother, Lorena, and I did only a few months earlier. This time we would not stop at *Young Times* and speak with Mr. Aspin or order a hamburger at *Sutter's.* Instead, we were on a mission to buy clothes, lots of clothes for school. Downtown was where everyone shopped back then and JCPenney was where most shopping needs, for us anyhow, were met. Shopping downtown had a special meaning for me a few years later as Petula Clark sang her 1964 hit song, *Downtown.*

One of the things I remember most about Penney's was the pneumatic tubes the store employed that sent messages and other information between the various floors and departments. Marietta loved JCPenney for other reasons, such as, for purchasing most all our family's linens including enough bed sheets to cover what seemed like the entire state of Ohio. During this one shopping trip alone and supposedly just for third grade, Grandma would also buy plenty of underwear, "mutande," for me to last at least until my 18th birthday. Her philosophy seemed to be that a guy could never have too high an inventory of cotton underclothing, especially of the quality produced by JCPenney. Granny seemed somewhat addicted to the 100% cotton that JCPenney used to produce its underwear. Grandma wanted the satisfaction of knowing she was sending me off to school in comfortable-fitting cotton briefs as well as T-shirts. In her mind, a sign of a good parent was sending their kid off wearing an updated foundation. Sending me off to a new school with a full belly wearing new underwear was all she felt was needed to be considered a successful parent of an American child. I was becoming her second chance at being an American parent. I would give a lot of thought to my JCPenney's underwear while growing up especially knowing that few others could match my inventory of clean undergarments. Certainly, Grandma Mary succeeded in purchasing all the other supportive garments needed to complete my school wardrobes, such as printed short sleeve shirts, stylish wool pants, and black leather shoes. No one wore sneakers, jeans, or shorts to school back then. We carried our sneakers, usually P.F. Flyers or Red Ball Jets, to school and only put them on in the cloakroom just before gym class. We wore our street shoes out for recess and I credit the hard leather tips of my shoes for allowing me to blast the ball further than almost everyone else during our daily kickball games. By the way, never before or ever since have I used the word, cloakroom. Harrison School was probably the last place where the word was necessary.

Another skill worth mentioning and recognized by most of her contemporaries were Grandma's grocery shopping skills. Though Granny was considered a proficient grocery shopper by some, her skills in this area would often haunt and embarrass me to death as a child. She meant well but some of her tactics were world-class embarrassments to her young American grandson. They were antithetical, with no malice intended, to Mom's approach to shopping up and down shopping areas. For instance, I detested it when granny began attempting to bargain down the price of items she felt were too "dear." She was, by the way, the only one I ever heard use the word, dear, meaning too expensive, and using that word itself embarrassed me too to no end. Mom would have never expected to pay anything but the ticket price. When Granny did it and bargained, I associated her approach with being Italian. I drew this conclusion as she mostly attempted bargaining down the price in Italian-run establishments likely because she could do it while speaking her native tongue. I also figured her shopping approach was perhaps the way it was done on the main streets, "La piazza cittadina," or town square, back home in old Tussio. For instance:

Grandma: "Puoi darmelo per meno (You can give to me for less,) itsa too dear?"

Storekeeper, Patsy Ricco: "Coo Mahd, non possa fa." (godmother, I cannot do it).

Grandma: "Itsa not so fresh, vedere (see)," as she pointed out an obscure bruise on a banana or pear. "Mio marito (husband) isa on pensione (pension). "non siamo ricchi, lo sai," we are not rich you know."

Patsy Greco: "Si, Io le sai (I know), maybe I can droppa the cost-a ma un po (just a little), ma only justee for you."

Grandma: "Mille grazie, sa un santo," thank you, you are a saint.

I always wanted to cringe, dry up and disappear when she began to bargain because bargaining, especially in the middle of the store, was not all that American or acceptable even in the 50s. The other thing that she did that embarrassed me, even more, was to tear off a couple of grapes or other small pieces of fruit and taste them before buying. She would grab something and nudge me repeatedly to taste it for myself while stating, "Provalo," try it. I was sure we would be arrested for shoplifting or something as this little habit of hers thoroughly humiliated me. Grandma was not finished, no not yet. Next, I could look forward to her drawing undue attention to me in some way in front of the cashier who in those days always seemed to be a cute teenage girl. First, she would assume that if it was an Italian store then everyone must speak Italian so she would automatically speak in Italian and say some variation of, "Questa e mio nipote. Non pensi che sia bello." That is, this is my grandson, don't you think he is handsome? Fortunately, most of the girls had no idea what she was saying so they just smiled as they glanced at me and said, "Sorry but I don't understand much Eye-talian." This is when it should have registered with Granny that she once had a good thing with my Irish mother who at least had the gumption to learn the Italian language that these young Italian-American lassies had no intention of learning. Nonetheless, Grandma was surely skilled at her craft of shopping as she always succeeded at choosing the freshest foods while finagling the lowest price.

Shopping with Marietta, while sometimes embarrassing could also be interesting. For example, I recall shopping at a meat market called

Baisley's. Grandma and I used to walk to the store quite often as she needed someone to help her lug the large amounts of fresh meats back home. My father was at work and Grandpa Giuseppe was likely picking worms off his tomato plants so Marietti and I set off on foot to walk downtown. I can still hear Marietta say, "Jovy, via al balla della villagio," (some slang form of "away we go to the village). Before you knew it we were off to a store called "Baisley's Meat Market."

Baisley's was in the center of downtown. It was not a very spacious storefront but it was usually bustling with activity. It was so busy that the first responsibility we had upon entering was to grab a numbered ticket from a special machine situated in the middle of the store and then wait for our number to be called. Often the store was so busy that the machine was hidden behind customers. I enjoyed sitting on a bench watching to see those who knew what they were supposed to do from those who had no clue. There was always a poor soul or two who waited forever for their turn only to find out they needed a number to numerically be served. Even as a youngster I internally laughed at the poor saps who lost time and their place in line because they did not know the game. I was not dastardly as I eventually would pitch in to help a few poor souls, particularly lost patrons like little old ladies who seemed incapable of figuring out the system for themselves. So, when I was tired of watching people suffer I sometimes reacted charitably and pulled a number out of the machine and handed it to the lost patron. This would occasionally earn me a pat on the head, a smile, or maybe a nickel or a dime for my assistance. Being a spoiled Italian prince I scoffed at the change since I was accustomed to receiving crisp 20-dollar bills from both relatives and family friends having done nothing at all to earn one. I did, however, smile, and courteously jam the coin in my JCPenney corduroy trousers trying to appear gracious. People in those days had not begun to warn kids against talking to strangers. Suspiciousness and lack of trust in all strangers would not rip through our culture for a decade or two to come.

There always seemed to be an interminable wait no matter what time of day a person shopped at Baisley's. The meat must have been worth it because the place was always humming with shoppers. As I waited I would often snoop around the cooler to see what exotic cuts were in the case hoping to see an oxtail, a mess of chicken feet, or some gross type of animal innards. If there was nothing too exotic like a goat's head hanging from a hook I could usually count on there being a healthy display of liver, kidneys, and maybe something like chitterlings, that is, some animal's intestines, filling up a shelf. I would usually imagine that the chitterlings were purchased from some freak, like Jack The Ripper, or were part of the special effects in a horror movie. As a kid, I remember seeing a movie called, *Blood Feast,* where the main character, the killer scientist, would grab people and pull their tongues clear out of their heads by the roots. There was usually a beef tongue on display in one of the coolers near the liver and I imagined that it was some guy's tongue that was freshly yanked out of his mouth by the mad doctor in the movie. Only children who have a lot of time on their hands can imagine gory stuff like that.

Italian grandmothers in those days, especially mine, cooked almost every cut of meat so it was not unusual for one of the listed innards to eventually end up on our dinner table. No worry for me since I was never required to eat anything except what I wanted. I was a strange kid because I enjoyed liver but not regular stuff like my grandmother's homemade pasta. On pasta nights or almost any night, she would cook me a separate meal if I did not like what was on the main supper menu. I even got to eat my dinner on the floor in front of the TV watching cartoons like *Yogi The Bear* and *Deputy Dog or Popeye The Sailor Man* on a show hosted by a Cleveland actor with pointed ears named Barnaby. The only thing that would distract me from my dinner was a nightly telephone call I began to receive from a new third-grade classmate named Antionette Emilia.

For some reason, Antoinette began to focus on me, maybe because we both hailed from Italian backgrounds or maybe she was just bored and wanted attention from the new kid. Well, she received attention but mainly the negative kind from me. Everyone in our household thought it was really cute when she began her nightly calls. When she telephoned I was mostly rude to her as she yammered away seemingly about nothing yet she persisted to call despite my continued unfriendly tone. I would even hold the phone out for all to hear before someone would instruct me to at least pretend to be polite. I had to curtail some of my rudeness because of the number of people who craned their necks to listen in on our conversations. These calls went on almost every evening for the entire school year. Now as an adult, I cherish the memory of those calls wishing I would have appreciated them at the time as it was a real compliment that someone gave shit about me besides family way back then.

So, why did a prince like me eat separately? I guess I did what was comfortable and the worst thing of all, which remains one of my wife's favorite stories, has to do with my early attitude toward my grandmother's home-cooked Italian food. Watching so much TV at the time taught me that real Americans did not eat homemade pasta and polpettes (meatballs) the size of baseballs, not at all. Real Americans seemed to prefer canned spaghetti and meatballs produced by *Franco America* or better yet, *Chef Boyardee.* Yes, I am embarrassed to say I ate canned "Spaghetti With Meatballs in

Tomato Sauce" while everyone else in the house ate the authentic pasta made by my grandmother. Crazy, yes I know but I was a kid living in a bilingual home who wanted to be a real American. Fortunately, my eating habits have matured as for decades I have only eaten the homemade variety.

My grandmother, as stated, really knew how to shop for food and that included her Baisley's forays. I remained clear of her bargaining whenever possible as well as her frequent demands to taste cold cuts before purchasing them. I learned quickly that the way to stay clear of embarrassment was to leave Mary's side as soon as we entered certain stores like Baisley's allowing her to make as many demands on the butcher as she wanted while I hid out of sight. While she waited and rehearsed her bartering approach, I tooled around the store trying to blend in with the rest of the shoppers. I left Grandma by herself to dicker for the best meats the store had to offer. She never left it to the storekeeper to choose which cut to package up for her in that white butcher paper tied with a string. She preferred being the one in charge of that. Her eyes were focused from the start of the transaction on the choicest cut of meat in the cooler. If she did not see a piece of meat or cheese to her liking, Grandma simply asked for another one, one that she surmised was a choice and purposely hidden behind the counter by the shopkeeper perhaps promised to someone of higher status than her.

"Meester, please, you can give-a me one, bedder one, from-ma da back? This one is-a no fresh enuf. I wanna fresh-a one from-ma da back," she would ask.

Grandma sent countless butchers to the backroom to find her the prime cuts and the meat cutter usually complied returning with what she considered the premier choices. Grandma knew which meat was the best, almost a virtuoso of meat to fat marbling as she was not going to settle for second best. Of course, this drove me nuts so I just scampered around looking for loose change on the floor or better yet sticking my head in and out of the frozen fish cooler while writing my name on the newly frosted glass. Besides, if I was lucky there would be a frozen octopus near the top of the case allowing me to pretend I was Captain Nemo diving down to the bottom of the sea to wrestle with it.

Why should she not expect the best? Muttietta knew meat for many reasons but had a particularly trained eye due to the years she and Giuseppe owned their meat market in the center of town. They owned their store during the later years of the depression. Not being the most creative entrepreneurs of their day they simply named the store the "Reid Avenue Market." A catchy name I know but a practical one for its day especially since it was located on Reid Avenue. During that time, they sold meat, made sausage, and displayed other Italian foods while simultaneously renting out some of the upstairs bedrooms to boarders. Between the store, the roomers, and my grandfather working at the steel mill, they were able to eat well enough and pay the bills during some of the worst years of the Great Depression. My father said that although revenue earned from the store and the boarders was sufficient to get them through most hard times, he and my grandfather would still occasionally hike out to the woods and dig out a woodchuck from its lair. This put a little extra meat on the table. Dad assures me that they ate the woodchucks themselves rather than including the animal's meat in their homemade Italian sausage.

It was during these years that one of my grandmother's younger brothers, Rudolpho immigrated to the US and he soon joined my father working at the store. My father and Rudolpho also lived with my grandparents, sharing a bedroom in the store and making room for three when my great-grandfather, "bisnonno," my grandmother's father, ventured to the US to make some money to send back to the remaining family in Italy. Due to my dad having to work at the grocery, he often lamented that he was prohibited from playing football for Hawthorne Junior High School. Instead, my grandfather laid down the law and made him continue working to help make ends meet. In place of football, the cousins, Rudolpho and Louie, both less than 16 years old at the time, had fun driving an old beat-up truck while picking up supplies or delivering groceries to customers. Neither of them had a driver's license but there was limited enforcement of driving laws back then.

The store was eventually sold in the early to mid-1940s. When World War II broke out my father enlisted in the Navy. Soon after that Rudolpho married and he too began working at the steel mill and thus had no time to devote to working in the meat market. Years later I would have the good fortune of growing up surrounded by a few aunts and uncles and cousins including Rudolpho's son and daughter serving as my surrogate siblings. We spent much time together, sleeping at each other's homes and never really having to sweat it out at the steel mill as our parents did. My cousin Geo put up with my screwing around as we spent many days trying to capture frogs in nearby woods or throwing the football back and forth in the middle of the street. Geo was good to me even though I was four years younger than him. The only time he ever messed with me was when he decided to trick me into eating some hot pepper seeds. I will never forget how it was impossible to stop the stinging once those seeds hit my tongue. Another memory from those days involves spinning in circles on their red leather rocking chair hoping to make a few dozen revolutions before being yelled at by my uncle. Strangely, when we got boisterous my uncle usually yelled at my cousin instead of me. I was always getting away with murder in those days in almost everything I did even when I was caught red-handed.

Regarding the store, without Dad or Rudolpho around to help make ends meet, as they were an available source of cheap labor, my grandparents sold their depression-era meat market for a minimal profit and bought a couple of nearby homes, rented them out for a few years and soon flipped them for resale. My father is not around anymore but until his last days continued to tell stories originating from his days in the Navy. His uncle, Rudolpho, only two years his senior, died years earlier, way too young, from cancer the likely result of smoking way too many filterless cigarettes.

Though Marietta was an excellent cook and host, one thing Granny was not very good at, however, was dealing with my teachers and the school. Education, while one of her top priorities for me, was out of her league, particularly since her English was so limited making it impossible for her to negotiate a public elementary school and meet with teachers. Therefore, Dad was the one charged with attending teacher conferences but that was about all the interaction that occurred between home and school. The rest was up to me to parlay and that included entering Harrison Elementary School alone that first day of class. Walking the halls the first morning at Harrison and searching for my third-grade classroom is a memory that periodically recycles through my mind. It was early September and most schools back then began classes the first Wednesday after Labor Day. That would make the date September 9, 1959. I think of that day fondly even though it was a little scary at the time.

Before finding my new classroom that first day, I got lost and started my experience at Harrison looking confused and bewildered. My father could not afford to take a day off of work just to cart me to school so it was up to me to find my way to my new classroom all by myself. In those days, kids were expected to be independent in many areas and it was often their job to find their way in many things. Right or wrong kids back then learned to fend for themselves a little more especially because children had not yet become more precious to parents than survival itself. Do not misunderstand me. I was loved, boy was I, but these were times before political correctness and worries about child abductions became the scary headlines. Besides, in 1959, most kids had two parents in their family with a mother remaining in the role of housewife. Moms, if anyone, were the key persons that were supposed to deal with schools, teachers, PTA's, and all kinds of other kid-related stuff. Besides, I already failed the scaredy-cat test months earlier on that morning I woke up to an empty house. I was not going to act like a baby again by whining about finding my new classroom.

After a hearty breakfast of toast and uova sbatutte (beaten raw egg yolks with sugar), sporting my new JCPenney underwear, black leather shoes, dress pants, and button-down shirt I was on the sidewalk early and headed for school. Once I arrived at school, the first person I met while searching the halls of the school was a second-grade teacher who gently pointed me up the stairs to my new classroom. "I am assigned to Mrs. Rabidau's class," I said flashing my entry papers, "my new third-grade teacher," as I hurriedly explained my assignment to this teacher who was all smiles while standing in the corridor outside her second-grade classroom.

Without knowing it, this teacher, Miss Ludnow, the one pointing me up the stairs, would by chance become a neighbor of ours ten years in the future, and to this day I am incorrectly reminded by my family that she was my best teacher. Somehow Miss Ludnow, who only gave me directions, was forever imprinted by my family as my best teacher so it became easier to just agree with the tale. Instead of arguing that she only gave me directions, I have learned to simply reply, "Yes, she's the best teacher I 'never' had," but no one hears the end of my sentence because usually the conversation has already moved on.

Conversations were always moving on in our mostly working-class city, especially in ethnic households like mine. In my household, where conversations swiftly moved along while mostly obscuring facts and sometimes intent on obscuring reality. That is if anyone was listening anyhow. This future neighborhood where Mrs. Ludnow lived was one more neighborhood in my hometown, West 29th Street, where I would eventually live when Dad remarried.

Meanwhile back in third grade, I finally made it up the stairs to my new classroom and by chance sat right in front of a "Spanish" looking kid with a spiky "butch" haircut. America had not yet begun to use present-day descriptors of ethnic groups, such as Mexican-American or Latino. To me, he was simply a Spanish-looking kid. I vividly remember that my new classmate's perfectly round head, which was plain to see due to his butch haircut, looked as if he was wearing a woman's swim cap filled with thousands of black pins sticking out from it. Each pin, that is, a strand of hair could easily be identified as every one of them was equidistant from the other.

As I sat down, my soon-to-be best friend smiled back at me and quickly volunteered his name. It was, "Rudy, Rudy Perez," he said. I still remember my first question to him after introducing myself. That is, I stupidly asked, "Is your father Jose Miguel Perez the famous wrestler I see on TV?" What a dumb question but an honest one since up to this point I had never met a "Spanish" kid before. I had seen "Spanish" people on TV. After all, everyone watched the popular for its day TV show, *Zorro*. But I was not referring to the star of the show, Don Diego de la Vega, but instead notably this guy, Jose Perez who wrestled on the local Channel 8, WJW. The Perez I knew always argued with Lord Layton, a retired wrestler who was the host of the popular wrestling program. These were the early days of people gathered around the TV set becoming emotional over the good guy getting his eyes gauged before eventually gaining an advantage over the bad guy and pommeling him into submission. In those days it had still not become widespread knowledge that the whole spectacle was phony. Who would figure that so many people would continue to be fans of this loony sport over 50 years later? I spent many hours explaining to my grandmother and her Italian friends that the whole phenomenon, of professional wrestling, was an act, a put-on. They never believed a word I said and instead were hypnotized by the violence as I saw them cringe in unison after each drop kick as their favorites, like Bruno San Martino, hailing from Pizzoferrato, Italy, was sent into the turnbuckle or given a mighty knee to the stomach. Pizzoferrato, it turns out, was just two hours from my grandparents' birthplace but it did not matter how far from their home he was born. As long as he was an Italian then he was their hero. Who would have known that one day I would move to Bruno's American hometown, close to Pittsburgh, and regularly see him honored on TV, often appearing in parades and various charity events? He remained a local hero for years after retiring from the ring.

Rudy, with a big smile on his face, corrected me stating the wrestler was someone else's Perez and took my stupid question right in stride. Rudy then quickly changed the subject and next introduced me to his good friend and neighbor, Dirk, who was sitting right beside him. Dirk, I would soon find, was a quick-witted guy, and that very little of anyone's stupidity, including mine, got past him. He could make us all laugh at a moment's notice and this often got us all into more trouble than was good for us. From that moment on Dirk, Rudy, and I were destined to become best friends and for the next nine years, we three and a group of other ragtag guys we would pick up along the way became buddies. No matter where my family moved, Rudy especially remained my pal and contributed to my having loads of fun while somehow getting away with tons of mischief.

For instance, I recall right from the start going to Rudy's house one Saturday morning to play. The three of us, Rudy, Dirk, and I decided, like most boys, that the first thing we would do was throw things at one another. Boys love using each other as bull's eyes. We aimed stones and rocks at one another for quite a while before noticing that the picture window of the neighbor's house behind us, and definitely in the line of fire, had a huge diagonal crack in it.

We did not wait to find out if the neighbor had already noticed. Without saying a word, we three began running as quickly down the street as we could. Little boys learn the art of nonverbal communication very early. Running away is probably associated with some primitive hunter-and-gatherer behavior that helped early Homo sapiens bring down large animals, or get away from saber tooth tigers. Through some nonverbal movement, perhaps only the raising of an eyebrow in a particular way, guys instinctively know when they should spontaneously start running for cover. It was no different for us, we saw the crack and even though we were new friends we understood that the sooner we zoomed away from that window the less likely it would be that we would be blamed.

The three of us were on the lamb for the very first time seemingly for hours before realizing we were becoming hungry. We rationalized that we would eventually have to confess to our crime anyway so we decided to return to Rudy's home and accept our punishment. When we arrived, however, everyone appeared calm even the neighbor whom we noticed was happily sweeping the stones off his sidewalk. This was not what we expected. Why were the police not there to greet us complete with emergency lights flashing and sirens blaring?

After collectively scratching our heads in disbelief we decided to be brave and investigate the situation a little closer. What we found, as we neared the cracked pane, was a thin wire tied diagonally close to the window. It was intended to support some type of vine but since this was autumn no foliage was clinging to it. From a distance, the wire gave the impression that the window was cracked. A sense of relief immediately swept over us.

Our antics matriculated from this little window adventure to making crank phone calls, ringing doorbells before running away and every little boy's favorite, throwing snowballs at cars. There is no way for me to recall how many windows we broke at the old boarded-up stove plant or times we broke into cabooses parked on the tracks next to King's Woods. Strangely, we were never caught for any of these minor delinquent behaviors and now as an adult, I am proudly the only person I know, except Rudy and Dirk, who has ever been inside a real caboose, that is, either legally or illegally.

We three were safe having escaped our first escapade and were now friends bonded for life. We had escaped the first of many situations that could have if known by our parents, set them wisely against our continued association. Our collective adrenaline high from that first play date would somehow addict us to risky behavior for many years to come and we would remain friends forever.

In school we tended to control our behavior, relatively speaking, instead saving most of our wild semi-criminal energy for after-school activities. Besides, in those days teachers were very strict and corporal punishments of all sorts were clearly at their disposal. Back then ears could be twisted, gum could be put on noses, and kids could be shaken. Most mild forms of humiliation were fair game and certainly, bottoms could be liberally paddled with or without witnesses present. We even knew a few kids who received swats on their bare bottoms, oh my! Early in the school year, smart kids learned just how far to push and recognize their teacher's limits.

Even though Rudy, Dirk, and I considered ourselves the "Houdini's" of Harrison School by extricating ourselves from trouble and recognizing the limits, we occasionally earned episodes of "Shaken Student Syndrome" administered by Mrs. Rabidau. Mrs. Rabidau, our third-grade teacher, made a habit out of taking misbehaving students in each hand and shaking them back and forth as if she were cleaning the floor mats of her 1955 DeSoto. A "milkshake," we called them and I recall her grabbing Rudy with her left hand and Dirk with her right on one particularly cloudy afternoon for something stupid they did. Shake, shake, shake, back and forth, in and out with all her might resulting in their heads bobbing back and forth and their brains banging against their craniums. They could have died from Shaken Baby Syndrome had it not been for their young youthful pride. Who knows whether any of us, especially Rudy and Dirk, who experienced the "milkshake" now present memory problems due to old age or maybe Chronic Traumatic Encephalopathy (CTE), the modern-day term for concussions experienced by football players knocked in the head too many times. Each time I see an episode of *The Three Stooge's* conking heads I am immediately transported back to Mrs. Rabidau's milkshake machine.

Of course, the three of us managed to earn a paddling by the principal the next school year when the teacher grabbed Kenneth by the scalp while twisting his head around emulating the twist of an owl's neck. Or was it our making fun of Larry for spitting on his desk and then sucking the mess back up as we had to put our heads down on the desk each day to give the teacher a respite? I can say that few things in life have physically hurt more than three swats from the principal's paddle. Rudy and I never let Dirk forget about his dramatic crying out as the paddle connected with his behind. Guys never forget stupid stuff they witness happening to one another. We all keep a secret listing of crazy stuff to bring back up at opportune times. Fortunately, each of us has a list of dumb things to be busted about that equalizes and thereby levels the playing field.

None of us can remember our parents being informed of our school-related infractions either. Even the paddling went unreported home. Teachers in those days, it seems, chose to handle most disruptive behaviors themselves, internally. In the '50s and '60s, there was still this basic unwritten agreement between home and school that if a kid did something wrong then teachers had permission to wield any punishment short of maiming. A well-conceived punishment, it was agreed, usually settled a guy down culminating in many future weeks of stellar behavior. Thus, parents were on a limited need-to-know basis regarding their child's daily antics in school. Schools mostly allowed parents to read their newspapers and eat their supper in peace leaving them to believe their kids were focused, happy, and active learners in school. Teachers and schools still knew best in those days so there was little need for a parent to question school personnel beyond, "We hope Johnny is behaving in school."
With friends like Rudy, Dirk, and many others at Harrison Elementary, I knew from the start, the school was going to be a blast. Living in my grandparents' home was also shaping up to be

extraordinary as well. Living with two elderly people should not have been so eventful but it was. These two people never broke a rule and seldom left the house, yet people, relatives, and countless friends gravitated regularly to their door. As was said, there was hardly a day that went by that someone did not stop for coffee or knock on the door to deliver cookies, cakes, or maybe a pound of parmesan. Who knew? Almost everyone was inspiring and generous in some way but there were certainly the personalities like Joe and Feliciana Cappello and strange other ones like Georgio all of whom remain in my playbook of memories. Even though Georgio was not my favorite for obvious reasons I hold no animus toward him. Instead, he, like others are part of a great personal story. As my number of friends multiplied back then, my fun experiences also increased making my childhood extraordinary. Good or bad these experiences all helped shape my personality and my life. Perhaps that is why I relish the memories so openly.

Goodbye Jack

Let me jump back a little here before I go on. Eventually, after flipping a few houses around town for the most profit, my grandparents bought a rather large home on Hamilton Avenue in the city. They purchased the house in 1951 and I was born shortly after they moved in. It was in that big house, my mother told me, that the marriage began to unravel almost immediately. As if things were not difficult enough, given all the issues I listed, that is, Mom being Irish, young, and then the elopement with my dad, she also began feeling psychologically harassed by one of the boarders, my father's cousin, who, as it turned out, was emotionally disturbed. His disturbance caused him to eventually drink some lye, while living in the house, thus killing himself. Before he ended his own life, however, he decided to make life miserable for my mother and one of the worst things he did was kill her cat, a tabby cat named Mr. Whiskers. The cat was a source of comfort for her as she tried to adjust to this strange and nutty new environment miles away from her life back in Philadelphia. The sick cousin thought it was a good sport to place the dead cat near her bed, so it was the first thing she saw upon waking up one morning. This unfortunate event should have been a clear sign to everyone that not only was Jack sick but that he also symbolically represented a situation, a marriage, and a living arrangement, that was just as difficult as he was.

Strangely, however, people did have a bit of a sense of humor over Jack's demise. As a result of his death from drinking the lye, each time thereafter when something broke in the house, such as a dish falling to the floor, a chorus of "Goodbye Jack's," would be repeated in unison from everyone within earshot of the broken object. My grandfather was the first to coin the phrase as he possessed, in addition to many other behaviors, a rather dry and sometimes screwy sense of humor. In our house, automatically repeating the phrase, "Goodbye Jack," soon became second only to responding in unison, "God Bless You," after someone sneezed. My grandmother used the phrase so often around friends, relatives, and even her boarders that the words seamlessly flowed out of their mouths from habit if they were fortunate enough to be visiting when something smashed to the floor.

I admit, my ancestors surely had a strange sense of humor. "Goodbye Jack" lasted as a trademark phrase throughout the rest of my grandparents' lives. Living in their home I surprisingly thought that the phrase was universally repeated whenever something broke and no matter where it crashed. It was, however, only our relatives and friends of the family who liberally, and shamelessly I might add, used this phrase. Most people probably did not know the exact origin of the remark but repeated it anyway because it sounded right. I even Googled the phrase just to see if it was ever popularized beyond our family but all I could find was "Goodbye Jack" referring to Jack Bauer, a character played by Kiefer Sutherland on the TV show, *24*. The phrase referred to the end of the series in 2010. There were other mentions of the phrase but they had to do with either saying goodbye to Jack LaLanne after his death or a disco remix of a song title. Strangely, my grandparents were ahead of their time by creating a fitting phrase that symbolized an unusual ending.

My grandparents' humor did not end with the phrase, Goodbye Jack. There were other similarly humorous situations and one involved an aunt of mine who laughed so loudly and with such a distinctive guttural trill that she sounded much like one of the high-pitched songs of the robin. Each time I hear robins trilling, especially as they are busy building their nests and rearing their young in the spring, I cannot help but say, "There's Aunt Adelaide." My grandfather was the first to point out the association between my aunt's trilling laugh and the song made by robins. Spring in our household would officially begin when my grandfather noted the first robin he heard singing. He would then take pride in announcing to all, except to members of Aunt Adelaide's family, "And There-isa Aunta Adelaide-ah." My wife thinks I am nuts but I just have to repeat the phrase, almost superstitiously, each time I hear a robin's trill. It is as if Aunt Adelaide is nearby and I am just minutes away from the family I knew growing up.

Certainly, I realize that I repeat the phrase less out of habit and more because it brings back a happy memory. I loved my Aunt Adelaide and miss her so I figure that the habit, besides making my wife crazy, is my way of staying in touch with my aunt, her family, and thus a good part of the past. Thanks to her laugh and my grandfather's wit, each time a robin is disturbed and makes that high-pitched trilling sound I get to think of my aunt, uncle, and cousins and our growing up together in the 50s and 60s.

One evening my wife and I were walking our dog, Lily the Malamute, when we heard for the second time a robin trilling nearby. Also, for the second time, I automatically blurted out, "And There's Aunt Adelaide." My wife, exhausted from hearing me repeat the familiar phrase, started to berate me by saying, "Joe, will you please quit repeating that already?" In the middle of her reprimand, she accidentally dropped her cell phone and it shattered as it hit the pavement. At that point it certainly seemed appropriate and what else could I say but, "Goodbye Jack."

Oddly, until 2010 I had never seen that big old house where I was born, where my parents' marriage began to unravel, where Jack killed the cat, where Jack drank the lye, and where the phrase, "Goodbye Jack," was first coined, oh my. This was the mess that Jack built. Few believe the following story but strange events continued to haunt my family at this old homesite. We had not lived in that house on Hamilton Avenue since the 1950s but in 2010 an in-law's brother innocently rented a room in the same place. Needing somewhere to live, he by chance happened on to this property in a city filled with many other rooms to rent. His locating and choosing the house was random and he knew nothing about our family's previous ownership or history in the dwelling.

It was therefore quite eerie that of all the houses in the city, it was in this house where he not only decided to rent a room but then subsequently died quite mysteriously. His death, happily, had nothing to do with drinking lye as Jack had 60 years earlier. It was also a plain old-fashioned coincidence that he rented the room and died in the Hamilton Avenue home. To my knowledge, no one created any macabre phrases such as "So long Tito," or anything like that over his death. However, and wherever it occurred was less important than the sadness that led up to the tragedy.

Because my father lived in so many homes throughout his life in our hometown, as well as, a few moves to nearby cities, I decided to devote one of my visits with Louie to driving around and snapping pictures of all the houses where either he lived or my grandparents previously owned. While most of the homes were still standing, some were in a rather poor condition and their Reid Avenue Grocery no longer existed. It had been torn down some years earlier. The house on Hamilton, where Jack and Tito both died was fortunately still standing, although, when Dad and I parked in front to take its picture, we immediately noticed that it was not doing so well. We were surprised that this once majestic house was now in the "Serious

And Need Of Repair" category. It required a new paint job, the bushes needed trimming, and the garage was leaning over ready to fall apart. The house also appeared much smaller and less elegant than I had imagined. My father was disappointed too when he saw it stating, "It was once a beautiful home when we lived in it." I admit that I was disappointed too when I saw it as we both mourned its condition.

While I was growing up, the house was often discussed in a way that led me to believe that it was considered the flagship dwelling of all the homes bought and flipped by my grandparents. Now its glory days had passed. No longer was the house considered a gem. It was not even a home where most people would care to live. Therefore, standing outside this once dignified home and gazing upon its deteriorating condition, and with Louie, my father, standing by alongside, it seemed relevant to repeat the only appropriate thought that came to mind. That is, due to years of conditioning we automatically and simultaneously announced in unison, "Goodbye Jack." After taking a few pictures of the house we hopped into my car and drove away.

The Interesting Cast of Characters

After I was born my grandparents decided the grand home on Hamilton was too much work so they built a much smaller brick house on a street a few blocks away from the one on Hamilton. I was old enough by this time to have a few recollections of the home and at least one of the men who rented a room in the house. Of course, Mom, Dad, and I lived there as well. Looking at the house as an adult it is hard to believe that the place was large enough to house us all but my grandparents were determined to continue making extra cash by renting out rooms. The guy I remember who rented with us during the years on Allison was a fellow incorrectly referred to as Mr. Moon. He was a very nice and soft-spoken man who as it turns out was gay. No one knew he was gay or at least if they suspected that he was, his sexuality remained his business. These were the days of letting bygones be bygones as long as no one flaunted certain characteristics associated with their lifestyle especially those that were considered to be against church teachings. My grandparents were quite liberal in their way but not so much to embrace open homosexuality, I am guessing, especially during the 1950s. As long as a person was pleasant and followed household rules, I refer back to the gift-giving rule, for example, then individuals had free access including dinners, coffees, and inclusion in holiday celebrations.

Mr. Moon, Grandma's Italian-American mispronunciation of his real name, that is, Mr. Mumm, lived with us for a few years while working at an Ohio insurance company. On most weekends, I found out later, he would head back home to New Castle, Pennsylvania, his hometown, to be with his partner. Following my grandmother's lead, everyone introduced to Mr. Mumm also began referring to him as Mr. Moon, even though all knew his real name was different. Mr.

Moon fell in line like almost everyone and just smiled and accepted the new surname. Accepting your name being mispronounced seemed to be part of the package when living and visiting with my grandparents. People through the years got used to my grandparents' mispronunciations of at least some part of their name. Most everyone considered Marrietti's flubbing up of their name to be endearing. A garbled name was a small consolation given all the rewards one earned for being part of my grandparentts' extended clan.

Eventually, Mr. Moon was transferred back to New Castle and would occasionally stop by our home for coffee and some dolce, sweets, when he traveled back to town on business. It was during one of Mr. Moon's visits that he was brave enough to cart along with his partner, Arthur, and it was during this trip that the dots were officially connected. It did not matter. Arthur was greeted just like everyone else. "Arturo, siediti e mangia (sit and eat), you too skinny. Mangia, hav-a some more to eat. Eat-a una toto cookies. Take-a sum mo. Mangia." I mention Mr. Moon and Arthur's sexuality because it warms me to think that my grandparents, even in the 50s, looked past certain issues siding instead with variables that mattered, that is, a person's basic humanity. Their model taught me much.

Shortly after Mr. Moon's departure from our home, my grandfather, who seldom made demands, decided they had made a mistake by building this new home because he had limited space to grow his tomatoes, "pomodore." So, it was not much longer before we schlepped off again. Before I knew it we were moving to the next house, the one I mentioned and located on 21st Street, just a mile or two away. By the age of three or four, I would live in three different houses and my mother would pack us up as we caravanned right along.

Now, here it was, 1959, post-divorce, and for the second time my father and I had moved into the 21st Street home where I would make friends with Rudy, Dirk, Anton, and a nutty group of other guys, many of whom would become lifelong buddies. The next three years would be spent living in that 21st Street home only now possessing all the freedom to terrorize not only the neighborhood but the overall general vicinity. Those years would be fun-filled and memorable due to making so many good friends and having such a wide run of the neighborhood.

The cast of characters continued to frequent our home due to my grandparents' generosity and gregarious nature. For example, there was a guy fondly referred to as Farmer Gray. He likely had a real name besides Farmer Gray but I never knew it. The name, Farmer Gray, seemed so relevant to me since there was a farmer named Mr. Green Jeans who starred in a popular TV show of the times called, *Captain Kangaroo*. I think that I enjoyed Captain Kangaroo so much because I felt my home life mirrored the Captain's Treasure House. On the TV show, there were regulars like Farmer Green Jeans and the Captain who also welcomed unusual daily guests as well, such as *The Banana Man*. As an only child, I was now living in a Captain Kangaroo sort of world where all kinds of characters would almost mysteriously drop in. Once, sometimes twice a week, Farmer Gray would pull into our driveway with a few dozen eggs and maybe a sack or two of potatoes or maybe some peaches. Whatever was in season graced our home when the farmer visited. It would also not be unusual for him to have a few chickens crated up in his back seat. Farmer Gray would usually be greeted in the driveway by my grandfather who quickly informed Grandma that the farmer had arrived. The farmer was the only one to refer to my grandmother as, "The Misses." The Misses would drop everything and promptly fix him a snack and quickly bring it out to the farmer while he remained seated in his car. Grandma Mary knew the farmer was on a tight schedule and would not remain to chat in the driveway for very long. I never saw Farmer Gray step out of his car. It was eventually explained that he was too arthritic to walk very far on his own. Instead, to accommodate his needs we would gather around the Farmer's car as he drank his coffee and ate his toast and Italian cookies. I don't know why but I hung around too because there was usually something interesting, even to an eight-year-old, about having this old guy drive up and socialize from the driveway. There he would perch in the seat of his 1946 Oldsmobile Dynamic and thrill us with stories from the farmlands that surrounded our hometown. Of course, it helped that Farmer gray always had a kind word and maybe a quarter or two to toss my way before heading down the road to deliver eggs to some other trusty customer. I often wondered how many breakfasts and maybe lunches too that the Farmer ate as he made his daily deliveries.

Ten years later as a teenager, I remember visiting old Farmer Gray down the road in a quaint lake village. Farmer Gray was very ill it was explained and was in hospice care and under the supervision of some relatives. It turns out that he needed to sell his farm and was now sick to the point of no return. He had delivered his last egg. This would also be the last time any of us would see him alive. Even my grandmother accompanied us on this visit which was a relative rarity since she likely had a mild phobia against leaving the house for very long periods. It was plain to see that gone were the farmer's energy and recall of farm stories was limited. He had no fruit or eggs to barter and could barely manage a smile. Farmer Gray was just able to sit up long enough to eat a pizzelle cookie or two that Grandma packed for him before he became too tired to follow the conversation. I often wondered if I witnessed his last bite of one of my grandmother's luscious pizzelles.

Visits like that one, to an old friend, as well as welcoming guys like Mr. Moon and his partner Arthur taught me that most everyone was on an equal social plane in our home with the exception, certainly, of priests and doctors who occupied a higher status position of their very own. A visit to the sick guy who delivered your eggs was just as important as visiting a close relative. That is what my grandparents were like. They were loyal and if you were their friend they would be yours forever. Farmer Gray died shortly after our brief visit likely from some disease that attacks old people. I will never forget how we all gathered around his old tan Oldsmobile while he ate his breakfast and delivered a simple sermon about life in the country. Right there in our driveway on 21st Street, we were able to keep abreast of the weather, and crop yield per acre and determine if it would be a good growing season for tomatoes. The farmer was like having our own *Farmers' Almanac* on four wheels. We did not need the Internet back then. We instead had people like Farmer Gray to keep us informed. Strange what a little kid remembers. I guess I still miss people like him today.

Mexico or Bust

I even miss that old driveway. That driveway on 21st Street was frequented by many people in those days and it was the site of numerous activities. Groups of us, kids from the neighborhood, played kickball on it and we were often disappointed when the inflated rubber ball impaled itself on the razor-sharp top of the chain-linked fence my grandparents installed. We had many punctured balls in our garage as a result of that fence. I also spent hours catching tons of bumblebees in clear glass containers in the flower bed alongside the blacktop. I learned that bees especially enjoyed snapdragons as I watched the fuzzy plump creatures open the mouth of one flower, climb in, and almost disappear before reemerging dusty with pollen before heading toward another. Catching bees in the 50s for no good purpose was stupid I now realize. However, catching the bees without getting stung was an adventure, a personal skill, and something for an only child to pass the time. I became pretty good in those days both at catching bees and passing the time.

Another thing about that driveway that remains sharp in my mind is the day I said goodbye to my father and Giorgio as they drove off on an adventure of their own to Mexico. This too was in 1959. They planned to drive from Ohio to Mexico in Giorgio's 1957 Buick convertible. Here were Louie and Giorgio heading west, two single guys, as if they were the prototypes to TV stars, Tod Stiles and Buz Murdock who would travel west on the popular series, *Route 66*, which would premiere a year later in 1960. Dad and Giorgio planned to be gone for three weeks and would return overflowing with tales and conquests mainly engineered, I figured, by the tall and handsome Georgio. Their best story from the trip would involve meeting some attractive Mexican women who invited them to a traditional

Mexican wedding. My dad, ever the photographer, took many pictures of the event proving to one and all that Giorgio's prowess with women was growing internationally as he had now acquired girlfriends in Italy, the United States, and Mexico. My dad must have done well enough in the lady department too, thanks to Giorgio's assistance and as evidenced by some of the snapshots. Needless to say, my father was not very specific about the subject of women when around me. Today, besides some snapshots of their trip to the Southwest, I still have a buckskin jacket, complete with spangles, that could have been worn by a rather young Daniel Boone. The jacket was safely kept in the cedar closet in my grandmother's house to stay clean and insect free but like so many new things, protecting it became more important than using it. The coat was never really worn by anyone except by me but only for purposes of picture taking. It, like most things considered luxuries, was to be savored and kept for special occasions. I eventually grew too big to wear the coat as I waited for the exact special occasion to come. It never did. Now I still have that old coat, and it remains brand new, hanging in my closet more than 60 years later. The jacket has become a symbol of Dad's cross-country adventure with cousin Giorgio so many decades ago.

Another fellow who regularly visited our home on 21st Street was a man name Orlando Scamorzes, but we all just called him Orlando. Orlando visited three to four times per week as I grew up and I remember enjoying his company. Orlando not only slipped me $20 bills for no reason but he also seemed to genuinely like me. By the way, Orlando was another one of the many people who slipped me the cash I believed partially as a way to pay back my grandparents for all the pasta and care they gave them. Orlando was an outgoing kind of guy, loud and boisterous, often grabbing me and propping me up on his knee while telling everyone what a good boy I was. My grandmother and Orlando's spouse got along quite well and considered each other best friends. Dinners together with Orlando and his wife were frequent and we all shared many important life events such as First Communions, marriages, funerals, and, of course, holidays of all sorts. Simply buying a new lawn mower in those days could end up as a dinner celebration. There are many snapshots, taken by my father, of me sitting on Orlando's lap as the whole bunch of us ate homemade gnocchi in my grandparents' dining room on 21st Street.

Another way our families interacted was via my grandfather puttering around at one of Orlando's many cheap hotels after retiring from his job on the blast furnace. In those early days, I could never understand why my grandmother was often angry at my grandfather for doing so much work for Orlando. She got mad, I surmised, because Grandpa would leave in the early morning, walk to the hotel, do some maintenance work, and usually arrive home without getting paid for his labor. Being recently retired, I assumed that working part-time for Orlando gave Pepine a purpose for living. It provided him with something to do each day, for example, in the winter when he could not enjoy his garden. Now that I am also retired, I can understand my grandfather's desire to remain busy. As long as my grandfather was contributing to something, especially work-related he was happy. He complained to Grandma that he was not doing the work for the money anyhow and in his way explained that he was instead working to retain his mental health.

Orlando was quite the fast talker and we all assumed was also very wealthy. He was carefully not ostentatious with his money so he projected the image of just another regular old working-class schmoe in town. Not being confident regarding how Orlando made all of his money, our family rightly assumed that some of his dough came from illegal sources. We all found out later that he was a little more than just an average wheeler-dealer or common flim-flam man.

When I was young I had no idea exactly how Orlando made all his money except that he owned a couple of run-down hotels and area nightclubs. As I got older, however, I became suspicious. My suspicion became reality when one of his hotels burned down and another was eventually raided by the police. The raid uncovered that along with illegal gambling, 5-10 prostitutes were also rounded up in the sting.

Our family overlooked some of Orlando's involvements with crime but when he got nabbed for running prostitutes we did not see much of him anymore. Orlando's high-profile crime was a surprise to my grandparents making it tough to remain friends with him after that. Once, before being nabbed for the prostitution issue and when I was around 16 years old, Orlando offered me a job as a bouncer in one of his nightclubs. My grandmother nixed that idea right away and I thought she stepped in due to concerns for my safety. At the time I was a little disappointed but did not complain that much about it. I was, however, honored to be recruited and felt like quite a tough guy just for being asked. Thinking about it today, I likely would have gotten the tar knocked out of me the first day on the job had I ever taken on the role of the bouncer. Besides, after watching every episode of *The Sopranos,* at least twice, I now know what a poor idea it would have been to mix it up with someone involved in crime. When watching *Godfather II* I marvel at the physical likeness between Orlando and one of the characters, Don Fanucci, who ended up getting killed in Italy by the young Don Corleone. Orlando, like Don Fanucci, may have had a mean side but he never showed it while visiting our home. Instead, Orlando was a likable old fellow who enjoyed our company, Grandma's pasta dinners and trips to the backyard to assess my grandfather's tomato plants. As a kid, I enjoyed Orlando too.

I missed Orlando when he went off to jail. When he was paroled a few years later due to illness, he and his wife moved away. We heard that Orlando died of natural causes shortly after moving. I often think about him and the many other colorful people who stopped at our house for "una tasse di caffe," a cup of coffee, and a little conversation. Carted along with them might be, for example, a bag full of zucchini exchanged for a shot of whiskey or anisette. They would share a couple of stories about their day and off they would disappear until their next visit. That was the way things were done back in our driveway and also in our home. The group of people surrounding us was large and varied in those days and they kept life engaging and entertaining for a boy with lots of free time on his hands.

No Home Alone

****

By now I was anticipating the arrival of both Stripes and Hipster as they circumnavigated the track. All I had to do was look to my right to see if they were emerging from the far corner of the oval. Certainly, they would be loud enough to regain my attention as they neared and awaken me from my memories. Sure enough, I soon heard them rounding the bend just ahead of a slender young woman whom I concluded must be on break from some nearby college. One could almost always determine college kids from all the others since they were not only younger and slimmer but they also seemed much more determined than the rest of us to perform some type of difficult workout. They were frequently seen engaged in the newest exercise techniques, as well. For instance, this young woman was holding two light weights, one in each hand, as she took elongated lunges, alternating one leg after another. I could see the frustration build on the student's face as she tried to pass the two older women who ere ntent on their conversation and not attending to their position on the track.

Stripes: "Some kid in our neighborhood was questioned by the police the other day. The parents were so embarrassed and all the neighbors were wondering what was up."

Hipster: "What's up with that family? Did you hear anything? Why, what do you know about the boy?"

Stripes: "Spends too much time alone. His parents are always somewhere else so he's mostly outside with too much freedom, just hanging out looking for mischief, I guess. I won't let my kids spend time with him that's a-l-l t-h-a-t I k—n—o—w a——b—-o——u——t h——i........"

That's all she knew. I wondered if people thought similarly about me when I was that kid. That is a lie, I know many people were concerned about my behaviors as I often noticed their looks or overheard the gossip. They did not know how to intervene on my behalf or at least I do not think anyone ever did. More likely people wanted to intervene on my grandparents' behalf. Just like the kid that Hipster and Stripes were describing I had too much time and freedom to do as I wished. There were no responsibilities, and no list of chores for me to complete each day so I was always available for fun. There was, however, one big difference between the boy the two women were discussing and me, and unlike that kid, I was never left home alone. My grandparents were always in the house. They seldom left the house together.

There was a major reason that my grandparents were usually home and the reason was mainly my grandmother. During the rare times that Mary went visiting, I would see her squirming around in her chair from the first moment after she sat arrived. Normally it would take an important event, perhaps a birthday or a christening, to get her out of the house especially if she was out for purely social reasons. Once she arrived at the destination she was never comfortable as she would begin plotting, coming up with reasons, excuses really, to return home. I can still see Mari-etti fidgeting in her seat while balancing a cup of coffee on one knee and a piece of cake on the other all the while developing a nervous scowl that enveloped her entire face. As soon as we arrived she would begin the entreaties about needing to leave and get back home. "I'm-a no can stay-a too long," she would say as she entered the house. Excuses such as the dog needing to be fed or go out to pee, or that she, Grandma, had to get up early the next morning to make bread or some other recipe were immediately introduced upon arrival and while removing her coat. She put the host on notice right from the very start. When Granny eventually got desperate to leave she looked for a way to make her entreaties heard, for someone to take her excuses seriously. That is when she pulled out some of her best excuses to leave. One of her best excuses usually involved something physical and one of her favorites was that her arthritis was acting up. The conversation usually included something like the following iteration.

Grandma: "Comare, Ima no can stay too long, you know, mio cane (my dog), Ginger, she's a no feelin-ga too good.

Host: "You stay, mangia, yu jussta got-a here, whatsa matta, the dog she gonna be okay."

After sitting for only a few more minutes,

Grandma: "Devo dare da mangiare al cane," I have to feed the dog

Host: "Comare, the dog shesa so fat no gotta feed for a week. Hey you, Angelina, geeta da Comare ecco (here) anudder piec-a da cake, come on-a hurry uppa."

Some of Grandma's other successful lines designed to help her get back home were:

"I gotta leave a-soon, to hang out some wash, the wet clothes. Its-a no good to stay-a wet."

She would save her best excuse and use it if all other reasons to return home failed.

Grandma: "Yusta giva me only una droppa da caffe. Me-a rhumatisma (rheumatism) itsa botta me so much. I gotta go back-a-home subito (soon) for my pills-a. La medic (doctor) dice (says) I gotta rest."

The last excuse usually brought the unsuspecting hosts to their knees. How could anyone deny an older woman comfort from her Rheumatoid Arthritis? Through time most hosts caught on to the game and came up with ways to keep her calm a little longer. As usual Granny eventually won the debate. Her entreaties paid off. She made life so miserable that my dad would have to take her home early from most social events. He might return after dropping his mother back at home but she would win by leaving way earlier than was considered polite. My grandfather, in the meantime, seldom complained, he just followed along with whatever decision was made.

It was not until I got older and became a psychologist that I began to better understand the causes of some of my grandmother's behaviors. That is, she was significantly more anxious than normal and she likely suffered from a bit of agoraphobia. Perhaps she could have been classified as possessing a full-fledged anxiety disorder but there would be zero chance anything would have been done about that anyhow. I can just see Zia Muttietta showing up for a counseling appointment. She would surely meet with the psychologist carting along an overflowing dish of ravioli or maybe some fresh sausage and peppers. After nibbling on the food for 10 minutes even the psychologist would be asking for the recipe and perhaps feeling a little sorry for Grandma. She would be excused to return home early once she explained her need to take her daily dose of Milk of Magnesia necessary to control sensitive intestinal issues. The next visit she might take a cake along and instead of discussing her fears, the conversation would likely focus on the frosting or custard filling. When I was young I did not comprehend her difficulties but I did have a sense that they were somewhat out of her control. I conjectured they were more than the idiosyncrasies of an older Italian woman even though I did feel that some of her issues were driven by culture. I never pressured Grandma to stay away from home knowing beforehand that our visit to most anywhere, except a grocery store and a few others destinations would be curtailed.

Grandma: "Tu sai, capisci, Jovy, (You know, Joey, you understand)?"

Me: "Yah, Grandma, I know."

Dr. M. and Chloe

My grandmother's arthritis and numerous other ailments gained her a significant amount of attention. Grandma was, for the most part, quite healthy but she did have bonafide health concerns. She often used her health to garner periodic sympathy from others. Sometimes granny seemed to need much more, however. I could never understand why she wanted the type of attention that health issues commanded but she did and one of the ways she obtained sympathy was to regularly visit her doctor. Marietta looked forward to her regularly scheduled physician visits. Going to the doctor was one of maybe four reasons, including grocery shopping, that got her out without having to pry her from her home. One of her early doctors, for example, was an African-American MD in town and my grandmother thoroughly enjoyed her visits to see him. I thought nothing of these visits at the time, they were so regular and were seemingly always a part of her life so they were seldom questioned. Visiting the doctor was just something older people did, especially Italian women, I figured since Maryetta and her friends all seemed to practice the same behavior. It was, strangely, after reading Toni Morrison's book, *Song of Solomon*, that my grandmother's situation with the doctor seemed all the more interesting.

Toni Morrison grew up Chloe Anthony Wofford and attended the same high school as my father. She was 11 years younger than my father so they never interacted but he was proud that he went to a school that graduated someone as famous as Morrison. Upon reading, *Song of Solomon,* I believed that one of the characters in the book, the city's only black general practitioner, was modeled after the same doctor my grandmother loved visiting. In her book, Morrison referred to a few people and places that local people recognized as being taken from the city. One of those fictitious characters she wrote about was a physician, a character who practiced medicine on what became known to local African-Americans in the city as, "Not Doctor Street." As the story goes, officials in town did not like people addressing their mail to "Doctor Street" as this was the name that only blacks popularized. Officials did their best to get people to call the street by its official name, Main Street. Blacks on the other hand decided to rename the street, "Not Doctor Street," in response to the city's denial of the street's nickname. In more than one of her books, Toni Morrison referred to real places in the city so that is why I associate the doctor located on, Not Doctor Street, possibly with Dr. M., my grandmother's physician.

Grandma loved going to Dr. M. and I think that he must have enjoyed my grandmother's visits too. She was always ready for her appointments with the doctor and must have seen him at least once per month. On the days of her visits, she began getting ready early and was usually found sitting and waiting for my father at least 60 minutes in advance of her scheduled appointment. Even though it was only a 10-minute drive to the doctor's office, if Dad did not pick her up at least 45 minutes before her appointment, he would receive a stern correction from "Ma," when he finally arrived.

Grandma: "Louie, where-a you bin? I'm-a wait a-too long. Come-e on let's-a-go. Andiamo, I'ma- gonna be late."

Dad's response, instead of letting it go since it was the same complaint each time:

Dad: "Ma, we got plenty of time. Calm down, I'll get you there on time."

Grandma: "What's a matta yu? You no think I'm-a calm a down? Yu the one who's-a late. You come tak-a me late all ah dah time. Tutto il tempo, all the time."

Right next to her, waiting to be included, would be a nicely packed bag of one freshly made Italian delicacy or another, perhaps homemade rolls or slices of pizza, maybe some meatballs and sauce too that I am sure the doctor looked forward to as part of each of Grandma's visits. Somehow, her general anxiety associated with leaving the house never interfered with her regular physician appointments. She began primping in the morning and seemed to almost rehearse all the new ailments she would present to the kind Dr. M. making sure that nothing was left out. I believe that Dr. M. understood my grandmother's special need for a physician's attention whereas other doctors did not. To me, Dr. M. served as more of a therapist to my grandmother than a primary care physician. Seeing Dr. M. was like one-stop shopping since he took care of both grandma's physical and mental health needs at the same time. Like clockwork, Zia Marietta arrived home from her appointments refreshed and equipped with all the latest news regarding her health. She would report that the doctor felt she would live to be 100, that her twisted bowl required only minor attention, her arthritis would benefit from rest, and her "sugar-IB," Granny's Italian accent for " sugar diabetes," would need to be monitored.

In addition to her regular visits to Dr. M., we could also count on him recommending, at least once per year, that she formally be admitted to our local hospital for a week's worth of necessary observations and tests. While in the hospital, Comare Muddyetta received the attention that she thrived on. From her hospital bed, she would welcome an entourage of visitors as if she were royalty. Each friend and relative trooped to her bedside lavishing her with gifts, well wishes, and hopes for a speedy recovery. Grandma would be in her glory for a minimum of 5 days. It was as if her hospital visit was her way of replenishing her stamina, justifying a much-needed rest from months of cooking, cleaning, and ministering to the needs of others. Some people planned regular trips to Florida for their rest and recuperation but Grandma enjoyed spending a yearly week in the local hospital. The hospital was her vacation as she returned home renewed with a spring in her step as she was once again ready to meet the needs of her world, a world that she pretty much owned. Granny gained all the respect and attention she seemed to need from spending a few days away from the usual daily grind of her life. Thanks to Dr. M.'s attention, the floodgates were open, Grandma's life was recharged and countless family members, boarders, neighbors, and friends could once again continue to enjoy fresh pasta, baked goods, and kind-hearted socialization the type they grew to expect from my Grandmother. For another year Grandma was ready to crank out cakes and cookies, can tomatoes, and boiled noodles. Thank heavens for Dr. M.'s ministering. What an involved woman, my grandmother.

Aside from those doctor visits and a few other outings, Grandma seldom left the house. Therefore, I was never left home alone. But there was one other quirky example of an acceptable reason for my grandmother stepping out besides seeing her doctor or completing food shopping. The other time Comare Muddyetta enjoyed socializing away from home was to attend wakes. Maria did not look forward to people dying or anything as macabre as that but since people tended to pass away she felt she might as well attend their wake. Somehow missing a wake would not hold up to scrutiny in her tiny friendship community anyway so attendance seemed to somehow release her from the self-generated guilt that other forms of socializing may have engendered. Who knew? Why she needed a sanctioned reason for going out and enjoying life is a mystery but then Aunt Mary would not have been so interesting if she had behaved like everyone else. Grandma would gladly attend a wake looking forward to dressing up in one of her many black dresses that were quite the rage back in the old country of Italy. Grandma would even wear her false teeth pulling them out of their snug resting spot on her, comeau, before slapping them smartly into her mouth. This was one of the few events where she would even wear jewelry, and costume stuff, also sporting those cheap screw-in-the-back earrings seldom seen anymore. Marrietta went so far as to put on a little lipstick and a modest amount of rouge rubbed into her cheeks also for added effect. After all, she could not have the person in the coffin looking better, more alive, than her.

Once all dolled up she would enter the funeral home like royalty and after offering her condolences to the family she would settle into a comfortable armchair next to her similarly attired and adorned friends, Biagina and Feliciana. Those two women were almost always also in attendance as the three of them pretty much knew all the same people. This female triumvirate would quickly begin sharing all the bad news since the last wake they all attended. Before becoming too comfortable, however, it was customary for the mourning group to shed a few tears before maybe munching on a cookie or two, followed by spreading all the latest gossip surrounding their poor Italian friend who had recently bitten the dust. Somehow, I figured, as I sat bored on an overstuffed hideously upholstered piece of furniture, that internally she felt absolved by Christ himself for attending the wake. It was somehow okayed from God above that she attends the wake since the occasion could not be considered recreation but instead something even the holy father would approve of. I believe that deep down Grandma and her pals believed that there was a passage buried deep in the bible that legitimized and perhaps even blessed their attendance at wakes and funerals. It was a no-guilt social day sort of speak. For example, "To everything, there is a season, and a time to every purpose under heaven: …A time to weep, and a time to laugh; a time to mourn, and a time to dance; (Ecclesiastes 3:1-4-King James version).

Another minor and yearly task that would get Maryetti out of the house besides those mentioned was picking tomatoes at nearby farms. Picking tomatoes, like attending wakes was not considered recreation so leaving her home was okay. While my grandfather planted a rather large and healthy garden, Grandma required five or six additional bushels of the fruit to produce all the sauce she felt was necessary to get through the hard Ohio winter. Grandma always had enough canned tomatoes in her fruit cellar to last more than three years but one never knew when an apocalypse or perhaps a tsunami would strike. She also needed to be prepared for any tomato emergency such as a sudden blight or maybe an invasion of locusts. After all, history was on her side. One only needed to dial up what happened to the Irish during their Great Potato Famine of 1845. Nonetheless, Grandma's fresh tomato sauce stockpile was second to none and served as another source of conflict brought up each year by Dad and my grandfather, who seldom weighed in on most topics except politics. After my father married Hanna she too would join the chorus of individuals criticizing Grandma's inventory of overflowing homemade canned goods lining the walls of her tidy little fruit cellar. Grandma, after the yearly argument, expectedly ignored her critics who lamented to no avail that she had enough canned tomatoes lining her cellar walls to feed all the people who died in Pompeii. Grandma instead and as usual coaxed Dad into driving her and her friends, usually good friends Biagina and Domenic Spolano, to a local farm on a chosen Saturday in late

August to pick the largest, juiciest, reddest tomatoes that money could buy.

As a seven or eight years old I looked forward to accompanying them on their yearly pilgrimage out to the farm. As they picked pomodore, tomatoes, I knew that they would be too focused on picking to pay much attention to me. I also knew that as the charming young prince of the family, I would not be required to take part in any of the labor involved with tomato picking. Work was for others and not for little Jovy. Therefore, I was free to set off on my own to locate some trouble. The farm experience represented another fine example of how I could find mischief all by myself almost anywhere without the help of others.

As my Dad, grandparents, and the Spalanos bent over filling their bushel baskets with juicy red tomatoes I searched for juicy hot mischief. One of my favorite rebellious acts while visiting the farm was chucking tomatoes at a group of cows conveniently lined up in a pen next to the tomato field. Each time I connected with one of the Holsteins the cow would let out a hardy, "Moo!" I must have thrown 50 or 60 ripe tomatoes at the unsuspecting bovines and I cannot remember anyone ever storming out of the barn to complain about my actions. I must have carried on with this senseless activity for what seemed like hours without being noticed. Certainly, I am now embarrassed by such a stupid and juvenile act not to mention the likely torture of innocent farm animals, but when you are less than 10 years old a guy is fairly clueless. The cows were too easy of a target to pass up. One year I remember my target shifted to a group of hefty hogs who replaced the cows in the pen. The pigs, unlike the cows, enjoyed eating the ripe fruit even though it might mean being banged in the ribs or conked in the head by a well-thrown sphere.

When my family had picked their share of tomatoes I simply rendezvoused with them as they loaded the car with the spoils of their day's labor. As we drove home through the country I would gaze out the window focusing in on the red barns, many emblazoned with the familiar chewing tobacco sign, *Mail Pouch*, printed on their roofs. As we drove I was the perfect little angel sitting comfortably in the back seat gazing upon the lucky farm animals like sheep or horses or some other domestic animals that escaped my accurate pitches. Driving in the country was itself a form of entertainment back in the 50s and early 60s so I looked forward to the ride home after a hard day of lobbing tomatoes at helpless farm creatures. All in a day's work for a spoiled little Italian-American boy hailing from the city.

As we continued our drive home, windows rolled down, I listened as the crew of adults analyzed the day's picking versus previous picking trips. The comparisons went on and on until we pulled into the Spolano driveway on Washington Street delivering both Domenic and Biagina safely home. Besides targeting the farm animals I also recall how big and ripe the tomatoes were. They remain the best tomatoes I ever tasted. Before leaving the Spolano's driveway plans would be made to meet up the next day to can the fruit while they remained fresh. I knew that canning day would be less exciting as Biagina, Domenic, and my grandparents would work tirelessly while preparing what seemed like hundreds of jars of tomatoes. The pomodores would eventually be transformed into the best homemade pasta sauce on earth. By the way, in our home, we called it sauce. We had nothing to do with calling it, *gravy,* as everyone seems to call it in New Jersey. I think it was on the TV show, *The Sopranos*, that I first heard pasta sauce called gravy, and have scoffed at the term ever since. Why I scoff at calling it gravy instead of sauce I do not know but I kiddingly warn people from New

Jersey to never substitute the word gravy for sauce in front of me. This, of course, is a silly argument but one that marches on nonetheless.

After the canning was complete, the new jars would be dated and neatly shelved in what was called the fruit cellar even though I never recall any fresh fruit being stored in the room. The only fruit in our fruit cellar was found in a can and it could have been stored almost anywhere. The canned fruit was neatly lined up next to many other cans of just about every vegetable ever produced by Mr. Del Monte. The items that needed storage in the fruit cellar were prosciutto, homemade sausage, and large balls of provolone cheese, waxed and attached to a traditional rope all hanging from a joist hook. The provolone was always the size of bowling balls and they had the most pungent smell of all the items stored in the cellar. The smell of the fruit cellar in our basement will always be part of my memory as I am transported back in time when entering an old-fashioned Italian store like the one that is located 30 minutes away from our present home in Pittsburgh.

It was also in our fruit cellar in one of our houses, the one on the lake, that I recall slowly downing a bottle of a sweet wine known at the time as *Bali Hai.* The wine was continuously advertised on TV during the 60s and was promoted by a plump Polynesian woman who stated at the end of each commercial, "*Bali Hai, you like*?" The commercial was likely associated with the release of the musical movie, *South Pacific*, in 1958. The bottle was opened after someone thought it timely and perhaps even sophisticated to gift it to my grandparents. Maybe my father or someone had a small glass of it to be polite or simply to see what the advertised product tasted like. Being too sweet for the Italian pallet, the remainder of the bottle was stored in the cellar with only me taking an occasional sip of its sweet nectar. After the first taste, I was hooked. I loved sneaking down to the cellar for another swig whenever no one was looking. Eventually, the bottle mysteriously emptied. When the empty bottle was discovered months later it was concluded that the wine must have evaporated or something. I certainly agreed with the suggested reason since the conclusion seemed the only logical explanation for its disappearance. I shrugged my shoulders in agreement when the conclusion was drawn. Where else could the wine have gone? I realize speaking at length about *Bali Hai* wine, canning tomatoes, and fruit cellars is a strange thing for a guy to fondly recall about his childhood but they were all part of my Italian experience. Picking tomatoes, attending wakes with old ladies, and listening to stories about trips to the doctor's office was simply part of my life with my family, especially my grandmother. These events made Marietti tick with Pepine following silently right along. Me too. That is where I was fortunately immersed through my early life and I enjoy retelling the stories.

Jimmy, Putt, and Dently

Mischief was my life while growing up. I have established that by now. It should also be established that I was not the only one or the only instigator that caused neighborhood turmoil. My friends could be dastardly too and somehow we all tended to get away with murder. I began making pals all over the area while living on 21st Street. My friends, just like me, enjoyed taking part in the craziness of various sorts. In addition to Rudy and Dirk living a few blocks away in one direction and Anton and Guido living in another, a few guys lived just down the street. For instance, a pal we named Jimmy the Sausage and another fellow we called,Puttaralla lived just a few houses down the street. Both of these guys were two years my senior but they let me tag along with them anyhow. They were just two of a growing list of compatriots in the mild misdemeanor department during the three years I lived on 21st Street with my grandparents. Jimmy and I always hung out together and given that he hailed from an Italian heritage, his family and mine were quite chummy. Sending food from one house to the other was a common occurrence and served as a way to cement our friendship. Jim and I spent many fun days hanging with each other doing everything from sneaking into his uncle's room and snooping through his stash of nudist magazines to throwing snowballs at passing cars. I remember a short discussion Jim and I had about being confused with a guy wanting to become a priest yet ferreting away nudist magazines. Our discussion about snowball throwing was much more intense.

Jimmy also had a grandfather, Pietro, who nurtured a healthy grape arbor and used the grapes to make dark red wine only slightly more drinkable than the wine produced by Joe Cappello. Pietro also had two rather large casks down in his basement right next to an old grape press and we would regularly bend down, put our mouths under the tap and turn on the knob. It did not take long to fill our cheeks with the strong red brew. Fortunately, none of us enjoyed the wine's flavor so we never really became intoxicated after having a couple of tastes. That was not our intent anyway. We simply drank it as another way to give the world our middle fingers and to have something else to snicker about. Had the wine tasted like the Bali Hai, the sweet wine I drank some years later in my grandparents' fruit cellar, we may have likely become, as the Italians say, "ubriaco," that is, drunk. Pietro suspected we were sampling his concoction from time to time and referred to us as, "diavoli," devils, but he never snitched on our parents. He instead shook his fist and chased us away using a fly swatter with a sly smile pasted on his weathered old face.

When we were not drinking Pietro's wine Jimmy and I enjoyed poking fun at our friend, Puttaralla's, last name. We liked to say things like Puttaralla never puts his toys away, instead like a golfer he "putted" them away. We then in unison pretended to use a golf putter to swing into the air mimicking how a golfer would putt them into place. This was stupid but we did it all the same anyway. We never got tired of doing the putting routine followed by hysterical laughter. Naturally, this drove Puttaralla crazy but he remained our friend despite this harassment. I still do the Puttaralla routine today and it drives my wife crazy. Each time I hear the phrase, "Put it away," I break in and change it by saying, "Let's putt it away instead," and go into my classic golf swinging motion. My wife often wishes she had a real golf club to whack over my head when I begin the routine.

If the three of us were not pelting someone's garage with apples, we were regularly permitted to sleep out all night in a friend's garage which always included taking it upon ourselves to plan raids on neighborhood gardens. After finishing our 16 oz. RC Colas and large bags of Snyder of Berlin Potato Chips we particularly enjoyed raiding the gardens pilfering carrots, peppers, and occasionally zucchini. Once we timed a sleepout to coincide with the ripening of the fruit from a fellow's coveted fig tree. He carted the fig tree back from Italy years earlier nurturing it for years so it would finally bear fruit. Unfortunately, we got most of the figs before the poor sap could harvest them himself and we joined right in with all the wondering and conjecturing regarding how the fruit suddenly disappeared. We agreed with the popular opinion that an errant raccoon must have stolen the figs as it marauded through the neighborhood late at night. Unfortunately, this was one year that our fellow paisano enjoyed only a precious few of his coveted figs since they ended up in our young bellies as opposed to his kitchen table. We were infantile meanies for some reason when we were young always pulling off terrible acts and snickering about getting away with them. We must have relished the adventure of creating neighborhood mysteries and sitting back and appearing just as astonished about the thievery as everyone else.

There was a fourth guy that we hung with fairly often as well. Dently was his name and he lived a little further down the block. I would often hang out with Dently if Jimmy and Puttaralla were not around. It would not be unusual for me to start the day playing with Jimmy and Puttaralla and later hang out solely with Dently. Dently was three years older than me and quite bright. He was not only older but he also came from an upper-middle-class family. I think his father was an engineer and perhaps a foreman in the steel mill, being the only college-educated adult in the neighborhood. Dently's family had, it seemed at least, more money than the rest of us and we drew this conclusion based on the number and kind of toys he had down his basement. He not only owned one of those Lionel train cities set up in a room devoted entirely to the electric train but he also had tons of other toys including everything from army men to plastic swords, shields, and Roman helmets that we could use to dress as gladiators. We would spend hours sword fighting in the back yard coming inches from losing an eye or ear while engaged in make-believe battle.

Perhaps due to his environment, Dently knew things that the rest of us had never heard about and he taught me many things that I would not have been exposed to in my family. For example, Dently taught me the wonders of mixing saltpeter (potassium nitrite) with sugar and when lit it would create miniature fire bombs that we used to make our war games more realistic. This guy even knew how to order wick, flammable fuse, through the mail that we would attach to little plastic tubes to make explosives for added fun. Not bad for a guy who was only 10 or 11 years old at the time. We would attach the small incendiary devices to some expendable rubber war figures, such as rubber army tanks, jeeps, or a group of soldiers, and whoosh, up they went in smoke. These were the days when there was a constant running of war movies on TV so Dently's little bombs were right in line with contemporary media and represented our miniaturized version of what we saw on TV.

Dently found that while he could order the wick through the mail he could not order the saltpeter. The saltpeter had to be bought at a pharmacy but this consumer barrier was no problem for Dently. Dently told me that he was too old to buy the saltpeter. He would look suspicious. So he instead trained me to visit the local pharmacy on the corner of 19th and Oberlin Avenue to buy the chemical. I can only wonder what the pharmacist must have thought when an eight-year-old, me, stepped up to the counter and asked for a half pound of saltpeter. Saltpeter has many practical uses, I found out later, besides the production of fireworks. For example, it was widely rumored to induce impotence in men and assumed to be a secret ingredient placed in the food of soldiers to control their sexual desires while on the battlefield. Even for a conspiring street-smart and maturing fella like me in 1959, that information was a little beyond my knowledge base. That, however, was not true for my older friend Dently who taught me all about it. He not only knew all about saltpeter's varied applications but he knew how to mix the chemical to create these little fire bombs. He also realized that my age and innocence would not raise alarms with the pharmacist. Just in case I was questioned, Dently coached me to say it was for food preservation, another one of the many obscure uses of saltpeter. Dently was a bit of a prodigy for a guy his age.

Had our bomb-creating behavior been judged by today's standards, we would both be identified as potential arsonists or worse yet terrorists. In the 50s, however, we were just a couple of adventurous kids out to have a good time. After all, it was the height of the "boys will be boys" era. So we created countless little incendiaries as we merrily blew up Dently's toy army concentrating mainly on blowing up the Nazi soldiers while luckily never getting burned, figuratively or literally, ourselves. Years later I heard that my precocious friend Dently took advantage of his obvious high IQ. Dently used his skills to become a prominent surgeon at the Cleveland Clinic and was able to use his abilities, honed right there on 21st Street, to save many lives.

Harrison School (Again)

While I often played with Jimmy, Puttaralla, and Dently I still had surplus time, compared to most others my age, so much so that I was almost continually searching for more adventures to keep me busy. If Jimmy, Dently, or Puttaralla were busy then perhaps there were other things happening elsewhere so I went out exploring the area to find them. One place where I could usually find excitement was at my school, Harrison Elementary. There I could usually find a big game of *Capture The Flag* taking place on the front steps of the building as there were usually all kinds of kids hanging around playing some type of game. The bunch at Harrison mirrored, in many ways, the group of kids starring in the *Little Rascals* from the *Our Gang Comedy* series we watched on TV each day. The series played most afternoons between maybe 4:00 and 6:00 right before the evening news programs. Just like the Rascals, the group hanging around Harrison was multi-cultural with local kids corresponding to many of the characters in the series. For example, there was a guy named Scarucchi who could have played, "Chubby," in the series, and a girl named Patti who could have easily been Darla. All the guys, as young as we were, swooned over Patty as she acted coy and cute just like Darla did toward Alfalfa in the series All the boys wanted Patti's attention but only the lucky ones were invited to kiss her under the fire escape. I considered another guy, Billy Deternio as Butch the Bully because more than once he taunted me and tended to steal my new English Racer bicycle whenever I was not looking. A guy in our neighborhood especially had to be tough even against a bully who might be older, bigger, and tougher. If that was not possible then he had to find a way to deal with the problem himself like identifying someone willing to protect him from ongoing abuse. In those days there were no anti-bullying campaigns nor adults to intervene. Billy only stopped bullying me when an older kid, Georgie Castile came to my rescue and I repaid him by giving him a ride home on my bicycle whenever he asked. Another guy, living just across the street from the school was the quintessential spanky character because everyone paid attention to him and seemed to enjoy his company when he was allowed out to hang with us, knuckleheads. He hung out at the school sometimes but not as often as the rest of us. Years later he and I would end up being together again but this time by attending the same college. The Alfalfa character belonged to a guy named Francisco whom everyone liked but seemed to always end up the buffoon no matter how much he tried to be popular.

Mostly, everyone seemed to get along well enough at Harrison School. There may have been some arguing and bullying but I never remember any real fighting taking place. It was not, however always that way. Harrison was not safe at times until a couple of brothers, Teddy Eckles and his brother Pat were eventually loaded into the back of a police paddy wagon, hauled off to jail, and never heard of again. They got caught breaking into a local hardware store and were likely turned in to the cops by one of the kids they were in the habit of torturing.

No one ever defaced the school with graffiti either but there was one time that Rudy and Dirk entered the school after hours just because someone left a door unlocked. They got caught by the school's custodian, Rudy's neighbor, Mr. Dicky, and both were banned from the playground for two weeks. Meanwhile, the rest of us continued to enjoy a variety of games at Harrison. Most often there were numerous and varied games all going on at the same time. Usually, a kickball game was in progress on the basketball court with some form of tag, hopscotch, jump rope, and many other old-time games like four square taking place nearby. A kid's importance and status were measured by how fast he could run or how far she could kick a ball. If you could do both you were hot. Even if you could not run the fastest or kick the farthest everyone was included and we all had a great time. After a game of *Capture The Flag,* probably the most fun game of all, it was not unusual for someone to show up with a basketball or football and begin choosing sides for a quick game before it got too dark to see. My early life, as I think back and especially as I grow older, was defined by games such as kickball and other sports, especially football.

Oh, Boy! Did I Say Football?

Our games varied in the side yard of Harrison Elementary School but our favorite became, at least Rudy's and mine, was football. Most often we played pick-up football games at the school in preparation for someday joining an official team. Rudy and I felt so superior when the older guys fought to have us on their side. Sometimes for fun and when they could get away with it, the older guys would use us as secret weapons against unsuspecting teams from other neighborhoods who thought Rudy and I were just a couple of puny little kids from down the block. Instead, our teammates would hike the ball to Rudy who would quickly fade back before delivering a perfect spiral to me as we all ended up laughing at the naiveté of the other team while falling into the end zone. In those days Rudy had a great arm and I had descent speed for a short skinny kid and this earned us both a bunch of statuses and a way to feel good about ourselves. We were fortunate to have some natural skills for a game that in those days was quickly replacing baseball as the national sport. Football probably had, at least in the short run, a major effect on whom we would become.

I fondly recall a day during a distant September, we had both just entered fourth grade, when Rudy picked me up on a Saturday morning on his way to football practice. Football was becoming so exciting to Rudy that he would get up early enough on the weekend to attend an organized practice. Usually, we spent the day together hanging around Harrison School playing football but now Rudy had managed to find a way to play the game in a more organized way. Rudy had already been playing on the team for a week or so when he thought to grab me to see if I also wanted to try out for the St. Peter's CYO (Catholic Youth Organization) football team. I had never heard of CYO and Rudy explained that all he knew was it was affiliated with our church and he was having a whole ton of fun playing. There was no need to ask me twice. I quickly dressed and with Rudy on the handlebars of my blue English Racer, the bike Billy Deternio used to steal, and me peddling behind him, we sped toward the practice field. Off we rode to the start of what would become a small-time but glorious football career for both of us.

As we arrived at Cities Field, it was clear that the team I would eventually join was not an assemblage of the town's best athletes. The team was also not the most organized either. It became immediately clear that the phrase, "Tryout for the team," was an over-extension of the words since the team would accept any kid who was not in a wheelchair. From the potpourri of equipment to the antics of the players milling around, it was clear that St. Peters football was going to be more about fun than winning. From the moment I parked my bike and Rudy began putting on his pads, a chorus of wisecracks could be heard between the guys. Most were directed at Rudy and me as we arrived after practice had begun. "Good that you finally showed up Perez. Did the tortillas come off the fire a little too late?" Another guy chimed in, "Who's this guy with you your personal chauffeur?"

Finally, the wisecracks began spilling over to just about everyone else on the field as the spotlight finally moved away from us. This friendly jabber continued until the two coaches blew their whistles calling the practice to order. The coaches were Mr. Boraccio and Mr. Di'Amato. Both coaches were first-generation Italians, just like my father. In fact, Mr. Boraccio and my dad graduated together. In the early '60s, churches in the city continued to be located in ethnic neighborhoods with St. Peter's remaining composed largely of Italian Americans. Most of the guys on the field, as a result, had

Italian surnames as well, such as Scupolli, Campanella, and Trataglia. Some guys on the team were not Italian but since they lived in the neighborhood and were Catholic they were allowed to play on the team.

The team was considered ragtag from the start. Other teams, such as St. Stanislaus, Polish, or St. Marys, Irish, were better prepared and equipped but St. Pete's, in those days, was not a wealthy parish and it was saving every donated penny to build a new church across town. The out-of-date equipment I saw scattered around was a good representation of the church's limited funding of its football team and probably its lack of status in the community, as well. For example, most of the helmets only had a single face guard for protection and some of the guys were forced to wear helmets that were not only too large but some were even without any face mask at all. Few players had all the updated protective pads that were required for safety and for those that did not, well they simply wore whatever was assigned no matter if it fits them correctly or not. Most of the guys were accustomed to playing tackle football on school grounds, without pads, so any amount of protection was better than nothing. For the chance to win a spot on the St. Petes football team, I would have played without any helmet or maybe even in my underwear. I loved football and playing it competitively, on a team, seemed like the greatest thing ever.

For most of the morning that first day I sat on the sidelines watching the older players, many of whom were already in junior high school. The players mostly screwed around and only intermittently played serious ball. Most of the guys seemed to be practicing to be comedians rather than football players and barely a few of them had any real athletic talent. One of the guys who seemed to be the team leader was a Black kid named Darnell who would run and make great catches then pretend to stomp on imaginary defensive players. The behavior always seemed to make the rest of the team laugh so Darnell did it each time he made a catch. Two other unofficial team leaders were twin brothers, tight ends, who did more messing around than playing football. They made as many jokes as receptions and both were vying for the title of team-designated comedian. Who knew that these brothers would grow up to become quite wealthy making their fortune in the local construction trade? The quarterback was a tall blonde guy named Robby Stizak who seemed to be one of the few serious players on the team.

After watching the team's antics, as the players drove up and down the dusty field, Rudy introduced me to the coaches and asked them if I could play along with the other guys. Coach Di'Amato, who spent much of his time chewing on the end of his Predroni cigar, said I was still too young (Rudy was six months older than me and just made the cutoff) to officially be on the team but he saw no harm in allowing me to take part in the practices.

Most of the fellas were in fifth through eighth grade and Rudy and I were still in grade four so I was particularly starry-eyed being able to play with the "big" boys. When I got a chance to step in and play, I vividly recollect the surprised looks from the coaches. They seemed to be impressed as they shook their heads praising my skills especially given my age and size. As I look back on this early recognition, it catalyzed an eight-year love affair I developed for the sport. Football defined much of my early life, from grades 4-12, and when I think back to my days as an athlete they seem to describe the life of an entirely different person. That is, I find it hard to believe that I simply loved playing football that much and that I devoted so much time practicing and playing the game.

That day, unfortunately, near the end of my very first football team practice, Rudy caught a long pass from the quarterback, Robbie Stizak, and as he fell to the ground he broke his collar bone. Neither his injury nor my breaking my hand as a regular member of the team a year later interfered with our love for the sport. Rudy and I would go on to play many games of football apart as well as together for the next eight years. Rudy played even longer earning a scholarship to an area college to play the sport. We continued to love the game despite its potential for injuries. Now that I am older it is easy to also criticize the sport. In many ways, football is a nutty game since it can easily cause lifelong injuries. I have a couple of them myself. The famous comedian, Dick Gregory, summed up football by joking something like, "Would anyone line up two rows of brand-new Cadillacs across from one another and then step heavily on the gas pedal." Usually, most sane people respond with an emphatic, "No." That summed up football for Gregory but not for thick-headed guys like Rudy and me.

Even though I was not officially allowed to play in games that first year the coaches gave me a weathered uniform to take home and use only in team practices. My dad was all in favor of me playing organized football especially since he was not allowed to play as a kid. My grandmother had reservations and worried I would get hurt but she did not put up a big squawk against my joining the squad. Besides, the little prince wanted to play the sport so I did. Grandma usually worried I would get hurt almost any time, no matter what I did, so convincing her that football would be safe was not too difficult especially since she knew very little about the sport. On other safety issues, Grandma was not so understanding. For example, when I turned 16 I bought a small Honda motorcycle and she refused to speak with my father until he made me sell it. I persuaded the kid who sold the cycle to me that he ought to return the money. Everyone lived happily ever after from that decision.

So I played organized football from grade 4 through my senior year of high and the game seemed to define me, at least partially, for those eight years. The same applied to some of the other guys too, especially Rudy. Now, as I think back on it, football may have cemented our ongoing friendship through all those early years.

Galen & King's Woods

From my home base, I began to fan out around the neighborhood. Included was football, my friends in the neighborhood, there was Rudy, the gang at Harrison School, and then there were my Italian friends, Anton and Guido. I think it was this freedom and independence, probably way too much for a kid my age, that raised eyebrows with some of the people who used to gather at my grandparents' home. Fortunately, in this neighborhood, I never hung around with anyone who was involved with any major crimes. We mostly engaged in petty stuff. At least that was our conclusion. Given our freedom, we got ourselves into what we considered the ordinary stupid stuff kids get into when they are unsupervised. For example, Rudy and a guy named Galen, and I used to regularly harass the hobos who hung around the rail yard at a place called King's Woods. We took great pride in lobbing rotten apples or rocks in the direction of unsuspecting guys who rode into town on the rails. On more than one occasion we also enjoyed breaking into the cabooses of parked trains while never really finding anything of worth in their cupboards except for flares. We, of course, stole them and lit them up to first throw one or two at each other and then maybe throw a few at bums before running away while laughing like maniacs. We never gave thought to what would have happened if someone, maybe a hobo or railway officer, caught us. Nor did we think about how hurt we could get if we fell from the top of boxcars we regularly climbed as we jumped from one car to another playing tag. I drew a line, however, when it came to some of the potential dangers in the railway yard. For instance, I would not hop on to a moving train because I was always fearful that I would slip and the train would cut off my arm or leg or something worse. I did have some standards. So if a train was moving I steered clear of it. We three enjoyed real-life trains in those days while hanging with other guys like Dently introduced me to toy trains set up neatly in his basement. He and I drove those trains while Rudy, Galen, and I had the real thing. The only thing we could not do was drive the locomotive or pull the engine's whistle and we would have likely done that too if we could have found a way.

One of my fondest memories, one that is often recalled by both Rudy and Galen is when I invited the guys over to my house for lunch for the first time. I figured that after a full morning of harassing the hobos at King's Woods that the fellas and I could use a quick pick me up. My grandmother had no forewarning that I would be showing up with two new and hungry friends but that never mattered to her. Grandma was always prepared with a well-stocked refrigerator plus she enjoyed feeding people and that was what endeared her to almost everyone. On this day she would forever endear herself to my two good pals.

The thing that Rudy, a Mexican-American, and Galen, an African-American, remember is how my family, especially my grandmother, welcomed them both into our home. Racial issues continue to make headlines all over the country but in the late 60s, a minority guy had to wonder if he would be accepted into the home of a Caucasian friend. No problem for either in this case. Instead of racism, my grandmother told us to wait while she prepared something for us to eat. We cooled our heels messing with my toys and chasing my dog around the backyard. To my friends' surprise, in about 20 minutes Grandma clomped up from the basement with three well-done T-bone steaks each one large enough to feed Fred Flintstone. On another plate, she had a stack of hand-cut French fries the likes of which I have never tasted by anyone else, except perhaps the fries made by *Berardi's* and sold at *Cedar Point Amusement Park*, a popular and well-known destination in Sandusky, Ohio. Certainly, there was Grandma's traditional green salad, soda pop, and other delicacies including an assortment of Italian pastries to wash everything down.

Rudy and Galen said they had never eaten so much in one sitting and enjoyed retelling the story about my grandmother's surprise steak dinner. While serving up a huge T-bone defined my grandmother, it also defined my grandfather too. Even though I never remember my grandfather cooking, I do remember how he enjoyed the company and the audience my friends provided for his stories. Grandpa had a habit of telling the same story over and over but this never stopped people from listening to them again as he merrily repeated each tale. He probably told a few of his favorites to Rudy and Galen as they sat gorging themselves by his side of the kitchen table.

For years my grandfather told the same stories repeatedly. He had a list of at least 40 stories, poems, and comical quips he pulled from his memory and delighted in sharing with anyone who would listen. The kitchen table doubled as Pepino's stage and the diners were his captive audience. Grandma cooked and Grandpa served up the entertainment. Most of his stories originated from his experiences in life either back in Italy or working in the steel mill in our hometown or coal mines of Western Pennsylvania. One of the introductory quotes that he used as a segue into his routine was a saying a Hungarian guy said to him one day while they worked up on the blast furnace. That phrase was something like, "Ninc munka ninc elelmiszer," translated as, no work not food. After he explained the phrase in great detail he usually began repeating stories about his dad's occupation as a forest ranger in Italy. I do not remember much more about my great-grandfather except that he was a ranger in a park surrounding Tussio as Grandpa never expanded beyond his limited description. Next, my grandfather would talk about how he was the smartest kid in the village school that he attended. He was very proud of his education as he learned to read and write during a time when few others had the luxury of doing the same. I have a copy of Grandpa's Certificate of Exams dated March 3, 1892, from the Scuola Elementare Pubblica Mista Del Comune Prata D'Ansidonia, that is, the name of his elementary school in his home region, Prata D"Ansidonia. On his certificate, he earned all passing marks and was promoted to the next level. He was proud of his schooling and enjoyed proving to people that he learned something important while in Italy as he began reciting a few Italian poems, some of which were well-known classics in Italian. The poems were recited in what he and others considered "proper Italian" and the sound of his verse seemed different even to me compared with the various Italian dialects that most of his countrymen spoke in our home. I never understood the poems but remember how the poems touched a chord in many visitors as I noticed them wiping away more than one tear from their eyes during Gramp's recitation. Native Italians can be very emotional people. Someone was sure to inform me, after Zio Pepine's recitation, that my grandfather had a sharp memory and was a very wise man. I simply smiled and agreed. I knew that their conclusions were only partially correct. Giuseppe had a good long-term memory for some things but his short-term memory was by this time unfortunately sliding. Grandpa's repetition of the same stories was not some small-time issue related to an aging man. Eventually, we learned that Grandpa's difficulty was diagnosed as Parkinson's Disease and this became quite evident later as the disease progressed and he developed a pronounced shaking of his right hand. The shaking did not bother him that much unless he was eating soup. He tried to spoon up the broth but the shaking frustrated his efforts usually ending with him loudly proclaiming, "son n'ma bitch-a."

One of Grandpa's more colorful stories was about a ditch digger named Mingo who fell into a pit that was for some reason filled with dung. Mingo did not get out of the pit without first swallowing a mouthful of the pit's contents. Therefore, each time someone, especially my grandmother proclaimed that her stomach was too full to eat anymore, my grandfather would emphatically pipe in and say, "Si, maybe she's-a full like-a Mingo." I can still see my grandfather almost doubled over belly laughing along with the crowd as if it were the first time the tale had ever been told. Pepino just loved repeating the phrase, "Full like-a Mingo," and it almost seemed that Grandma was the Abbott to Grandpa's Costello, that is, his straight man feeding him the lines so he could repeat the comical phrase yet again.

Si Pepine had another favorite, about an Italian guy who wanted to buy some cheese, formaggio, but he could not communicate his needs to the storekeeper in English. As the Italian man was about to leave in frustration he muttered his exasperation in Italian, saying something that sounded like "che checchese," meaning, I give up, and then the English-speaking shopkeeper replied, "Oh, so you want to buy some cheese? I got plenty, come back." He would tell these stories as if they were being told for the first time and he always gave the best laugh ever too. One could not help but smile and feel a bit of Grandpa's merriment.

Besides his usual stories, the only other thing my grandfather would mutter about was politics. He was a die-hard democrat and union man. Grandpa was always up to date on the news because he read the newspaper from front to back each day while sitting at his desk in the living room. He hated Richard Nixon and credits himself with predicting that, "Signore Tricky Dick," would eventually be, "fired out." Grandpa enjoyed predicting and promoting the idea that every republican should be, "Fired out."

While I cannot recall which stories my grandfather told Rudy and Galen during their historical inaugural steak dinner, I am sure he mentioned how people from every nationality worked side by side in the local steel mill where it seemed most of the men in our hometown were employed. My grandfather had a repertoire of stories that he borrowed from almost every nationality because he worked with a multicultural group. Most of his stories were work-related because work is what a guy like my grandfather knew about. Hard work defined him and his generation When it came to life, a man was measured by his work ethic and according to Giuseppe, a man's ethnicity or the color of his skin was secondary. Grandpa's invitation to eat at his table even included Republicans if they were judged to be hard-working and pleasant. Rudy and Galen were especially safe since my grandfather would have surmised, from his work-related experience, that a Mexican-American and African-American would-be Democrats and not Republicans back in the late 50s and early 60s.

Rudy and Galen somehow devoured their whole steak, most of the French Fries, and the salad. They relive that lunch each time we meet up as adults giving me a chance to share my stories involving the best tamales or the best mac and cheese that I ever enjoyed at their respective homes.

Growing up Italian means that food is more prominent than stories. Who does not know that now, "capisci." During the 60s, however, information of this sort was not as widely known. My impression while growing up was that "American" families did not necessarily emphasize food as much as we did or celebrate eating together, weekly at regularly scheduled Sunday meals. If it was Sunday most Italian-American families that I knew were eating together usually at noon or so. Most Italian-Americans I knew worshipped in church each Sunday before sitting down to a multi-course meal that could not begin until everyone, whoever that included, was at the table. My family, like most Italian-Americans, was Catholic and they tried their best to have me follow the Catholic doctrine as well. I was even convinced that I wanted to become an altar boy when I was in fourth grade. I was doing well in the altar boy training department by memorizing the numerous Latin prayers required during the mass and also learning all the choreographed moves up at the altar designed to assist the priest throughout the service such as,

"Ad Déum qui laetíficat juventútem méam."

My downfall, and certainly there was going to be a downfall, came when I was caught trying to play a rock song on the electric bells situated on the altar as Father LaBelli stepped back into the church during one of our training sessions. The bells were not designed for rock music, of course, but instead designed to use sparingly to add emphasis to various individual portions of the liturgy. If the rock music was not enough, the last straw came when Dirk and I were later caught wrestling under the communion table by the same priest. Getting caught wrestling so embarrassed me that I decided to quit the training rather than face the head priest, Father O'Deo, to explain our antics. Confessing my behavior to the assistant priest was bad enough but now I was too chicken to face the lead priest too. So instead of facing up to my crime, I quit my short career as an altar boy before things ever got started. I made up some excuse or another to explain to my dad and grandparents why I quit. Dirk decided to quit shortly after I did too but he was not about to leave empty-handed. He left only after drinking a bit too much of the sacristy wine followed by stealing a rather large plastic bag full of unblessed wafers, the communion hosts, that had not yet been turned into the body of Christ. He guiltily handed them out to his friends, including

Rudy, Anton, and me as we met up one day in front of the old church on 17th Street. The whole group of us, derelict heathens, ate the majority of the unblessed wafers knowing fully well we would certainly all end up burning in hell when our time clocks were punched. Hell is where we all belonged anyhow after this little rebellious act. At least if we all ended up in hell together we figured we might be able to have a little more fun together when the devil was not paying attention.

Without the altar boy gig to study and train for I continued to have too much time and was increasingly becoming the neighborhood drifter. When I was not with Rudy and Dirk I was with Anton and Guido. It did not take long for Anton, Guido, and I to become just as big annoyances in their neighborhood as Rudy, Dirk, and I were menaces in their neighborhood. I had a BB gun, for instance, part-time, that I borrowed from my cousin, and being boys we thought nothing of shooting anything nonhuman, such as cats, squirrels, and birds as well as street lamps, posts, and construction signs. In those days we always seemed to get away with these minor offenses even one time inadvertently killing a few prized homing pigeons belonging to Anton's neighbor. The neighbor suspected we did the deed but our parents, especially my grandmother, thought we were angels. She and Anton's mother would yell down anyone who tried to pin a crime on any of us. Therefore, the neighbor was told that someone else must have killed his birds and he smartly chose to believe them. For extra measure, a rather large plate of pasta and meatballs and freshly baked Italian bread also went a long way to smooth things over. We delivered the pasta and bread as a sort of peace initiative and the neighbor even invited us into the house for some cookies.

By the time we got tired of playing with the rifle, neighborhood wildlife remained hidden until nightfall and there were no unbroken bottles left in any of the alleys nearby either of our homes. Looking back, our possessing any type of weapon that could kill or maim was a particularly stupid idea. Fortunately, after messing up with the pigeons we realized that even a BB gun could be lethal and we never aimed it at another animal again. We found that we were not so tough after all and did not have the stomachs to hurt helpless creatures. Maybe that is why neither I nor any of my friends were ever interested in hunting or hurting any sort of animal for any reason. Fishing may soon, in fact, be erased from my list of "manly" hobbies.

Slowly, after becoming friends with Anton, he and I began to hang out with other newly emigrated Italian kids and their families. Family visits were a common form of entertainment between friends and it was not unusual for large groups of people to converge at a different Italian household each week. Since Sunday meals remained commonplace too, afterward, during the years we lived on 21st Street, it became a custom for the group of us, mostly Italian guys, to get a ride downtown to watch a movie at one of the three theaters in the city. It was during these Sunday dinners that I honed some of my skills of fighting off my grandmother's onslaught of forced feeding because I knew I had to finish eating early to hurriedly get out the door.

The Sunday meals could become protracted events. Grandma would get up early on Sundays to begin the cooking process. She never went to church with my grandfather. Instead, Muddietti concluded that God understood that she, who never committed any sins, was not worthy of notice. She believed God wished for her to remain at home to prepare the meal. Each week's Sunday menu consisted of soup, pasta, meatballs, and often a roast. Lamb was served on Easter, while ham, beef, or pork turned up regularly after people helped themselves to hearty meatballs or a bit of sausage. God, she wagered understood her absence.

The conversation was brisk around the table and sometimes became heated as one never knew who would join us at the table besides regular family members. If only those who espoused the democrat's doctrine sat at the table then the conversation was peaceful and loud. If, however, a more conservative voice spoke up, such as, Uncle Rudolpho, then all hell broke loose. One could expect any sort of verbal fireworks to occur when popular liberal doctrines were challenged. It was during these heated discussions that I found it easier to corral someone into carting me off to a downtown movie theatre. Attending Sunday matinees had become a regular part of the Lord's day.

A group of us loved attending the movies together on Sunday afternoons. These were the days of watching Steve Reeves playing Hercules or Goliath, and he and his muscles became our big heroes. I have lifted weights and attempted bodybuilding all my life thinking that maybe someday I would develop biceps as big as Reeves'. All my efforts have been in vain because my arms have never gotten very close at all to those of Steve Reeves. Now as I age and watch my muscles deteriorate, having little control over Mother Nature, thoughts of those days trying to be like Steve Reeves are becoming particularly challenging.

Two new Italian friends, Rocco and Mariano, eventually began to join Anton, Guido, and me on those movie-watching Sundays. The new brothers moved to town shortly after I had become friends with Anton and Guido. Just like Anton's family, they invited us to their house to help with their adjustment to the U.S. Unlike our parents,

Rocco and Mariano's parents imposed rules governing their kid's whereabouts so when visiting their home we had to toe the line a little bit more. Anton and I felt lucky that our parents were not like Rocco and Mariano's mother and father requiring them not only to follow rules but also to take Italian language lessons on Saturday mornings. Now, as an adult, I wish that the language rule would have been imposed so I could better speak Italian. When you are 9 or 10 years old though a guy has other preferences besides learning a foreign language, such as, running loose and terrorizing the neighborhood.

The bunch of us enjoyed attending Sunday afternoon matinees at one of the three downtown theaters. One of the theaters was palatial and we loved scaring ourselves by imagining what it would be like to have the giant chandelier, that defined the space, fall from the ceiling onto our heads below. We plotted the best way to duck out of the way to survive a chandelier catastrophe. The movie theatre was a large venue and a spot where the mischievous among us could more easily initiate some type of mischief. Seldom did anyone ever get thrown out of the place. With all the screwing around taking place it serves as a mystery how we could ever remember the plot of any movie? Maybe that is why we often attended the same movie more than one time. I cannot count the number of empty popcorn boxes we flattened and threw into the air just to see its shadowy reflection up on the screen. Certainly, an added laugh included hoping the airborne box would ultimately land on some poor schmuck's head as gravity forced it to fall to the theatre's seats. The toughest part was trying to keep a straight face as the theater usher shined his flashlight at our faces trying to determine which one of us threw the box.

Our theatre-going system included getting a ride to one of the movie houses, watching the show, eating popcorn, wreaking havoc, and when finished walking home down the main street. As we were growing up, most main streets were amid a major decline. Independent department stores could not compete with the larger retailers and strip malls being built just at the edge of town. Shopping plazas were all the rage and soon included "malls," enclosed spaces that would be built dealing a final blow to many central city retailers.

It was our habit to walk home and on the way gaze in the windows of the remaining storefronts. Because it was Sunday and Blue Laws remained in effect, there were only a few stores open for business. As we walked, there was usually a planned stop at the display window of a men's apparel store.. Although it was closed we spent a minute or two gawking through the plate glass window at the latest styles. Next, we made sure to stop at a variety store further down called Jussine's where we hoped to linger at the candy counter long enough to capture a glimpse or two of the covers of the "adult" magazines usually on display. Sometimes, depending on where we were headed, we would also stop at Kranak's for a Coke and a bag of chips to assuage our growing appetites before being deluged with more pasta when we arrived home. One of the owners of the store was a good friend so we often got a little extra flavoring in our cherry Cokes. It usually took us a long time to walk home, and the trip's length was dependent on how fast we were thrown out of stores like Jussine's or the local Army Navy Surplus Store, both of which got away with staying open on Sundays. The Army Navy Store would only let us linger for a few minutes before throwing us out. We usually got even with their impatience and disrespect for us by sticking chewed gum inside army helmets or melted chocolate bars inside of new boots then internally feeling ever so proud for our revenge.

Soon, however, the duration of our trips home would become dependent on a new behavior, a habit that Mariano developed. As the five of us walked down the street having fun while looking into storefronts, suddenly Mariano, out of nowhere, would turn around and walk back first five, then ten, and ultimately twenty or more paces behind us before turning to walk back in our direction. At first, we waited for him but after his behavior became a routine we figured we would never get home if we kept waiting for him. Besides, this weird performance, like other behaviors committed by any of us, was considered outside the confines of standard acceptable behaviors and thus qualified, according to the informal "adolescent boy's codebook," you guessed it, for ridicule. Soon we would wait for Mariano to head back and then we would run the same number of paces ahead thus doubling the distance between him and us. Eventually, we were so far in front of Mariano that he could never catch up to us.

This game lasted for quite a few weeks before his parents realized that we always arrived home much earlier than Mariano. After asking questions and finding out what was going on, Rocco and Mariano's parents stopped their sons from attending our Sunday matinee excursions. We never knew what happened to him but slowly Mariano stopped hanging around with us all together. After a few months, Rocco and Mariano's family bought a new home, an upgrade, in a nearby suburb of Cleveland, and we never saw either of them again.

Today we recognize Mariano's behavior for what it was at the time, that is, Obsessive Compulsive Disorder or OCD. In 1960 no one knew anything about OCD as every kooky behavior of almost any kind was simply labeled as one's personal choice. If a guy acted goofy we believed it was his choice to act that way. We simply labeled it screwy behavior that demanded an equally stupid response from us. Our treatment of Mariano adds to the list of ever-increasing acts encompassing our shameful responses to almost serious issues. In retrospect, it equates to one of several behaviors we are now embarrassed having ever practiced as kids. While each of us found ourselves at times the criticizer as well as the criticized, it is also likely that some poor soul among us ended up with a greater share of the razzing. Perhaps due to our early experiences, many of us have made it a priority to correct some of the numb-skull acts we perpetrated on our friends with many of us going into the helping professions to assist others and maybe even to help explain things better about ourselves.

I think most of us, myself included, likely met one or more of the classifications listed in the psychiatric, *Diagnostic and Statistical Manual of Mental Disorders*. Fortunately, the first manual did not include the kinds of nutty behaviors we exhibited at the time, such as Attention Deficit Disorder, Conduct Disorder, and Learning Disabilities. Without a proper psychological classification, we were most likely considered as simply run-of-the-mill PITAs or "pains in the asses." Throw in a few spoiled, disrespectful, unsupervised, and lazy behaviors and some of us could easily qualify as good old-fashioned juvenile delinquents. We never knew if Mariano was ever taken to a doctor or psychologist for an assessment. Years later we received word from someone that both Rocco but especially Mariano fooled us all by becoming quite successful, engineering we heard. We were happy for him and despite what could look like cruelty, we relished the short time we had growing up together with the brothers.

During those three years living on 21st Street, I was fortunate to have so many playmates. Friends like Rudy, Galen, Anton, Jimmy the Sausage, and Dently. Although I would remain friends with some of the guys especially Rudy and a few others into adulthood, I would lose touch with Jimmy The Sausage, Dently, and numerous friends from around Harrison School. This especially occurred shortly after moving away from 21st Street a second time. It is funny how some friendships are like library books that are checked out, returned, and never read again. Friendships have a way of ending but the important memories remain.

Moving, Always Moving

****

Stripes: "I am enjoying this walk but I'm a little tired."
Hippie: "Why is that?"

Stripes: "We are planning our move to the lake house in a couple of weeks. We have been making lists, packing up summer clothes, and having to plan for every contingency. You know how that is. A nightmare at times."

Hipster: "Too much for me. Sometimes it takes so much work just to make sure everyone is happy and has all their needs met. I remember w-h-en I w- a -s g—r—o—w—i—-n——g u————p n———e—————-a————-r..."

In 1961 I was 10 and it seemed that the next move was usually right around the corner. By now I could remember moving four times and sure enough, the next move had to do with Dad's job. Like many men in town, my father was continually getting laid off from his job at the steel mill. He would work a few years, maybe only a few months, and then, "Poof," he would come home looking downtrodden announcing that he had been laid off again. My father would then begin the waiting game never knowing if or when he would be called back to the mill. It could be a few weeks or a few months but not knowing when he would be called back to work was stressful for us all. He and I were fortunate in comparison to others because we had my grandparents serving as our safety net. Living with them, when Dad was only collecting unemployment checks, helped with the finances and we never really had to worry about housing, food, or other expenses.

Each time Louie was laid off the precariousness of his job was highlighted as he restarted the process of considering alternative employment. Layoffs were a fact of life for him and they were becoming increasingly monotonous. They were a continual reminder that finding steady employment elsewhere was an option to consider. Maybe a new start could solve the layoff problem? But where would he work? Where could we go? Dad was not aware of it then but now, in hindsight, he was part of a national trend that was beginning to sweep the country. That is the slow disappearance of higher-paying manufacturing jobs especially those that did not require specialized training or a college degree. All my father knew was that he was psychologically exhausted from being at the mercy of others. His lack of job security was unnerving and he wanted to break free and find employment that would be more secure. He was frustrated from being a drone for those at the top who cared more about the company's stock price than its personnel.

Dad became particularly unnerved over one of his layoffs occurring when I was in fourth grade and he finally convinced my grandparents, or so he thought, to move to Arizona. His recent trip to Mexico with cousin Georgio, by way of Arizona, confirmed his belief that Arizona was where the action was and where he could find steady work, work that would sever his dependence on the whims of bosses and the stock price of the company. My father wanted independence and security and he was betting that Arizona was the place to fulfill his dreams.

At first, my grandparents seemed to finally agree with my father's lust for moving to Arizona. They indicated that they would be willing to move if it meant that Dad could find steady employment. They understood the negative effects that being laid off has on a man and they hated to see their son, their only child, upset as he began the daily wait to be recalled to work. So they all three made a decision and spent much time plotting a move southwest. During this time my father sent away asking for numerous brochures on various ventures and businesses that he dreamed of running as a means of starting over in Arizona. Louie seemed particularly enamored with donut franchises that were becoming all the rage in the early 60s. Strangely, had he chosen the right one, perhaps say, Dunkin' Donuts, he might have done quite well. I remember looking over what seemed like piles of brochures Dad collected on the newly thriving donut industry. There was Mr. Donut, The Whole Donut, Country Style Donuts, Krispy Kreme Donuts, donut this, and donut that. In our hometown, I distinctly recall regular trips to a place called, *Bob's Donuts*. Thinking of biting into one of Bob's cream-filled sticks still brightens my day. I loved donuts but as a kid, I could not envision being part of a donut empire. I could only imagine my grandmother somehow entering the picture and turning the business into an Italian donut franchise. Had she started a donut empire, maybe naming it, *Nonna Maria's Dolce Donuts*, then there was the hope of big things to come. "Mangia, Cowboy! Mangia!" could have been their Arizona motto. Believing that my father could somehow become an overnight businessman was another thing altogether.

As I later determined, my father's idea presented my grandparents with a major dilemma. It turned out that secretively they did not want to move to Arizona and had no intention of packing up and schlepping thousands of miles away from their home. Moving from Italy to the United States was hard enough and they did not wish to start all over again. I figured that Grandma and Grandpa somehow had to appear to agree with my father yet tactfully squeeze out of the deal. They had to figure a way to back away from the move, find a substitution, or create a compromise perhaps that would make everyone happy. After much scheming, they somehow happened onto a surefire way to shut down their son's plans.

Instead of a move to Arizona, they latched on to another of my father's top wishes in life and that was owning property on Lake Erie. After some deliberation, somehow, my father located a vacant lot just inside of the city limits and right on the lake shore. With the empty lot purchased the family set out to plan and ultimately build a new home. Their house plan was to construct a duplex so we could all live on one side and collect rent from the other. In this way, my grandparents could continue their life as landlords. They would build a house large enough for us all to fit into and the other half, a little smaller, would be large enough to bring in adequate income. So just before I bought a set of spurs and as I dreamed about the pony that was promised to me if we moved, the land on the lake was bought and blueprints were drawn for building the new home.

Let me add a little background here. My hometown was probably the last city in the country to realize that a resource, Lake Erie, made good sense to develop. With manufacturing dying quickly all around the city, a resource such as a lake, in our case a Great Lake, could be a major boost to the local economy. In 1962 there did not seem to be much emphasis on the direction of lake development and tourism. The lake was polluted from years of dumping manufacturing waste directly into it and its adjoining rivers. Mills that were situated up and down a river in the middle of the city emptied waste directly into the lake's waters for years. As a result, the fishing was poor, those fish that existed were considered unsafe to eat, and people were beginning to shy away even from swimming at any of the many beaches that lined the coast. There was little reason for anyone to make any money from the natural resource right in our city's backyard. Therefore, any schmoe, any working-class folk like my grandparents, could afford to buy the property and build a house directly on the shoreline. That luxury would never be available today for people who fell into my grandparents' income category. Land on lakes is finite and is usually too expensive for most retired working-class families to afford. In 1962, especially since Lake Erie was ignored, they could easily manage the cost of not only purchasing property but also paying cash for their next home, a ranch-style duplex situated approximately 50 feet from the lake.

Sitting around the dining room table on 21st Street, the same table where many people ate homemade gnocchi and slurped up gallons of pasta e fajioli, I remember the deep conversations that took place with a local contractor who spoke with a thick German accent. Hahn came equipped with blueprints of what would become the duplex built to the specifications designed by my grandparents. It was soon planned that the groundbreaking would begin in September 1961.

It was exciting watching the house being built. We saw the heavy machinery dig the cellar, men lay the foundation, and witnessed the cement blocks being carefully placed against the dark clay walls. One frigid evening in January 1962, Dad and I ventured out to the construction site after dark. To a 10-year-old boy, the house seemed to be so far away from our home in the city and the temperature felt significantly colder than any weather I ever experienced before. I remember standing inside the skeleton of the house that evening in what would become the rental side of the duplex. At this point, only the exterior walls and roof were built with plastic sheeting serving in place of glass in the windows. It was already dark and the wind was howling off the water with nothing standing in its way but the plywood and plastic. This would be the first of many winds I would feel blowing off the water, up the bank, and through my clothes. Winds like those off of Lake Erie are the type that someone must have felt when they first coined the phrase, "bone-chilling." Standing in that future living room with only the thin walls protecting me, I could hear what sounded like a cyclone outside and see the lights of a small trailer park sign across Lake Road swaying back and forth. I could not help but wonder what it would soon be like to live in this house all year round, especially in the depth of winter. Who would be my friends and where would I go to school? Would I see my old pals and remain friends with them? What freedoms would I have way out on the lake road away from those things that had become so familiar to me? Questions, many questions that would be answered soon enough.

So just as Jed, Granny, Ellie May, and Jethro moved to Beverly Hills in 1962, our family did the same but only west to the banks of Lake Erie on the way out of town. While not as contrasting a move as, *The Beverly Hillbillies*, our immigrant working-class Italian family's move to the lake could be likened to buying Waterford Crystal glasses only to fill them with Budweiser. My grandparents were always practical people and had limited appreciation for a lake view and had zero interest in swimming, fishing, or boating. The lake to them was an "attractive nuisance" but it was all the bargaining chip they needed to keep Louie and me in town. Louie always loved the water, hence his joining the U.S. Navy in World War II and considered owning a sailboat one day for himself. Sailing represented another reason he traded away Arizona for remaining on Lake Erie, however, anyone who knew him for two minutes would readily conclude he would never follow through on something like that. Besides, my grandparents were, especially my grandmother, petrified of the water, and drowning was at the top of her list of fears. Had my father bought the boat she would have found some way to make him feel guilty enough to never attempt to sail the high seas. Anyhow, by then the main reason for the move, that is the layoff, had changed. Almost on cue and as usual, he was called back to work right before the first shovel full of dirt was dug and before he could summon the nerve to take the plunge into the donut industry. All those donut franchise pamphlets were stored and destined to gather dust on the bottom of our glass bookcase filled with other books and materials no one ever read. The pamphlets ended up shelved next to Dad's old photography textbooks as well as his 1941 class yearbook.

Growing up, the local steel mill was almost always the topic of conversation around the kitchen table. There was continual discussion of departments, such as the rolling mill, coke plant, blast furnace, union contracts, and crane repair shop, as well as other topics like foremen, union contracts, etc. It seemed that almost every guy in town, as few women worked at the mill in those days, had some experience working either for the steel mill or a subsidiary. If it was not discussing the latest reason for a layoff, men were discussing the installation of a new piece of equipment or worst of all, a serious injury or sometimes even the death of some poor soul who was in the wrong place at the wrong time. The steel mill served for years as the city's biggest employer and while it provided work for thousands of men, and later women as well, it is considered by some to be a distraction to the town's long-range progress. Today the mill continues as a major employer in the city and a fickle one at best. When it is up and running it provides a great opportunity for a worker possessing few skills to make a good living. However, it remains more unreliable now than ever before. The mill historically raises hopes by moving into hiring mode and then dashes them without a blink of an eye by laying off workers. Just as folks become confident of a full recovery and consistent paychecks, then wham, layoffs occur en masse. Dad was laid off in the 50s and 60s and my brother-in-law was laid off in the 2010s. One can almost blame the mill for distracting the community from modernizing and updating to a more contemporary business.

Back to our new home on the lake. Here we were again with Dad getting a call back to work and it happened just before a planned dive into the donut industry. The callback was a good short-term solution for him and a wonderful long-term solution for the rest of us. No one knew how long he would work until the next layoff but few questions were asked. His black metal lunch bucket was right where he left it and it was once again called into action. Growing bored and surviving on unemployment checks was a terrible recipe for a person therefore returning to work, even though he knew he would likely be laid off again, was the best thing for Louie's mental health. Plus we were now moving to a new house within the city rather than to Arizona and there was much to look forward to. I griped about having to move again but moving across town was much better than across the country. Plus, while I did not know it at the time, the move would provide me with more friends and crazy experiences than would likely have been found if we had shipped off to Arizona. I did not foresee it but I was on my way to having one heck of a good time for the next few years with three crazy fellows I would soon meet. For the world, I would not change any of the fun I had with that trio of characters.

I recall my father picking me up that last day at Harrison School in his little gray Italian car, a 1959 Lancia Appia. My father had bought the Italian-made auto from a friend at a weak moment in his life as he had too much time on his hands during the layoff. Louie always prized Italian cars from afar and when the Lancia became available he jumped at the chance to finally own the auto of his dreams. By the way, my father was the only person I ever heard of who owned a Lancia in the United States. It was a beautiful car but it continually malfunctioned which Wikipedia should use as the defining feature of any Italian automobile. "Sorry, signore ma she'sa broka don, no funzione" is a familiar phrase to the owners of Italian autos. I owned a Fiat in the mid-seventies and out of frustration I kicked the bumper of the four-year-old car. Half of the bumper crumbled and broke off. This sounds like a stereotype but it is the truth. When it ran it was fun but it seldom ran.

The most defining feature of Dad's Lancia, the car he loved to show off to friends, was the car's doors. When opened, the front and rear compartments were both unlatched in the center as if one were operating French doors on the way to meeting Maximilien de Robespierre or someone equally elegant. Vive La France. Then when let go, the doors would close and fully latch all by themselves. To Louie, this characteristic was the height of quality workmanship that Ford and Chevy could only dream about possessing. This feature alone gave him the superior high ground when explaining the positive features of foreign car ownership which most others defined as looney in the early 1960s. Louie took great pride in his knowledge of the superior workmanship put into Italian autos. While it was great that the car's body had integrity, it is unfortunate that the same level of quality was not engineered into its engine and other running parts. It did not make much sense to me, at age eleven, to engineer a car with great working doors but ignore the most important features, that is, the quality and durability of the engine and transmission.

Due to the Lancia often breaking down it was eventually sold. This enabled Louie to make another creative car purchase, that is, a 1962 fire engine red Chevy Corvair, probably the worst car ever manufactured in America. Its repair record made Lancia's reliability seem as sound as today's Honda Accord. I do have a few fond memories of the Corvair. Dad allowed me to sometimes steer the car and often shift the gears too as he stepped down hard on the clutch as we drove home to the house on the lake. There is nothing a boy wants more than to drive a vehicle of any sort as they move into adolescents.

My dad was a good man who did things for me that I will always appreciate. He, for instance, spent hours carting me to recreational activities with my friends, such as Cedar Point and, swimming at the beach. Dad would sit, maybe read the newspaper, while my friends and I swam and attempted to drown each other, one of our ways of aving a good time. One of my favorite memories is riding an old wooden roller coaster at a now-defunct amusement park called Crystal Beach Park. The coaster was so old that it was torn down while I was still young to make way for a new housing complex situated on the bank of Lake Erie. He and I must have ridden that roller coaster 30 times over the years as he and I often went to the amusement park before it was sold. How wonderful the memories of my visits to Crystal Beach with my father!

Skeeter, Paulie, and Freddy

Buying the car and moving into a newly built home across town were all happening near the end of my fifth-grade year. Just as no one considered walking me to my classroom that first day at Harrison no one gave a thought to allowing me to finish my fifth-grade year at the school either. Therefore, on Monday, May 7, 1962, with one month left in the school year, I would enter Masston Elementary to finish fifth grade. I hated leaving Rudy, Dirk, Anton, and my friends back at Harrison and had to hold back tears as moving seemed to be a regular part of our life up to this point. While I do not recall how or when it was done, my father must have preregistered me at Masston. All I can remember is being dropped off at the school, finding my way to the office, and sitting there while waiting for my class assignment.

Throughout my life, however, just as things seemed so unlucky or unfair and as I would reach the precipice of my whining, somehow luck reemerged. That is exactly what happened on my first day at Masston. Masston was a fairly new school when I attended. It seemed quite sprawling as it was built on a large piece of land in the middle of newer housing developments within the city. Unlike the two-storied Harrison, Masston was only one story with more than one class per grade level. My first day at my new school would be a day I would always remember. As I sat inside the glass-enclosed office playing with my fingers while waiting for my class assignment, out of nowhere I heard a tap on the window behind me. I was surprised to turn around and see a familiar face. It was an old friend, Gregory, from 21st Street, who like me was an "ex-pat" from the old neighborhood. His family had recently moved from Harrison to Masston as well. There he was behind the glass, grinning from ear to ear right back at me and I immediately recall feeling the strain of the new environment begin to drain off. Seeing Gregory, aside from helping to decrease my fear of entering a whole new environment, helped me begin to realize that our family moves around the city were beginning to pay some dividends.

Gregory's excitement, more like exuberance, was difficult for him to contain. He was giddy about my entering Masston and I could not quite figure out why my enrollment seemed so important to him. Strangely enough, Gregory was one of the first guys I hung around with when I moved to Harrison Elementary. Rudy was the one who introduced us and we would all regularly congregate behind Gregory's family deli to play kickball. It was right behind Rintower's Deli on 21st Street and Hamilton Avenue that I developed some sound kickball skills and I would soon find out how that skill and others would translate into being accepted into my new classroom.

Like any kid would be, I was nervous about meeting my teacher and classmates but this immediately vanished when I entered the class that first morning. When the door opened and the students saw me standing next to the school secretary, the entire group exploded with cheers and applause. I was overcome with surprise and wondered why the kids in this school were so welcoming. It turned out that within minutes of Gregory seeing me in the office he had spread the word that a youthful version of Jim Thorp had just enrolled in the school. This new kid, me, Gregory explained, would tip the athletic scales of victory for whichever classroom was lucky enough to get him, that is, me. My friend communicated that I was a fairly good athlete and since there was a major competition between one fifth-grade class and another at Masston, he was hoping I would be placed in his room to help them secure victory. When I walked through the classroom door the students seemed to know they would soon achieve school-wide athletic prowess. I was to be their superhero before ever smacking a ball or tying on my "Red Ball Jets." If they had control over the "Wheaties" cover, my face would have immediately been slapped on the front of the box. Sometimes in life, you get lucky and other times not. This placement fell into the "lucky" category and my fortunes did not end there.

That very same day we went out for recess and as it was spring a softball game was planned. It was customary that the kids from one class would play against those from the other grade five classroom. Softball was probably my worst sport but my chest was already extended as I was granted so much positive regard that I could only exude self-confidence.

It was not too difficult for me to feel superior. Within just a few short minutes of my entering the classroom, I was able to reliably size up my competition. I hated to stereotype but I moved out of the type of environment that usually produces good athletes in ball sports like football, basketball, and baseball. That is, I moved from a lower-income, working-class, and multicultural neighborhood, into a White relatively privileged one. It should be noted that this was before all the middle-class White kids began to improve their athletic skills by being continuously enrolled in seasonal sports camps and travel teams. My quick assessment of the competition was that it was quite limited at Masston and that notion was immediately proven.

When it was my turn at the plate, Gregory had made sure I was the clean-up batter, I grabbed the first bat tossed my way. After making a couple of practice swings I stepped into the batter's box and toed home plate. I remember gazing at the anticipatory smiles on the faces of my new classmates hoping that I would not disappoint them.

Then, all at once, the very first pitch was on its way. It proved to be a perfect lob directly over the bag. Then, without hesitation, wham! The perfect blooper was easily smacked directly out to center field over everyone's head. I recall not even having to run my fastest to tag all the bases on my way back home. Back at Harrison, I might have hit the ball but I certainly would not have earned a home run.

It was my first homer at my new school and I was the school's newest hero. While all the girls screamed, as if I were a member of the Beatles, Gregory beamed and strutted around like the "cock on the walk." He proudly accepted numerous pats on the back not only for his role in my placement in Mr. Peroni's classroom but also for being such a wise judge of athletic talent.

As I said, moving was starting to pay dividends. In addition to the enhanced home life provided courtesy of my grandparents, the numerous family moves, all within the same city, continued to influence my early life. The friends I made, per neighborhood, many of whom remain lifelong buddies, helped form lasting memories of the intense kind that bring on goosebumps when I think about them today. Pairing these variables with my hometown made for a really interesting childhood with the Masston school story representing just one example. These experiences, acquired for close to a decade, have often come in handy for me for the last 50-plus years and will, I hope, for many more years to come. There are seldom times when a story originating from my days growing up does not find its way into present-day conversations ultimately allowing me to surprise new friends with a bit of crazy childhood trivia.

Although I was lucky to be somewhat athletic, as this helped me to make friends and assimilate easily into each new school, fitting into my new neighborhood, which I would soon find, was not as easy at first. Being on the lake our new home was a natural playground for a boy but it was missing one essential ingredient and that was kids my age to hang with, or so I thought. We had moved just far enough out of town that it was difficult for my old pals to regularly visit and there did not seem to be any nearby kids for me to amuse myself with. Our new home was situated on a small access road just across from a major highway with businesses in the area and only a few homes close by seemingly occupied mainly by adults. I no longer lived in a neighborhood and all there seemed to be around our new home was a small motel, a roller skating arena, and a home for aging citizens. It may have taken me a while but I would eventually strike pay dirt in the friend's department with three guys who would make the crowd back at Harrison School seem like model citizens.

On 21st Street I lived close to Harrison Elementary so I walked to school. In those days students could still walk home for lunch and my grandmother was always there to serve up all my favorite canned foods or better yet bologna sandwiches which were my favorite. I ate enough bologna in those days to have hopefully pickled myself with preservatives to secure a long life to come. Now that we lived on the lake, instead of walking to school I would catch a school bus out on the highway in front of our home. Taking the bus helped me identify three guys who had the potential of becoming my new playmates. The three guys, two of them brothers, and another named Freddy rode the bus with me and two of the three were also in my new classroom. Freddy was friendly and lived the closest. He was in my class at school, had failed two grades, and spent a few periods each day attending a special education class as he had an intellectual disability. He was already friends with the only other characters, brothers who lived within walking distance of my new home. The brothers were, Skeeter, my age, and Paulie, who was a year older but had already failed one grade in school himself. It did not take long before the four of us began spending time together not only in class but also after school. We would almost immediately begin to chalk up adventures many of which were fraught with risks and sometimes even perils of various sorts.

Freddy lived alone with his mother in a small trailer park located across the street from our new duplex. His mom and dad were divorced and I never remember meeting or even hearing much about his father. Freddy's mom was a school teacher and she tried hard to do well by Freddy but he had his challenges and the three of us, Skeeter, Paulie and I, slowly became one of them. Due to Freddy's limited aptitude, few kids wanted to hang around with him so she was stuck with him hanging around with us or nobody. We sometimes took advantage of Freddy but for the most part, he was our friend and while tending to be more of a follower than me, he kept up with our shenanigans and was a good sport.

Where Freddy lived in a trailer park, Paulie and Skeeter lived in a mansion. Their home, situated on two acres of prime lakefront property, was at least 5,000 square feet with six bedrooms, seven bathrooms, and countless other amenities. Their home was unusual for the early 60s in our hometown and was considered one of the nicest houses in town. We especially enjoyed the pool table located in their finished basement imagining ourselves as budding Minnesota Fats. While all four of us were knuckleheads we represented almost the full socioeconomic spectrum of city housing. Our friendship would last only three years but those years were jammed with some of the most memorable zaniness of my life. Once again it was our freedom during the time together, including frequent sleepovers, that allowed us to build numerous memories that were in many ways similar to those I enjoyed on 21st Street.

With three of us living right on the lake shore, much of our days together were spent fishing, swimming, or just skimming rocks. We would maraud up and down the beach and docks looking for spawning carp to catch with our bare hands or rats to shoot with our slingshots. We would purposefully get sunburned waiting for our skin to peel and like chimps peel each other's back competing for the longest piece of peeled skin. More than one time we stupidly swam in heavy surfs with usually one of us coming close to drowning. It scared us but we did not seem to care and kept doing it anyway. In the winter we would risk our lives by climbing in and out of volcano-like ice drifts near the shoreline remaining aware of the potential to fall through the ice at any time. We even tried ice fishing a couple of times but the howling wind off Lake Erie was way too much for ding dongs like the four of us to endure.

Our quartet had, it seemed, more freedom than was reasonable for kids in the fifth grade. This was a theme that I was of course already used to. When we grew weary of hassling the old Black men fishing off the dock at a nearby company pier by day or staging fake fights close to the highway after dark, bringing traffic to a screeching halt, we traveled widely around town, favoring the East Side of the city. The East Side housed the site of a business owned by Skeeter and Paulie's father. Before moving to the lake their family lived on the east side so the brothers knew everyone in that area of town. This may not sound like much but we covered many miles of territory for boys our age and our travels would likely be frowned upon by most parents today especially when our primary mode of transportation was hitchhiking.

Skeeter and Paulie, like me, were technically blue-collar guys who had moved to a wealthier section of town. While my grandparents were not poor and had successfully scraped out a living by working hard and renting rooms, Skeeter and Paulie's dad had made millions by being in the construction trade. They were a little closer to the story line of "The Beverly Hillbillies" than me because they had recently moved from a modest home in the blue-collar East Side of town to their mansion on the Lake Erie shore. Their new home was surrounded by similar large and expensive properties mostly owned by doctors, lawyers, and other professionals. I soon found out other neighborhood kids, many our age, were already forbidden to hang with Paulie and Skeeter and later me after I had joined the group.

Skeeter, Paulie, and I, however, had more in common than money and lake homes. Like me, these guys were Italian-American. In addition they were allowed lots of freedom to come and go as they wished. Given their family's income level they, like me, had everything they desired including pocket money. The brothers, however, were also different from me in other ways. Most notable was the difference between us in academic areas. For example, neither one of these guys ever cracked a book or did any homework and as a result did rather poorly in school. I, on the other hand, did my best, earned okay grades, and always completed my work on time. Another major difference that existed between us was how far outside the law we would travel. I had my limits but Skeeter and particularly Paulie seemed like they were enrolled in an apprenticeship program for a life of crime. These two thought nothing of committing petty crimes of various sorts such as shaking down poor souls for minor things like hamburgers from McDonalds.

When we were ten years old, however, there was very little comparing and contrasting going on between us. We left the sociology to others and all I knew was these guys were fun, their parents treated me like a king, and in some ways, the situation was not too different from the guys in the old neighborhood. Now, when

I think of Freddy, Paulie and Skeeter, I mainly think about all the great times that we experienced together most often through the mischief we created and realize how lucky we were to escape incarceration or worse. For instance we got drunk a few times and usually smoked packs of cigarettes together and thankfully pot and other drugs had not yet become popular. Instead, Freddy, Skeeter and I stuck to smoking Lucky Strikes.

Certainly cigarette smoking was not good for any of us either as the dangers of smoking cigarettes was beginning to become an issue. Skeeter enjoyed smoking much more than Freddy or I, but we smoked along with him anyhow spending much of our time devoted to figuring ways to either buy or steal "smokes." We mostly smoked unfiltered Lucky Strike cigarettes as this was the brand smoked by Skeeter and Paulie's parents. I still remember how Lucky Strikes were advertised on TV as being better than other brands. They were supposedly better and the company acronym said so, that is, "LSMFT" or "Lucky Strikes Means Fine Tobacco." We assigned a different meaning to LSMFT, that is, "Loose Straps Means Flabby Tits." We loved repeating that phrase and then breaking into uncontrolled laughter each time LSMFT was mentioned on TV. Infantile, I know, but we were growing boys.

When we were not smoking or calling up girls on the phone in the middle of the night we, especially Skeeter and I, were likely hitchhiking to the East Side of town. We hitchhiked all the time and only occasionally were picked up by sketchy drivers. Mostly we were offered rides from friendly lawful people who kindly drove us all the way to our destination making sure we arrived there safely. There were a few crazed type drivers who picked us up, but fortunately we never met up with any murdering perverts or worse. Besides we had already developed plans to deal with the weird types by being sure to always carry an easy to open pocket knife as a form of protection.

Skeeter and Paulie loved the East Side of the city and they seemed to know every nook and cranny, and everybody within the 12 block radius of their old home. Even as a kid I often thought that their neighbors on the East Side probably threw a block party in celebration of these two budding delinquents finally moving out of the vicinity. Unfortunately for the neighbors, Skeeter and Paulie kept on visiting their old stomping grounds and now they brought two additional chumps, Freddy and me, along with them.

One of the favorite things we did on the East Side was to hang out around their father's various businesses, the cement plant and construction company. Paulie and Skeeter's dad owned acres of property and all types of work vehicles from cement trucks to backhoes to dump trucks of various sizes. The construction business was located on one side of the street and included a rather large warehouse set up to repair the many pieces of machinery and vehicles belonging to the business. The cement plant was on the other side of the street, down a dusty road.

After a hard day of hanging around the East Side causing mayhem, we would often drink sodas and hang around the maintenance garage hassling the workers while waiting for Skeeter and Paulie's father or mother to drive us home. When we were not doing that, we created a couple of other foolish stunts to pass the time and add a little more adventure to our ordinary delinquent lives. We pulled two of our favorite stunts, more than once, after working hours or on the weekends when the plant and garage were closed. Both these games included purposely breaking into either the cement plant office or the garage where the machinery and vehicles were repaired. After deciding where we would hide, one of us would call the cops on ourselves. Freddy was often coached to be the caller because he had already gone through puberty and thus his voice had transitioned to become deeper. "Hello is this the police station," we coached him to ask. "I would like to report a possible break-in at the Ready-To-Build maintenance garage."

While we waited for the police to show up, we would find a hiding place and practice being silent and still. After only a few minutes the police would arrive with the four of us securely settled in our spots. We always made sure to perch ourselves where we could see the cops but not vice versa. The four of us thought it great sport watching while the cops made a cursory search of the premises. After a perfunctory check, they always concluded that it was likely a false alarm and would soon leave. We loved the adventure and our only worry was that our hearts might be pounding so loud that our positions would be given away. As crazy as it sounds, I can still experience the extreme rush we felt as I recall the creative yet dangerous stunt the four of us committed on more than one occasion. After the cops left we experienced such a sensation of power and superiority. Then, of course, due to being notified by the authorities, Skeeter and Paulie's father would arrive shortly after the police left to check things out for himself. We would by then have circled around the building making it appear that we had just happened by and were only too pleased to accept a ride home.

Our creativity was second to none as we nearly did the same thing at the cement plant, naturally never pulling the stunts on the same day since we were nuts but not totally stupid. Our favorite place to hide at the cement plant was up in the drums of the cement trucks. We would each choose a truck and scramble up to the top where the cement was mixed and then climb down the ladder into the drum. It felt sort of like being in a submarine while we watched for the cops. When the police drove in we could stick our heads up ever so slightly out of the drum just enough to see them searching. We had to hold back our snickering the whole time they circled around looking for the "intruders." I remember being especially aware of laughing when in the drum because it was hollow and sounds really reverberated around inside. If you enjoy the sound of your voice in the shower then you would really love hearing yourself singing while in the mixing drum of a cement truck.

We thought this feat was so exciting. Now I think about how messed up our adolescent minds must have been. Rebel, rebel, rebel, all the time rebel, that is what we lived for it seemed. No matter who I hung around with rebellion against something or someone was the theme. Fortunately, we never got caught and no one ever was seriously injured from our wise ideas. We obviously wasted much time that the police could have been doing something useful but we never gave that a thought nor would we have cared. Perhaps if we had gotten caught and disciplined for some of these irresponsible acts our future delinquent behaviors might have been curtailed. No luck, we just kept doing crazy things like this for fun while never getting pinched.

Just as my life was filled with excitement on 21st Street my life on the lake was becoming filled with more thrills than anyone should have been able to experience in three short years. Life around Skeeter, Paulie, and Freddy was anything but boring. I slept over Skeeter and Paulie's house on many weekends because they had a TV in their room during a time when that was only a dream in most kids' minds. We would eat pizza and tune into a local Cleveland TV show featuring a nutty character called, Ghoulardi. Starting in 1963 this crazy disc jockey from Cleveland created one of the funniest programs ever and it was called, *Shock Theater*. By performing amateurish and foolish pranks Ghoulardi became a Cleveland legend as the program aired for only three years. He did anything that came to his nutty mind both during and between segments of old scary movies. Ghoulardi, who sported a fake mustache and goatee, dressed in strange hats wearing a white lab jacket, he soon became a cult hero in the Cleveland area. From his trademark superimposing himself onto the screen running from dinosaurs in old cheesy horror movies, to his weekly pizza eating contests, Ghoulardi soon became a legend. Everyone tuned into the show and waited for their favorite segment, such as the pizza eating contest. Usually a guy named Mariano "Mushmouth" Pachetti won the pizza contest although I still laugh thinking about how a German Shepard, brought on during one episode, was the only contestant to finally beat Mushmouth's string of consistent wins. Ghoulardi also made fun of a nearby suburb, Parma, and did so due to the high percentage of Polish people who resided there. These were the days of Polish jokes and Ghoulardi capitalized on the subject. He got away with playful joking about Parma at a time before political correctness went into full swing. Who knows? Maybe Ghoulardi's joking about Parma somehow imprinted the city on my mind as years later I would marry a woman who was from Parma. PARMA (add a little polka music here)?

People of all ages waited for Ghoulardi to come on Channel 8 on Friday nights at 11:30 pm right after the news. He quickly became more famous locally than the cult classic films he aired. His local fame likely surpassed contemporary programs, such as, today's *Game of Thrones*. We looked forward to Ghoulardi's *Shock Theater as* Skeeter and Peter's and Skeeter's house was suited perfectly for watching as it was so big that we had a whole wing to ourselves to laugh and make noise without bothering anyone.

In addition, we were trusted to sleep outside overnight when the weather was cooperative. At least once we talked Freddy, who appeared older, into riding my bike to a local store to buy some wine and other goodies. During one of our sleep-outs, we all got so drunk on *Richards Wild Irish Rose* wine that we set off hitchhiking in the middle of the night. We were fortunate that no one stopped to give us a ride since we had no place to go anyway. I woke up the next morning having wet my pants and I will never forget how hungover we all felt. Besides being dangerous this whole stunt was really stupid behavior and I must say that after getting so sick from the booze I began to analyze my behavior admitting that maybe we were going a little too far for 11-year-olds.

Later that fall, as the weather began to get cold and a freezing wind blew off of the lake, Skeeter and I got ourselves into another mess through no fault of our own. One evening, when we were in sixth grade, Skeeter and I walked down Lake Road and made a stop at the home of one of his many questionable friends, an older guy who at 16 had already dropped out of school. Our home town was a conglomeration of socioeconomic groups spread throughout city neighborhoods. There were not many areas in our city solely considered exclusive. Therefore, while my questionable friends, Skeeter and Paulie lived in a million-dollar neighborhood, only a half mile down the coast was a low-income trailer park also situated on the lake. That is where this derelict friend, Trailer Guy we called him, lived. One conclusion that could be drawn about my hometown in the 60s was that there was little housing discrimination due to race, gender, class, or socioeconomic status. Everyone could live anywhere no matter their income level or job classification.

As usual, the Trailer Guy's parents were not home, one of the reasons that we sometimes hung out with him. We figured he was some kind of a loser since he had already quit school at age 16 and spent most of his time doing nothing. We were 11 going on 12 years old and well on our way to becoming just like him but of course we did not think so at the time. We tended to hang around his trailer since we never had much to do and we knew Trailer Guy would let us in and share his cigarette with us. We knocked on his door and after hearing his familiar grunt we walked in and made ourselves at home. Skeeter and I sat on one side of the small living room and smoked cigarettes while Trailer Guy and his friend, a new guy named Wiley, also around 16, sat on the other side. They were drinking beer but we were not interested. Besides, we did not yet like beer and I had already sworn off most alcohol after drinking the bottle of *Wild Irish Rose* the previous summer. We were only interested in smoking cigarettes and keeping warm since it was really cold and windy outside. We thought we would hang out in the trailer and warm up while considering where else we could go to waste time.

We were just smoking and talking mostly about nothing when out of nowhere and for no good reason at all Wiley, a skinny runt who was proud of being from West Virginia, began picking on Skeeter. Skeeter, short with limited muscle tone, was somewhat smaller than Wiley. Skeeter did have a sharp tongue and usually kept out of fights due to threatening to call his tough older brother and his numerous close associations with other petty hoods around town. Wiley, an obvious screwball, was new to the area and either did not know or care about Skeeter's background. He tried but failed to talk cool and spoke with a southern accent so we figured he must be new to the area and thus too stupid to understand the rules in the city. Wiley seemed to project a chip on the shoulder type of attitude, a common behavior we were used to, but slender or not he seemed to possess a seemingly crazed personality. While we were not winners ourselves we always figured that anyone with a southern accent came from a lower class than us and could thus be disregarded. Wiley was perhaps trying to make up for his second-class status, we guessed, by picking on Skeeter for no reason at all. The beer likely also played a major role in his aggressive style.

Wiley soon informed us that he was a "West Virginia boy through and through," and thus knew how to take care of "punks" like Skeeter. He began to make verbal threats, kept getting in Skeeter's face and then began throwing fake punches in Skeeter's direction. Next, he slowly began to physically push Skeeter around. All this was going on with the subtle encouragement from the older Trailer Guy whom we thought was our friend. Instead of intervening to stop his dopey buddy from bothering Skeeter, Trailer Guy was finding the whole performance rather entertaining. I could not understand why this was happening but as I look back at it today it probably had something to do with the alcohol, boredom, and Wiley trying to look special in the eyes of the Trailer Guy. In other words, the situation had many of the major elements, beer and too much unsupervised time, that are part of a formula comprising the top 10 reasons why so many teenage boys get into trouble in the first place, us included.

Finally, after this had gone on for about 10 minutes and when Wiley grabbed Skeeter and put him in a headlock for the third time I had had enough. I swallowed my fear and got up, grabbed Wiley off of Skeeter and pushed West Virginia Wiley down on the couch. Wiley swore and threatened us but Skeeter and I were able to get out of the trailer as fast as we could without getting beaten up. Wiley might have been a punk but from the way he was acting I thought that he was tough given his age and beady eyes. Thus we got out of there while we were still safe or so we thought.

Skeeter and I had not gotten very far walking down Lake Road when Wiley and Trailer Guy ran up behind us as we neared our city's sole McDonald's hamburger joint. Trailer Guy had apparently convinced Wiley that we made him look bad. Now Wiley, not wanting to look bad in front of Trailer Guy, informed us that he was, "Here to get even." Wiley had lost respect and loudly informed me that he was going to get even, "By kicking your ass," he announced. Here we were faced with a situation that was common while growing up in our home town, that is, fighting. Growing up there was seemingly always a threat with a possible good old ass kicking being just around the corner. This type of situation could be expected almost any time for little or no reason at all.

Now only 100 yards away from that trailer park on a busy highway as cars went racing by and with the lights of a McDonald's casting shadows down around us, a fight was about to occur. There we stood, a skinny thug from West Virginia, Trailer Guy, Skeeter and I and it appeared that we had a fight on our hands. My heart was pounding because I did not know what to expect from this knucklehead who was now threatening me. I might have been afraid but something told me not to wait. All of a sudden Wiley stepped forward and, bang, without notice I cracked him squarely in the mouth with my left hand knocking him to the ground. I had learned this trick, a quick offense, years earlier from a guy named Donald at Harrison School after he punched me squarely in the face on his first day of class.

I was just as surprised by the result of my action as was Wiley. My initial fear had luckily turned to anger and it all seemed to settle in my left hand. Now the adrenalin was pumping and fear gave way to confidence. I wolfed at him to get up and get some more but he remained on the turf in a daze. This one punch was enough to settle the feud sending Wiley not only to the mat but also back to the trailer to lick his wounds and perhaps his ego. As the Trailer Guy helped Wiley stand up and while pulling him back home, Wiley turned, while rubbing his and jaw threatening us by yelling, "One day I'll git ya when y'all ain't a lookin." We never saw Wiley after that night and smartly decided to quit hanging out with Trailer Guy.

This one punch made me a hero to Skeeter and it was my first of what would become many tough guy gestures. Skeeter told everyone he met that I smacked an older guy and knocked him to the turf. I felt like the guy in the 1961 hit song, *Big Bad John,* who used his left hand to send a guy, in our case a guy from West Virginia, not to the "Promised Land" as mentioned in the song, but happily back to the trailer for another beer. I envisioned Wiley holding his next beer up against his swollen jar to ease the pain before guzzling it down.

As I look back on this event, Wiley was probably a really screwed up kid. At the time, he was just another of the many morons we needed to learn to deal with as we aimlessly bopped through the city. In our town, guys like Wiley and the Trailer Guy were everywhere and they were not exceptions. We knew we were going to regularly run into these types of nincompoops in our circle of relationships, and we never knew when we would next be threatened by one of them. We had to learn to either take care of the situation ourselves or find a way to avoid them.

As adults, we now realize that guys like Wiley were bullies who had problems of their own. Maybe they were experiencing family issues or worse. There always seemed to be a Wiley nearby as we grew up. When we were young a fight could brew at any moment over literally anything. Fighting was seemingly always a possibility usually for no reason at all. Danger from fights notwithstanding, I had such a good time with Skeeter, Paulie, and Freddy and strangely the possibility of a fight brewing added to the excitement. We may have been a group of misfits but we sure had a great time together. Freddy was the first one of us to move away. After he moved in seventh grade we never saw him again. I, fortunately, moved away in grade eight, luckily perhaps, before it was too late. After I moved I only saw Skeeter and Paulie occasionally as our friendship dissolved as they went to a different high school than I did.

Decades passed and as an adult living out of state my wife and I regularly visited my family who had moved a few miles west of my hometown. While visiting, I enjoyed reading my hometown newspaper checking to see if there was any news about former friends. In one edition, as I checked the obituaries I was stunned to read one that immediately caught my eye. I took a double take on the obituary because it did not seem possible. The article said that my old friend Paulie had suddenly died. He, we, were too young for this to happen. Being only in our forties we were not yet on deck to pass away. Dying was something that happened to older people it seemed to me. There was no listing regarding a cause of death. I was immediately saddened by the news and my mind began taking me back to those crazy days when we were kids growing up with Lake Erie as our back yards.

I considered attending Paulie's wake but I never did. I still feel guilty for not trying to contact the family to offer my condolences but I had not seen either Skeeter or Paulie since we were maybe 14 years old so I decided against making contact. I felt bad about Paulie dying so young especially as I thought back to all the life he and all of us had back then. I admit that I continue to cherish my time with Freddy, Paulie, and Skeeter however short it was because growing up around especially Skeeter and Paulie was a continual thrill. Each time we got together was an intriguing adventure where anything could happen and something strange usually did.

A year or so after I read Paulie's obituary I was visiting my dad this time by myself. My wife and children were back in our home, now in upstate New York. At the end of my visit as I set off for home and instead of heading down the major highway, I decided to take the long way home. I purposely set out to drive through my home town and view our old neighborhood to check out how the area had changed since my last visit a few years back. So down Lake Road I drove from my dad's new condo heading east right past the duplex my grandmother built to save us from moving to Arizona. I drove slowly past the buff-colored brick house my grandparents built in 1962 and stopped for a minute or two in the driveway as I needed to turn the car around on the dead-end street. Little had changed except the mountain ash trees they planted decades earlier were now much taller than they were when I was just a kid. Gazing at the house was so nostalgic returning so many memories. As I needed to make time and head home I was back on Lake Road again and soon passed the mansion where Skeeter and Paulie once lived. As I passed their old house where we had so many wild experiences, I noticed a young guy, maybe 13 or 14 years old, standing on the shoulder of the highway sticking out his thumb for a ride just as we had done decades before. The kid could have been Skeeter, Paulie, or even me 30 years earlier.

I never pick up hitchhiker's but for old times' sake I decided to stop and pick up the young man. After a little small talk, I asked him where he was coming from and where he was heading. He said he was going home to the East Side. He then pointed back to the big house on the lake and said something like, "I was just visiting my relatives." Without saying a word I felt a chill run up my spine, and

I felt I knew it all. He did not have to say another word as I knew all about him. No questions were needed, no explanation was necessary, I knew the whole story. I simply nodded my head in recognition without saying a word. Without the kid knowing it I was likely a small part of his story. I repaid a favor, I drove the young man all the way to his front door.

Tony Pisano and Va Va Voom Jackie C.

****

Coming around the track again. So what will it be this time? By now I was using the talkative walkers as my personal nostalgia machine. What will the topic be this time as they pass by and will their gabbing give me another story line to ponder? I was prepared and knew that the slightest word or reminder would send me right into dreamland and back to a life I passed through years ago.

Hipster: "I can only wonder what my in-laws think. During every visit someone is in their kitchen talking away. We have to share our visits with their whole neighborhood. My husband is used to it, you know. He never bitches. He's a wimp. I threaten but I buckle and go right along, don't want to cause trouble."

Stripes: "Is it that bad? I thought my in—l-a-ws w—e—r—e ge—t-ti—-ng u—nd—er m—-y s—-k—i-n……. s——o t——-o—m——-or r——— - ow……".

We may have moved to the outskirts of town, that is, to the lake duplex in 1962, but we did not lose the visitors. Some of the visitors from the old neighborhood had dropped out due to distance but we also gained many new friends. It was as if our move represented a spin-off of a TV sitcom. There would soon be many who would join the cast and begin to make life on the lake as interesting, if not more so, than before. I continued to enjoy some of the old crowd, cousins, Biagina, Uncle Rudolpho and Aunt Adelaide and the others but a new group would soon emerge adding new bits and interesting quips to our story lines. By the time we moved into the new home Giorgio had already moved back to Italy leaving a trail of broken-hearted women behind. In spite of the way Giorgio treated them, a couple of the women he promised to marry remained friends of the family often stopping by for small talk or to take part in holiday celebrations. They had grown attached to my grandmother and while they mourned the loss of their Giorgio they were not willing to also end their relationship with Giuseppe and Maria. Other folks like Joe and Feliciana Cappello were mainstays as well and we continued to enjoy their company on most weekends. Living on the lake, only three miles from our home on 21st Street, must have seemed like the other side of the moon to my grandparents as they could not drive. It did to me too as there would be no more walking trips with my grandmother to Penny's or Baisley's. There was not even a sidewalk available forcing me instead to walk alongside the busy highway as I went over to hang with Skeeter and Paulie. I will never forget how cold it was walking on that dark road in the dead of winter with that Lake Erie wind blowing through my soaked wool clothing wet from sledding or some other activity. Instead, our move seemed to open the gates to a whole new social scene that welcomed a colorful group of people. To a certain degree it was almost as if we had moved to an entirely new community. Location, location, location, as some of these new people were a surprise to me but represented a mixture of old as well as new, a fresh batch of people for my grandmother to feed and for me to build memories.

For instance, shortly after moving into the new home a fellow named Tony Pisano began stopping by each morning. He did not call before arriving, as most people simply dropped by in those days and Tony simply drove over to say hello, "Ciao," and have a cup of coffee. Mr. Pisano was a very wealthy guy, and like Orlando Scamorzes he gave no outward appearance of his wealth. One would never know that Tony was the successful local entrepreneur. Here was another Italian immigrant who struck it rich in the new world by using both his back and his brain to carve out a living. Tony was a mild mannered, honest and reserved fellow. Tony, like many Italians, including Skeeter and Paulie's father, made his money through the construction trade. Never meeting him before moving to our new home I did not realize that he was a family friend. I recognized his name immediately after the first introduction because of my continual pilgrimages around the city. That is, one could not help but notice his last name stamped on most of the city's sidewalks. Each rectangular sidewalk, mostly in the city's newer neighborhoods had a small, perhaps 3" X 5" corner of the panel stamped with the guy's last name, for example, "Pisano 1959," imprinted into the cement advertising who laid the walkway and when. To me, Tony was almost as famous as a movie star. We did not know anyone important in town, no politicians or doctors or anyone like that but now I knew Tony the sidewalk guy. Somehow knowing him, the sidewalk fellow, gave to me a sense that our family knew someone of importance. We had a little prestige that I did not otherwise recognize.

We began to get used to Tony's early morning visits. Like clockwork Tony parked his modestly priced compact car in the driveway at about 8:00 a.m. each weekday. Then he walked around the back of the house as he always entered the kitchen through the sliders facing the lake. Newly retired, he always knocked twice on the slider before entering. Tony would sit at the end of the kitchen table, where almost everyone learned to sit when paying a quick visit. Tony would peer out at the lake as Marietta immediately poured him a cup of coffee. Like most, he would also be offered a shot of whiskey or maybe an Anisette to accompany the coffee which he seldom turned down. There was not a day that went by that a plate of pizzelle or Italian anise cookies was not included in the morning routine. Tony enjoyed the coffee and one or two cookies before having to defend his plate against my grandmother's attempts to feed him more. "Mangia Tony, mangia, bere il caffe (drink the coffee)," she would say each day as if it was his first ever visit. Tony was kind to me and I enjoyed the banter, mostly in Italian, between him and my grandparents. Tony always complimented me on my comprehension of Italian saying he wished his kids understood the language as well as I did. I could follow most conversations but never seemed able to respond in Italian except for the basics so I just shook my head and listened. Tony often patted me on the head, said I was a good boy and sometimes slipped me some money, just as others seemed to do. He did it just for the fun of it. He wanted to thank my grandparents for their hospitality so he slipped me money and other times overpaid me for cutting his grass when his regular guy could not do the job. Much of the conversation revolved around Tony's retirement and the amount of time he now had to fill each day. Tony kept us abreast of his health and how his family was growing. He and Grandpa spent much time sharing their secrets on how to grow the best tomatoes, zucchini, and eggplant just as was done between Grandpa and others, and in the summer they swapped each other's crops. Food was the cornerstone of most conversations and I knew that Tony would soon be on his way as the conversation moved toward what his wife was cooking for dinner that evening. In some ways the conversation was formulaic so it was not hard to recognize the beginning, middle and end of a day's visit. Tony's visits usually ended abruptly as he stood up and made his way back out the same set of sliders that he had just entered less than 15 minutes earlier. Tony usually left about the same time I went out to the highway to wait for my school bus.

Grandma: "Tony, why you no stay a lilla more. Mangia la pizzelle, com-on, sit, 'a siede.' Yu justa come-a here. 'Sediamo."

The funny thing was that Tony seldom stayed longer than 15 minutes as he seemed to have a hard time relaxing, "Si rilassi." He enjoyed getting out of his house and needed a destination and our house was one of the places that fit his schedule and helped to pass his day. We were just down the road from his place and a few houses down from his daughter and son-in-law's new home. Filling his day with other Italians of his generation met one of his needs. I got the impression, even as a kid, that Tony was uneasy with retirement. Before retirement his day was jam-packed with meeting construction deadlines and making sure his employees put in an honest day's work. He was now doing his best developing a schedule that suited him and we were glad to be on his itinerary. On days when Tony did not show up my grandparents worried a little but knew that he often skipped a visit for one reason or another. My grandparents knew that Tony would explain his absence during his next stop for a coffee and "biscotto." His routine became our routine and we looked forward to his daily visits.

Another new character joining our family's life after the move to the lake was a neighbor who lived in a home next to ours. She and her daughter, a few years younger than me, were to become new players, seemingly ever present for the next decade. Grandma had a way of adopting all sorts of people no matter what their station in life. She found a way to somehow envelop them into her web of free food and hospitality. My grandmother noticed the neighbor and her daughter soon after they both moved next in. A woman living by herself without a man apparently was code to my grandmother for, "lonely woman who needs to be nurtured and fed." The woman, Jackie Carleton, seemed nice but one look at her should have indicated to most anyone that this was not just any lonely helpless woman. In those days, people would have described her as, "built," and quite willing to flaunt it too. She stood out the moment one saw her as she was always dressed to kill, including short dresses and spiked heels that took full advantage of her hourglass figure as she daintily exited her pristine white Cadillac. I realize that the terms I used to describe Jackie could be considered inappropriate by some but they described her perfectly in terms of the language of the day.

Jackie was a secretary at a local firm earning a salary commensurate with that of most other secretaries at the time, that is, very little. People were still called secretaries in those days as there were few positions of this sort defined as "Administrative Assistant." Yet, here was this woman, possessing no formal education, close to 40 years old, a single parent, wearing short designer dresses, stiletto heels, driving a newer Cadillac and renting a home on Lake Erie. Everything about Jackie screamed, living beyond one's means. Grandma, bless her, looked past this window dressing at first. She simply concluded that here was a woman with a child in need, another couple of people she could feed and support. Jackie was able to exit her car that first day unmolested by Marietta. However, before closing her car door on the second day Grandma was right on the scene. I can still see Muttyetta looking through her plate glass window on the edge of her chair scoping out her new neighbor's arrival. Granny was patiently waiting for her new neighbor to pull into the driveway. Soon Jackie arrived and before she could exit her vehicle, "Missee, you lika tha pasta, la spaghetti. I give yu una piatta, a dish, just a lil-for a taste," Jackie, who would refer to granny as "Mrs." from that day on by both she and her daughter for the remainder of their friendship, said, "Why sure," as she was surprised in her driveway.

This was how Grandma made her first introduction to her new neighbor who adjusted her tight-fitting clothes after closing her Caddie's door. What a sight, Grandma in her torn dress and unzipped rubber boots handing a large plate of pasta and meatballs to the elegant Jackie in her snug white silk blouse suggestively unbuttoned to display her gold accessories. Food was my grandmother's calling card, her greeting and well-meaning approach to befriending anyone in her orbit who was willing to eat her food, which included everyone. Everyone was eligible for a dish of her pasta and no one, not anyone that I remember, ever turned down a dish from old Aunt Mary. In the 1960s few seemed to whine about their diet anyhow and certainly no one ever told my grandmother, "Oh, sorry, Comare, but I can't eat that, I am glucose intolerant and trying to reduce fat and carbs."

From that day forward Jackie became one more addition to the regular lineup of frequent visitors who stopped by for coffee and she was always available to accept almost daily dishes of pasta, tureens of "minestra" (Italian soup with vegetables), even pans of pizza fritte (fried dough) or whatever else was on the day's menu.

To a young guy, reaching adolescences and soon to be a teen, I was somewhat enamored with Jackie, realizing from the start that she was not just some ordinary spinster. Jackie was shapely and sexy and was not at all ashamed of advertising her figure. Jackie knew what men wanted and was prepared to figuratively sell it. She was confident and as I soon figured out was quite proficient at twisting any male around her finger. I never complained when Grandma said, "Jovy, porta questi piatti next-a door, por Jacka (take these dishes next door for Jackie)."

Jackie was no fool and like nearly everyone, realized that to remain on my grandmother's good side she needed to be nice to me. Maybe she would have been nice anyhow but I felt comfortable around her and I think that was because she treated me as an adult. Jackie asked my opinion about things and was not afraid to summon my assistance with tasks around the house. In front of Comare Mary she fawned over me being sure to mention what a good and handsome boy I was. She knew nothing about my shenanigans down the lake or on the East Side with my trio of hooligan friends. What Jackie did know was that complimenting me was a sure way to get closer to my grandmother, a goal she was intent on massaging. Later, when I was in high school Jackie even made a habit of calling me over to help zip up her dress when she was getting ready for a night out. Certainly, this was confusing to an inexperienced young guy because it was not clear whether this was just an innocent request for help or whether I was expected to make some kind of move. Nothing ever resulted from these little dress-zipping episodes but they sure added spice to my teenage fantasy life.

As mentioned, Jackie's most prominent characteristic, besides her figure, was her control over men. Jackie knew how to get all she wanted from guys. For example, shortly after moving in and throughout the time she was our neighbor, we found that Jackie spent most weekends entertaining her wealthy married lover. Jackie was this guy's mistress as he would pull his Cadillac into the driveway, open the garage, drive in, and then close the door behind him remaining with Jackie the entire weekend. Often the pair would not emerge from the house until late on Sunday afternoon when it was time for the fellow to head home. If they drove anywhere they always drove Jackie's Cadillac. Grandpa, the king of nickname assignments, began calling her lover, Signore Zucchero, meaning, Mr. Sugar. Signore Zucchero was quite wealthy, it appeared, and at least two decades older than Jackie. He lived in a Toledo suburb in a rather ritzy home also on the lake. Some say his money originated partially from a hefty trust fund that he supplemented from operating a high-end business with his wife. Our family was never quite sure where the wealth originated from but it was well-known that he and his wife were loaded.

My grandparents also suspected that Jackie got her appliances repaired, perhaps a metaphor, free by the same repairman who fixed ours. In those days appliances were still repaired, instead of replaced, requiring an occasional new tube or wire of some sort soldered back into place. When the guy fixed our appliances it took him approximately 30 to 45 minutes to complete. When the same fellow fixed Jackie's he stayed around for two to three hours. My father and grandparents suspected that the repairman was focused on more than the appliances as were most men who seemed to associate with Jackie. We assumed that Jackie paid very little cash for most services rendered and this plus Signore Zucchero's aid helped her to enjoy the finer things in life in spite of her minimal secretary's salary. Grandma was not entirely naive concerning Jackie. Marietta was not a fool. She questioned Jackie's behavior but she could not refrain from sending stacks of pastries, plates of lasagna and even an occasional panettone (sweet bread) over to feed Jackie, her daughter and, Signore Zucchero when his Cadillac was safely parked in the garage.

Jackie was always thankful way beyond appropriate and gushed with compliments toward Granny as well as toward me. As feeding Jackie and her crew became habitual, Grandma had to soon ward off criticism from my dad, grandfather, and eventually others regarding the rate and amount of food she sent over to her new neighbor. Grandma could not control her generosity and this was cause for many family disputes. Soon there would be further criticism over feeding the boarders, as well, in addition to Jackie, when my grandparents eventually began renting out dad's and my bedroom.

Let's Move Once More

Yes, we eventually moved again but this time it was only my father and I doing the moving. During my seventh-grade year, my father must have begun to get over his divorce from my mother and perhaps was a little lonely so he decided it was time to begin dating. He dated a few people and I remember going out to dinner at a restaurant for the first time in my life as I tagged along with him and his date. We went to a Chinese restaurant and on another day to an amusement park. I assume he decided to take me along when he thought things were getting serious with a woman. Fortunately for me, these auditions only lasted for a short time because one day Dad hit pay dirt. He was introduced to a woman born in Germany who possessed her green card and like him was recently divorced. Her name was Hanna and she had a daughter, four years younger than me, named, Jeannie. Hanna was a friend of the German-American contractor who built my grandparents' lake duplex so a little matchmaking must have taken place along with the blueprints. I do not remember much about my father courting Hanna except that he came into my bedroom one day to tell me that Hanna and he intended to get married. Having in most cases limited opinions about most adult business, I simply shrugged my shoulders and accepted this dictate. He asked if I had any questions and I had only one, "Will we be moving again?" and his response was, "Yes." Here was a situation I should have paid more attention to because Hanna and I would remain in continual conflict for years to come. It would take a couple of decades, becoming an adult, and rising a family of my own before our relationship improved.

Marrying a woman from Europe was similar to Dad's opinion of foreign cars, that is, they were of higher quality than the domestic variety. Who was to argue given his experience with his first wife, my mom? Dad seemed convinced that foreign-born women, like foreign autos, were superior to their domestic sisters. Hanna fit the bill as she grew up in Germany during World War II and knew first-hand what hardship was all about. A person first meeting Hanna was certainly impressed that she, if anyone, was built both mentally and physically to take on any hardships firsthand. Hanna was a rather tall, broad, and attractive woman who was not afraid to look you in the eye and let her opinion be known. Her past must have taught her to never take anyone's nonsense because she had been served enough of it during the war and more when she experienced heartbreak from her first marriage to an American. Her past taught her to not take any gruff from anyone and most people recognized that in her personality. She was tough and she was just that much of the time. This quality would come in handy for her as she set out to become a member of our family. Any woman married to my father would need toughness and thick skin not only with my grandmother but also when dealing with me, the Young Prince of the Lake Shore.

Hanna would have to stand up to my grandmother and all of my grandmother's idiosyncrasies if she wanted her marriage with my father to last. In addition, since she and I did not get along right from the beginning she had a doubly difficult job facing her. Thinking back, it is amazing that she said yes to my father's marriage proposal in the first place. But Hanna was strong-willed and confident if she was anything and likely felt she could withstand anything including my insolence. Hanna was good at recognizing a good man in my father and must have decided she was strong enough to put up with any of my nonsense. Our relationship, however, teetered from the beginning before making her biggest mistake with me. Hanna realized that I would need discipline, which I suppose I did and told someone that she was going to make some changes as she trained me to toe the line. Whether or not she said those words did not matter. Once I heard them it was all-out war. From that point on my stubbornness would be tested right up against hers. Imagine two billy goats banging horns as they vie for dominance. That was Hanna and this was the case from the genesis of our relationship. This little spoiled Italian boy who was reared as the prince of the city was not going to relinquish his throne so easily. The mainstay of my plan, if there ever was a plan, was to simply ignore Hanna's attempts to make changes as I had ignored all previous attempts at control from practically everyone else. I had years of experience ignoring rules so all I had to do was to continue just as before while adding Hanna to my ignore list.

I would soon learn that Hanna was a worthy opponent but my efforts would be reinforced by joining up with you guessed it, yes, Granny. Horns were going to soon get locked as Grandma Mary would meet a worthy opponent who would become an occasional obstacle of hers not allowing Zia Muttietta or me to always get our way. Grandma intended to hold on to her position of power as well. She was not about to cave in and permit another woman to manage her life. After all, Marietta had years of practice dealing with competition from other women, and now here was this "German" woman storming in to take away both her son and also her grandson, both of whom she had nurtured for years. Butting heads was something that both Grandma and Hanna were comfortable executing and the only question was who would blink first. So began years of tested wills filled mainly with small battles that would mostly end in a draw. Until the very end, of course. Strangely, I think that in time it was concluded that both women cared deeply for each other but both were strong-willed believing that their opinion was the correct opinion with neither one seeming willing to compromise.

Just as my father had eloped with my mother he pretty much did the same thing with Hanna. The only difference this second time was instead of Philadelphia they headed to Washington DC for an abbreviated honeymoon. After first getting hitched by a local justice of the peace in our hometown they headed off for their honeymoon. Neither Jeannie nor I attended the brief ceremony, nor were we invited. Not only were we not invited neither of us even knew when the brief ceremony took place. Afterward, there was no party, no cake, and no visitors in congratulatory mode. Could someone contrive a stranger way for two families to merge? This all happened around Thanksgiving, in 1964. Thanksgiving went off as usual as if nothing big had just occurred, that is, a marriage, and I took the whole situation right in stride. Limited celebrations of some holidays, American holidays, were common and understandable in our home as my grandparents were still mainly, "Italian." They never seemed to understand the whole Indian/Pilgrim thing. Christmas was downplayed too since decorations and trees were impractical so they celebrated only enough to make sure I was not shortchanged. I did not complain that much because I was distracted and placated with tons of gifts and money. I did have questions about the differences between our family celebration and the ones I saw on TV but ultimately I had to accept the situation.

Somehow, it took becoming an adult to realize the sheer madness of the way that Dad and Hanna married. I asked my father why he decided twice to run away to get hitched and he responded that it was simply the practical thing to do. He had already told me this about his marriage to my biological mother as I reminded him that his previous approach seemed to fail. He just shrugged and said it would work out better this time. I understood the concept of practicality but not to the extent adhered to by my father. How he located two women who would be satisfied with a bare-bones marriage is also a mystery to me. Louie was lucky enough to identify two of the few women in the world satisfied with a zero, no-cost wedding. Dad was a good man in many ways but he never really understood the concept and importance of social convention.

Right from the start posturing and territoriality between Grandma and Hanna began. One of the biggest issues between them was Maria's almost obsessive need to feed the world. This got her in trouble before and it would get her into trouble again and again even though it was the behavior that most positively defined her. Grandma had her ways and she had practiced them for decades but Hanna decided to face the impossible and attempt to make changes anyhow. Hanna's refusal to accept Grandma for whom she was set off mild fireworks between the two matriarchs for the remainder of their lives together. Since there was no way to intervene I often found myself sitting back and watching the two spare over just about everything. Their interaction could almost be considered a spectator sport. The matches, Granny vs Hanna, were similar to the competition between Mohammed Ali and Joe Frazier. There was no one match between the women comparable to *The Thrilla in Manilla* but there were a series of mini-fights over time that were certainly considered a spectacle.

Announcer: "Ladies and gentlemen, LET'S GET READY TO RUM**BUUUUUUUUUULE**."

Announcer: "Now, introducing the champion,- the fighter out of the red, green, and white corner wearing her signature ripped gray dress complete with tomato sauce stains and sporting her unzipped black rubber boots. She fought her way through the Great Depression and withstood her son marrying an Irish-American woman from Philadelphia. She has a record of 20 wins and 0 losses. Logging in at 4’ 9’’ and weighing 150 pounds please put your hands together and welcome,

GRANDMA MARRRRR-**RY**."

Announcer: "Now introducing the challenger—fighting out of the red, blue, and gold corner, wearing Birkenstocks, costume earrings, and a pearl necklace, sporting a multi-colored dress with an eagle emblazoned on it. Hailing from Haan, Germany, and fighting her way to the US not letting a little altercation like World War II or a divorce break down her spirit all while serving as a single mother. Now, having built a record of 15 wins and 1 loss, standing at 5' 9" and weighing 165 pounds please welcome the challenger,

HAAAAAN—NAAAA."

As I hinted, one of the important areas to point out that served as a constant source of arguing between the matriarchs was Grandma's treatment of her new neighbor Jackie. Hanna was wise to Jackie from the beginning and did not care at all for her. Few women of the 60s would accept a person like Jackie. These were not days when people were accustomed to allowing bygones to be bygones. These were the days when strong judgments were still being made regarding the morals of certain people. Therefore, the doling out of food to people such as Jackie by my grandmother was a particularly irritating situation for Hanna and truthfully to others too. Many people knew that Jackie was not very genuine and that her character was questionable but no one, as I said, was ever ostracized or left unfed by Granny. Once she accepted a person into her informal club they remained a member forever. But who could blame Hanna? Jackie was the type of woman most wives would not trust around their husbands given her continual coquettish demeanor. It was therefore irritating for Hanna from the start to see food regularly delivered to Jackie's door often before the rest of us sat down to eat our dinner.

Hanna could not stop herself from injecting her opinion into the arrangement and this always ended in the same argument.

Grandma: "Jovy, portare questi piatti (take these dishes) por Jackie and Signore Zucchero."

This statement was usually followed by Hanna saying:

Hanna: "Ma, I 'vish' you vould stop diss, Jackie don't need it," or better yet, "Oh Ma, how many times do 'vee' have to tell you to stop already vith dah food for Jackie and her boyfriend. He's a millionaire. Let him pay for her dinna. He already gets enough, 'free' from her, anyhow."

Nothing was ever changed or accomplished from these arguments. The same criticism of Grandma's behavior went on for years. It was a predictable argument from week to week. Maryetti shrugged off the remarks as I was summoned from the cheap seats to deliver Jackie's food despite the ongoing squabbling. I felt like a pizza delivery guy being given two opposing directions to the same house. I chuckled to myself each time I knocked on Jackie's door with a dish of pasta.

Roomers Again

Soon after Dad and Hanna married, he and I moved out of the lake house and into Hanna's one-story ranch home on the other side of town. I would now live with Dad, Hanna, and Jeannie. Within days of our departure, it seemed that my grandparents began renting out the bedrooms that we left vacant. Serving as landlords was what they knew best and it qualified them as successful small-time entrepreneurs. Our departure allowed them to continue to pursue a business that brought in extra money. Renting out space got them through the hard times before and they enjoyed the labor attached to the work in addition to the extra income. Renting gave them purpose so almost immediately after we moved out Giuseppe and Maria began renting to guys who hailed from all walks of life. When renting the room, boarders were aware that they only rented the bedroom but to their surprise, they would soon find that they received more for their rent than simply clean sheets and towels. Grandma could not keep herself from feeding most of the fellows too. I say most because some of the guys simply were private and preferred to eat out at restaurants rather than accept Granny's invitation. The vast majority, however, enjoyed the food given to them as well as the socialization offered as they incredulously realized that they struck it rich renting a room from Joseph and Maria.

Now, in addition to feeding Jackie, Mr. Zucchero, and Jackie's daughter, Carlina, whom my grandfather had nicknamed, "Boo Boo" after Yogi Bear's diminutive sidekick, there would also be boarders to feed. This would surely add to the confusion at meal times as a whole new layer of issues to argue over began to emerge. Hanna especially, with my father's backup, would go literally nuts criticizing my grandmother for now adding boarders to the list of guests taking part in our weekly meals. If that was not enough to irritate Hanna and Louie, my grandmother further fueled the situation by inviting many of the boarders to sit with us during meals. Hanna would blow her stack over most of these new invitations. I say most of the invitations because my grandparents, fortunately, rented to some very nice gentlemen who were mannerly, personable, and often quite interesting. Eventually, family members began to enjoy conversations with many of the men and, just like Mr. Moon, some boarders became almost like family members. If a fellow was neat, socially appropriate, and occasionally repaid my grandparents in some way for their kindness and generosity, then Hanna and my father were more likely to embrace the guy and not complain about their presence at our table. But there were others.

For example, one particular fellow, a guy with a disability, seemed to be ever-present when food was being served and he became a particular source of disagreement between my grandmother and parents. The guy's name was Albert and he was hard of hearing and could not express himself very well. Albert tended to mumble and pretend to understand but due to his hearing loss and likely lower intelligence, Albert was unable to keep up with his end of most conversations. Albert was a tall bald guy who was a janitor at a nearby auto dealership and in his spare time was a goalie on a local roller-skating hockey club. I remember seeing Albert walking all over town years before he ever rented from my grandparents especially when Skeeter, Paulie, and I hung out at the roller-skating arena. I think Albert caught us stealing from the arena one time and pointed us out to the manager. Albert observed us taking turns boosting each other up high enough until our mouths fit neatly under the nozzle of the Hires Root Beer barrel located behind the refreshment counter. The manager then nabbed us and gave us a stern lecture about stealing and sanitary conditions. After the lecture, he sent us on our way. He never called the cops or even our parents. Luckily, Albert did not recognize me when he rented his room, and even if he did it is unlikely he could have adequately explained the situation to my grandparents.

Albert was a peaceful fellow but since he could not hear very well he mostly ate quietly. He simply sat and smiled a lot most often chewing with his mouth open. Most people, not only Hanna and Dad, did not enjoy Albert's company at the table. The real problem, the one that finally got Albert banned from eating along with us was his lack of cleanliness. It became obvious that he did not shower as frequently as he should nor did he use deodorant. That was the final straw and my grandmother submitted to the pressure to remove him from the list of dinner guests since even she could not stand the odor. Grandma was, however, persistent and creative. She could not stop herself from feeling sorry for Albert and thus continued feeding him. She also was not timid about telling him to shower more often. She saw to it that Albert took better care of his hygiene. A compromise over the dinner routine was somehow reached and it included feeding Albert after everyone else had completed their meal. So when we were finished eating and retired into the den to watch TV, Grandma would slink into the hallway, knock on Albert's door and say:

"Alberto, you wanna eat a lilla bit, 'Vieni a mangiare,' come to eat, have som-a-ting."

Grandma got a kick out of Albert learning a little Italian in addition to getting his belly full. Albert was never fussy about what he was served nor did he ever turn down a meal. He was always ready to eat no matter what Granny cooked. He ate anything put in front of him and he ate it with gusto. This system went on for at least 10 years.

The day my wife and I spent surveying the auction items spread across the den floor I noticed a silver-plated candy dish that played a significant role in a previous incident involving Albert. I immediately recognized the dish as being the same one my grandmother accused Albert of stealing a few years earlier. Grandma pulled me aside at the time and whispered that she had begun noticing that things were missing from the house and she specifically mentioned the silver dish during one of my weekends home from college. I found the whole accusation strange at the time but pushed her concern aside explaining that I could not believe that Albert would steal anything but especially not a silver candy dish. Although Marietta's behavior seemed a little suspicious at the time, I thought that her accusation was the result of her imagination. She strongly reiterated her concern that Albert had taken the dish because he was the only person besides herself living in the house. By this time my grandfather had already passed away and she was living alone with Albert being the sole boarder. Naturally, an all-out search ensued after she made the accusation but the bowl was never located. From that point on Grandma began to distrust Albert. Slowly, I found out later, she began blaming him each time something could not be immediately located. My father did not believe Albert stole the dish either. Now, here we were, Deb and I years later and almost magically the dish was laying right before us alongside all the other memories being readied for sale. I realized that had I been able to hide up in the attic, as I did when I was a child, I would have known right where to locate the dish and saved Albert from the blame. I would have known the inventory so well I could have saved Albert's reputation.

Eventually, after my grandmother kept imagining that Albert was taking her things, Dad acquiesced and had to tell Albert's guardians that they needed to find him another place to live. My father was not convinced, nor was anybody else, that Albert was doing anything wrong so my father trod lightly as he offered some phony reason for Albert's need to move. He did not explain that my grandmother no longer felt safe with Albert living in her house. In her mind, Albert was a thief and had to leave. In retrospect, we were becoming concerned with Aunt Mary's strange behavior concluding it was beyond the norm. Without proof, we worried that she had begun to develop dementia or some other sort of mental health issue and was becoming delusional but no one seemed to grasp the severity or reality of that concept as yet. Since our family never questioned a doctor's conclusions they simply accepted whatever Zia Muttietta's physician diagnosed and it was unlikely that the doctor was even informed of Granny's unusual behavior. This condition would eventually lead to my grandmother's placement at a local senior care facility where she would complete the rest of her life.

After Albert moved away, people reported seeing him walking the railroad tracks or walking down the highway just as he had done for decades. Albert's guardians, fortunately, found him another place to live not too far from my grandparents' home. It was only a few years later when we heard the sad news that Albert had died from an aneurysm. My Dad and Hanna attended the wake. Albert was 57 years old when he passed away.

Albert's death occurred years after I had already moved into my new home with Hanna, Dad, and Jeannie. We moved in together in 1964, and although I remember much of my life growing up, I, for some reason, do not recall many specifics surrounding the move out of my grandparents' home and into a new life with a stepmother and sister.

I was only 13 years old and this move represented my sixth move all within the same city, my hometown. Once again we were moving to a different area of the city, a new environment where I would have to identify and somehow develop a whole new friendship circle. Here I was moving again this time with a new family with my biggest worry being finding friends. I knew very little about where I was moving and whom I was going to be living with. In those days parents spent little time considering the sociology attached to blending families so there were no family meetings associated with the move. Instead, as Peter, Paul, and Mary once sang in their John Denver song something like, "Bags packed and being ready to go." One day I was a lake guy hanging around with a couple of pals auditioning for space in the local jail and the next I was shipped across town to parts unknown. What would I do for excitement in my new neighborhood where I thought I knew no one besides who could compete with the thrills created by hanging with Skeeter and Paulie? Traveling around town with that pair was a continual adventure.

I simply recall that after settling into my new home I immediately began scanning the neighborhood for a cohort of friends. I remember standing out front of the house thinking something like, "Ain't this some shit? Who lives around here that I can call a friend?" The place seemed sterile. The grass was mowed, shrubs sheared, trees nonexistent, and the houses looked all the same. I wondered whether I could locate the craziness that I was used to. No lake, no school playground, and nowhere to hitchhike toward. I did not know it yet but as boredom began to set in, and as it took a few weeks of experimentation, I would soon get lucky once more and somehow team up with a few interesting guys in the new neighborhood. As it turned out kids were living nearby whom I would team up with and it only took a few weeks to locate them. Soon it was concluded from this move, that no matter where I lived there would be a cohort of other knuckleheads just like myself to befriend. I would soon come into contact with guys from St Peters, the football squad I started playing on back in fourth grade with Rudy and others. Fortunately, the church had moved into its new buildings only a few blocks from my new home into a new complex that included a school and playing fields.

At first, I did not think the guys in the area would be my type. Hanna did set me up to walk to school with a guy, RC, who played on the football team and who lived nearby. His mom and Hanna worked together as cooks in the cafeteria of a cross-town elementary school. He and I began walking the mile each day to and from Hawthorne Junior High School. It was the middle of grade 8 and RC was a great guy but I was savvy enough to know that my delinquent tendencies would not be the type of influence his parents would appreciate. Having someone to walk with to school certainly helped out a lot as I began to feel shell-shocked from being transplanted in what seemed at first like a foreign land. During that period, while not in school, I was frantically searching the area for friends, guys that were used to the type of freedom and nuttiness that I relished. It took a few weeks but I eventually hit pay dirt. After a short period, I located a group of peers who would remain my friends throughout high school and some who continue to be friends even today. After hanging with guys like Skeeter and Paulie and before them Rudy and Anton I needed to find a group that shared a few of my rebellious characteristics but not so much that it would land us all in jail. Fortunately, after a short search, I found just the right match for my interests.

The first guy I started to hang with was a guy named Mac, a player on the football team who lived two blocks away. Mac went to St.

Peter's Catholic so we never attended the same school until high school. Becoming friends with Mac was at first surprising. Up to this point, I only knew him from football where he spent the majority of his time screwing around and his screwing around really irritated me.

In those days I was socially unruly but crazily serious about football. With football, I followed all the rules. PI was a football nerd if there was such a thing and perhaps, as a result, my teammates elected me as their team captain. As captain, one of my jobs was to lead calisthenics during warm-ups before practice. Being dedicated and committed to my leadership role, I remember how it angered me to look up each practice and see almost everyone doing their designated exercises except Mac. Instead, he was usually immersed in laughter while simultaneously distracting all the players around him. Mac could not do a simple jumping jack without adding a dance step or maybe a pirouette, any nutty thing just to gain a laugh. My job, as I defined it, was to refocus him before he disrupted the entire team. My efforts always ended in defeat as it did not take long to learn that even if Mac shaped up it would last for only a few seconds. Soon, Mac would be cracking new jokes and messing around while smiling from ear to ear like the Cheshire Cat in Disney's version of, *Alice in Wonderland.* Usually, by this time Coach, Mike Di'Amato would notice Mac's unruliness and intervene. While taking a long drag from his Italian Predroni cigar Coach Mike would yell, "All right Macroski, 50 laps." Mike never got anyone's name exactly right and always seemed to call Mac, Macroski, for some reason. Mac's real last name was, "Macroni," but we always called him Mac. Some of us concluded that Mike preferred calling him Macroski since he would rather consider Mac Polish rather than claim him as a fellow paisano. Mac, like many of us in town, was at least 50% Italian by ethnic background and thus from the "correct" nationality given that

St. Peter's Parish continued to remain the Italian Catholic Church in town despite its new location.

One's ethnic background was an all-important characteristic in my hometown. After providing your name, the second step in any introduction was a discussion designed to reveal your cultural heritage. One was not comfortable engaging in further conversation until each person's ethnic origin or origins was somehow revealed. These introductions were toughest on people who claimed membership in more than two ethnic backgrounds, especially if one of them was British. In my town, if you were English then you were nothing at all except a "Medigan," that is only an American, a person without an all-important ethnic identity. I was lucky enough, by the 1960s, to possess only two cultures both considered acceptable in the city, that is, Italian and Irish. So I was mostly okay, I was safe by birth. By the 60s it was becoming acceptable in our town to be a combination of Italian and Irish but that was not always the case as evidenced in my parents' generation.

Smart people learned quickly to reveal only one or two nationalities when questioned about their cultural background even if that was a fib. A really smart guy led off with the ethnic background he felt most proud to relate to as the city was filled with a multitude of varied cultural and ethnic groups, that is, Italian, Polish, Czech, Puerto Rican, Slovenian, Ukrainian, Mexican and African, followed by many other ethnicities. Of course, no nationality was any better than another but it seemed in our town that differing status was assigned to certain backgrounds depending on whom one was speaking with. Though not likely the case anymore, back then an uninformed person who was multi-ethnic would stupidly respond to the question about his cultural identity by saying, "Oh, I am Heinz 57 variety, ahee!" Once these words were uttered you were disregarded and figuratively filed in the dead letter bin. Admitting that you were Heinz 57, which is a conglomeration of backgrounds, was tantamount to saying you were only "English." Everyone was American, that was already assumed but in our hometown, ethnic origins were important, and being equipped with that knowledge somehow helped tell your story allowing others to fill in the blanks. Knowing a person's ethnic background seemed to provide people with some type of background, a bridge. It leveled the playing field. One's ethnic origins helped others know much about you before saying a word. In the 60s, words such as stereotyping and bigotry were hardly known to exist let alone their definition understood. Thus, claiming to be only an "American" placed you on another team, shutting others out, indicating you were uninformed and perhaps even from another planet.

Coach Mike, for example, who let everyone know he was 100% Italian, was a pleasant old tough guy. He was short and stocky, like most Italian-American guys of his generation, who, like me could only take so much of Mac's shenanigans before exploding. But Mac was endearing. Even after blowing your stack over his behavior, you continued liking him. We all enjoyed Coach Mike too. A fellow who minced no words if he felt a player was not giving his best. Mac and I reminisce into adulthood regarding a particular time that we ran into Coach Mike at Yaya's Pizza Parlor, a favorite hangout of ours. We recall running into him a few years after graduating from the CYO league. One evening Mac and I noticed Coach Mike standing in line to pick up his pizza while we were at a nearby table enjoying ourselves. As soon as he recognized us he smiled, said hello, and asked how we were doing. After a little small talk and for no reason at all he bent over and gave us some money followed by saying, "You's guys take this and enjoy yourselves, but be good." Something about the twinkle in his eye told us he still cared about us years after we stopped playing on his team. We were considered family to him. In those days there were not many people who looked fondly upon our bunch, or so we thought, as we concluded that adults tended to hone in on our hoodlum tendencies and not look beyond that. Certainly, we gave people a reason to judge us in this way but we did not want the recognition smashed in our faces. Recalling Coach Mike's unanticipated kindness, I guess, communicated that he saw something good in us where most other people did not. That is probably why we appreciated the gesture from this stocky little Italian guy with a big stomach and a bigger heart. Now each time Mac and I get together Coach Di'Amato is fondly recalled in our conversation.

Of course, Coach Mike's assigning 50 laps to Mac due to his screwing around is also discussed at our get-togethers. Running laps was not much fun at the time but Mac never seemed to mind. He could not stop himself from laughing and joking around even as he circled the field, usually by himself. His extended nonsense usually earned him a few added laps, enough to eventually wipe the smile from his face. It took about 60 laps before Mac would come close to being serious. By the time he completed his penalty laps, football practice was nearly complete but this would not stop him from repeating the same behavior during the next practice. Mac would return to the field the next day and continue messing around earning himself another 50 or more laps. This cycle never seemed to change.

That was Mac and our initial interaction should not have built a strong foundation for what would become a new and long-term friendship however somehow things worked out as we began to hang out together each day. Living just two blocks away, Mac would soon become one of my best friends. Our new relationship began when we by chance met out on the street one day and he asked me what I was doing in his neighborhood. I pointed out my new home just down the block. Mac smiled and generously invited me to hang out with him and a couple of other local guys. He said, "don't worry, I'll take care of everything." From our previous interactions, Mac should have wanted to remain clear of me given my propensity to act like a drill sergeant on the football field. He was outwardly confident and a wonderful jokester and he knew just about everyone and everyone seemed to enjoy Mac's company. I would soon find that his craziness on the field was only the tip of the iceberg and his style was just what I was searching for in a new friend. Thankfully, Mac was forgiving and a friendly sort of a kid, a risk taker I suppose and he took his chances with me too. I began to believe that there was hope in my new living arrangement after all. I would also find that even though I moved around the city, it seemed that no matter where I landed bean brains like me seemed to abound. Mac and I found we were not so different from one another except for our differing attitudes on the football field. We turned out to be just two peas in a pod as we were on our way to becoming small-time troublemakers and big-time friends.

Doubl'in Back

Since home life was not a happy place for me I spent most of my time with friends like Mac and we had fun comparing notes on our family backgrounds. Mac, like me, had grandparents who emigrated from Italy. Being from Italian households gave us much to compare and similar traditions to joke about. We both enjoyed laughing at many of the Italian-American lifestyle behaviors we shared in common, such as the total emphasis on pasta, tomatoes, and grapes. He and I enjoyed comparing the number and kind of fruit trees our grandparents had in their backyards as well as the number of tomato plants lining their gardens. We also discussed our estrangement from what we considered the regular American culture or at least what we surmised was the culture. Mac and I concluded that most Americans cooked upstairs and that real Americans sat on furniture without clear plastic covering placed over it to keep it clean. Being Italian, we felt, made us a little different from the other "true American" types, especially the ones who served as our TV role models. We mostly joked about the comparisons between our homes and what we considered the normal American households of our classmates and this tended to cloud our self-concepts.

TV comedies highlighting family situations were on the rise during the 60s. No one on the popular programs, *Leave It To Beaver* or *Ozzie and Harriet* spoke with an Italian accent and I never saw piles of pasta or mounds of meatballs on their dinner table. Instead, their dinners consisted mainly of pot roasts, potatoes, and peas. When Ricky Nelson sang he played the guitar, not an accordion, and as he crooned he sang to a mostly blond-haired group of girls. In addition, few women in Rick's audience even had black hair like most of our relatives. Certainly, none of the girls had the telltale sign of a mustache growing from their upper lip as many of our female Italian relatives did. Plus there were few serious Italian guys on the tube who came from families like ours. Sure there was Frankie Avalon, Bobby Darin, and Bobby Rydell but they were just beginning to emerge and just slightly considered Italians. There was only one bonafide Italian guy on TV who spoke with an Italian accent and on the program, his name was, Mr. Bacciagalupe. Mr. Bacciagalupe had a starring role on the *Abbott and Costello Show* and it turns out the last name means, "Fool," in Italian. Real Americans, I concluded from watching TV programs, were those without accents and people who ate roasted chicken and beef as well as their Italian food out of cans or boxes. Besides, I always wondered if Italians emigrated to the US for a better lifestyle or to live in a place where their names were not so literal. Imagine growing up with your last name "Caporaso" (shaved head), "Falaguerra" (make war), or everyone's favorite, "Pelagatti" (peel the skin from cats). One has to admit the last names sound much better in Italian where the meaning is camouflaged to Americans. Thus the exodus to the U.S., "Andiamo tutti?"

Mac and I had a good time comparing families and joking about our common culture. We liked to bitch about them too but deep down we felt pride in our heritage and knew that our families loved us very much. He got to know my family and I got to know his. Mac enjoyed my grandparents too and he certainly had a field day calling me "Jovy," after hearing Marietta's accent as she mispronounced my name during his first visit to her home. Grandma also warned us to, "watcha da machine," one of her stock warnings to me each time I left the house. I figured she used the word, "machine," to describe automobiles since one of the Italian words for autos was "machina." A one-trial learner is what Mac turned out to be. He only needed to hear my grandmother's phrases a single time before they became lodged in his memory bank forever. He jokingly used the mispronunciation against me from that time forward. It was things like this that made it evident that we would become close friends and that my grandmother would continue to affect my life in some way or another long into the future and likely forever.

An example of Mac's ability to hold onto crazy stuff in his memory has to do with another standard phrase he pulls out of his lexicon each time we meet. The origin of the phrase was total all my doing. The phrase is, "I ain't 'doublin' back," and that was something that came out of my mouth way back in grade 9. It all started during one of our morning walks to high school. Mac, one other new friend, Luke, and I were on our way to school. We had just stopped to pick up a third pal, Corto, but he had overslept again so away we three went without him. I think it was Luke who said something like, "Let's go back a couple of blocks so we can take another path to school." The new route, I recall, was intended to pass by Mora's house, a classmate Luke wished to impress. The change in route, I concluded, would make our trip longer thus increasing our chances of being tardy. I prized punctuality even as a teen while Luke and Mac were pros at being late, at least to school, and thus usually did not care about the time.

Due to the anxiety created by the suggested route change and the prospect of being tardy, I swiftly blurted out the now memorable phrase, "I ain't doublin back," which has become as famous in our circle of friends as JFK's phrase, "Ask not what your country can do for you…" has become to the baby boom generation. Almost before the now-infamous phrase was totally out of my mouth I knew I was in trouble. Luke and Mac seized onto my phrase immediately just as sharks seize on to the smell of blood in the ocean. They both nearly doubled over in laughter and I knew that my little faux pas, my impulsive verbal blunder would go on to live a long and embarrassing life of its own. Mac particularly focused on everyone's blunders as he could write a book filled with the silly phrases we all muttered at one time or another as we grew up. Mac had an uncanny ability to remember many nutty things we all said or did and pull them from memory at opportune moments making everyone laugh. Making people laugh in a variety of ways was Mac's calling card and recalling faux pas' was just one of the ways he was comical.

I guess like most teens we joked, razed each other, and often complained about family and hometown. Family dysfunction seemed to be our trademark, a sort of binding characteristic common to us all. Dysfunction was the common factor securing most of the guys into what would become a critical brotherhood that was burgeoning in size. Family dysfunction of one sort or another leveled the playing field and gave each of us something in common. Some of the family issues facing our entire group of friends included alcoholism, divorce, mental illness, poverty, adultery, loneliness, abuse, and suicidal ideation. There was something for each of us to complain about. Satisfaction at home varied but we all had our issues and for a group of guys, we listened and empathized with one another. We became peer therapists as we believed that we were the only ones in the world confronting such heavy issues. Surely we learned later that everyone has something to complain about but in our egocentric minds, we believed we had it worse than practically everyone else.

Mac's introduction of both Luke and Corto to the group would form our new neighborhood quartet. Both Luke and Corto, I soon discovered, were very much like the other friends that I made back at my home on 21st Street. They, like me, complained about family life and spent as much time away from home as they could get away with. Luke lived a few blocks over and Corto's home was right on our way to school. Luke was a tall good-looking guy that all the girls wanted to get to know. Corto was a quiet inward fellow who went along with most of our nonsense and created craziness of his own. Luke's main problem was a lack of self-confidence largely the result of a family that continually criticized his every move. Corto was a retiring kind of guy who would come up with some of the most astounding ideas that seemed to be pulled right out of the sky.

The four of us began going everywhere together. We spent time boxing down Luke's basement using an old pair of boxing gloves given to me by one of my father's best friends. While looking for something down my basement recently, I was surprised to find the one remaining pair of those gloves underneath some other items at the bottom of a cardboard box. Seeing those old torn-up mitts brought a tear to my eye. When we were not boxing we often enjoyed skateboarding up and down Mac's driveway. Soon the four of us began attending sporting events, dances, and hanging out at our favorite pizzeria, Yaya's. We ate many pizzas over the years at Yaya's and then sat around the small restaurant as long as the management would put up with our antics. Usually, we found a way to thoroughly piss off the owner and staff usually ending many evenings of fun by being thrown out of the place.

Moving often within the city and now between families was difficult for me, however, its value was beginning to pay dividends. Here was a chance, I found, for at least some of my friendship groups, made through numerous moves, to begin to merge. Hanging now with Mac, Cato, and Luke would combine with others guys, that is, Rudy, Galen, and Dirk, and later include others, such as, Anton. We would slowly mix into a single unit, a brand-new crowd, a sort of nuclear fusion of friends. Rudy even grabbed a guy from the high school football team, Chase, and introduced him to our growing family of friends. We enjoyed Chase right from the start as he quickly became a great pal. Chase fit in well and like us was happy to be out of the chaos of his home and into the screwy world of our new group of misfits.

Chase grew up in a large family with one income provider, that is, his mother. Like us, he complained about family issues and wished things were better. Money was tight in Chase's family and as a result, he lived in public housing. Being one of the few Caucasian families in a largely African-American and Latino housing project, Chased learned how to interact with all types of people so joining up with us was easy. Even though he lived in a tough neighborhood, I never remember Chase getting involved in any negative racial incidents or becoming involved in a fight or argument with anyone. Chase had a tight relationship with his siblings and together they made things work.

As mentioned our best spot to hang out was YaYa's Pizzeria which became a central gathering point for most of our group. Soon after our friendship group expanded, a new hamburger franchise called Sandy's Burgers was built just across the street from the pizzeria. We quickly scoped it out as another place to be seen and soon we started hanging out there too. While Sandy's was in business it became our unofficial headquarters for a couple of years. Unfortunately, Sandy's Hamburgers was created during the hamburger boom days when many entrepreneurs felt their fortune would be made in the burgeoning fast-food burger industry. Like many hamburger hopefuls, it was eventually absorbed into another hamburger franchise and only lasted in our hometown for a few years. We enjoyed many hours of mess-ups inside Sandy's, such as, threatening the manager and promoting food fights. Who knows, perhaps our behavior had something to do with its eventual demise in our neighborhood.

Sandy's was very convenient for us as it was situated on the outskirts of our compact little ranch home allotment. It was also convenient since friends working the counter habitually slipped us bags full of free food unnoticed by the less-than-competent management. One time a weasel-faced little guy named Franky handed us maybe what seemed like $100 worth of hamburgers, fries, and milkshakes to us just because he was angry at his boss. There was a lot of food in the bags as a burger in those days was only about 65 cents. We were able to feed all of our friends and anyone else who walked through the door of the shop that day. Best of all, Sandy's managers usually ignored our continual presence so we did not have to worry very much about being thrown out. When they did on occasion toss us out, we would indignantly leave and cross the street to Yaya's where with time we would be thrown out of there too.

Sandy's was also on a busy street with big plate glass windows so just by driving down the road, a guy could see if his buddies or better yet, girls, were situated inside. To make it even better, a vacant field was located right beside the street where we could play football while working up an appetite. When enough female spectators gathered on the sidelines we would call the game and go hang out with them at Sandy's.

Mac and I often laugh, being slightly embarrassed by our immaturity back then, particularly over one football game that involved Chase. Chase was known for turning up late for most things so one day we thought we would teach him a lesson. Before a scheduled touch football game across from Sandy's, Mac and I had enough time to hatch a little scheme before Chase arrived. We had been playing for about an hour before Chase finally showed up at the field and wanted to be included in the game. After busting Chase for being late again, Mac and I said we were tired and began taking a break from the football game. We informed Chase that we were going to eat the snacks that we had previously bought at Sandy's. So Mac and I each grabbed our prearranged Sandy's hamburger bags and prepared to eat our burgers. We were certain that when Chase saw us eating he would surely ask for some of our food. As was usual, Chase was hungry and soon asked us to share.

Mac grabbed one of his bags and pulled out a burger and began eating it. I told Chase I had more than enough and would share my food with him. I threw him one of my bags containing an extra hamburger. What Chase did not know was in place of the hamburger patty we had substituted some dog poop and placed it between the bun. Chase had a big smile on his face as I threw him the bag. We could tell his mouth was watering and it was all we could do to stop ourselves from laughing and giving away our little secret. Chase quickly reached in and unwrapped the "hamburger." His expression soon changed from anticipation to revulsion as he immediately knew something was not right. His smile quickly turned into the face of someone who had just confronted a skunk.

After throwing the "poop" burger at us Chase began to run after Mac and me attempting to make us pay for our little joke. Due to our laughter, it was tough to keep ahead of him, and soon the three of us were wrestling around on the grass laughing until we could laugh no more. As disgusting as this little prank was it represented the type of thing that bonds guys together. It is a story we never forget and it always makes us laugh. The group of us quickly became best friends and it was an added dividend for me that many of my new pals welcomed old buddies into our whole new friendship circle. Life at home may not have been that good for most of us, we may have felt somehow cheated, but we had developed an extended family of old and new buddies as we headed toward more memorable days together in high school.

Frontpage Granny

****

Hippie: "I like living here in this little burgh but if it weren't for Facebook I'd never know what's going on around town. No newspaper, no communication."

Stripes: "Yeah, where I used to live there was a daily, we heard about all the DUIs, divorces, all the gossip. Only silence here. We'd probably get blackballed by the local clubs and boards if we complained. You know h-o-w so-m-e of t—h—o—s—e lo—ng ti—-m—-e b—-a—b—-e s r——e—-m—-em be———r……."

Newspapers, hard copy newspapers like the dinosaurs will soon become a thing of the past. My generation still enjoys reading the hard copy but progress, and technology will likely win out leaving only online stuff to read. I used to look forward to relaxing while reading the morning newspaper, the *Rochester Democrat and Chronicle* and resented having to stop reading it when it was time to head off to work. As a kid I first began enjoying the paper after being introduced to a section titled, *Tell Me Why.* The article highlighted topics such as the reason birds sing and then it would go on to explain the process so that even a kid like me could comprehend the answer. I always had to wait until my grandfather finished reading the paper before I read and then cut out the article. In high school, the egocentric side of me looked forward to scouring the sports page to determine if I was mentioned in articles analyzing the results of our high school football games. I always hoped that the newspaper would picture me making a tackle or report on a great play that I initiated. What an imagination! That never happened but my dad did gather up a series of articles from various sources that wrote of my play on the field and he subsequently created a small scrapbook for me. After being surprised that my dad took the time to form the scrapbook and after showing it off to my friends, I lost track of the memory book. Years later I found out that it was eventually thrown away during one of Dad and Hanna's many moves. I remember how nice it was that he took the time to build the scrapbook for me. He did not seem like the kind of father that would do something sentimental like that but he did and it fooled me. Even though I scratched my head wondering what got into him, I had to admit his gesture was thoughtful. In the scrapbook, there were snapshots of me on the football field and a few others pictures such as one of me being caught watering some plants after college graduation while working maintenance for the county. It was a particularly hot summer day when a local reporter took my picture as I sprayed my overheated face with a hose. Yep, it was captured with a caption saying, "The Spray That Refreshes." The article brought me 10 seconds of fame. For one afternoon I could see myself plastered on the front page of everyone's newspapers even gazing at myself as I parked in front of a Lawson's Dairy Mart viewing my mug through the glass of one of those newspaper vending machines.

There was, however, a much better story that I included in my scrapbook, one that would be highlighted years later and it had nothing much at all to do with me. No, the best story of all, one published by a small local independent newspaper that still brings a smile to my face and a chill up my spine when I sit down to read it. It makes me the happiest. Fortunately there was more than one copy made of the article and it remains among my most prized possessions. Each time I read the article it not only makes me smile but it also makes me proud but unfortunately a little melancholy as well. The article immediately entered my mind as Hippie and Stripes once again came sauntering by. The article was about my grandmother, Grandma Mary.

So here is the story. Years after building their house on the lake, the one that saved us from moving to Arizona, a "For Sale" sign appeared on a rather large plot of land right next door to my grandparents' house. The land was owned by our elderly neighbors, a couple who planned to move and retire to Florida. The parcel of land represented one of the last undeveloped spaces on the lake shore so it sold rather quickly to a developer. When it was announced that the new owner wished to build a small apartment complex right next to my grandparents' bedroom, Mary and Joseph went nuts. No one in the family liked the idea as the project would surely block the sun and worse yet be butted up close to our property line crowding my grandparents' home. My whole family was upset over the entire issue as they tried their best to stop the sale. Since our house was a duplex there was no way to block the multi-family zoning of the area so within a year of the sale the apartments were constructed snuggly up against our yard divided partially by one of those ugly privacy fences.

The two-story apartments were built on the west side of our home and as a result, obscured what used to be an unobstructed view of the sunset over Lake Erie. Since my grandparents were practical Italians and were not that interested in sunsets they were indeed more upset by other issues associated with the arrival of the new housing units. For instance, the issue that they most began disliking was that some of the people living in the apartments began allowing their children to walk across my grandfather's pristine lawn, the lawn that he labored over for hours including the digging out dandelions by hand. Like many Italians, the dandelion greens, "denti di leone," did not go to waste but instead ended up in a wonderful salad each spring.

In addition, some of the children in the complex began to cross our backyard to climb trees located in a vacant lot area on the other side of our home. Lawn maintenance was something my grandparents valued. The sunsets were for Americans to cherish but for Pepino and Marietta a green lawn, without weeds, a lawn where my grandfather painstakingly picked out the dandelions in the spring for salad, was more important. Therefore, after much complaining and fretting a plan was hatched to halt the migration of apartment tenants and their children crossing our sacred green space. The solution, a very simple one, was the sole brainchild of my grandfather. His response to the problem must have come to him in the middle of the night. So, without mentioning a word to anyone, and right after finishing his piece of toasted Italian bread and a daily cup of coffee, laced with a hefty portion of *Carnation Evaporated Milk,* Gramps headed to his toolbox. There he collected his metal snippers, hammer, and a few other tools including a narrow paintbrush and black paint. From this equipment, Giuseppe created two thin sheet metal signs, one for each side of the yard. Each sign, measuring approximately 5 X 12 inches each, spelled in handwritten black paint, was the now famous phrase: **NO TRESPASSING**

As soon as the paint dried, Grandpa pounded both signs into the lawn, each facing outward and one on each side of the backyard. We all sat silently inside the sliders, the same sliders where we waited each morning for Tony Pisano to show up for his morning coffee. Once the final whack of the hammer landed and after the signs were securely in place we all let out a sigh of relief as a solution to the problem was finally at hand. There was nothing to do but wait. So we all just waited to see if the signs would work by warding off the pesky trespassers. The signs would be the first things anyone from the apartments would see as they considered traversing our backyard.

I remember being opposed to the signs, embarrassed I think, but my opinion was abruptly ignored by family members determined to put an end to the high crime and misdemeanor of trespassing. The signs, at least to my surprise, almost magically managed to have the intended and I might add immediate effect. The signs were surprisingly successful as they turned away all would be trespassers. We saw interlopers stop dead in their tracks as they began to traverse what they previously considered the no-man's land between their apartment and the small empty lot on the other side of our house. People actually read the signs and took them seriously and the apartment dwellers were now scared to cross over the property from that day forward as though they were a part of the children's book, the "Billy Goats Gruff" and afraid of the "Troll." Pepino's simple plan was the hit of the day and his chest was visibly enlarged with pride. Go figure?

However, the signs had an unintended secondary effect, as well, and the effect could not have been predicted. The story goes like this. Some years later, after the signs went up a long time, a middle-aged couple moved into town to start a brand-new newspaper. The newspaper was designed to compete with the already established, *City Journal*. Of all the luck for my grandparents, the newspaper's main purpose was to emphasize all things positive and local. That is, the couple wrote about area restaurants, new houses, places of interest, and anything new, fun, and good about the city. One day soon after the publishers moved into the apartments next to my grandparents, one of them stood outside her apartment and noticed the rather threatening signs posted prominently on her next-door neighbor's lawn, that is, my grandparents' lawn. "What a grouch," she thought. What happened next was also unexpected and morphed into a heartwarming story, printed in the long-defunct newspaper.

Instead of explaining what happened, I will let the following article, reproduced in its entirety, speaks for itself:

"Good Neighbors: Mary DeMeis
Metropolitan, February 3, 1982

(Editor's Note—When you are talking about what is good about this area you can't overlook good neighbors. This is a friendly place and even strangers notice it as soon as they walk down the street. If you have a neighbor you'd like to tell us about write to Joanne Scrivo, % Metropolitan News Magazine 1374 E. 28th St.)

By Joanne Scrivo
When we first moved into our home on Shore Drive more than five years ago I wondered what sort of grouch we had moved next to. For in the yard a few feet from our property was a "No Trespassing" sign.

It wasn't until one of the first warm days of spring when I saw Mary DeMeis. She was doing what only a few of us do anymore. She was hanging up clothes. Without a twinge of guilt, I turned back to my book and let my automatic washer and dryer take care of my job as I lay on the ground, soaking up the warm sun's rays.

Suddenly, I heard the lady call, "Honey, honey. You catch cold, you catch cold." I hastened to assure her that the sun was quite warm and I was in no danger of getting a chill. But a few minutes later she was back outside calling again to me. "Honey, honey, You come over the here and lay on my patio so you no catcha no cold."

This was the "grouch" who had intimidated me with her signs! As I got to know "aunt Mary," I found out that the signs had

been placed there by her husband who had recently died, in an effort to keep children out of her yard so that they wouldn't climb her trees and fall from them.

Mary lives on one side of the huge duplex her husband had built when homes were built like the "Rock of Gibraltar." Although crippled by arthritis she keeps the house antiseptically clean. It is filled—but not cluttered—with memorabilia and pictures of her family and friends. There are pictures of her lovely roses which my husband, Bill, took for her one sunny day. That was the day that cemented our friendship, I think.

Mary came from the Abruzzi province in Italy and she has never learned to read English. Her speech is a charming mixture of her native tongue and English and she's not always easy to understand. But she is patient and doesn't mind repeating when she knows I've missed the point of what she's saying.

Although she loves to cook, it's not often anymore she has the strength and fortitude to make one of her homemade pasta dishes from scratch, of course. But one of the nicest Christmas gifts we got this year was a huge bowl of gnocchi, a potato-pasta made in a bullet-like shape. Mary makes a mild sauce which never comes back to haunt you.

Although she hasn't done any canning for several years, her pantry in the huge basement has shelves lined with jars, the contents of which are still being used for her sauces when she does cook. And when she bakes, she uses her full-sized kitchen in the basement which always stays cool, even on the hottest of summer days.

Time was when things bustled around Mary's home. But even with her two boarders who have lived in the house for many years, it is pretty quiet now and too large for her to continue keeping it in the immaculate way she insists upon. So when she is able to sell it she will go live with her son, Louis and his wife Hanna. Mary also has three grandchildren.

When that time comes Bill and I will miss her occasional pasta dishes and the traditional breads she sends over when she feels up to baking, but most of all we will miss the warm and friendly lady who won't let us leave her house without having something to eat and drink; who knows very little about the world's problems and cares less' but who cares for her friends as if they were her own family. (The End.)"

In some ways my writing about my grandmother is redundant. The *Metropolitan* story explained it perfectly all by itself. The article captured my grandmother and the essence of her personality effectively endearing her to so many. Grandma Mary was also a contradiction as she knew how to get things done and done in her own way. She was the sweetest most generous person and there it was printed for the entire city to see. The newspaper article was published some years after my grandfather had passed away. and my grandmother went on living but she was lonely. Loneliness did not stop her from continuing her regimen of working, cleaning, and cooking for her boarders and obviously even the neighbors who moved into the apartments that blocked the sun and who got to enjoy the meany with the "No Trespassing" signs.

I fortunately salvaged the one remaining copy of the long forgotten, *Metropolitan News Magazine* article highlighting my grandmother's story. I have it framed and prominently displayed in my home. I smile each time I pass it by. The article represents a small piece of tangible proof of my grandmother's time on earth and her uncanny ability to make a friend from a total stranger.

Gents

****

The two women who were walking and gabbing their way around the track kept feeding my recollections of the past. One memory transitioned to another, however, I did not need to rely on the two walkie talkers when it came to one of my favorite stories. I waited but nothing the walkers said transitioned my mind into thinking about the Gents This story often popped back into my head all by itself. How can it not? It was not long after moving in with Hanna and Jeannie followed by meeting my new friends, Mac, Corto, and Luke that Rudy came up with a new idea. Our bunch caught the tail end of the gang era that peaked in our hometown in the late 1950s. When we were in grade school, older guys, mostly high school aged or slightly older, would travel around town looking tough wearing their club jackets. Each club had their own look. The toughest White guys, for instance, all seemed to sport Duck's Ass haircuts and stylishly kept a toothpick hanging out from the corner of their mouths at all times. Maybe that is why I began the habit of keeping a toothpick in my mouth as I coached my son's little league team. Soon my son's friends nicknamed him, "Razor," to get a dig in due to my toothpick habit. Without me knowing it, a professional wrestler named Razor Ramon sported a toothpick in his mouth during TV broadcasts while spouting threats to good guy wrestlers, as well as, the audience. I quit the habit of sucking on toothpicks when I found that out.

Gangs, clubs as they were often loosely called, in my hometown were broken down mainly by race or culture. Early clubs included the Mexican Kings, Southerners, Bishops, and Cavaliers, that is,

Mexican, Puerto Rican, Black, and West Virginian, respectively. So one day, when we were in ninth grade, Rudy dropped by to excitedly explain that he was thinking we should form a club of our own. He had recently spoken to a local youth organizer whose task was to transform city potential gangs into groups of law-abiding citizens. The mission, he explained to Rudy, was having young people learn to do something constructive with their time rather than hang around doing destructive things. In ninth grade we were too young to work and since none of us spent much time studying or engaging in useful hobbies, we seemed to fit the criteria for budding young delinquents. The newly implemented Vista Program signed into law by President Johnson, was designed with a group of unengaged scalawags like us in mind. If we joined Vista, we were told, we would develop skills, such as, leadership and would also travel together on fun filled outings. Field trips were included we surmised, to teach that it was better to prevent delinquent behaviors rather than create them. The Vista leaders also figured that with supervision our graduation rate would also increase even though none of us ever considered quitting school without a degree. Most of the guys were not very studious but not one of us ever considered quitting school. Even the dumbest and most inattentive guys in our class seemed to find a way to graduate in the 60s so we were not too worried about that. Sometimes, in those days, smart but unmotivated students attended summer school and that included a few of us. A few of the guys, for instance, were considered poster children for summer school attendance being forced to enroll due to seldom completing homework during the regular school year. These guys were hoping, we figured, for an immaculate graduation bestowed on them from heaven to help them earn their diplomas. God must have intervened and been looking down on some of my buddies because guess what, all of them did graduate. Perhaps God spoke to a few of them and said, "If I help you graduate you must promise to become religious men," and that intervention, we joked, may serve as a reason why Mac joined the seminary and Luke became a prominent preacher after high school. Corto must not have been paying attention even to god as he, unlike Mac and Luke, missed a religious calling.

Forming a club worried me at the time, especially wearing jackets around town during a time when clubs continued to spell trouble. I eventually warmed to the idea since Rudy's ideas were hard to deny. After deciding to move forward with creating the club, Rudy and a few of us began forming a list of guys to recruit followed by creating procedures designed to organize ourselves. We found out that much of this was already outlined by the lead Vista manager that Rudy negotiated with, Mr. Szartek. Rudy said, after running things by Mr. Szartek, that he would begin looking into jackets to represent our club but we first had to gather guys together to agree on a club name and logo.

It did not take long at all to recruit a ragtag group of wannabe "hoods" for the club. Aside from most of us originating from at least slightly screwed up families, another chance characteristic of our club was its multi-cultural composition. While we did not set it as a goal or requirement for membership, the club was becoming, what could have been called the Rainbow Coalition since we looked like a microcosm of the city, that is, Black, White, and Latino. Without giving it any consideration we were developing into the early pioneers of multiculturalism. Certainly, none of us had heard the word "multiculturalism" or "diversity" nor had we given any thought to being a mixed-race group of guys, it just was, and that is simply how it formed. The best consequence of not emphasizing our racial make-up was that none of us had to sit through any of those lectures concerning how we are all really the same color inside. We were already on that page. What we did find out was if somebody called any one of us the N-word, spic, wop, or hunky" then it was as good as calling our mothers the name, "playing the dozens," as it was termed. If names were flung then the loud mouth shooting off his mouth would have to pay a price for his disrespect. So while we never said, "Wow, wouldn't it be really profound to form a multicultural club, one which emphasizes diversity and equality," we just simply were. Later down the road race would sometimes become an external factor that we had to deal with but it was never an issue we dwelled on during the formation of our new club. Soon enough we would confront outside forces, somewhat racially charged, that would interfere with our club's harmony.

Besides, most of us felt life was against us in some way so that even the White guys in the club felt a little like quasi-minority members. The teenage years, for us, were as close as the White guys among us would ever feel similar to a minority member in America. Adults tend to treat teens, especially countercultural groups of guys like we were, with suspicion. Given a guy's neighborhood, teens of any color tend to be profiled, feel disrespected, and are sensitive to negative adult expectations. While realizing that being a profiled White teen is not anywhere near the same as a profiled minority member, many teens figure, and we were examples, "Why not do crazy things since adults already expect it?" So we often did.

Here we were, a group of numbskulls, not particularly sinister, who were forming a club usually reserved for tough guys. In addition, we were a club represented by marginalized groups, many of us, Black, Latino, or poor White. As I think back, not only were we perceived as "punks," but we were a mixed-race group of punks at a time when that kind of thing was still highly frowned upon especially in White neighborhoods. We, on the other hand, simply thought of ourselves as a group of guys who wanted to be a part of something new, something bigger and hopefully fun. Soon we found out that while a club could be fun the variables of race, class, and not appearing very tough, were also a magnet for trouble particularly when we were separated out on the street. This would become an issue as we meandered together through our mainly White working-class environment.

To keep things moving forward, Rudy set up a meeting with Mr. Szartek in his office. Szartek explained that we would be assigned a supervisor, a Vista worker, who would attend our meetings scheduled for Saturdays at a central housing project. We were told to begin choosing a name for the club and at the first meeting our membership would vote on officers and begin establishing bylaws.

That is exactly what we did as the group of us met together for the first time on a Saturday morning. Guys joined for various reasons, mostly to have a good time with new and old friends. Luke, who enjoyed basketball brought in a guy named Brad from his sandlot basketball team. I mention Luke and Brad specifically because some of the guys recall that playing basketball served as a major impetus for us initially forming the club. Rudy reminded me that he conceived the idea of the club partially since Brad, Luke and he spoke about finding a way to play basketball indoors on Saturdays during the winter.

I found out years later, as an adult, that Rudy and another guy, Rafael, wanted to form a club of their own partially since by doing so they could relieve the pressure they were feeling to join an all Mexican-American club in town called, the Chicanos. By becoming members of another city club, Rudy and Rafael felt the Chicanos would leave them alone. As one thing led to another these were some of the factors that led to the formation of our new club.

Therefore, on a Saturday morning in 1966 in the activity center of a housing project on North Central Drive, Rudy was voted in as president, our new friend Chase became the secretary, and our old buddy Dirk the treasurer. I became Sargent of Arms. After considering several suggestions for a club name and after much discussion, we agreed to call ourselves, Gents. Also on that first morning, we not only incorporated but also created a list of rules. Recently an original rule sheet was uncovered and those rules written in 1966 were:

"Club Rules
1. No Fighting!
2. Pay dues
3. Come to all meetings.
4. Every meeting a fine of 20 cents must be paid if you have no excuse for absence.
5. For talking out of order a fine of 10 cents must be paid.
6. There will be no loaning of sweatshirts.
7. Must act as a good citizen.
8. New members must pledge for one week, <u>within reason</u>.
9. Discussion of club business will not be expressed outside of the meeting."

Strange to have an original list of rules written over 50 years ago found tucked away behind some old memorabilia. Not so strange is that I remember that few of the rules were ever followed. It is somewhat laughable imagining that the threat of a 10 or 20 cent fine would stop anyone from breaking any regulation. We had secret rules as well and one was a paddling for any major infractions the officers deemed serious. The paddling rule was unwritten simply because it would not have been accepted by the social workers assigned to our club. Thankfully, a total of one paddling was administered, to our disgrace, as a paddle was broken over Brad's behind for some stupid rule infraction that had to do with basketball. That stupid act remains one of those awful behaviors to regret with all of us wishing that it never happened, especially me, the Sergeant at Arms. As adults we recognize the inappropriateness of our behavior and have apologized to Brad numerous times. Brad's a good sport as we try to laugh it off as best we can.

No one knew it at the time but this small-time incorporation, the forming of the Gents would provide a rather large group of us with something to reminisce over for many decades into the future. The club which lasted no more than a year and a half would give between 20 and 30 guys a story to replay repeatedly to their families and to each other as we periodically meet at school reunions. It still brings a silly smile to all of our faces and to the faces of many others, such as the girls whom we hung with, whenever we see a picture of our designer Gents jackets or simply hear the name "Gent" used in casual conversations. The Gents has remained a glue continuing to bind us together over many years.

Being a member of our new club did have its costs. The biggest problem associated with the club was the negative attention our coats brought on us. Wearing the coats down the streets of the city seemed to flag us for abuse. We soon found that unless a guy is big and tough looking, wearing club colors served as a catalyst for criticism motivating some to do things like throw out crude insults or worse yet empty beer bottles from passing autos.

Our first major threat began with a challenge that involved Mac and Luke. One evening as they hung out at, Sandy's, a group of older guys confronted them and began ridiculing our club jackets. Profanities flew, and Luke ended up getting punched smack in the mouth. Outnumbered, we were later informed that Luke subsequently feigned a heart attack or something equally ridiculous to help him get safely away. Luke left Mac to fend for himself as these would-be thugs liked Mac and used him to deliver a message to the rest of us. The message they wanted Mac to relay to all Gents members was to quit hanging around Sandy's, "since we were stinking up the neighborhood" and they did not like us hanging around with their girls. They further threatened that if we did not quit hanging around the area we would all pay a stiff price.

When the remainder of the club members heard what happened to Luke and Mac we were all naturally angry. A transgression of this sort could not be overlooked, oh no, this could not happen to one of the Gents. After all, how could we be seen in public, in our stylish navy-blue jackets, if we were made fools by a group of guys who sported penny loafers and madras shirts? I, due to my big shot position in the club, was therefore assigned the job of contacting the ring leader of this group of wannabe tough guys for purposes of challenging them to a rumble. Rumbles were actually a thing of the past by 1966 but we felt compelled to reincarnate them to meet our present situational needs. We concluded that if these Bermuda shorts wearing bumble-pins could disrespect us then we would never gain any status or respect from within our little community.

I called Kenny, the fool who punched Luke in the face, from Luke's kitchen table with Mac sitting right next to me. I had earlier discussed our situation with Rudy who had already hatched the plan. I called Kenny and angrily informed him that we were looking for revenge. Naturally, I threw in a few expletives for extra emphasis, and he was told they had better show up at 6:00 at a local park where a gang fight would settle the score.

Most of Kenny's friends were neighborhood guys, middle-class White guys who never broke rules, were probably even listed on the honor roll, and disliked our competition for girls in what they considered was their neighborhood. These were intolerant guys who did not like minority kids, especially those cavalier enough to bop through their neighborhood wearing club coats and wishing to hang around their babes. While these boys in madras were a year older than us, I could be as brazen and threatening as I wanted since none of them were particularly tough. Certainly not like some of us thought we were.

We had all previously enjoyed the movie, *West Side Story,* while growing up but our level of rumbling experience was fashioned nowhere near the caliber of the rumbling illustrated in that tale. In fact, we only knew about rumbles from screenplays and from watching TV having never really taken part in any, at least as of yet. We thus were not very sophisticated in the gang fighting department. To prove my point please notice that we were meeting during daylight hours and not at midnight as did the Sharks and Jets in Stephen Sondheim's story. We were also scheduled to fight in a public park not underneath a secluded highway bridge as was done in the musical. Apparently, we had a lot to learn about gang fighting. We planned to do our best and did not know it beforehand but we would soon surprisingly become slightly more educated in the fine art of the rumble.

All club members were called and most agreed to assemble at the park according to plan at about 5:30 on the chosen day. There were about 20 Gents assembled in the park as Mac, Luke, Corto and I arrived and we immediately began making plans for how things would go down. Rudy assembled us and we began planning. His idea was to not give them a chance to set up but instead to rush Kenny and his friends as soon as they arrived then proceed to pound them all into submission. In those days we were simply talking about a fight designed to coerce guys to give up and apologize. We were not looking to permanently maim anyone.

The trouble with fights contemporarily, I have found out since getting older, is that individuals can be seriously injured or even die from a single punch. When a guy is in high school, at least in the 1960s, we never considered that anything like that could happen. We figured a bloody nose, maybe a loose tooth, a few sore muscles and an "Okay, I give up," would be all that could happen. Most of us did not brandish knives or guns back then and even if they were in someone's pocket at the rumble they would not be taken out and used. We were still living in the good old days relying on our fists to get the job done.

Finally at about 6:00 p.m. we were surprised to see three cars pull up at the park loaded with guys who, when they opened the car doors, were not the ones we expected. Many of the guys who emerged turned out to be members of the Southerners, a mainly Puerto Rican club from across town composed of really tough young men in their late teens and early 20's. As these older and much rougher looking fellows came toward us they either picked up sticks or already carried baseball bats, chains and who knew what else. We looked at each other and said, "Whoa, did not expect this, now what?" These were not the toughs we wanted to fight for many obvious reasons. Luckily, quick-thinking Rudy stepped forward and greeted one of the guys with, "Hey Chico, what's happening." Rudy recognized Chico as a friend of one of his cousins. In addition, this guy Chico, it turns out, would never mess with Rudy, we found out later because he knew the reputation of one of Rudy's older brothers. It turned out that Rudy's oldest brother, Francisco, was a past president of the

Mexican Kings, a defunct club that became defunct, partially, because most of the members were either dead, maimed, or in jail. Chico would easily know that fighting Rudy would cause him more long-term trouble than it was worth.

The gang took a long deep breath while Rudy, Chico, and a few others began sorting things out. Kenny, it was figured, panicked a little after our discussion and called Chico to help he and his pals deal with our threat. He apparently knew Chico from working with him on some summer job and promised Chico a stash of liquor if he brought some reinforcements to the fight. In our hometown there was almost always a group of guys who were ready to fight in a moments notice for little reason and for any amount of payoff. Fighting chumps like us for booze was, in fact, enough of a payoff for guys like the Southerners without much else to do.

After a little deliberation, it was decided that Rudy would choose one of us to fight Kenny since Kenny seemed to be the main big mouth who started things from the start. A one-on-one fight was felt to be the best course to follow due to the apparent politics of the situation. So far it seemed our little rumble was somewhat following the plot line of *West Side Story* including some prejudice but without the interracial romance interwoven. So, with little fanfare and minus the Leonard Bernstein background music, Rudy nominated me to fight Kenny. After all, as has been established, I was the big shot Sergeant at Arms.

It is nearly impossible for most of my present friends to believe that in those days I was a quasi "tough guy." I was strong from weight lifting, in good shape from playing football, and had a quick trigger temper. I was, much of the time, pissed off about something much of the time too. These skills and attitudes were a recipe for a good old-fashioned fight and fighting seemed to follow me around for a short period of time in my adolescent through my early teen years. Give a kid freedom to tool around at all hours of the day or night in a place like our city and it would eventually lead to the growth of many questionable but sometimes practical skills. One of them for me was fighting. Where we grew up there was always a healthy supply of dim wits who loved to pick fights for simple reasons. I already mentioned that. Therefore, a guy always had to be prepared.

One time, for instance, after the club had formed, similar to the time with Skeeter and Wiley, we were sitting in Yaya's Pizza Parlor eating pizza, drinking cokes, and being wise asses. As usual we were lingering way too long after eating our food not to mention making wise cracks and emitting too much noise. All of a sudden someone must have complained to the manager about our boisterousness because she sent over a well-built waiter, three years our senior, who ordered us to leave. We never liked being commanded to do anything in those days, even when we were wrong, which we were most of the time, and this time would be no exception. Of course, we gave the fellow some lip and we refused to leave. Therefore, the waiter guy grabbed a friend, Dario, by the arm and tried to pull him out of his chair toward the door. At this point, my temper sprang into action and I stood up, grabbed the tough guy by his jacket, pushed him against the wall and lifted him into the air. As his eyes got really wide like slices of pepperoni the manager yelled, "Call the cops," which got my eyes real big too so I dropped the tough guy and we all ran out of there as fast as we could.

This little tête-à-tête added to my growing tough guy reputation. My friends, especially Dario and his older brother Santiago, were simply thrilled with my intervention and we all laughed and relived the episode for many days to come. "Hey, did you see that guy's eyes when Joe lifted him up against the wall," as they all guffawed as we walked down the street. "Yah," someone said, "his eyes looked as big as his pizza's," added another. "I thought he was going to shit his pants," the last guy chimed in. "It would have only improved the pizza's flavor." That little fracas seemed to simulate a scene from all the western's we had grown up watching as kids. Maybe that is why that little memory is often recalled when some of the old Gents get together. Play the song here from the movie, *The Good, The Bad The Ugly.*

Pretty impressive is it not? Nowadays, I would probably be arrested for putting my hands on this fellow and causing a scene in the pizza parlor but we got away with lots back then. That has been established too. It seems people were not as touchy as they are today. A few weeks after the pizza parlor episode we eventually returned to eating Yaya's pizza after we figured things had cooled down. I could certainly understand why they wanted us out of the joint because we were usually disturbing customers and taking up seats. This is the same place where Luke bent over a few weeks earlier and a knife, followed by a chain, fell out of his coat pocket. This little item was witnessed by the manager and a few patrons as well. I marvel at the patience the proprietors of Yaya's provided to us and thank them now in absentia for their tolerance of our behavior. We enjoyed many good times there. By the way, we loved the pizza. It never tasted like shit. It remains the best pizza ever. PS, believe me Luke never intended to use with the knife or the chain either.

One evening, not long after the Yaya's Pizza affair the same group of us, including Mac, Dario, and Santiago, plus a couple of other guys were walking on the way to playing basketball over at St. Peter's Church. We were bopping along, minding our own business, a few feet in front of a group of older guys and we were sporting our new club colors. Soon we heard the guys wolfing at us from behind and they were not shouting out compliments. We had seen the group around the neighborhood before but most of us did not know any of them personally. Mac, as usual, knew the bunch and its leader, a big mouth named Rusty. Mac, I will mention it again, seemed to know everyone.

We were just minding our own business, pushing and knocking each other around as always, when suddenly, from the group behind us, we loudly heard, "Hey Mac, why don't you and your 'Spic' Gent friends quite smelling up this street and stay the hell out of here." Sound familiar. This guy, Rusty, we found out was not a very accepting person and also disliked Mac for his joking around attitude. He apparently decided, after seeing our new club name displayed on the back of our coats, that now would be a good time to put us all in another tight situation. Dario and Santiago were half Puerto Rican and given our looks, Gents' coats, and all, we were all being tested by Rusty and his toady friends. We kept walking after he insulted us but I began feeling the familiar pangs of adrenaline pumping through my head and knew we would likely not escape without a confrontation. With my head pounding, I seriously felt like bygones were not likely going to be considered bygones by the end of the evening.

As we entered the foyer that separated the church from the gym, the same foyer where Mac and I were notorious for making so much noise that we regularly got thrown out of the church during Sunday mass, Rusty repeatedly directed more derogatory remarks toward us. The result was he and his cronies laughed uncontrollably like chimps right in our faces. My temper being what it was back then and becoming increasingly sensitive now that the club was becoming a lightning rod for wisecracks, I knew that Rusty's challenge could not be ignored.

It was right there in the church foyer where I came unglued. Most importantly, it was in the vestibule where I blurted out the now famous phrase, never to be forgotten by friends, particularly Mac. Somehow the devil must have invaded my body or perhaps it was the result of my prior sinning in a holy space that caused me to spew the embarrassing phrase from my lips. As if things would not turn out bad enough that evening I had to turn, look Rusty squarely in the eye and exclaim,

"All right, 'big daddy' let's take it outside."

These words, this short simple sentence, especially the pairing of the two words, "big" with "daddy," would become particularly memorable. You see, this short word construction, "big daddy," had not been uttered by anyone since the end of the 1950s. The famous tough guy movie star, James Dean, star of the movie, *Rebel Without A Cause,* himself, had he been alive at the time, would certainly have been too ashamed to repeat that corny phrase again in public in the 60s or otherwise. But not me, no not me. Now, here it was 1966 and somehow that short phrase was the first phrase that popped into my adrenaline-filled brain as I maneuvered myself right in front of Rusty's big fat face is a mystery to me. Though I was focused on Rusty, I could somehow tell that the rest of the guys were torn between preparing for a fight or beginning to laugh uncontrollably over the inane sentence they just heard stumbling out of my mouth. For a brief second, they must have been conflicted about which direction to head. Should they remain on my side or out of embarrassment scatter pretending that they were not at all associated with me? "Big daddy," must have caused them to question their very own hearing as they could be seen scratching their heads and toeing the linoleum. Did they hear me correctly and did I not just dig us a bigger hole to crawl out from? The hackneyed phrase, "All right big daddy...," that burst through my protruding lips that evening would become another entry in Mac's phrasebook right alongside, "I ain't doubling back." He would add this locution to all the others used forever as friendly taunts on his friends and especially me for the rest of our lives. By now I had likely said so many silly things that a whole chapter with my name on it could have become part of Mac's potential bestseller. Once uttered they could never be erased. They immediately became history.

Fortunately, the boys supported me as we took it outside and Rusty and I prepared to fight. Being impatient and having had enough of the criticism that seemed to be increasingly bestowed upon us, newly ordained Gents, I did not hesitate. I did not hesitate before directing my left fist squarely at Rusty's face, approximately right in the same place where only a few minutes earlier he was uttering racial pronouncements. Rusty ended up on the ground, flat on his back, and I quickly jumped on top of him. My second punch missed its mark and my fist smashed instead against the pavement. There would be no third punch because the next thing I knew there was a young priest grabbing my cocked arm saving Rusty from what I hoped would be a second smack to the other side of his big dumb mouth.

We were separated, lectured, and all sent home. I left with a stinging right-hand absent a few layers of skin that had scraped off of my knuckles when my hand missed and slammed into the blacktop. Upon reaching home, I recall sitting at my desk and feeling my temples throb. My heart felt like it left my chest and entered my head. Heart palpitations were pounding away inside my skull as the adrenaline continued to pump through my brain as I felt as if Poe's,

Tell-Tale Heart, had entered my cranium. I sat at the desk in my bedroom reliving the fight and fretting over my use of the phrase, "Big daddy?"

Apparently, overnight, word about the fight had quickly spread throughout the school. By the next day, I was surprised by all the attention I received and was confused to hear that the fight was technically not over. The rumor spread that Rusty, a senior, got beat up by a freshman and his classmates were now laughing madly at him. Luckily my expression, "Big daddy" was less interesting than Rusty getting slugged to the pavement by me so I heard nothing more about that phrase except a few snickers from the guys. Rusty, as a result, wanted a rematch to recapture his self-esteem and we were scheduled to meet after school a block from the school to settle things. I felt the fight was finished, my swollen hand seemed to prove that to me, plus the adrenaline had leveled off and I was no longer crazed. Becoming crazed seemed to be necessary, a major motivator when it came to my altercations. I was beyond worrying about using any outdated 50s slang but I was pleased to learn that one of the football coaches got word of the after-school fight and made sure nothing occurred. Soon things settled down and the whole Rusty affair was forgotten as life moved on.

Now, back to the *Gent's* big gang fight. There I was chosen by Rudy to protect the integrity of our club. My fighting was about to be tested again as I stepped forward to collide with Kenny. Before the fight began, a circle formed around us, and just as we were to begin the brawl we all simultaneously heard a high-pitched voice yell from across the street:

"You boys had better get out of here. I've just called the cops."

As we turned around we saw a neighbor woman wearing an apron and sporting large curlers in her hair, a regular style of the day, waving her fist in the air while warning us to clear out. Unlike the manager of Yaya's, this woman had really called the police. As we began to hear sirens in the distance, everyone automatically began to scatter. Soon the sound of sirens were blaring closer followed by the appearance of two patrol cars attempting to encircle the park. That is after I saw the backs of Chico, Kenny and the others running to their cars with sticks and bats flying because no one wanted to be caught carrying anything that could be construed as a weapon. There was something ironic about seeing guys, tough one minute but now all running away like spooked gazelles. We twenty or so Gents also transformed into wimps commencing to swiftly dart through the brush and the yards, jumping over a nearby stream and hurdling over logs trying to find places to hide until things cooled down. Everyone luckily escaped that afternoon and we survived another day with no one having to suffer the consequences for being dodoes.

Gents Turned 60

None of us gave much thought to our future as we escaped from the police that afternoon of the gang fight. Who could project that forty years later many of us would gather at a thrown together birthday party designed to celebrate most of us turning 60 years old? The party was held in the old downtown Elks Club Lodge by Rudy, Mary Lynn, his wife, and a few others. It was great seeing members of the gang and a ton of friends from the class of 1969. Turning 60 would have seemed like an eternity to a group of 15-year-olds when we formed the club but it would eventually serve as an excellent reason to get together once again in our old hometown. That night in 2010 a number of us reminisced about the club and someone brought up our ill-fated and fortunately interrupted gang fight. Assembled would be a representative group of Gents and other old guys whose energy had begun to decline along with their testosterone. The previous tough demeanor we loved to project years earlier by this time had waned, now replaced by the love of family and dreams of retirement.

Strangely, that night at the party, and it seemed almost destined, I by chance shook hands with Kenny, greeting him as a friend after all these years. This was the same Kenny who helped instigate the gang fight. He was certainly someone I did not expect to ever see again. It turned out that he had married a woman from our graduating class who was like us also turning 60 years old. I had not spoken to Kenny since that crazy afternoon so many years earlier in the park as the guys circled us as we prepared to fight. I wondered if he was replaying our near fisticuffs in his mind as we now stood across from one another holding up beers instead of our fists. I wondered if he, like me, was just as happy the fight was interrupted and looked upon the handshake that evening as something that should have occurred decades earlier. I did.

Later that same evening, eight old Gents had the opportunity to pose for a picture. Together one more time, the photo is now nestled among my most prized snapshots of all time. As if the evening had not gone far enough to raise our collective nostalgia, one of the guys, Jimbo, had brought along the only remaining original Gents jacket and it was held up prominently in the center of the shot. Possession of the jacket seemed to somehow serve as historical evidence of our club's existence. The coat seemed to scream out its need for cataloging and placement in a local museum. The jacket was our time capsule. We could not have been any prouder that night with that coat unfolded in front of us as it sort of represented our own personal Stanley Cup.

No sooner had the picture been snapped when one of the guys, Rafael, pulled out a bag filled with T-shirts. Obviously, there were more surprises in store. He had decided to amaze us by superimposing a picture of our 1964 junior high school football team on the back of the white shirt and on the front was the Gents insignia, spelled in old English lettering and complete with top hat, white gloves, and cane. We were transported back to a day when we considered ourselves chic and hoping to leave an imprint on our hometown. Now, as much as we wished, only traces of our old selves existed but we were still friends whose bonds were secured decades earlier partially by that club. Now, for a few hours, we had the chance to feel dapper again.

Rafael was surprised when I told him I was not on the junior high football team instead remaining on St. Peters CYO. That hardly mattered to him as the picture flashed, #37-Chase, #36-Rafael, #27-

Brad, #51-Teddy, and #48-Rudy. All of them in the picture were destined, but did not know it at the time, to become Gents The picture was as clear as the day it was taken and we all marveled at the passing of time.

When we were teens we had no notion that someday we would turn 60. As teens, perhaps we looked forward to becoming 18 allowing us to vote, or 21 to legally drink real booze. Those were the only two age-related thoughts we had back then. Now it was different and while few would wish to return to the life we had as teenagers, we could not help but long for some of that adventure and youthful energy left behind so many years before. As we began turning 60 and while mingling with our friends and classmates, we simply sucked in our guts and earnestly tried to recall being young so long ago. We toasted a lot of things that night ending with one symbolic toast, "Long live the Gents," we all yelled as the photo was captured.

More Reminders

Much of what happened in my early life, the friends, the experiences were due to my grandparents. That could never be forgotten. Not only did they influence who I am today but their lust to move within the city allowed me to meet and become friends with so many different groups of people throughout my hometown. Now, before me on the floor of Grandma Mary's den were so many possessions, objects with life history attached. It was difficult for us to focus on any one object for very long due to Grandma's newly developed paranoia and her worry that we were out to steal her possessions. The grandmother I knew during my life was not the person standing next to us. This grandmother was obviously feeling substantial paranoia and her generosity had turned to possessiveness. Where she would have almost forced us to take anything that we wanted, she was now quite protective of every article readied for sale. Any focus on a particular article seemed to cause her to conclude that we wanted to take advantage of her. This was never a behavior I witnessed as a boy growing up in her household. My wife and I needed to tread lightly and keep our distance so we would not raise my Grandmother's suspicion and cause her to believe we were visiting only to poach her things.

Panning the room we could not help but notice the numerous doilies she knitted as I, a child, sat nearby playing with my Tonka Toys. Close to the doilies was her sewing box filled with needles, thread and the hundreds of buttons she salvaged over the years and used to so skillfully sew and repair clothing. Seeing the buttons reminded me of a game she taught me on one memorable rainy day when I was bored and could not escape outdoors. Noticing my boredom, Grandma began by threading a large two holed button with a folded piece of thread. She then tied a knot and while holding each end of the thread with both index fingers, began to spin the button around and around. When the thread was taut, one was supposed to pull outward in an accordion-like fashion and the button would first spin in one direction before winding up and releasing to spin in the opposite direction. Neither of us knew it at the time but someone had named the game, *The Dancing Button*. I remember marveling to myself, how does she, my grandmother, know about the game, any game as I was forgetting that at one point she was once a child herself followed by becoming a mother who raised her own child, my father.

How I wanted to salvage some of those buttons for old times sake but I refrained. The buttons were nice but the doilies were a work of art. Knowing the amount of hard labor that went into crocheting each one of them, my wife and I hoped she would offer us a few to save and someday give to our children. Instead, none were offered and we knew better than to ask for anything or risk being labeled as modern-day carpetbaggers. By this point Grandma believed that the world valued her possessions, doilies, buttons, pots and pans and that they would bring in a hefty price at the auction. We would later find out that the entire box of at least 100 hand-knitted doilies sold for $5.75 and her sewing kit with hundreds of buttons, crocheting needles and other things for only $3.00. My wife and I later thought that we should have sent someone in our place to bid on a few of the items we cherished but it never crossed our minds. Disappointed, we moved on knowing that we were not only missing out on memories in the form of possessions but more importantly witnessing the breakdown of the personality of someone we loved.

The difference between the Grandma we knew and the one before us was staggering. Even the quiet that had now replaced the regular sound of activity in the house was so very foreign. Boarders long since gone were always controversial to family members but we could now feel their absence. My wife and I missed the chatter associated with their random coming and going and knew the person who missed them the most was my grandmother. Renting rooms was Marietta's lifeblood and while he never admitted it openly they were simultaneously enjoyed by Giuseppe too. Renting rooms gave them both something important, at least to them, to do. Renting, while difficult, gave them a purpose and certainly a secondary social life. It kept their minds sharp while never having to face boredom. Others did not seem to understand why my grandparents continued to rent rooms late in their life but my wife and I did.

"Muttietta, why you renta dah room," I would hear her friends ask. "Troppa lavoro, too mucha work, troppo lavoro," people would chant.

I can still see my grandmother's face after hearing the question for the hundredth time. Depending on who was providing her with the unappreciated advice she would do one of two things. Maryetti would usually give her famous shrug, tilting her head to one side while squeezing her toothless lips together. Silently she was communicating, "Tough shit I am doing it anyhow." If it was someone in the family reminding her that she should stop renting, Granny might blow her stack and move into full defensive mode. This latter response was usually reserved for Dad and Hanna. Talking loudly, incorporating multiple hand gestures, with no one really listening was considered a hallmark of many Italian-American households, including ours. My family represented the poster child for such behavior and to the newcomer this everyday behavior was at first difficult to comprehend. Were people angry, was a fist fight about to brew? Newcomers sometimes could not determine if the yelling was serious or not. When we first began dating, my wife, for example, needed to excuse herself from the dinner table retreating to the bedroom to lay down because the heated discussions upset her stomach so much.

"Whatsamatter with-a Debbie, where she'sa go," Grandma would ask.

"She'll be right back," I would reply.

"Maybe she'sa no like a my pasta, maybe no eat'ta nuf. She'sa so small, skinny, she-sa eat you know, como una gallina, justa-lik-a dah chicken, all-a skin and a bones. Jovy, go. Ask her if'fe shes-a wants una pesito, a small piece ah dah cake, go on ask'a hu."

I usually checked pretending to ask my wife if she wanted cake but instead simply asking her if she was okay. After her very first retreat to the bedroom I fully knew the issue. You see she grew up in a quiet, subdued household where Japanese culture was likely on the opposite end of the decibel continuum from Italian culture. People ate just enough in her family, never gorging themselves and never forcing food on anyone else. The conversation around the dinner table in her household was polite, tempered, and never boisterous. People listened to one another too which was certainly a departure from what I grew up facing. When I returned from the bedroom I reported to everyone that everything was fine, a little tired is all, and that she had enough to eat. I told them she required time to digest her food or some other excuse.

I did not dare relay that her stomach was upset because of the noise and chaos that was a regular part of life around our dinner table. Peaceful arguments were part of every meal and could occur over most any subject. It took some getting used to before a newcomer felt comfortable during one of our meals. For example, simply hanging a shower curtain could develop into an explosive discussion and create an argument that would last for two or three dinners, perhaps even for years.

Dad: "Ma, why did you hang that brown shower curtain?"

Grandma: "Whatsa matta with-a that-a one?"

Hanna: "Ma vee told you. I vould buy one with brighta colors, maybe flowers. It vould make the room feel light."

Grandma: "I'ma like-a that brown-a one. 'Mi piace quello marrone,' I like-a the brown-a one, it-sa no getta dirty," she would respond.

Hanna: "Flowers von't get dirty, they look brighter."

Decibels now increasing.

Grandma: "I know how to decorate-a too. Itsa look good. Yoo no think-a da room she'sa bright now?"

Dad: "We'll go buy a new one."

Grandma: "Im-a no wanna new one. You make-a mia crazy, pazzo, Luigi. Marrone, mi piace marrone." It would get even louder.

Hanna: "Vhy you gettin mad for? Vee'll get a flower one, it's brighta, you'll see."

Grandma: "Ah, Maddone (the Virgin Mary, Madonna) I'm-a gonna die, a heart attack, Louie. I'm-a no want a fancy one. I lik-e the browna one. No buy me one with-a the flowers, I'm-a like the brown-a one. Mi fai male al cuore (my heart hurts)."

The argument surrounding this topic would go on throughout the remainder of dinner with tempers flaring and voices raised. The dinner table was not for the faint-hearted in our house. Newcomers needed to develop a tough skin developed only after attending a few dinner table conversations like this one. Guests needed to experience more than one heated conversation before they fully realized that no one was going to be stabbed or disfigured. The shower curtain disagreement would be revisited for at least three future dinners with my grandmother winning a battle and Dad and Hanna teaming up to win a few battles of their own. My wife and I would hear about, The Great Shower Curtain Fiasco, along with many others, for years to come.

Grandma: "Jovy, there was-a nothing, niente, wrong with-a the browna curtain-a, no?

Me: "Sure Grandma, the brown one was good."

Grandma: "Whatsa Hanna do inna my buseeness. Shes-a maka me pazzo, crazy. Yu fatha too, pazzo." Etc., etc., etc.

My grandmother was also an expert at swooping in, just over the left shoulder of distracted diners and refilling their otherwise partially completed plate with more food. She purposely hurried through her meal and then sat focused with an eagle eye toward everyone's dish, except Grandpa's, waiting for an opportunity to fill an emptying plate. Marietta might even create a distraction and when a guest was not looking she would expertly flick more food onto their dish. The newcomers who had already forced themselves to finish their first overly loaded helping of lasagna, for instance, would now wonder how to remain polite and somehow finish the surprise portion. Usually, there was a lot of joking over the surprise assault but the poor guests was still left with the dilemma of what to do about the extra food surprisingly plopped in front of them. Rookies did not know how to politely appeal, "Sorry Mrs., I can't eat anymore, I am so full." Experienced patrons smiled and took a few more bites before saying something like, " I need a doggy bag for the rest." I stood guard over many a dish for friends and others whom I pitied and saved them from the onslaught of my grandmother's expert dish-filling pitches. At times, and under extreme conditions, I even had to raise my voice yelling,

"GRANDMA, SIT DOWN, NO MORE, ENOUGH, 'BASTA,' THEY DON'T WANT ANYMORE!"

Granny would then slink back to her chair in temporary defeat, assume her moping posture complete with shoulders pulled inward and lips pinched and puckered out. Muttietta was never fully defeated because when no one was looking she would self-release herself from exile and renew her attack. At first I had to protect my soon-to-be wife from Grandma's airborne attacks toward her plate. Eventually, she learned to fend for herself but in the meantime, she needed my protection against Muttieta's food assaults. My soon-to-be wife would eventually harden to the animated table wars learning how to assert herself when necessary, have her opinions be heard, and protect herself from the stress that the animated discussions had on her digestive system. It would not take her long to build the necessary resilience required in becoming an honorary, "Italian."

In addition to the dish-filling behaviors and heated discussions around the table, other things sometimes drove people crazy. My grandmother was entertaining but I also understood how her generosity could sometimes be annoying to family and guests. For example, we would all be ready to sit down to enjoy a quiet supper when suddenly a renter would walk through the kitchen, and immediately Granny invited the guy to sit and eat with us. Before the first meatball could be popped into a dish my grandmother would say something like,

Grandma: "Meestair Bruce (for instance) you lika lilla to eat, sit down, sit down right-ova here, ecco, Meestair, hurry uppa you," she would say.

Renter: "No, Mrs., I already ate," he might respond.

Before the guy could make it to his room, Grandma would grab him by the arm and say,

"You too skinny, man posto eat-a, fa forte, make strong, mangia, sit down right ova here, ecco. Jovy move, get una sedia, getta a chair, 'dare il posto,' por Meestair Bruce seeta down, sieditti."

The family was ready to dig in when out of nowhere the meal was halted almost in mid-bite and the musical chairs, designed to accommodate the boarder, would begin. Everyone would have to almost force a smile and move aside to make room for the new guest. I did take some sick pleasure watching the steam begin to pour out of people like my dad, uncle, or Hanna. I enjoyed scanning the table knowing the fireworks that the invitation would cause when the renter retreated to his room. A mainstay was my grandfather being bent over eating. Pepine never moved he just ate. He never really was engaged in most of the drama associated with my grandmother's incessant feeding frenzy anyway. Grandpa Giuseppe would just continue to slurp up his food as he was used to doing for years and simply ignored the musical chairs and the ensuing arguments. Dad did not say very much either, at least at first. This would change in time as he needed to support Hanna who never gave up trying to change her mother-in-law. Since Hanna and I did not get along I took masochistic pleasure in seeing her face redden and could envision the top of her head blowing off to release the steam. Sometimes, however, I was disappointed because Hanna accepted the guest depending on who the boarder was. In this case, Mr. Bruce, a rather sophisticated guy possessing a college degree and being of Germanic heritage, was readily accepted. Therefore, he was considered high status and was in the "automatically acceptable" category in terms of surprise dinner guests.

There were plenty of roomers who fell outside the acceptable category too. Some of them were downright jerks who we were all forced to sit with over countless dinners in my grandmother's kitchen. Even I had to agree with some of Dad and Hanna's assessments regarding a few of the characters Grandma invited to eat with us. For instance, there was a guy who owned a souped-up Pontiac GTO, the muscle car of the 60s era, who never seemed to have any money for rent but was always ready to be fed. Once he asked me for money to pay his rent and I, out of weakness and stupidity, gave it to him. I was partially repaid with a collapsible cue stick complete with its own carrying case which I never used. He also allowed me to borrow his GTO for a whole day. My friend Johnny Boy and I drove the car all over town one afternoon trying earnestly to find some girls to impress. We unfortunately only succeeded in acquiring a speeding ticket from a park ranger at a nearby park called Mill Hollow. Turns out that neither the cops or any girls were impressed with the car or our driving style.

There was another fellow named Bobby who drove a new Cadillac and made a lot of money working at the nearby Ford Assembly Plant. He was best known as a little twit who took great pleasure in pretending he knew everything. He had no friends that we knew of nor any acceptable hobbies and thus had way too much time on his hands. So Bobby-boy spent most of his time waxing the Caddy in the driveway. Unfortunately he was short, unattractive and also quite cheap. Worse of all he had no personality and this may have contributed to his habit of traveling to Gentleman's Clubs in Cleveland for lap dances and who knows what else. . Of course, he seldom offered my grandmother any extra rent money for his food and this only strengthened the family's dislike for cheapskate Bobby. It was because of these behaviors that my grandfather secretly renamed Bobby, "Meester-a Stronzo," or translated, Mr. Asshole.

The dinner table was the center of the universe in our home and it historically entertained all types of people, friends and relatives, over the years. Some of the boarders who joined us for dinner were great personalities and others not so much. Over time, the roomers sitting with us during meals became commonplace. Grandma could not feel comfortable if someone passing through her kitchen was not fed. If they refused to sit and eat then she would fix a dish and take it to their room. In addition to the boarders, many others regularly joined us for food and socializing. One of those people was an elderly woman we all referred to as Aunt Celina. She would be dropped off at noon on most Sundays and remained in my grandparents' home the entire day. Aunt Celina Lakoshma was Polish-American and thus not really a relative. She was usually smiling in spite of her extremely bowled legs, rheumatism, and wobbly gait supported by using a wooden cane. In addition, Aunt Celina had no bottom teeth but had a big jaw making her appear very much like Popeye the Sailor Man. At first greeting, Celina seemed quite affable but after the first meeting with her one was not fooled again by her smile. She seemed quite caring but never stopped talking and worst of all, complained about everything. A smiling complainer was what she was. Aunt Celina was probably the most negative person one would ever meet and because of her attitude she said some of the weirdest things imaginable. Once, when we were watching Mutual of Omaha's *Wild Kingdom*, starring a guy named, Marlin Perkins, she came out against saving the Bengal Tiger. Aunt Celina's view was simple, "Why spend time and money saving a tiger? What are they really good for anyhow?" she blurted out for no reason. My wife and I could only look at each other with astonishment. How do you respond to kooky stuff like that? I remember just walking away but I never forgot the story.

Hanna used to get upset that old Aunt Celina spent each Sunday with our family over but became unnerved when she visited at the same time as Joe and Feliciana. This was a real circus with Aunt Celina in one corner complaining about everything from her aching bones to the cost of cottage cheese as Feliciana became increasingly drunk imbibing on bottles of Stroh's beer my grandmother kept offering to her. Celina would complain and Feliciana would simply nod her head understanding very little English and caring even less about whatever Aunt Celina was gabbing about. Aunt Celina kept on talking and it never seemed to phase her that no one seemed to listen. She simply jabbered away. The room could have been focused on the snaring of a black rhinoceros as a Kenyan driving a Range Rover got closer and closer but Aunt Celina would simply keep talking about her back pain. In no time she would switch to her dislike, say, for women's latest fashions,

"I can't understand why any woman would want to show off her behind wearing those mini dresses," she once added.

Someone might make a head shake in what seemed like an agreement with Celina but it was more likely just an act of being polite or shooing a nat away from their face. This would only encourage Aunt Celina to continue. Later, after all the guests had finally gone home, the family would reminisce about Feliciana getting drunk on the Stroh's and their annoyance with Aunt Celina's continual diatribe throughout the episode of *Wild Kingdom,* which by the way, continued into *The Ed Sullivan Show.* I knew from observing the situation numerous times that no matter what was said, processed, or concluded during these after-party bitch sessions that the entire scene would replay itself the very next Sunday. It was certainly comical and entertaining much of the time from my vantage point laying on the floor taking it all in.

Hanna: "Ma, vhy you keep givin Feliciana Strohs?"

Grandma: "Im-a no give-a hur too much-a da birra. She's expected the beer. Whas-a matta, she's a like to drink la birra."

Hanna: "Yes you did. If you don't vant her drunk don't give her no more beer."

Grandma: "Whadyou wanne me to-a do, say, no, be a bad persona in-a my own house. Shes-a wan-a drink, Im-a giva to hu."

Hanna: "And vhy do you inwite Aunt Celina here every Sunday? Can't vee have dinner with only our family, just one time."

Grandma: "Im-a no invite-a hu. She's-a come- all-a by herself-e, no invite. Dia, troppo domande (God, too many questions)."

This back and forth would pretty much sum up the recurring weekend conversation. But Grandma defied her critiques week after week doing just as she pleased in spite of the objections. Through living in my grandparents' home I developed the skills of a circus ringmaster similar to the role of Don Ameche, a TV host of a popular TV program in the 60s titled *The Big Top*. I enjoyed daydreaming seeing myself as Ameche and suddenly appearing in our living room during one of the dramatic interchanges between Hanna and Grandma. I would burst in wearing Ameche's traditional ringmaster's black cape and top hat, shove Dad aside and begin announcing the death-defying act of Hostile Hanna vs Mighty Muttietta locked in the Big Cat cage with Hanna throwing Stroh's bottles at Grandma and Granny throwing one of Aunt Celina's inedible and usually overcooked fruitcakes at Hanna. Winner would take all. The competition for who was the ultimate boss or "capo" of the "familia" would go on for years with neither of the matriarchs really claiming the title, until that is, many years later.

By now it is obvious that there was usually someone visiting or something interesting going on in my grandparents' home as life came to us, it seemed, rather than the other way around. Our home was transformed daily into a modern-day frontier way station and instead of welcoming people like George Washington or Nathaniel Hawthorne, we welcomed characters such as Tony, Feliciana, Aunt Celina, Biagina, Jackie, Signore Zucchero, Mr. Bruce, and scores of other colorful individuals all of whom enjoyed the food and expression of strong opinions about subjects they knew nothing about but were nonetheless assured that their viewpoint was correct. Headaches, "mal di testa," were never a factor, unless you were new to the scene like my wife was at first but even she learned to survive in the maelstrom of activity that was my grandparents' home.

While Grandma's generosity was occasionally a source of irritation for some family members, I really enjoyed her near addiction to giving people food and so did most others. I have to say I cherished the arguments that would invariably ensue over her obsession with feeding the masses. I also have to admit that I cared about all the characters who frequented our home, even Aunt Celina. Life, especially for me, would have been so regular, downright boring without the chaos that was enmeshed in our meals and social life. Grandma's preoccupation with food distribution made her the most eccentric character of them all. It defined her and it was her purpose. If there was one behavior that described Marietta it was her consistent need to feed the world. If there was one behavior that described her husband, Giuseppe, it would be his tolerance for whatever my grandmother wanted. One never knew who would be joining us around the kitchen table and that was one of the ways that living with them was so intoxicating.

Fighting Coach J

Boisterous Sunday meals continued at my grandparents' table no matter where we lived. The other constant, at least for me was football. The snapshot of the junior high football team, the one that Rafael superimposed on the newly created Gents T-shirt at our little birthday reunion served as proof that we were not imagining our lives as early football geeks. Included in the team picture that Rafael printed on the t-shirt was a locally acclaimed coach, Coach J, who was both respected and feared by his players. His teams won numerous championships during the years he coached the junior high team during the 1950s and 60s. His winning ways were the result of his toughness and coaching acumen. Coach J was stern and gruff if he was anything and his never-take-any-prisoners reputation both on the field and in the classroom was widely known. Most practical students would toe the line whenever they had any dealings with him whether it was in class, study hall, or on the playing field. On the football field, Coach J incorporated high standards and any player who did not contribute 100% was first physically knocked around and if he still did not shape up then he was knocked off the team. While many students feared Coach J, other guys, those who followed his rules, idolized him and became good football players.

Seeing the team emblazoned on the T-shirt was fun but it was immediately noticed that some of the more colorful guys were missing from the picture. Absent from the T-shirt picture, for instance, was Donald, a guy who punched me in the mouth our first-time meeting at Harrison Elementary School. Donald entered our school after the year had already begun. On his first day in third grade at Harrison, I noticed Donald breaking one of the school's steadfast rules, that is, not standing silently in a straight line before the entrance bell rang. Instead, Donald was running all around the lawn committing every infraction from throwing stones up in the air to turning cartwheels on the lawn. All I remember doing that morning was gazing at Donald with astonishment and the next thing I saw was his fist heading straight for my face. I was glad when Donald entered our class and we all became close friends.

Years later, Donald was technically a member of the Gents too but none of us recall him ever attending a meeting. He was our member in absentia. Simply listing the guy as a member of the club had its benefits. That is, including Donald in our membership was enough to keep most reasonable guys at bay because Donald's short fuse and propensity for using his fists was well known. In other words, Donald's reputation was usually considered a deterrent against many would be antagonists.

Now gazing at Coach J on the back of Rafael's T-shirt caused me to immediately focus on a wild intersection of those two short fuses, that is, old Coach J's and wild man Donald's. We could not have predicted it when we were back in junior high but Donald, not particularly known for his leadership skills, would angrily lead us, in just a couple of years, into a serious confrontation with Coach J. That confrontation strangely enough would occur right in the coach's very own team locker room.

As we left junior high school Coach J simultaneously ceased coaching the junior high squad and become the head coach of the cross-town high school football team. In tenth grade, our high school junior varsity football team played Coach J's junior varsity team in a hard-fought game and we lost by just a few points. Cross-town rivalries had a long history resulting in an overflow of emotions before, during and after most contests. Donald would capitalize on our elevated levels of testosterone and lead an almost spontaneous uprising due to believing, as did the rest of us, that we were cheated out of the win and that the loss was due to racism. Never has a contest developed into such a chaotic mess as this one and it remains hard for me to believe that it did occur.

As background, our team was composed of a much higher percentage of minority members than the cross-town team. Donald was Black, as were many other teammates and a number of our players were Latino. Most, if not all of the cross-town team members were White and hailed from sociologically higher strata than our players. This combination of differences paired with intense emotions would set off a firestorm of stupidity difficult to emulate today. Had this whacko situation occurred in any community nowadays it would immediately become local front-page news if not develop into something viral.

During the game there were a number of penalties that seemed unfair to us. We went into the game with a preexisting chip on our shoulders believing that the majority of our community favored the other school due to demographics and racial composition. Many of our players complained about racial slurs directed toward them during the game and that those inappropriate comments were ignored by the referees. We lost the game that day, I am sure, due to a number of factors but by only a few points. At the time our sentiment was that we lost due to cheating, favoritism, and racism rather than skill and that made us all irate and crazed.

Donald, usually quiet, was noticeably very angry after the contest. Actually, Donald was somewhat agitated as he took the loss in an uncharacteristic manner even for him and we found out for the first time how sensitive he was about racial injustice. Donald took hold of the situation and morphed it into a leadership role we had never seen before. Donald then capitalized on our sentiment by making it plain that he was not going to allow a group of White guys not only to abscond with the win but also insult us with racial remarks. We all symbolically yelled in so many ways, "Yes, sir," to Donald's conclusions and demands! "You're right! We are not going to take it." So after we showered, perhaps unconsciously realizing the need to smell fresh as we engaged in civil disobedience, approximately fifteen of us walked a few blocks down the street and marched directly into Coach J's locker room proceeding to verbally accost some of his players.

It did not take very long at all before the sheer lunacy of the situation was realized. We found out quickly that our fifteen guys could not match up against their entire football team, which by now included their varsity teammates totaling more than fifty players plus coaches. The amount of disturbance we created immediately alerted Coach J who angrily exited his office and confronted the group of us. We were quickly commanded by him, as would be imagined, to leave the locker room immediately or pay the consequences.

At this point, the rational ones among us began to think that leaving would be a smart idea. All of us decided to leave quickly but not Donald. Donald, we should have remembered, possessed many attributes but none of them, especially when he was mad, included being rational. Nor did he suffer from an overabundance of patience. Instead, Donald yelled something back at the coach daring him to make us leave. Coach J, we figured, never took much disrespect from anyone, especially from a football player, and made an incorrect yet expected decision to begin physically pushing Donald out of the building. This decision likely contributed to the coach experiencing his very first slug in the mouth from maybe anyone but certainly his first from a school-aged football player. This punch was considered by most of us in future days as "The Roundhouse Heard Throughout The Stadium." The first punch was Donald's best and as the fight filtered out to the street, beyond the locker room, Donald began getting the best of the coach. Punches from Donald's fists were quick and accurate while the coaches were lumbered and seemed as though they were delivered in slow motion. Donald was able to throw three punches by the time the coach was able to unload his first.

Fortunately, the fight was eventually interrupted by Coach J's assistants who likely were as astonished as the rest of us. The fight would have ended sooner if everyone, including Coach J's assistants, were not so stunned by the complete folly of the situation. Luckily for the coach, Donald was wiry and his arms as skinny as beanpoles, so his punches, while they connected, did not do much physical damage.

By this point, the rest of us had cooled down and were looking for a quick exit route. Our crusade into the opposing team's locker room was looking more like a suicide mission than anything else and the severity of the event was becoming apparent. We began wondering, especially after Donald decided to box the coach on the sidewalk in front of the stadium, what the consequences would be for our little foray into the world of lunacy. Unexpectedly, our team was not severely penalized as a result of this fracas. In those days events were not sensationalized or politicized as frequently as they are today. In this case, a group of guys simply lost their temper and chose to lick their wounds by doing something nutty like storming a team in their very own locker room. Crazy notion, yes, but admittedly a strangely creative one. Our coaches certainly were informed about the crime and they gave us all a stern warning. Amazingly there were no major suspensions of any sort. A couple of players reported back that they had inadvertently overheard our coaches enjoying a hearty laugh over Coach J's obvious butt whooping but they had to outwardly project a more adult-like response in front of our team members.

If this situation occurred today we would all be either thrown off the team, minimally suspended for a few games, or perhaps suspended from school. Coach J's coaching career would most likely be finished and the local media would have a field day covering the whole event. In the mid 60's no one got excessively excited over the situation or at least the episode was able to be sufficiently hidden from the public. More than likely Coach J wanted to keep a lid on the fight since he kind of experienced a whooping by a 15-year-old not to mention first grabbing Donald from the start. Draw your conclusions regarding which method is best for dealing with this dopey event and thank heavens cell phones and social media had not yet been invented.

While there were no major consequences paid for our actions, we did learn a few lessons. We learned that storming the opposing team's locker room was a recipe for disaster, that Coach J was not as tough as he projected, and Donald was a looser cannon than any of us ever reckoned. We also had no way of knowing it at the time but the fight Donald had with the coach served as perfect foreshadowing for his future. Donald's temper would sooner than imagined get the better of him. Fist fighting was what would eventually and unfortunately kill him. That is, Donald was unanimously chosen three years later, while a senior, as a first-team conference linebacker. Donald's football skills were also good enough for Ohio University to attempt to recruit him. Sadly, his grades were considered too low and since he did not have the money or desire to first attend a junior college, he decided against a university education altogether. Instead, Donald enlisted in the Army and went off to fight in Vietnam. Upon returning home safely, he promptly got into his last fistfight at a late-night party in town. After once again getting the best of his opponent and believing the fight had ended the guy returned from his car with a gun and shot Donald dead. This fellow, unlike Coach J, sought out his amends and scored.

Donald's scenario, his death, is now played out way too often in some form or another every day with similar themes across the country and that is certainly unfortunate. Too many loose cannons are out there letting anger and emotions rule. I must admit that in many ways our kookie escapade was somewhat laughable as well as crazy. I have never heard a similar story about a guy leading his football squad to a revengeful fight in the opposing team's locker room. This event was just another first-of-its-kind tale that causes me to shutter today as an adult. I sometimes question myself over this and other similarly imbecilic things that we did. Foolish behaviors that marked our early lives. I ask myself, "Did we do that?" It is fortunate that boys eventually do mature and acquire some sense before it is too late. Maturity and sensibility were not reached soon enough for some including Donald. It is situations like this one, from our past, that leads me to conclude that Forrest Gump had nothing on many of the adventures experienced by my friends and me.

We were involved with many unusual situations growing up that were certainly memorable. We, in some ways, "grow'd like Topsy," that is, without direction much like the slave girl in Harriet Beecher Stowe's 1852 novel, *Uncle Tom's Cabin.* We were not beaten like Topsy but we disregarded rules and had too much freedom some would say. Most of us had parents who cared and we all had safe places to go to after performing some very secretive and stupid stunts. Maybe that is why none of us got into any serious trouble.

We lived by kids' rules when we were out together but did not want to hurt and embarrass those who cared for us at home. Alternatively, one of the rules we followed as friends was never expecting much sympathy from our buddies when we did get caught committing some knuckle-headed act. An example of this contrary behavior is summed up by an occasion when a group of us, "Real paisanos," got into a little more substantial trouble than normal. As I previously mentioned, the event I am referring to was the only time that a group of us got hauled in by the police.

Five of us were out looking for something to eat after attending a movie one Sunday afternoon when I was maybe 15 years old. We were still in the Gents but were not wearing our jackets at the time. The trouble we caused had nothing to do with the club as we innocently immersed ourselves into trouble this time all by ourselves. Besides me, Guido, Anton, and two older fellas who had recently moved from Italy to Canada before settling in the United States were involved. Their family was following their father from city to city due to his employment in some type of construction business. These new guys, James and Arno, were two and three years older than Mac and me respectively. Why they hung around with us was anybody's guess but they were a riot to be around and we all had tons of fun together.

On this occasion, I think it was Anton who asked me to accompany the group to the movies. His plan for us was to go see a show and then instead of walking directly home, we would head off in the opposite direction toward a McDonald's located on the lake. That is exactly what we did when the movie ended. After buying our burgers and fries I suggested that we continue walking to a nearby spot and eat rather than hang around the McDonald's parking lot. Because I used to live in the area, this being the same McDonald's where I had punched the guy, Wiley, in the mouth a few years earlier, I knew the environment quite well. I easily persuaded the group to follow me, the self-proclaimed "know it all." So I led the way behind the burger joint heading down the shoreline. I planned to walk around a restaurant, cut behind some boat houses, and then walk down the coast through a few backyards. This was pretty much the same route that Skeeter, Paulie, Freddy, and I took many times before. I remembered a nice dock where I figured we could sit in the sun and enjoy our food without being hassled.

As we began tromping along my suggested route and while marching through some backyards, a guy, an adult, suddenly began running toward us like a maniac, yelling for us to get the hell off his property. This never happened to me before when I lived just down the lake. I felt indignant as though I sort of owned the land myself long before this loudmouth moved in. Skeeter, Paulie, Freddy, and I were never pestered before when we hung around the area so why now? After all, this was the same yard where a few years earlier my ne'er-do-well friends and I along with about 20 high school guys and girls watched as a big guy called, Country Boy, got beaten up in a fight by a much smaller fellow than himself. It turned out that to even up the odds the scrawny smaller fighter snuck a pair of brass knuckles on his right hand and only needed one good whack to neutralize his oversized opponent. As only a few years had passed since I traversed the area, I figured that things probably had not changed that much. Therefore, I got incensed as the guy ran at us yelling crazily for us to vacate his land. We nonetheless tore out of the guy's backyard quickly not wanting to tangle with the lunatic. In no time we found a spot to eat our lunch a little further down the beach. I was embarrassed and upset with the guy's attitude toward us and certainly knew the fellas, my paisanos, would let me have it. I was not "the big wheel chief of all things" who was going to introduce them to my old stomping ground on the Lake Erie shore.

"Hey Joe," Arno yelled, "want to tell us a little more about how you know this place like the back of your hand, or is it more like the back of my ass?" They all had a good time ribbing me.

After skipping a few flat rocks in the lake followed by walking along a nearby pier, we bypassed the maniac's backyard and started walking home, back down Erie Avenue toward Lake Park. To get to the park we had to file directly in front of the maniac's house. As we walked by, we noticed the bean brain outside of his house waxing his car. When we saw him it was almost automatically decided that we should all razz him in revenge for chasing us off his property. We felt safe since we were all on public land, the sidewalk in front of his house. So we simultaneously began yelling at the moron saying things like, "Hey, din-a-ling get off of my property," and "You are an ……," insert your preferred profanities. We all had our fingers and knew how to use the middle one to make a point while directing them liberally in the direction of the short-tempered blowhard. Given his obvious short fuse, we knew our antics would get the desired effect. The guy again went ballistic and appeared crazed. If it had been a cartoon, such as *Popeye*, smoke would have shot straight out of his pipe and the pipe would have begun spinning around in circles like a propeller. Seeing his anger explode we took off as quickly as we could while figuring that we had seen the last of the jerk.

Arriving at Lake Park that sunny afternoon shortly after razing the car waxing property-owning bonehead, we sat down on a bench to rest and began watching a men's lawn bowling league. The old guys played on a smooth green lawn manicured beautifully by the city. Most of us just took the court and the old guys who played the game for granted. Now as I think back, having the beautiful playing field, the court, that was prominently displayed right on the lake for everyone passing through to see added a little class to the city. The green lawn with the smartly dressed players represented the city's own little Currier and Ives photo. It was something for all of us to be proud of too but we never gave that much thought as kids.

Anyhow, we were just sitting on some benches cooling off when I scanned left viewing the ever-present lighthouse, and then as I scanned right, toward another of the city's markers, an oversized Easter basket, I let out an audible, "Uh Ooh!" The angry fellow that we had just fingered was driving his partially waxed car toward us followed closely behind by a police cruiser. Since we had no place to run we just sat there looking straight ahead and hoping we would be overlooked. No luck, the unsettled car waxer immediately pointed us out and soon the officer asked us all to step over to the curb right next to his patrol car.

A cop standing with an adult, who was obviously a bonafide taxpayer, would signify to most wise kids that the officer was going to side with the grown-up no matter what had just transpired. It was also customary to most informed guys that we should expect and absorb a certain degree of attitude from the officer as he began to interrogate us and tend to show off for the taxpayer. As the officer settled down to business, the first words out of his mouth were sternly directed at Arno, the oldest of our group. The cop said, "So, what is your name wise guy?" That is when Arno mistakenly responded, "So, why do you want to know that for?" I still remember the simple phrase as if it were spoken yesterday. Police officers are by nature impatient with kids, as a sign of power, maybe, and knuckleheads like us, who deal with them more than once should know this. Therefore, most smart kids know they should just politely answer the questions without asking other questions. Arno, being from Italy by way of Canada, had not yet developed this knowledge so he answered the cop's question with a question which is something one should never do.

The officer sternly responded with, "Okay smart guys get in the car. We are going downtown." All I could think of was the popular TV program of the day called *Dragnet* where the star character, Detective Joe Friday, might confront the culprit with, "I've dealt with dozens of smart punks like you guys before and it always ends the same. See, you think you are so smart, smarter than the law but it never works out for punks like you. No sir, never in your favor. There is always someone smarter than you and the law ends up winning. Officer, take these smart-mouthed stooges downtown and book 'em." You could have heard a pin drop in that car as we drove toward the station. The ride downtown was only 10 or 12 blocks long but it seemed like miles. As I sat squashed in the back seat of the patrol car with my partners in crime, I remember thinking, "Boy am I going to get it this time." Fortunately, the whole affair did not amount to anything. The police had a lot more to do than mess with a group of trespassing smart-mouth teens. The maniac taxpayer was probably simply happy that we got hauled to the station to teach us a lesson. The only consequence of the whole affair was that each of our parents received a call from the police telling them to come to pick us up. I can still see my father entering the police station on that ill-fated sunny afternoon. As he came through the front door I heard him address the desk sergeant saying, "Hey Tommy, I hear you got my boy down here." Growing up and living your whole life in a smaller sized city had its benefits. People get to know one another over time. It turned out that the desk sergeant and my father graduated from high school together. Of all the dumb things we did, substantial things, being nabbed for trespassing and name-calling was almost ironic. It turned out that as a punishment we were required to stay clear of one another for a few weeks. We had to swear we would never trespass again and to stay away from the knucklehead with the temper. Our parents mostly threatened us predicting that we would all end up in prison if we kept misbehaving but nothing much other than that happened to us over this little screwball incident. We got off easy once again.

We newly minted trespassers reminisced over this experience for some. However, shortly after our little brush with the law, James and Arno's family moved again and this time to Toronto, Canada We heard that the brothers eventually became big-time building contractors just like their father. We promised ourselves to get together someday in Toronto so we can all laugh over again concerning our tiny brush with the law right on the shore of Lake Erie. Anton and I pledged that if stopped and questioned by the police while visiting Toronto, we would at least have the common sense to instantly provide our names when asked and be sure to never answer a police officer's question with a question. The likelihood of ever seeing James and Arno again is unlikely but the memory of that day is recalled at least by me every so often and it seems to always bring a smile to my face.

I was lucky as this was the only time I was busted by the cops. My friends and I did plenty of stupid things, many of which broke laws of various sorts, nothing too serious but we somehow always escaped. I knew the limits of my misbehavior and would only go so far before a buzzer went off in my pea brain and my conscience kicked in. A large part of that conscience had to do with my grandparents. I knew that if I went too far and got into real trouble I would break their hearts, especially my grandmother's. Although I was slow to admit it she cared for me when I needed it the most and was largely responsible for teaching me about citizenship while providing a positive model of everlasting values. Those values would direct me in a positive direction for the rest of my life. She and my grandfather were excellent role models and taught me respect even though it took a long time for me to appreciate it.

I do not believe that anyone ever told my grandmother about our little brush with the law. There was no need to upset either her or my grandfather. From then on I was not an angel but remained careful and mindful that my behavior would not only hurt me but also hurt others, especially those who devoted much time and effort to my development.

“Towels To Furniture

****

Back at the gym, I kept on rowing and thinking about old times. Here I was living in another new city, closer to my children, both grown, married, and beginning to raise families of their own. My wife and I, never envisioning that we would move so often were now hopefully living in our last new town. I once swore off moving particularly after changing locations so often as a kid but here we were living in our fourth city.

As I rowed on, my thoughts could not stop visiting the past as the two women continued to circle the exercise track. Besides, I still had a few more minutes promised to the rowing machine. I kept on thinking about my grandparents, my upbringing, and my hometown and how my grandparents represented goodness and sharing. Now, of course, I knew that could have given me less freedom and spoiling but things turned out for me in the long run. The good they modeled fortunately outweighed the bad. They spent their life working hard. My grandfather began as a coal miner and ended working as a scaffolder, a boilermaker, in one of many blast furnaces belonging to U.S. Steel. Similarly, my dad worked as a pipe fitter’s helper for the same company first working shifts before settling for a lower wage so he would only work during daylight hours. Both never missed a day of work and were grateful to be employed. Grandma, well I have explained what she did from morning until night, clean, cook, and be charitable. Neither of my grandparents or my father, however, ever wanted me to follow in their job-related footsteps. From my earliest days I never questioned what I would do after high school as my family's message to me, almost a dictate was that I was headed for college. My grandfather's words still ring in my ears.

"Jovy, you go to the college-a school someday. Si? You go, study hard. Use a yoo brains, be smart. Be the doctor or lawyer. No breaka tha back 'com'e' (like) me enna yoo fodder (father)."

There was never really a choice so I grew up always figuring that I would attend college after high school. That was the same message most of my friends received from their parents as well. In the meantime following the work ethic of our families and with a desire to make a little money of our own, my friends and I began holding down a series of petty jobs in the off-season while still attending high school. On a few occasions some of us even worked together. In fact the first two jobs were scouted out by Rudy who contacted me and together we convinced another friend, Rafael to join us. The two jobs turned out to be the most memorable places we ever worked.

A little background-Rudy, as it turned out, became a father at the age of 15. Certainly this was not planned but it happened and he needed cash to help support his new child who lived across town. I still remember his surprise phone call to me one afternoon. We were just 14 and in the ninth grade when Rudy called quite upset. Rudy came right out with it by saying his girlfriend, a good friend of ours, was pregnant and that he was the father.

Rudy needed money for obvious reasons and began locating possible jobs to help support what would be his new daughter. The available positions were not easy or always fun but Rudy was wise. He must have figured, why suffer at these jobs alone? While he needed money from a job he wisely figured, why work at a place and suffer all by himself. Nope, Rudy talked Rafael and I into joining him for our first mutual employment that turned out to be one of the hottest and dirtiest jobs I would ever have.

The first position entailed working after school at an industrial laundry where we unloaded and sorted all types of dirty linen. Each day, after schlepping there after school, our job included separating laundry and linens including dirty table cloths and napkins from restaurants. Other bags were filled with items such as, towels, diapers and soiled sheets from long-term adult care facilities. It was a grimy, smelly and sticky job separating and collating those sacks especially as the sultry humid summer approached. The plant was also sooty and hot lacking air conditioning and employing only a few overhead fans to keep the air circulating. The number of bags we opened each evening varied and seemed never ending and we could not go home until each bag was fully sorted. We were never certain about what we would find inside each sack. As we opened them we learned to be cautious as the tablecloths could be filled with anything from leftover spaghetti to chewed-up steak. Nursing homes seemed to relish sending us adult diapers complete with human waste wrapped inside. Along with the filth and garbage in the bags, each time we opened a sack we never knew what other extraneous items would be discovered inside. For instance, one time we opened a bag and out jumped a couple of rats and another time we found a set of forgotten dentures tucked inside the sack. We hated the job, not only because it was nasty but also because it paid so little. The job taught us how impossible it is to survive and get ahead making a minimum wage salary. In those days we were making $1.52 per hour. The money, after taxes, was hardly worth the time we put in, except of course, for the memories.

Despite its drawbacks, the three of us did have some really fun times while working at the towel supply. For instance, a recent conversation I had with Rafael reminded me that we worked alongside an older guy named Floyd while at the laundry. He must have been in his forties. Floyd, we figured was not very skilled and that sorting bags at the towel supply was the best job he could muster. We often joked around with Floyd and he continually warned us not to screw around too much or we could be fired. He was forever nervous about losing his job but that did not stop any of us from messing up as much as we could.

One evening, for instance, an opened linen bag revealed that the contents came from a Chinese restaurant since it smelled like soy sauce and contained many of those tiny parasols used in cocktails. We also found a large tea bag that must have been used to brew gallons of green tea. It measured maybe 10 by 15 inches long and looked like a mushy brown pillow. Soon one of the guys grabbed the bag and threw it to another as we found ourselves playing hot potato with the soggy industrial sized tea bag.

After throwing it around from person to person, Floyd began to warn us to stop or the boss, a stern old guy with a limp and a Slovenian accent, would yell at us all. As Floyd finished his warning, the bag was lobbed in his direction and just before the wet bag reached his open hands it hit a chain suspended from the ceiling. As the bag connected with the chain it immediately ruptured with the entire contents of sticky tea leaves splattering all over Floyd's face. When the bag burst the bunch of us also burst into laughter. Our laughter was soon curtailed because we heard the boss' shuffle punctuated with his continual singing of some Slovenian folk song. As he was about to enter our sorting area Floyd panicked, not knowing what to do since his face and body, from the waist up, was covered with wet tea leaves. Someone quickly threw him a soiled towel recently unloaded from one of the sacks, and Floyd used it to clean himself off seconds before " Oh-Ba-Ba-Deb," as we called the boss, rounded the corner. We called him Oh-Ba-Ba-Deb due to the repeated lyrics from the Slovenian folk song he sang not exactly under his breath which by the way usually smelled mainly of garlic and paprika.

The best story that came out of working at the *Towel Supply* company, however, had to do with Rafael driving us home one evening after work. Rafael was learning to stick shift a car belonging to Rudy's father. Rudy, without telling his father, was teaching us all, as we turned 16, to stick shift the auto. According to Rafael's recollection, it was a hot summer evening in June. While eating our dinner in Rudy's car, an olive green, 1959 Chevrolet Impala, Rafael talked Rudy into allowing him to practice his stick shifting by driving the four of us home after work. Besides Rudy, Rafael, and I, another guy, a rather crazy acquaintance with a Puerto Rican accent, also begged for a ride home. We were on our way to this guy's house to drop him off when a little accident occurred.

"There we were just minding our own business and tooling down the street," Rafael told the guys at a recent get together. Is this scenario starting to sound familiar?"

"Luckily we were driving slowly because I was having trouble coordinating the clutch peddle while shifting and changing the gears on the three speed on the column," Rafael went on. "Things were going real fine with the windows cranked down while we were all singing a Beach Boys tune, I think it was, *Help Me Rhonda*, when all at once, BAM! And I mean, BAM! Suddenly the car tipped to the left side and noisily thudded down to the pavement as we skidded fifteen feet to a dead stop," he went on.

Rafael then continued, "As we looked out the window on the driver's side we all saw the same thing. The left front wheel from Rudy's car went rolling down the street well ahead of us, all by itself, before settling 100 feet in front on someone's lawn. The wheel and tire almost knocked over some little girls playing hopscotch on the sidewalk."

I remembered the event clearly and recalled feeling as if I was in a Buster Keaton silent movie when it happened. Rudy and I almost simultaneously chimed in contributing how we all looked at each other as the tire rolled down the street, puzzled, as we sat there in the middle of the street in the lopsided Chevrolet. As we jumped out of the car to survey the damage, all we could see was the car's brake drum dug well into the pavement as we had skidded to a halt. There also, scattered around, were a few of the lug nuts that had come loose allowing the wheel to fly off the car. Being a warm, humid, Ohio evening, many neighbors were outside on their porches and our little mishap quickly drew a crowd. As people gathered around the car offering their opinions, Rudy searched for a familiar face in the crowd someone who would allow him to use their phone to call his father. Soon Rudy's dad and one of his older brothers arrived and they were happy that none of us were injured. They were just as amazed as we were, while scratching their heads over what had happened. Feeling that it was unlikely that the lug nuts all came loose at the same time we concluded that someone, perhaps seeking revenge against either Rudy or his father, decided that this would be a good way to get even. Since there was no investigation into the situation, we never found out any more about the incident. For quite some time after that Rudy and his dad were very careful while driving the car. They began checking the auto for any signs of tampering before cruising around town in the green Impala. The incident, a likely sabotage we concluded, represented another story that quickly entered our friendship's archival index.

We had numerous good times in that old 59 Chevy. I can still visualize that ugly green car rumbling down the road. Rudy frequently drove it slowly while leaning cool to one side in the front seat trying to make an otherwise unattractive vehicle appear slick. There was no reason, he concluded, for not acting cool even if the car was frumpy. Rudy seemed to drive that low luster olive green auto almost as if he was flamenco dancing with it. The car was truly unattractive but it always started and it took many of us countless miles around the city.

The towel supply was tough work. It was hot, dirty, and smelly. The hours and the pay was terrible too. The three of us headed over to that place after school for a few months and we never knew just when we would get home. The job served as a perfect example of the type of employment my grandfather warned me against. I knew from the very first hour of working at the towel supply that I would make sure I went to college. Fortunately, I had college as an option and so did Rudy and Rafael. I chose not to work very long at the *Towel Supply* but Rudy needed to hang on to the job at least until he found something better. So Rudy held on as bad as it was after first I and then Rafael quit. Soon, however, Rudy discovered a better place for the three of us to work.

While still asleep one Saturday morning, I heard a rap on my window. I continued to live with Dad, Hanna, and Jean at the time. The houses on the street were all the same style of ranch. They were typical 1950s suburban homes built on a concrete slab. These homes were created to prove that the American dream was alive and within reach of anyone willing to work hard and save a little money.

Theoretically, anyone was supposed to be able to afford one of these houses and we were the prototype for this assertion. My bedroom was on the ground floor at the corner of the house facing the street. I groggily awoke having heard, "Joe, you in there, wake up." I went to the window and was surprised to see Rudy's face smiling in at me. I asked him what he was doing awake so early on a Saturday. Rudy never awoke early when we were young so seeing him before noon scared me. The one thing I hated about hanging around with Rudy as kids was his sleep pattern. He would sleep well into the afternoon if his mother let him and I thus spent tons of time waiting for him to wake up and get ready to hang out. Now here he was waking me up early on a weekend morning for maybe the first time since we became friends in third grade.

Worried, I asked him what was wrong and he said, "Come on, want to make some money?" Having nothing better to do I responded, "Sure, doing what?" That Saturday became the first day of my employment at Mr. A's Furniture.

I quickly dressed and met Rudy out front. Once outside Rudy's first move was to point toward the street. He immediately motioned to what would become our furniture delivery vehicle, that is, a maroon, 1963 Ford Country Squire Station Wagon complete with faux woodgrain siding. Though the station wagon was only 5 years old, it had aged and looked fairly haggard due to the amount of cargo and furniture it had already delivered for Mr. A, the owner of the store. Besides, there was very little that could make a station wagon with faux wood siding look very cool.

Rudy and I had a big laugh over the vehicle we would soon be using to deliver couches, stoves, dining room tables, and even refrigerators to the store's customers. We were only 16 or 17 years old at the time so we enjoyed any form of transportation that placed us squarely in the driver's seat. We considered any driving, including delivery vehicles, as an adventure. Rudy indicated that the boss asked him to find another guy to help unload trucks, arrange furniture in the showroom, and deliver furniture sold to customers. I turned out to be the guy.

We quickly got in the wagon and "were off to see Mr. A, The wonderful 'Mr. A' in town." I did not know it yet but I would soon meet Mr. A. who in our city drew a likeness, a similarity to the character, the Wizard, in the movie, *The Wizard of Oz*. In our hometown Mr. A was a sort of business wizard, a legend, with a long and pleasant reputation. Rudy and I were thus, as the song goes, "Off to see the wizard."

When we arrived at the store and I saw the man standing before me I was immediately frozen in my tracks. I was thoroughly surprised by the fellow that would become my new boss since I recognized the aging man right away. Seeing him was such a surprise, how could it be? A coincidence, perhaps? I could barely believe that I would soon be working for this person who, without knowing it, was someone I had known many years earlier as a child.

Mr. A was not hard to forget. He was a slightly built man with a sunken chest. With his dark-framed glasses and bushy eyebrows and mustache, he looked an awful lot like Groucho Marx. Exactly, Mr. A was the same Mr. Aspin who previously owned *Young Times*, the exact store my mom, Lorena, and I visited 10 years earlier before my parents divorced. What were the chances? Here was the same guy who welcomed my mom, sister, and I into his store over a decade earlier. I almost had to rub my eyes as I thought that this could be a dream. It was certainly another interesting coincidence. Yes, my new boss would soon be Mr. Aspin. From the very first I knew our previous association would remain my little secret because I did not want to fill him in on the details of my parents' situation and likely he would not remember us anyway.

Now, with his old store closed for many years, I fondly recalled looking so forward to going into *Young Times* with my mom and sister especially if it included a cheeseburger at *Sutter's*. This new store, *Aspin's Furniture*, where I would soon become employed, was located less than a mile south of where *Young Times* used to be. Aspin's was newly situated in a less desirable section of the thoroughfare even by the main street's standards. Peddling cheap furniture to poor people, his latest venture, was now located closer in vicinity to his new clientele.

Aspin's Furniture was right on the corner of a questionable block being right next to a bar followed by a plumbing supply shop. There was also a thrift store close by followed by a vacant lot. The store backed on to an alley where we unloaded furniture deliveries from tractor trailers. In this section of downtown it was not unusual to regularly run into panhandlers and wino's hanging around outside the store. The decaying bar next door seemed to cater mainly to the downtrodden. The sidewalk in front of the furniture store, due to the indifferent attitude of the bar's patrons, therefore, usually needed a daily sweeping and hosing down before Mr. A. opened for business. This was due to the overnight appearance of broken beer bottles, puddles of urine and sometimes other bodily fluids smelling up the doorway.

Bizarrely, Rudy and I agreed that we rather enjoyed working in this type of environment partly because we ran into all types of colorful and unusual characters. Besides, we thought of ourselves as being unusual too, as well as, hopefully, interesting tough guys so there was never a worry about being in danger. Thinking so little of ourselves we rather relished, in a weird sort of way, lording over not only the area winos but also the numerous other far-out types who shopped at Aspins. We figured that while things were not great for us at home, our families did not have to buy furniture at Aspin's.

The one fellow that sticks out, as I think about the varied people who hung around the furniture store, was a wild looking man who never shaved or cut his bushy black and tangled hair. Considered by us as a local derelict, this guy, whom neighborhood people referred to as, Black Beard, possessed dark gritty skin among other unfavorable characteristics. We could not tell if his dark complexion was due to caked-on dirt or even coal dust since his big black beard covered the majority of his weathered face. His clothes stunk as expected smelling like a combination of perspiration, filth, and booze.

Black Beard usually wore all-black clothing, as well, thus the name. He wore the same clothes day after day, and we imagined from his appearance that he could have been a pirate of some kind in a former life. At first, he worried us since he appeared so wild and seemed to materialize from out of nowhere. He simply appeared from doorways that one minute seemed empty and the next, there he was. We got to know Black Beard since Mr. A. often hired him as a day laborer and he assisted us with unloading trucks when things got very busy. Through working with Black Beard, we found out a little about homeless people and specifically about him. There was a lot more to Black Beard than his scary appearance would first indicate. He was simply a harmless aging fellow with a drinking problem who pretty much wanted to be left alone. He was also homeless during a time when there was very little recognition of homelessness in our country. We found that he was not too different from any of us and with a little bad luck anyone could end up just like him. Black Beard made mistakes, plenty of them from the little he shared about himself. As a result, he had limited skills and spent more time drinking than finding ways to get himself out of his mess. Whenever I find myself feeling snobby or superior, I think back to unloading that furniture truck with old Black Beard. I often pay homage, fortunate really, to growing up lucky and not having to worry about my next meal. My home life built resilience through support and good role models and I was fortunate, maybe, to maneuver myself through the portals of life successfully not ending in a situation like Black Beard's, at least so far anyway. We began liking old Black Beard. Whenever we got the chance we brought him some leftover food and one time we gave him a sack of clean clothes including a black sweater for cold nights. Rudy and I enjoyed working with him and benefitted much more from our interaction with him than he likely did from us.

Mr. Aspin had few things to say as Rudy introduced us that first day. The only interchange between he and I was, "Okay as long as you're 16 and have working papers you are hired." That was fine with me because my social skills were not very slick and small talk with adults was nearly nonexistent. Rudy and I began working immediately. Our first assignment was to deliver a bedroom set to a family and we loaded up the Ford station wagon right away. Rudy and I placed a new box spring, still wrapped in its plastic on top of the car followed by the mattress and tied them both down with rope. Next, we laid the dresser on its side and pushed it in followed by sliding the boxed mirror in right next to it. The last piece to go on the wagon was the chest of drawers and we stood it straight up, back up against the car, on the tailgate as it was also tied down. Ford produced big station wagons in those days making it easy for us to fit tons of furniture inside. I doubt they intended for the wagon to serve as a furniture hauler but it did the trick. After loading the car, off we sped on our very first delivery.

As we drove down the road making furniture deliveries to various parts of the city, Rudy and I must have looked like a family of indigents moving into town. Even at our age, we thought it kind of a nutty way to do business, delivering furniture from a station wagon, but the customers usually did not care as long as they got their items delivered in one piece. Sometimes they appeared astonished when a couple of guys our age made the delivery but they never seemed to question the delivery vehicle. Perhaps Rudy and I, as young delivery guys, were more unique than our vehicle so the customer's focus was more on us than our means of transport. Most of our deliveries, it turned out, were in the southern part of town, the poorest section of the city. We guessed that since the customers did not have much money they were not exactly savvy consumers. Receiving their new furniture or appliances from the back of a station wagon was probably not out of the ordinary for them. We may have been wrong but we figured our delivery method correlated to the population we served and the quality of the junk Mr. A. sold.

Delivering from the Ford had other drawbacks too. More than once we were forced to pull the car over to the side of the road to either tighten the load or totally repack the cargo. Between the ruts in the road and our erratic driving style the packed furniture had a tendency to shift and occasionally require readjustments. Even with keeping track of readjustments, once a whole mattress and box spring set slid off the top of the car right into the center of the street while making a sharp turn during one of our early deliveries. Fortunately, no other vehicles were traveling through the intersection with us at the same time. Since the customer never realized their new bedding had just fallen into the middle of the avenue they readily accepted delivery without question.

Another thing we learned was that the older the refrigerator the more it weighed. There were times that we wondered if our strength would be enough to lug out a heavy refrigerator or freezer from an upstairs apartment. Rudy remembered a method that we employed more than once depending on it to get the job done. We used the method only in old apartment buildings with narrow messed up hallways and staircases. He reminded me that we would simply tilt the appliance on its side, usually a heavy refrigerator, get out of the way, and just let it go at the top of the stairs. Gravity slide it down to the bottom of the stairway like a sled thus saving our backs. This allowed us to conserve energy as well as bypass the potential need for a chiropractic treatment. Even though Rudy and I were fairly strong from playing football, maneuvering down narrow flights of stairs with an old stove or refrigerator was often a challenge. Therefore, occasionally the easiest way to get the appliance down to the first floor was to simply let it go.

Rudy and I also concluded early on that it was unfortunate that shoppers at the furniture store did not know that the furniture that they were buying was poorly constructed. Due to their lower income levels, they bought what they could afford and this usually meant the products had correspondingly lower quality. The items they purchased, we knew, were cheaply constructed and were not durable. In the long run, these poor souls would spend more on the furniture than wealthier people because the furniture and appliances would soon fall apart and they would be buying them all over again.

Occasionally, we removed old furniture after delivering it back to the store. The used furniture sometimes was resold making Mr. A. a little more money. He did this by selling the used stuff he received for free from customers and sold it again in his scratch and dent furniture department. One day we brought an old sleeper sofa back to the store. After looking at it Mr. A. said, "Put that divan in the alley, it's a piece of junk and beyond repair. Someone will take it overnight." We did as he ordered but later that day he asked us to cart it back inside since rain was forecasted and he figured no one would take a soaked couch. So we hauled it back in.

The next day, however, Mr. A. and a customer who appeared to be down on his luck came into the warehouse and Mr. A. sold him the very same divan he would have given away for free the day before. Strangely enough, he quoted the customer $50.00 for it and after bartering sold the divan for $35. We learned much about business while working in that furniture store.

Between deliveries, Rudy and I would take long trips around town simply joy riding and looking for people we knew. Deliveries took double the amount of time because of our little forays through the city. Rudy and I loved to take the longest and most round about ways back to the store. Luckily, Mr. A. never questioned our whereabouts or the amount of time we took for deliveries. As long as we completed our work he seemed fine with our performance. I have to say that while we often malingered, we also worked hard enough to get all of our assignments and deliveries finished and on time. No one ever complained about us or if they did Mr. A. never mentioned it.

After working at Aspin's for a month or so, Mr. A. asked Rudy and I if we could find a third guy to help out. The business was thriving and he was going to extend his hours. We decided to ask our buddy Rafael if he wanted a job and convinced him that working at Aspin's would be both easy and fun. Rafael was purposely not told very much about the job's responsibilities especially the part about delivering heavy refrigerators from the tailgate of a Ford Country Squire. We also neglected to explain that he would have to lug bulky objects, like sofa beds, up flights of stairs followed by removing the even heavier late model items back to the store. Rafael bit and soon the three of us would be furniture and appliance delivery "barons" working together again.

Rudy and I quickly introduced Rafael to the toils and benefits of our new role. I think the very first day we took Rafael on an easy delivery and made a side stop to my grandparents' house where Grandma cooked us up a few pork chops, fries, and salad. She sent us off with a sack of Italian cookies and we did her one of many favors by removing an old recliner and a coffee table that were gathering dust down her basement. Mr. A. did not notice our absence nor question the addition of the chair and table as we unloaded them upon our return. We placed both items in the used furniture showroom and most likely he sold them to someone at a reasonable price. Without knowing it we were becoming young entrepreneurs having set up a sort of win-win situation.

We three enjoyed the deliveries most of the time but really liked tooling around in that old Ford wagon. Cars and driving seem to be at the center of a guy's life during our teenage years. At least that was the case during the 1960s, and that is why automobiles bring back so many fond memories. I can associate several memories, complete with a time and date, to a particular automobile. For example, I associate the day Dr. Martin Luther King, Jr., died, on April 4, 1968, at 6:01 PM with my father's 1967 Buick Skylark.

The three of us were still working at Aspin's at the time. My plan was to leave work earlier than Rudy and Rafael and I was feeling superior because parked out on the curb was my father's black Buick Skylark. The car was waiting just for me to get in and drive it away. Earlier in the day, before work, I cleaned the car inside and out and even rubbed on a little polish to make the car literally glow. Just because it was a Buick did not mean it had to be totally dowdy.

I was departing from work early because I had a date planned with a girl named, Paula. Paula and I had been seeing one another off and on for some time and she, her friends and mine, enjoyed some really wonderful times together. I really liked Paula and we had lots of fun together so I did not want anything standing in the way of our date that evening. So right after work I remember getting into the car on what was a warmer spring evening and as I flipped on the radio to CKLW FM out of Detroit, the northern Ohio teen's favorite station in the 60's, I heard, instead of the familiar sound of Motown, a bulletin informing listeners that Dr. Martin Luther King, Jr., had been assassinated. I knew this would probably be a big news event but as a sixteen-year-old I had no idea just how big until later that evening.

Being an egocentric 16-year-old all I knew was I had a date and needed music to set the mood. I had to beg my father for the car, the only car in the family at the time, and I was not going to let another assassination stand in my way. The 60's involved one shocker after another and assassinations were becoming all too familiar. While Dr. King's assassination was breaking news, it did not totally dominate the evening's broadcast, as it likely would nowadays, so the familiar sound of Motown soon returned to the airwaves.

Before the music returned, however, I did hear a local report stating there was the potential for rioting in many cities, including my hometown, and officials were implementing a lockdown in certain areas of the town to prevent injury and destruction of property. I just wondered if the assassination was going to louse up my night given that I had worked so hard to obtain the use of the car. How out of it I must have been back then even as a sixteen-year-old thinking mainly of my date rather than giving the atrocity of Dr. King's assassination more thought.

Happily, my date with Paula went on as planned but on my way home I decided to proceed down the main street in town hoping to show off, to anyone driving along, that I had daddy's car. Traveling only a few blocks through the main drag I noticed that there were few cars on the road. This was unusual since on most nights there was almost bumper to bumper traffic up and down the avenue. Soon, in the rearview mirror I clearly noticed that I was being tailed by a local police cruiser. Next thing I knew was the officer suddenly flashing his lights indicating that I needed to pull the Skylark over to the side just as I was passing in front of the city's main post office, the same post office where my father caught the bus heading off for basic training and World War II decades earlier. I turned down a side street to get away from nosy passersby and the officer parked his patrol car next to mine making a motion for me to get into his car.

I noticed right away that the police officer acted strangely and appeared excessively agitated toward me. His behavior appeared animated beyond expectation for what I surmised was some puny traffic violation, whatever it was. Upon entering the patrol car the officer quickly began yelling at me at the top of his lungs for stupidly driving into a potentially dangerous city area. He said as a White kid I could be stoned or jumped because the "Negros" were rioting all over the place as a result of Dr. King's assassination. "What is the matter with you," he yelled? "Do you want to be part of a race riot?" His ranting continued for quite some time and I was having trouble holding back from laughing at his extreme show of drama. He finished by stating, "It is especially threatening in this town since Dr. King was shot at the Lorraine Motel. Don't you see what I mean?" I had no idea what he meant by that.

After he checked over my driver's license and finished his scolding, the officer made me promise to leave and drive directly home. I certainly complied and as I drove out of the post office parking lot I turned right instead of left, which would have been the quickest and most direct route home. Again I immediately saw the patrol car's lights flashing in my rearview mirror. This time he came to the window and yelled at me for not driving in the correct direction toward my home. I reminded him that if I had turned left I would be driving right into the "potentially rioting Negroes" and that is why he had initially pulled me over in the first place. He said, "Oh yea, forgot," and he directed me to drive on but indicated that he would be following me closely. He did follow me right to my front door making sure I drove into the driveway, parked in the garage, and went in through the side door. Only then did he pull away.

Maybe the officer was being diligent and kind but I thought the whole episode was quite strange because in our hometown there was only minor protesting and rioting that sad night. The officer, for whatever reason, seemed way too emotional over the situation. I simply tallied the event to my list of wacky childhood experiences. Now as an adult I realize that day in April 1968 was much more important than my need to continue on with my date. I am somewhat ashamed of my egocentrism and for not realizing the scope of what happened on that momentous and terrible day in our nation's history.

Do all teens think the way I did back then, being more concerned with personal needs than important national issues? Perhaps, some do. That was the way we were as teens, more concerned with our lives and how to have fun than we were with history. Hopefully, kids today, with greater access to information take global events more seriously than we did.

Our escapades at *Aspin's Furniture* store were numerous. Rafael was sure to lambast Rudy and me, kiddingly, in front of the guys at a future get together for talking him into the furniture store delivery business. I shot back that in those days "pretty" boys like him were not accustomed to breaking a sweat unless it was on the dance floor. I continued that he should thank me for helping him acquire his first and probably his last set of callouses.

There was some truth behind the comments I jokingly made to Rafael. Rafael was one of the handsomest guys in our high school. Most of the girls liked his looks and had it not been for latent and direct parental prejudice, Rafael was Mexican-American, he would have had all the girls swooning around him. Similarly, the girls felt the same about Rudy. Not only were they both good looking guys but they were amazing dancers during a time when new dances seemed to be created each week.

Dancing The Nights Away

Many of the guys I hung with through high school, including pals in the Gents, could dance quite well. At dances, and there seemed to be many of them during our teen years, it was customary to be dancing along with the music when suddenly a circle was formed around couples who were performing exceptionally well. This meant that a competition of sorts would soon begin with maybe another couple or often one guy (since it was always guys) after another jumping into the center to try to out dance the last one. Anything "cool" would be applauded. Guys would be seen doing the splits, and even flips were fashionable. Anything considered smooth or classy while keeping with the Motown beat was considered acceptable. When it came time to slow dance the best dancers would do the "Strand," with couples holding each other tight while trying to be as cool as possible.

During high school, it was easy to see that White guys could not dance as well as many of the Black and Latino guys and girls. After high school, 1992, someone produced a movie called, *White Men Can't Jump,* starring Woody Harrelson. In our hometown that phrase was at least partially true for White guys attempting to dance. Chase could hold his own while dancing but was nowhere near as good a dancer as Rafael, Rudy, and Davy. Certainly Luke, Mac, Corto, and I could dance a little but all our Latino and Black buddies stole all the girls' attention with their moves. Even though we were not as coordinated as the others we still took part in dance circles by jumping in the middle to show off. Instead of trying to be hip dancers, most of us White boys relied either on athleticism or comedy to get our share of respect and attention. Good or bad it did not matter, the bunch of us spent time on the dance floor screwing around and having a good time. I can still see Mac jumping into a dance circle and jerking around, head bobbing backward and forward making the audience laugh as he emulated a guy named Jeff Kutash from the *Upbeat Dancers,* a popular Cleveland dance troupe at the time. Mac would soon be pushed aside by a really smooth and serious dancer as the cycle continued. Mac's comedic dancing was usually a highlight of the evening adding to the fun that we all seemed to enjoy.

Though dancing was meant to be fun it could also spell trouble. For example, simply bumping into the wrong person on the dance floor could end in a fight. Another common way to get into a brawl was dancing with a girl that was considered off limits by another guy. Maybe they just broke up, maybe a Latino or Black guy was not supposed to dance with a "White chick," or some other complicated social algorithm. Simply dancing awkwardly was asking for trouble too as if dancing poorly signified some sort of a masculine challenge. If a person, especially a guy, could not dance well then it supposedly meant that he should know enough to stay off the dance floor. If the kid was so stupid as to dance poorly then it was common practice for him to be chased off the floor or worse yet, beaten down. Who knew, the rules were not always clear? Dancing was supposed to be fun but if a guy was not careful he could get the tar knocked out of him for breaking some obscure social mores. Dances were fun as long as a guy knew the rules. To be safe, a smart person never went to a dance without a group of his friends being close by for protection. Sometimes even following the rules were not good enough given the intricacies of life in our town.

For instance, Rudy reminded me of a time he broke that rule and went to a dance at the Hotel Horner without a group of us tagging along. Rudy said he attended because he was trying to impress an older girl who was visiting from out of town. The rest of us did not attend for some reason but always wished we could have been on hand during the melee that would ensue. The Hotel Horner was not a place where we ordinarily hung out as it had just recently opened for teen dances. After what occurred that evening it was never used as a teen venue again.

The hotel was owned by none other than our old family friend, you got it, Orlando Scamozes, the same guy who used to drink wine, eat pasta and slip me $20 bills. This was the same hotel where he was housing the prostitutes and ultimately what landed him in prison. The dance took place shortly before Orlando's place was raided and the prostitution ring foiled. Small world. In a city like ours, there was a blending of cultures and relationships that tended to overlap both in good ways and sometimes, obviously, in less than positive ways too.

While Orlando owned the hotel and before his arrest over the prostitution incident, he made the poor business decision to host a dance designed to collect money for some worthy cause or another. Knowing Orlando, the worthy cause was likely filling his back pocket with some extra cash. Nevertheless, as was customary where I grew up, the phrase coined by Claire Booth Luce seemed to always apply, that is, "No good deed goes unpunished." Have a dance to raise money in town for a charity and it would somehow lead to disaster? That is exactly what happened and leave it to Rudy to be smack in the middle of it.

According to Rudy and countless other witnesses that night, everyone was having a good time dancing. It was a mixed-race crowd and sometimes this added more tension to an event possibly due to the mistrust, jealousy, racism, social class differences, and general uneasiness between competing groups. Put these variables together with the age and maturity level of the crowd and it was almost impossible to successfully hold any type of event, such as a dance, without some knucklehead finding a way to mess it up. This particular dance at the Hotel Horner,would be just like all the others.

Things were going well at first according to Rudy. People were gathered in dance circles with guys jumping in and out showing off their dance moves. People were seemingly having a good time with everyone mixing and getting along. Then, for some stupid reason, a small Latino kid who did not like a particular White guy, who by the way was about the size of Andre The Giant, decided it was time to knock him out.

The big fellow, The Giant, was part of a local club the Bachelor's made up mainly of White guys. The giant kid was, along with his club members, standing around watching a dance competition. Out of nowhere and for no good reason at all the Latino kid ran up from behind, jumped high in the air and sucker-kicked the giant boy squarely in the back of his head. This became the catalyst for what turned out to be a major brawl. All the guys and some of the girls began pairing off and punching each other around. The fight was way too big for the hire-a-cops to control and soon the local police were on their way. The station, the same one where I was carted off a couple of years earlier for trespassing, was not too far away so the police were on the scene quickly to begin transporting people back to the local jail.

Rudy relived the whole story with us one evening as we drove around town reliving old memories. He reminded the whole car that he escaped without a scratch because after he threw a few punches he broke away from the grip of a bouncer just as the cops began to arrive. Lucky for him a good friend of ours, Pablo, drove by, pulled

Rudy into the car and they drove away just ahead of the law. Strangely, it was Pablo's younger brother who first started the whole brawl by attacking the Giant kid. It was rumored that Pablo's younger brother, Migo, decided to sucker-kick the Giant kid just for being a "Giant kid." That is how things seemed to happen growing up in town. Some guys would decide to attack another guy for any or no good reason. A guy could be punched just for eating popcorn in a way judged as incorrect by someone else. Imagine being threatened or knocked out simply because of the way you ate popcorn. In this case, it was because a guy watching a simple dance was considered too big. That is, however, what we all grew up understanding. The list of offenses could be staggering and some rules for keeping out of trouble were not able to be fully listed since rules were often created on the spot or changed at random. A good defense resulted largely not only from following the known rules but also from the associations one made. Luck was another major variable for escaping difficulty but one never knew if luck would be on your side or not. Therefore, practicing a little self-defense and having a trustworthy group of friends close by could come in handy.

The next day the melee at the Hotel Horner was front page news and served as another black mark stamped on our teenage years. Behavior like this did nothing positive for the reputation of the city either. People were not only arrested that night but a few ended up in the hospital. Luckily, most of the injuries were minor and I can only conclude that if that fight occurred today guns and knives would accompany fists and it is likely that people would have been more seriously injured or perhaps killed.

As we relived the tale in the car that one evening, Rudy, Chase, Mac, and I outwardly laughed over the old story as we reacted like our former selves. The difference, however, was we could hardly believe that our lives growing up included crazy events like the one Rudy relived. We could only thank our lucky stars that we were to escape such a nutty life. We had transformed into the adults who were now the incredulous ones. We could almost disbelieve that we were part of events such as the hotel fight as if we were the ones reading about it for the first time in the local newspaper. I need to pinch myself back toward reality as others, my wife, for example, remind me that today's headlines could easily have been about us, my friends and me had they been written many decades earlier. The guys and I agreed that we took way too many risks as kids and that our lives could have been very different had just one materialized differently.

How She Could Cook

****

Stripes: “The other night we finally got reservations to that expensive ‘Eye-talian’ restaurant in Pittsburgh.”

Hippie: “Which one, there seem to be so many new restaurants in town these days.”

Stripes: “People have been raving about it girl. You know, it’s Della Famiglia, I think, and it means like on a farm or from the table or something. You know with Eye-talians its ‘alla’ this or ‘una’ that. All I c-a-n s a y th at i t w a s r e a l......”

Not only was I forced to listen to these two women but they were now screwing up the Italian language. As I said I always hated that stupid pronunciation, “Eye-talian,” which makes me crazy each time I hear it. Hearing it from one of the walkie talkers was even worse as Stripes paired the meaning of the restaurant’s name, “Della Famiglia,” which really translates to, “of the family,” with the words, “Eye-talian.” Listening to her for those few seconds was like hearing someone’s nails running down a chalkboard. The restaurant’s name had nothing to do with farm to table either. Hearing the two loud talkers was almost too much for me to take. I had to hold myself back from jumping off the rower and teaching them a little something about Italian culture. I held my rising temper and figured that at least they were focused on a topic that was familiar to me and perhaps their jibber jabbering would provide me with some new restaurant tips as they blabbed about good places to eat in my new hometown.

Their theme at least kept me on track and played neatly into my mindless recall of the past.

For example, I had been clearly thinking, thanks to the walkers, about my grandmother's penchant for feeding everyone. Not only did she feed the masses but the food she prepared was of gourmet quality. I have never had better Italian food than from my grandmother. Certainly, I can be considered biased but there is 100% correlation between my conclusions regarding her food quality and everyone else's. She made the best homemade sauce, "sugo or salsa," and it was the best regardless of whether it was poured over homemade or store-bought pasta.

As another example, Muddyetta's homemade raviolis' could be considered a work of art. I spent many hours watching her roll out the dough, by hand, since she had no machine to do the work for her. On top of the dough, a dollop of her filling (locatelli, egg, ricotta) was dropped at two inch intervals before covering it with another layer of dough. Lastly she used a special tool with a serrated wheel to cut out the ravioli's. Her ravioli's were basically square with decorative serrations. None of this mezza luna (half-moon) shaped stuff. Her final result was substantial, that is, as large as the palm of a man's hand as it was now ready for boiling in the waiting vat of scalding salted water. Grandma always said about the cooking water, "salato come il mare," that is, salt it like the sea. I think of this phase each time I boil water to make pasta. Once prepared Grandma's work of art could have safely been placed on display at a venue like the Museum of Fine Arts in Boston. Andy Warhol should have painted a picture of my grandmother's raviolis in addition to his famous, *Campbell's Soup Cans,* 1962. Her food was artistic. It is almost too exhausting trying to find the words to describe just how overwhelmingly delicious her raviolis and everything else she cooked were. Her cooking equaled art. Just think of the best meal you ever had, make it Italian, and that would describe Marietti's daily menu. Her meals were also free. Now I pay top dollar for what I consider mediocre Italian meals, ones that are not nearly as tasty as Grandma's. The only Italian food that nears Aunt Mary's is the cooking of my relatives in Toronto, Canada. They really know how to make a braciole, lasagna, or rigatoni dish, rivaling Grannie's. Their various homemade salami and soppressata are the best ever too. I have pleaded with them for years to find a way to sell their food over the internet and if they did a fortune would be made. Imagine, *Harry and David* selling frozen ziti or gnocchi made by my relatives. This makes me hungry just thinking about it.

Another thing my grandmother made was fried dough and she was making it long before it was discovered and sold at almost every street fair and traveling amusement park. When the word got out in the neighborhood that Aunt Me-Etta was frying up a batch of what she called, "pizza fritte," fried pie, everyone found an excuse to drop over for a large piece and a cup of home-brewed coffee. Her pizza frites were large, like almost everything she made, the size of a dinner plate. Each one was fried individually in corn oil and always in her cast iron pans. My new stepsister, Jeannie, particularly went nuts overeating Grandma's pizza frites.

Marietta's homemade rolls were also a big hit but required tons of time to prepare. Even though they were labor intensive she simply enjoyed making them as they never failed to bring smiles to everyone's face. I recall her waking in the middle of the night to punch down the dough every couple of hours. There were many days that I awoke to the smell of her famous baked rolls. Hearing a knock on the door I welcomed friends like my old pal Johnny Boy or Chase who dropped by early on their way to work or school to arrive on time to butter up one or two of the golden-brown loaves. Johnny Boy was usually the first of many to arrive and be welcomed by the aroma of a warm bun the size of a small loaf of bread and piping hot right out of the oven. I can still hear my grandmother's command to my friends the day before:

Grandma: "Giovanni, come, droppa by, domani, tomorrow mornin for the rolls. Yes, yoo come-a early, before la lavoro, the work."

Johnny Boy: "Don't worry Mrs. D. I'll be here."

Sure enough, Johnny and everyone else would show up before the rolls had a chance to cool down. They stuffed themselves before work finding it hard to pull themselves away from the table and head out the door. But there were some concoctions, recipes, which were part of Grandma's menu that were not so universally appetizing, such as raw eggs cracked into a glass of homemade red wine. This strange drink was usually consumed at breakfast and only by hard core Italians myself not included. She also made what she termed, "uova battuto," or beaten eggs. Here she would separate the yolk of two to three eggs into a large wide-mouthed coffee cup, spoon on three to four heaping teaspoons of sugar, then with a tablespoon begin beating the eggs and sugar until the mixture turned a light yellow. This breakfast treat required the enlistment of those who would consume the drink after spending time beating up their own mixture until it was ready. When the egg yolks turned approximately the color of the sun it was ready to drink. The "uova battuto" could be drunk either by itself, with milk, or mixed with black coffee. Most people dipped toast into the drink and no matter how it was consumed it was terrific. Nowadays, a similar Italian dessert, zabaglione, is more widely known, however, this dessert also includes Marsala wine in the recipe. No one ever seemed to get sick from the raw eggs in those days but I would have second thoughts about enjoying this recipe today unless the eggs were pasteurized. Uova battuto was part of the daily menu back then but is now only a distant memory. I look forward to attempting to make my own rendition of the creamy egg mixture one day perhaps for my grandchildren.

Another food that Grandma occasionally cooked was tripe or "trippa" in Italian. Tripe, cow's stomach, was probably the grossest food on the family's rotating menu. I hated the smell while it boiled and it seemingly boiled forever in order to soften it enough to consume. When it was finally ready to serve, the tripe had the appearance of small rectangles of sponge dipped in marinara sauce. I think I would have rather eaten a sponge in those days than the tripe itself. I fortunately was happy they opened a can of *Beeferoni* for my dinner on those stinky tripe nights. Recently, at a family wedding in Toronto, tripe was one of the many dishes I discovered as I cruised the antipasto bar. Incidentally, I found the antipasto bars at Toronto weddings to be nearly the size of a tennis court packed with just about every food imaginable, especially, of course, Italian delicacies. Having not tried tripe since becoming an adult I decided to give it a try for old times sake. My eating repertoire had expanded somewhat with age and I was surprised by how much I enjoyed the tripe. I wondered if my grandmother's preparation of this organic meal would have tasted just as good today. Most likely it would have.

At Easter, "Pasqua," in our home there was the traditional baking of an Italian sweet bread known as "panetone." Grandma's was certainly the best and the only trick was to eat it soon after it was baked since it included no preservatives to keep it fresh. Waiting just a couple of days meant that the panettone would quickly become a little dry needing to be dunked in coffee to increase its moisture.

Italians enjoy dunking anything in coffee, especially "dolce," sweets, so the dry panettone was never a problem for most people in our home.

On Christmas Eve, "Natale," there was always "calamari" and "polpe," that is, squid and octopus. Back then most people raised their nose to the notion of eating either of these two ocean creatures. Admittedly, both animals are creepy looking making the thought of eating either one a little harrowing. Now many people, non-Italians and non-Mediterraneans, have learned to appreciate squid and more and more are discovering the flavor of well-prepared octopus. After getting married, my wife and I were always sent with dishes of Italian-American foods to my wife's Japanese-American parents who either ate it as it was prepared or if it lent itself, my mother-in-law turned it into a Japanese style rendition. Christmas Eve fishes, such as octopus or breaded smelt, for instance, could easily be transformed to an eastern delight simply by adding "shou-yu," soy sauce, and perhaps thin slices of ginger as well as adding a little spicy wasabi. I kiddingly believe that part of the reason my wife's family ultimately accepted me, a non-Japanese, into their family, had to do with the food my grandmother sent to their table. My grandmother's food paved the way for me serving as a sort of peace pipe or cultural bridge. How could I, a "nihonjin," a Caucasian, be so bad if I came from a generous home that cooked food as delicious as my grandmother's?

Paddling Polenta

One of the meals I looked forward to, that is its preparation, not its flavor, was "polenta." Polenta is cornmeal mush prepared in many Italian styles, one being with parmesan cheese and marinara sauce over the top. The polenta was only prepared a few times per year in our household as it required my grandfather's muscles to help get it cooked. Grandpa's help was necessary as the mixture required continual stirring while it neared readiness or else it would easily burn onto the bottom of its oversized pot. Cooking a large batch of this dish was labor intensive especially as the concoction thickened. As the polenta boiled in its kettle, it became denser and denser. Imagine paddling a canoe through cooked oatmeal and that is what stirring Grandma's polenta was like. Muscle power was necessary to make sure all the ingredients were incorporated correctly and kept a creamy, "cremeso," consistency.

Due to the thickness and quantity of the polenta, a special paddle or stirring utensil was required to dip down deeply into the large cooking pot. The stick was about three quarters the size of a baseball bat with the larger end flattened somewhat like a cricket stick. This paddle needed to be large because the pot was big and deep and the person doing the stirring had to work quickly. After watching polenta bubbling toward preparation I knew one of the reasons why my grandparents had such well-developed biceps. Stirring the polenta was like mixing concrete and I often thought that if it cooked long enough it could be poured into a form, shaped into bricks, and used to create a retaining wall.

Polenta was cooked in the basement where most of the Italians kept their real working kitchens. It seemed natural to Italian-Americans, those that immigrated from the old country, as Italy was referred to, that an upstairs kitchen was only for show. Upstairs stoves were for small clean cooking tasks, such as, brewing coffee or boiling an egg. Downstairs was the industrial kitchen. The basement was where the action took place from making homemade pasta to butchering chickens. The basement was the place to be for cooking, storing, and canning foods. Everything big happened out of sight and the basement was where miracles, turning raw products into delectable gastronomic masterpieces, occurred. Therefore, the basement was where all the utensils, the special boards for cutting out pasta, the various sized rolling pins, pots and pans of every shape, as well as heavy duty iron skillets for frying almost anything. My wife was always impressed by the large bowl of salt placed right next to the stove where my grandmother, who never measured anything, would grab handfuls of the spice and add it to whatever she was cooking. Deb reasoned that it was possibly the amount of salt we all ingested that kept everyone in our family edgy and hyper-animated.

When the adults were finished cooking, eating, and cleaning, then the basement opened up for my friends and I to take over. We played many games down in the cellars in each of the houses we owned especially games like Hide and Go Seek and one game that Guido and I created. This game was designed solely to playfully torture poor Anton as we incorporated the polenta paddle into our craziness.

The game required darkness so no lights were switched on in the basement. The game started after Guido and I situated ourselves out of sight downstairs. Next, Anton's role was to sneak down the steps attempting to locate us in the dark space after reaching the bottom. At least that is what we told him would happen. Instead, Guido and I planned to be hunters rather than the hunted seeking Anton out as soon as he was within striking distance. What we chose to strike him with was the polenta paddle that was conveniently located right next to the stove.

Because Guido and I were in the dark basement first, our eyes were accustomed to the darkness while Anton's remained blinded as he reached the dark basement floor. Anton was supposed to search for us but as he neared we would give him a good whack with the paddle before once again slinking out of range. This silliness would go on a few times before Anton gave up his search. Usually, Anton would yell out his plea for us to stop but our smacking him with the paddle was all in jest and we, including Anton, all had a good laugh over his protestations. Guido and I never felt bad about smacking Anton as we rationalized our torturing him was all in fun. Besides, Anton was older than us and given his size we concluded he had a higher pain threshold than we did. Thus, he was able to withstand a couple of good whacks with the polenta paddle without really feeling it. At least that is what Guido and I used as justification for our antics. Rationalization, well maybe, but we did this and many other foolish things growing up together while goofing around down basements, in backyards, and anywhere trouble could be found. The basement for us, growing up, was where it was happening once the adults finished the food preparation. The polenta paddle played a varied role in our families being used to both stir the Italian mush and also to stir up trouble accomplished through whacking our old friend Anton.

A little more on polenta. When my family made polenta enough was cooked to feed the 7th Fleet. To the novice it appeared that my grandparents were preparing way too much as they cooked the mixture. This was particularly so because most experienced eaters knew that only a small portion of the heavy cornmeal concoction was needed to fill one's stomach. This was doubly so since the overall meal naturally included a heavy tomato ragu, meatballs, and other "contorno," side dishes. However, in our home when polenta was served it was considered a special day, like All Saints Day or July 4th or something. Therefore, a regular friendship crew was invited over to consume the dish and they were invited not only because they enjoyed polenta but also because of their well-established gargantuan appetites. These were not just any people. Polenta meals included select folks, polenta eating champions who almost worshipped and prayed to the god of Italian grits. Two couples were always at the table with us for polenta night, and they were Joe and Feliciana, and Domenic and Biagina. There was a revolving group of other diners invited to fill empty spots around the table but they were invited almost as much to serve as an audience as they were invited as dinners guests. After all, cooking and eating polenta was special, almost a spectator sport. Newcomers were needed at each polenta dinner since without guests there would be no "WOW" effect. Newcomers were usually defined as those uneducated in the art of eating mass quantities of the Italian mush so it was fun playing to their naivete`. One of the newer guests, invited for the first time to witness the polenta gala, were my pals Rudy and Johnny Boy.

I enjoyed watching unsuspecting first-time polenta eaters, poor souls like Rudy and Johnny Boy, as my grandmother dished out the mush in oversized oval dishes that were reserved only for polenta meals. The rest of the year the dishes waited patiently in the cupboard until the polenta once again began to flow. These plates, "piatti," had a lip on them to hold back the overflowing polenta and sauce that would otherwise fall onto the tablecloth like waves of lava. The net contents of an average plate of polenta without meatballs could easily weigh in at two to three pounds. The unsuspecting diner, new to the polenta-eating world would have little idea regarding the difficulty attached to cleaning a plate full of the mixture. Most ordinary humans would be lucky to devour one-fourth of the amount that my grandmother heaped onto their dish. I usually waited and watched knowing that soon the guests' faces would turn from anticipation to dread as their stomach filled after only finishing a fraction of their creamy portion. What looked so good five minutes earlier now posed as an insurmountable obstacle as they began searching for ways to say, "Help, I can't fit anymore." Even before their faces turned green my grandmother would have already begun storm trooping around the table, replacing missing meatballs on dishes and beginning her running dialogue, "Giovanni," for example, "mangia, you no like-a da polenta? Go on eat-a some mo, you no full, mangia." In the meantime, Johnny-Boy, Rudy, and every other unsuspecting guest would be searching for the words to somehow get out of finishing their first plate full. Faces would soon begin to communicate, "Mercy on my soul, I give up. How do I get out of this?" Realizing they could not eat another bite, their entire body projecting pain, they began looking for someone to save them from hurting Grandma's feelings. When they slowed down or said they could not eat anymore Maryetti would usually frown and say,

"Whatsa matta, you no like-a my cooking, shame. Come on, eat-a some mo, fineesha tutti (finish all). Take some. Yu too skinny, en-a-how. Have another polpette, meata- ball"

A lucky newcomer would be saved, temporarily, if Grandma became distracted by the needs of someone else. After all she had others around the table who required her attention perhaps others who were not eating their designated amount. Granny's superb attention, after all, needed to be distributed fairly as there was also the first team of eaters, such as Joe Cappello, to deal with. He required attention even though he was more than willing to eat more. Of all the people I observed eating polenta at my grandmother's table, and there were many, Joe Cappello was by far the champion. Joe was short and stubby down to his bulbous fingers. I always marveled at his inflated digits and imagined that they were so chunky because as his stomach filled the rest of the food needed a place to go. When his round belly could fit no more food, his fingers, I imagined, were the last empty cavity in his body for food to be stored. I never saw his toes but concluded that they were most likely another food reservoir where excess food could be squeezed. I could never understand how such a short guy could eat so much and this was particularly true when polenta was served. If there was a polenta eating competition Joe would have won the prize.

"This year's IPEA (International Polenta Eating Association) first prize is awarded, for the seventh consecutive year, to the most profound polenta polisher of all time, a modern-day Tom Brady of the mush-eating world, to 'Jumpin Joe, The Cornmeal King,' Capelllll**oooooo!**"

As the eating continued, Feliciana would begin trying to stop Joe from eating after his third refill but Joe would scoff and make some remark in Italian, like:

"Quando finisci la bere birra io finirò di mangiare la polenta," that when she quits drinking beer he would stop eating the polenta.

Feliciana would then heartily laugh, playfully punch Joe in the tummy and they both continued what they had been doing. She did not intend to stop drinking beer, as it was too early in the day to do that, so she left Joe to plunder the remaining polenta. What a marathon it was during these dinners. Feliciana was always trying to guide Joe in one direction or another only to find that her entreaties were mostly ignored. Feliciana was the only person I ever met, by the way, who could have been mistaken for the famous actor, Peter Lorre who co-starred in the 1930s and 40s movies such as *Casablanca* and *The Maltese Falcon.* In the meantime, serious and stout Biagina, arms folded over her heavy bosom, partially to protect her plate from a surprise refill attack from her good friend, Comare Mutietta, but also communicating her negative judgement of Feliciana's drinking, was quietly absorbing the couple's interplay. Biagina was surely making mental notes of both Joe's eating and Feliciana's alcohol consumption so that she had gossip to spread the next day. Feliciana provided much gossip material as she was the only Italian woman I remember who drank anything but coffee. No elderly woman visiting our home drank beer and certainly not in the quantity that Feliciana consumed.

Meanwhile, on the other side of the table, I can still see Biagina's husband, Domenic, and my grandfather, ignoring the chatter with their heads bent into their plates shoveling in the polenta while never missing a beat. They would both finish their polenta much earlier than would Joe C. Usually, after my grandfather ate his fill he finished off his meal by then eating his salad. Without fail, Gramps enjoyed explaining to any non-Italian sitting at the table that eating salad at the end of his meal was the way it was done in Italy. He steadfastly believed that eating salad after a meal, as well as chomping an apple each day, sufficiently cleaned his teeth therefore preventing the need to see a dentist for a teeth cleaning. Grandpa credited the timing of his salads and ingestion of the apple for never needing a dentist scoffing at those who did. He repeated this dictum after each meal taking great pride in his oral hygienics philosophy and never recognizing that he just told the same story after yesterday's meal as well. Once his dental philosophy was fully explained, Grandpa would call up some old Italian parable from his memory and begin entertaining the crowd with his cracker jack poetry. Grandpa was his own best audience too since he heartily laughed after each one of his jokes and stories. It did not matter to him if he told it before because he enjoyed telling it again. Guests simply smiled while cleaning their plates and keeping a lookout for my grandmother's dive-bombing attempts to refill their dishes with polenta. By the way, I never recall Giuseppe needing to see a dentist so who can argue with his philosophy.

Eating was surely the main event in our home and any particular food item could serve as the day's theme. Whether it was homemade rolls, making sausage, panettone, canning tomatoes, or pickling melanzana (eggplant) whole days were devoted to the food of choice. One food item could often take up whole days ending with it as the main course at dinner. For instance, if fresh bread was being baked most of the day's conversation would revolve around yeast, dough, kneading and baking. A list of bread recipients would also be formed and each of us would be delegated to transport the bread item to the lucky beneficiary. Jackie was sure to get some bread and I usually was sent across the street to the county administrator's home with a loaf or two. A day or so later I would be called back across the street to pick up Grandma's dish now filled with something the administrator and his wife made to repay my grandparents. Anyone lucky enough to stop by would not leave until they tasted the bread and they surely were sent home with some to savor later. Part of the dough would likely be saved and turned into pizza incorporating some of Muttietta's canned tomatoes and Grandpa's homegrown basil.

As if food choices were not overly abundant around our house already, they diversified further when Dad married Hanna thus adding her German cooking touch to our crowded menu. Hanna was an extraordinary cook. Her German cooking was comparable to

Granny's Italian cooking. Hanna's emergence introduced gastronomical variation to our overflowing menu and new tastes and flavors to our household. The addition of German food injected another food philosophy and added debate regarding the world's best cuisines. Thankfully the one thing that Hanna and Granny agreed upon was cooking. Good food leveled the playing field and since their cooking originated from different cultures competition and jealousy was kept at a minimum. They may have argued over a way to prepare certain dishes but both enjoyed quality food, cooking and making people happy. Expense was never an issue with either woman and while they may have dickered over price both always purchased the best and the freshest items in overabundant quantities. For example, I remember eating five of Hanna's well prepared pork chops all by myself after a particularly hard football practice. Why she had five extra pork chops available after Dad, Jean, and she had already eaten dinner is an example of always being prepared with more food than was necessary. One never knew who would drop in or what surprises were in store.

Food was obviously celebrated by the two matriarchs. Sometimes the menu mirrored important events like a change in season, or a child's Holy Communion. However, any excuse to celebrate food would do. Perhaps obscure reasons, such as, the expectation of a sunny day, the distant call of a blue jay, or maybe the appearance of a low flying airplane, all could serve as a reason to cook up something special. Food was the family focus and it did not matter whether it was spaghetti or sauerbraten. If it was in season then it would soon materialize on the table and be the best anyone ever tasted.

Center Park

My grandmother and Hanna certainly held many discussions and debates over food preparation, correct cooking temperature or even the best way an item should be shelved. I presided over many friendly disagreements concerning food issues from the number of jars of canned tomatoes needed in the fruit cellar to the length of time required to roast a leg of lamb. There was never any holding back of opinions on almost any subject. In our household opinions dominated, no need for facts, and the only question was how to get your opinion heard. That has already been established. Discussions could get heated but most arguments were benign. They were simply part of the culture. Hurt feelings were temporary and for those lasting a little longer, well that would soon change as there was sure to be another new argument around the bend to take its place. That was the life I was used to witnessing.

Times with my grandparents were good. Life was smooth and loving, however, living with my dad and stepmother was mostly the opposite. I have no regrets now, no big deal, but back then it was a reason to bitch and I did a lot of that. Right or wrong I spent as much time out of the house as I could because it was not very pleasant or comfortable for me at home. Whether it was sports, hanging with the guys, or visiting with girlfriends I was happier away from my home. Similar feelings enveloped most of my friends including Mac, Luke, and sometimes Corto. The four of us spent much time complaining about our home life thus justifying, perhaps, our desire to spend as much time screwing off as we could. Before acquiring driver's licenses, the four of us spent countless hours hanging out in a nearby park, Center Park, where we often met up with a group of girls that we attempted to impress. The park was safe and being located in the middle of town it attracted all types of kids from various sections of the city. In the park, anything could happen, good or bad and it was up to us to determine what part of the continuum we wished to engage.

When we were not acting silly, trying in vain to rouse attention from the girls, we were mostly attempting to act cool and tough making sure that we were respected and not considered a group of chumps. Sometimes trouble had a way of finding us even when we were trying to stay clean. As was the norm in our hometown, turmoil was seemingly always nearby. For example, Mac got himself into a dilemma simply by trying a little too hard to be funny.

Mac had mentioned to us, many times, that before we all became friends he was well trained in judo. He often tried to convince us that he was a pretty good judo enthusiast but we mostly disbelieved him since he protested so much against our naysaying. One time he did make believers out of us by successfully using his judo skills on a bully who was older than us and who challenged Mac to a fight.

Mac, always the comedian, managed to keep himself out of most fights but sometimes even he had to defend himself against some of the toughs in the neighborhood. Admittedly, our buddy Mac had a way of shooting off his mouth attempting to be funny and garner attention. That is one thing we liked about him but to some kids outside our group, his behavior was considered annoying particularly if it was misinterpreted. Most people found his behavior funny and endearing too but sometimes while attempting to be comical his shenanigans backfired. Incredulous as it may have seemed to him, Mac was honestly confused when one of his actions was misconstrued. On this occasion a bully was told by someone, likely his girlfriend, that Mac spouted out something stupid about her rear-end. I recall that she sat on some paper and it lodged near the crack of her behind, one of those stupid things that seem to always make people guffaw. Mac could not help himself from pointing it out to a few of us figuring we would all have a little laugh and move on. Somehow the girlfriend must have seen us laughing at her behind and after identifying the reason, figured that Mac was the instigator and she likely reported her discomfort and the ensuing ridicule to her boyfriend. Those types of things were never ignored by boyfriends where we grew up and in this case, it was all that was needed for a fight to brew. Guys in our town were forever conscious of their honor and this situation required the bully guy, who did not like Mac anyway, to stand up as much for his girlfriend as for himself. Therefore, the bully fellow, after finding out that Mac was making jokes about his girl's rear end, challenged Mac to a fight. The issue, a simple piece of paper stuck to a girl's behind, would escalate into a showdown as the older kid wanted everyone to know that he was not going to put up with Mac's nonsense. So the bully fellow challenged Mac to a fight a few days in advance. He let it be known to one and all that Mac had better show up if he knew what was good for him. Nonetheless, Mac's desire to be the comedian had gotten him into another mess. As the famous old time comedian Hardy often said to Laurel, "Well here's another nice mess you've gotten me into."

Mac fretted over this issue for days claiming that he did not say anything terrible about the girl's butt so why did he have to fight? Mac noted that he only pointed out the obvious so why the big deal? He went on about having to fight this older guy who he, and the rest of us, thought was much tougher than Mac. Mac ruminated over how the girl misunderstood him and how the older guy would neither accept his explanation or his apology. Now Mac had no choice but to fight and hope for the best knowing that he would be the brunt of jokes for week's if he punked out.

Being forced to fight, Mac recruited Luke, Corto, and me as backups. We were to meet this bully kid and his friends at Center Park at 4:00 one humid summer afternoon before entering 10th grade. When we arrived, there were quite a few others who came to gawk, including the girlfriend whom we all agreed did have a sizable derriere that could have easily attracted a piece of paper as a magnet attracts metal. Certainly, her rear was capable of enveloping the piece of paper through no fault of her own. Nonetheless, she was front and center along with her group of gnarly friends, ratted-up hair and all. The bully guy intended to, we heard through the gossip mill, "Knock the smile off Mac's face once and for all."

As we neared the group, the circle quickly enclosed Mac and his foe, signaling the beginning of the long-awaited showdown. Anticipation was in the air and Luke, Corto, and I had no idea what was next. Mac, however, must have either secretly conceived of a plan, or maybe the stress of the moment simply overwhelmed him and triggered his surprise response. That is, without notice he surprised us all. Without hesitation, as if he had just returned from the Kodokan Judo Institute in Japan, Mac took matters into his own hands. Perhaps due to extreme anticipation, fear, or agitation, and before any words were exchanged or preliminaries decided Mac quickly grabbed the bully guy by the lapels and with one lucky judo flip ended the contest before it had a chance to begin. Mac erased days of fear and rumination while finally silencing the skeptics who doubted his judo skills and his ability to back up his Cheshire Cat smile.

The beautifully administered, Morote Seoinage (two-arm shoulder throw), knocked the wind thoroughly out of the thug as his back hit squarely on the ground. The fellow lost so much oxygen, as his back struck the tarmac, that a quick recovery on his part was impossible. Once the air returned to the big shot's lungs, Mac helped him up. Strangely, the fight Mac fretted over for days was completed in less than 5 seconds. The crowd, feeling cheated, eventually dispersed as the groups walked away in opposite directions. Mac, having temporarily learned his lesson, did not immediately break into his trademark smile waiting smartly for the crowd to first disperse before he did eventually smile but his face exuded more relief than happiness. Mac has repeated this story to me 20 times over the years. Mac still clings to the notion that he said nothing serious about the girl's butt and always follows up by stating, "I told you guys I took Judo lessons and you never believed me."

Another Park story revolves around our old friend Corto. I am not particularly proud of the story but it does illustrate some of the stupid things that friends sometimes do to each other. The story focuses on Corto and how he began, seemingly out of nowhere, to brag incessantly about a shirt he consistently wore for weeks during the same summer that Mac finally proved his Judo prowess. Corto became obsessed with a green shirt that he loved and began bragging that it was better than anything that any of us ever wore. No amount of kidding or complaining changed his mind and he began to drive us nuts over his shirt. We agreed, at the time, that his perseveration over the garment was strange but instead of ignoring him we eventually decided to teach him a lesson.

It was another hot summer day and Corto wore the green short sleeve shirt once again. The large group of us continued gathering in the evenings at the neighborhood park earnestly trying to impress the girls. The girls were a year younger so we felt it would be easier to impress them given our "maturity" level. One evening Luke, Mac, and I decided we had had enough of Corto's shirt talk and his ongoing diatribe concerning its superiority over any of our clothing. As we gathered in the park that sultry evening with our buddy Corto and along with the girls, a few of us conceived a plan to grab Corto and take his shirt away from him. The plan was supposed to be funny and get him to stop being such a bore over his shirt. We planned to find a way for him to take off his shirt and then the rest of us play keep away with it.

Unfortunately, our plan ended differently. Instead of taking his shirt, I acted in a characteristically wrongheaded way and on my own decided to change our original plan. Instead of tricking Corto into taking off his shirt so we could snatch it, I decided to run up behind him, grab his shirt with both hands and pull it over his head. If my behavior was not so insensitive it would have been humorous because when I grabbed the shirt with both hands, instead of it coming off over his head it easily split in two right up the middle. While this was not the plan, it made everyone except Corto laugh like frenzied baboons.

At the time, we thought the situation was great fun but as adults, Mac, Chase, and I agree that our little stunt stunk and I accept most of the blame. We reasoned at the time that Corto had it coming but even back then realized our plan was wrong. Especially now we recognize that it was an awful thing to do especially to a friend. We lament it, especially because of what eventually happened to Corto a few years after high school.

After graduation, we all lost track of Corto. We were busy with our own lives trying to fulfill our goals. Keeping track of others, Corto included, was not foremost on our checklists. There were just too many things going on so none of us kept up to date on Corto's plan or whereabouts after high school. As it turned out we should have been more aware of where he was heading.

A few years after graduation Rudy reported that he was walking down Broadway in front of the old Gelman Brothers fruit business when he noticed a bushy-haired, down-and-out homeless guy smiling up at him. The disheveled guy, sitting in a doorway, looked familiar. Rudy thought at first it was one of the derelicts we had worked with unloading trucks at Aspin's Furniture Store and he would have kept walking except for suddenly hearing a familiar greeting, "Hello Chi-Chi," a nickname only used by a few of his closest friends. Rudy said to himself, "Could it be," and it was, our lost friend, Corto.

Corto, it turned out had become a homeless person, the type of guy we used to call hobos and "bums" as we grew up. Some of the guys had heard rumors that Corto had hit the skids but no one seemed to believe it or know of his whereabouts. There were large numbers of downtrodden types of men who hung out at the rail yard near downtown and they panhandled near the numerous saloons located in the area. There were guys of all sorts, some without limbs sitting on the sidewalks selling pencils hoping for almost any coin a person was willing to drop into their cup. I recall one fellow who would sit outside Bailley's Meat Market and Grandma usually gave me a coin or two to plop down into his cup each time we entered the store. He in return handed out number two pencils for those donating. Now, grown up, one of our buddies had become just like the unfortunate men who dotted the sidewalk as we shopped in the downtown area. Hearing that one of our buddies, a former Gent had joined this unfortunate group of fellows was unbelievable and I am not sure any of us would have believed the rumors had it not been witnessed by Rudy.

Certainly, none of the guys ever aspired to become a homeless guy yet here was our old pal Corto immersed in the role. Rudy spent some time speaking to Corto on the sidewalk that one day. They talked about high school and both discussed what had gone on in each other's lives since graduation. Corto said he had had a little bad luck but living on the street was all right with him. Rudy did not think that things were just fine and asked if he could do anything to assist him. Corto simply asked for a little money and indicated that he would repay Rudy when his luck improved. Rudy gave him all that he had at the time, a few bucks, and some words of encouragement before leaving. Rudy mentioned the meeting with Corto sometime later but none of us, given our busy lives, had the time nor knew what to do to help our old friend. Besides most of us were away at college trying to build a life of our own. As it turned out none of us ever saw Corto again.

Without anyone knowing it, Corto's life after high school headed downward. We never knew whether he ever saw a therapist, if he was diagnosed with any condition, or if he enrolled in a program designed to help him deal with his situation. We suspected afterward that his problems were likely due to something serious like a quick onset of some mental condition or an addiction of some kind. We also learned later from one of Corto's family members that all efforts to intervene and assist him were rejected. Was the green shirt situation an early symptom of a future problem? Who knows for sure but we knew that our self-doubts and teenage egocentrism kept us from detecting or predicting Corto's future demise. When we were kids we thought he was just a little odd, particularly over the shirt issue. Corto's behaviors became fodder for us poking fun and screwing around with him at the time. Besides, each of us had a quirk or oddity of our own to deal with and we all expected the same razing treatment, even from friends. All busting, even toward friends, was considered fair play in those days and it applied to any guy who screwed up or acted weird in any way. If you made some kind of error, say farted in public or fell off your chair in class, then it was expected that others would playfully laugh and pounce on you too. Behaving like this toward your friends was supposed to be fun, at least most of the time, but likely it sometimes grew out of hand. In those days we felt everything could be decided, and controlled and nothing was due to a real illness. We had so much fun even laughing at ourselves most of the time anyway. Had we known that a real condition was plaguing our old friend, Corto, perhaps we would have trod more lightly with him.

There was a guy, for instance, that we knew named Joe and he had only three fingers on his left hand. He was therefore aptly named, "Three Finger Bob" and we used to piss him off on purpose and then dare him to give us the finger, finger. Of course, he only had one hand which still had the "finger" finger attached to it. We, therefore, waited for him to have his normal hand busy before we made him angry upon giving him the finger. We laughed crazily when he smiled knowing his other hand was too busy to give us "the finger" finger right back. It was one of those "gotcha" moments. But Joe never seemed to mind.

We did have a lot of fun with our old friend Corto. I still possess an old audio recording of him and together with Mac, and Luke we spent much time tape-recording all sorts of silly things. The most memorable tape recording involves the four of us getting together to create silly modified fairy tales on the 1/4 inch audio tapes we made on my recorder. Few people had tape recorders when we were in high school and the one I bought was of fairly good quality. The four of us made a series of tapes that we would play for our friends trying not only to keep ourselves busy but also earn a few laughs resulting from the product of our work. One story was a recreation of *Cinderella*. As the four of us worked on the final take of the recording, all of a sudden, in the middle of the tape, Mac was heard making fun of the way Corto slurred a word. While reciting the children's fairy tale that we had doctored up to be funny, Corto made a silly but memorable mispronunciation. Mac naturally brings up the mumbled slur whenever we discuss the old days of hanging with each other. Corto mispronounced a phrase about "mife (mice), mice for horses," which was part of a poem we read about Cinderella. Naturally, we still snicker at the phrase having left the mispronounced word in the final copy. The Corto mistake, "mife, mice for horses," has become part of our wacky history.

The bad news is that after seeing Corto, maybe a year or two later, Rudy got word that our old friend had died. Some say he died of exposure, or maybe an overdose of some kind, or even a street accident. We never knew for sure how it happened. Sadder yet he died alone. Corto was the first close pal to die and we wished that we could have helped. We hoped that Corto was resting in peace and was finally reunited with that green short-sleeved shirt that was hopefully, unlike Humpty Dumpty, successfully stitched back together again.

Cold Cuts

****

That one last day I finally had to ask Marietta if we could have something to eat. Gazing at all these memories spread out on the floor should have ruined my appetite but I knew if we did not eat something soon my wife's blood sugar level would drop and that is never a good thing. This may have been the first time in my life that I had to ask for food before my grandmother offered it. Ordinarily, the first thing my grandmother would say upon our stepping over her threshold was, "Sit, Ima cooka u both una steak, Frencha -fry. Itsa taka me cinqua minuti, sieditì," that is, five minutes, sit. Now I wondered what, if anything, Grandma had in her refrigerator to offer us given our rather cold reception.

I was relieved when Granny responded that she had numerous types of luncheon meat, as well as, fresh Italian bread. "Im-a shop 'ieri' (yesterday) at-a Fisher's," she added. Unfortunately, she had store-bought bread, not the homemade kind we longed for. At least she had gone shopping in preparation for our visit, and that was a positive sign. She mentioned shopping at the local Fisher's Grocery Store. Fisher's is where I took Grandma shopping many times before. It was the major grocery chain in the area and one of its stores was located just down the lake and around the corner from Granny's house. It seemed that each time we stood in line with her years earlier waiting to pay the cashier Fisher's Grandma would strike up a conversation with one of the checkout girls. It seemed that Marietta somehow knew all the cashiers but she had her favorites. Grandma especially enjoyed paying out with a familiar cashier whom I knew from high school and whom Granny was sure was sweet on me. It did not matter, however, which cashier checked us out since they all seemingly knew her as the sweet older woman with the broken English. “Missee, thissa my grand-a-son,” she would begin. “I’ma tell-a you bouta im. He’sa go to tha colleg-ia school, Bowling Green. You know the Bowling Green, no? Maybe he be smart, rich, one-a dees days, maybe.” Of course, I hated this at the time, embarrassed really, but it was going to happen no matter how I threatened Grandma Mary beforehand. “Please, don’t tell the cashier about me and college,” I would plead as we entered a line but as soon as we approached the register she could not help herself, “Missee questa e my grandson, he’sa hansom, no, una good-a boy?” Grrrrrrr. At least the checkout girl thought the little lady with the thick accent was cute.

Grandma enjoyed every type of luncheon meat and we always had a healthy supply in our refrigerator so it was no surprise that her shelves continued to be well stocked when we arrived that last time. This was the Grandma that I knew. It was a relief that she had not changed so much that she had given up on packing her refrigerator with food. I remember growing up eating tons of Italian specialties like capicola, prosciutto, mortadella, and salami. But Muttietta loved regular old Bologna, Headcheese, and other exotic cuts as well and I thought that I had seen it all until Dad married Hanna. I found out that Germans are at the top of the cold-cut hierarchy, they belong to the world’s cold-cut aristocracy as Hanna introduced many unfamiliar types into our already jammed arsenal of sandwich meats. Hanna introduced many rare types of wursts, such as eager wurst, Bierwurst, and Gelbwurst to our diet just to name a few. Some type of Thüringer was always available as was any type of ham under the sun, such as Black Forrest, Westfalen, and Alpine. Hams seemed to pack our refrigerator once I moved into Hanna’s house. Do not even get me started on what I consider to be the stranger types of cold cuts, for instance, cow's tongue and its preparation. Once a month, it seemed, I came home from school, lifted the top off a large kettle, and gazed upon an ugly cow's tongue boiling away on top of the stove. Hanna introduced more luncheon meats than most any non-german knew ever existed but I did not welcome being confronted by a cooking cow tongue on the range that very first time. I did welcome the 'gazillion' types of mustards unknown by most, that were now neatly stacked in the cupboard being ready to spread between two pieces of bread. Hanna also knew her bread and where to buy rare types of ryes and dark German styles that I had never tasted before. I found myself living in a cold-cut paradise after Dad married Hanna surpassing even Grandma who accepted defeat against Hanna's college bowl knowledge of cold cuts. Hanna beat Marietta hands down in the fine art of cold-cut diversity.

There were no exotic cold cuts in Muttyetta's fridge that one day during our last visit. There were just the regulars, Genoa Salami, and boiled ham one of her favorites. I can still hear her pronunciation, "bola ham." There was always American Cheese, "formaggio Medican," available in Grandma's fridge too. American Cheese seemed out of bounds as its quality was nowhere near Hanna'a Munster cheese or Granny's Parmigiano-Reggiano. By the way, no one in our home pronounced, "sandwiches," as "sangwiches. An Italian stereotype that did not apply to our home. Sure, we had provolone much of the time. It was almost law that an Italian-American had to have a waxed ball of provolone hanging somewhere in their house. But American Cheese? I guess my grandmother thought, "Americans," enjoyed American Cheese and so did she so having it on hand, to her, was the patriotic thing to do. She also learned that Americans ate Velveeta Cheese and somehow concluded that cooking with Velveeta was classy. I remember that I thought it was kind of funny, almost contrary to her modus operandi, that my grandmother had any thoughts regarding class or classiness with food or otherwise. I always got a kick out of watching her run a fork down the sides of a peeled cucumber before slicing it. Someone must have informed Granny that doing this was a sophisticated way of presenting them. The design on the cucumber, I imagined Granny thought, placed her squarely in the cooking ranks of chefs like Julia Child or a 1960s-70s TV guru, Graham Kerr who called himself, *The Galloping Gourmet.* I chuckled to myself each time she proudly demonstrated this little culinary trick for me forgetting that she demonstrated it to me many times before.

My wife and I sat and ate our salami sandwiches that day spread only with French's Yellow Mustard knowing things were not the same. We ate and we struggled with conversation making sure we did not say anything to make Grandma incorrectly suspicious of our intent. There was already a general silence in the house that we did not recognize and it succeeded in worrying us. The silence seemed to project that things would never be the same again. I would soon find out that was true.

Everything's Buzzin' Up Here!!!

We, the guys and I, were inseparable in high school. Our group was also fortunate to team up with a group of girls our age who lived in the neighborhood. We were never too far from Mary Lynn and her friends as our relationship started near the beginning of our high school years. The group of us spent many hours dancing, partying, dating, and attending sporting events together. Mary Lynn was the daughter of a fellow Italiano whom I knew years earlier, informally, when I hung around with Skeeter and Paulie. This was years before ever meeting up with Mary Lynn. Somehow there was a connection between Skeeter's and Paulie's dad, and Mary Lynn's father, card buddies maybe, so my two friends were no strangers to her father. At the time, her father, Mr. R, owned an Arcade downtown and since Skeeter and Paulie had the run of the city, the Arcade became a regular hangout on our circuit through town as we aimlessly meandered around town looking for adventure.

Each time Skeeter, Paulie and I headed downtown, we were only in sixth or seventh grade, we would find Mr. R. out in front of his Penny Arcade on Broadway, chewing on a stogie. He would always, in his smoker's gravelly voice, kiddingly greet Skeeter and Paulie with one form of vulgarity or another warning them that he was going to keep a special eye on them and their friends since he knew, "youse guys are big trouble." That warning was usually followed with something about how they, Skeeter and Paulie, would both end up in jail if they did not get an education and become somebody. He knew what he was talking about. Who knew it at the time but a few years later I would move away from Skeeter and Paulie, become friends with Mr. R's daughter, and hope that he would never recognize me as that other guy who hung around with those two guys he thought were delinquents studying to become felons.

One evening a number of us were sitting around Mary Lynn's basement. Her parents often opened their house to us as a place to talk, drink sodas, and crack jokes. To entertain ourselves that evening I had brought along my tape recorder, plugged it into the wall and we began listening to music, as well as, showing off the silly tapes, those same silly fairy tales that Mac, Luke, Corto, Chase and I had just created. After playing the tapes for a while, the recorder apparently began causing some type of electrical interference upstairs thus interrupting Mr. R.'s TV viewing. All of a sudden from upstairs we heard the now famous phrase emanating from Mr. R's gravelly voice, words that would last long after his innocent question to his daughter. Out of nowhere, breaking our lively basement conversation, Mr. R. yelled down the stairs the now famous question, "Mary Lynn, what is going on down there? Everything's buzzing up here." From that little innocent phrase, meaningless to most normal human beings, we all broke out laughing. It must have been the way the question was delivered, perhaps the result of Mr. R's gravelly tone, that somehow made it so hilarious to us all but especially to, you guessed it, Mac. When Mac was in the room it was certainly possible that something from nothing could easily be construed. Mac had a way of making nothing into something that would last forever. Mac did not disappoint us that evening down Mary Lynn's basement.

The innocent question emanating from Mr. R's gruff voice made a simple question humorous forcing us all to place pillows over our faces so our laughter would not be overheard upstairs. Mac has made certain that the phrase holds an important place in our groups' collective history since he is surely the first person to repeat it when he is anywhere near Mary Lynn and the rest of us.

Cars and Rodent Too

Our friendship circle continued to expand. Although our hometown was mid-sized, approximately 70,000 citizens back then, my friends and I must have known half of them by the time we were 16. Someone new was always entering the group, as well, and one new addition, introduced to us by Chase, was a guy named Rodan. Rodan would add a whole new dimension into our buddy system. It did not take very long for him to fit in and we soon began to spend much time with he and his family. Rodan also did not seem to mind when we nicknamed him Rodent either since he had given up long ago trying to fight against the obvious way smart asses like us joked about his name. Rodent also became an honorary *Gent* but he did not have much time to attend our meetings since he often was required to work for his father after school and on weekends. Rodent's father owned two small businesses, a professional house cleaning franchise and an appliance operation and both were run out of the family's home. Mr. Minor, it appeared, was not the best businessman but stayed afloat, most of us agreed, mainly because he kept his prices lower than his competitors and had a fabulous gift for gab. He was a fantastic salesman too having a perfected style of persuading shoppers to buy his products and services.

Another way Mr. Minor kept prices low, it seemed to us, was to hire young guys and subsequently seldom pay them or at least pay them late. When he occasionally cut checks he did not pay a guy all the money owed but instead usually promised to make it up to them in some other way. Much of the time, just before a mutiny over pay would ensue, Mr. Minor would write one or two of us a check and promise to pay the others in a few days. Rudy, more than any of us needed the money to help support his child, so the rest of us kept quiet as long as Rudy received his salary.

Mr. Minor sold appliances and much of the time he also owned the cleaning franchise. He would acquire jobs cleaning almost any type of building that got messed up due to any number of reasons. Often in the spring, for example, a group of low-lying lake homes located in a nearby resort community flooded. When this or any other large job occurred Mr. M. hired on a few extra guys and that is when I sometimes signed on to assist. There was a time, for instance, that we even helped clean a house where a letter bomb was mailed to the owner. When the letter was opened it blew the poor fellow to pieces. One of us, I think it was Luke, found the man's finger inside the globe covering a ceiling light. This finding at first grossed us all out until we thought of using the finger to really impress people at McDonald's. Unfortunately, our scheme was somehow exposed to the FBI and the finger was turned over to authorities so it never served as an exhibit designed to build on our grizzly status. We did enjoy impressing people with the story and told the tale many times over until those among us, with the weakest stomachs, protested loudly.

It was kooky experiences of this sort, as well as, simply enjoying Mr. Minor, Rodent and the rest of his family that kept us hanging around in spite of the faulty salary process. Our work was fun and part-time so we did not complain very much plus we were placated with food, drink, and a place to hang out. We were also kept satisfied by Mr. Minor's liberal policy for loaning us his vehicles. None of us had cars of our own when we turned sixteen so if we really needed to borrow a ride one of Mr. Minor's vehicles could become available. Much of the time we were also satisfied that Rodent had nightly access to one of his dad's work vans. He seemed to enjoy the role of chauffeur so he drove us around night after night for much of the time we were in high school. Rodent's access to the van helped assuage our need to be seen cruising through the city which was the ultimate custom of teens in town. In fact, Rodent and I were riding in one of those vans on an afternoon that he and I became small time heroes.

The both of us were driving around the city looking for girls to impress one cloudy afternoon having no luck as usual. We were just cruising through the city minding our own business and searching for something fun to do. We intended to spend, or should I say waste, much time engaged in this activity. All of a sudden Rodent pulled up to a railroad crossing on Leavitt Road noticing the warning lights flashing. After stopping we immediately saw a woman frantically exiting her car while taking the hand of her little boy. They rushed away from their car which seemingly was stuck on the railroad tracks. We may not have been the brightest bulbs on the block but Rodent and I immediately realized their car had stalled on the tracks as a train was barreling down toward it.

The tracks luckily were not installed with those safety gates that most have these days. Without having to say a word Rodent put his van in park and we both automatically ran to the woman's car. When we got to the vehicle Rodent placed the car in neutral and he and I began pushing it over the tracks to safety. Fortunately, we got the car out of the way of the train in plenty of time. The woman, though scared, was really very thankful and we subsequently felt like genuine heroes. I have to say I still feel proud for what we did.

After the train passed, we walked back over to the other side of the railroad tracks and retrieved Rodent's Dodge van still idling in front of the queue of cars. While a few bystanders applauded, our appearance relieved other drivers who must have wondered why there was no one sitting in the empty red van idling at the head of the tracks. We were giddy over our new role as heroes and could hardly wait to brag to our friends about what big shot celebrities we were. When we excitedly told a few friends the story about the car on the tracks, surprise replaced pride when we heard their flippant responses, "Oh really, so what other stories have you made up? When can we get going and doing something that's real, that's fun?" We were disappointed in their reaction but self-satisfied with ourselves for helping the woman and child even though our pals did not believe us. Soon Rodent and I gave up on hoping to impress anyone with our tale and I have seldom repeated the story since that day. Rodent, if you are out there, I am still proud of what we did and I bet you are too.

Certainly it is easy to imagine how important cars were to us back in the 60s. Guys with the best souped up autos had an inside track on attracting girls all of whom seemed to enjoy riding up and down the avenue through our favorite hometown route. Our route was set up very much like, Modesto, California, the city illustrated in the movie, *American Graffiti* which by the way was at theaters four years after our graduation. Drivers with anything from hot rods to the family station wagon followed a nicely laid out circuit in town which unofficially began at the city's lone McDonald's restaurant (that I already highlighted), circled through an A & W Root Beer diner across the street, then tooled east on Lake Road past the park. Right before the bridge, our route turned a hard right at what locals called the loop, following a path south while passing the numerous bars that lined both sides of the avenue. Most people turned around once they were propositioned by a visible bevy of the city's finest street walkers, that is, unless a guy wanted to stop and indulge. The women positioned themselves on the curb just a block down from *Aspin's*

Furniture. No one that I knew ever stopped their car to take advantage of the propositions but obviously some in the city found the recreation a necessity. At the end of the route, just beyond the working women cars were turned around and the trip reversed ultimately ending back at the McDonald's. Once back at McDonald's, if you were lucky, there was a vacant parking space and after parking people simply waited to be noticed. If all the spots were taken then one proceeded to drive down the same circuit again. It would not be unusual to drive the total circuit four or five times during a Friday or Saturday night. All of us looked forward to being invited for a ride in someone's car on a weekend and taking part in the circular ride to nowhere as we wanted badly to be seen and hopefully capture the attention of a special member of the opposite sex.

None of us ever owned a car that was considered cool in any way. Chase had a 1956 Chevy for a short period that was the closest any of us had to a muscle car but right after he bought it he blew out first gear. This caused the car to basically limp down the road until enough RPM's could be mustered from second gear to shift into third as the auto was finally able to fly down the road. Without a first gear there was no way that Chase was ever going to impress anyone with the speed he hoped would emanate from his 265 horse power engine.

Early on, Rudy, being the oldest and first to earn his driver's license, drove us around town in that ugly green 59 Chevy, the one that lost a wheel as Rafael practiced his three on the column shifting. Many times, Rudy with Mary Lynn and I with another close friend, Katie would travel the circuit through McDonald's but we were also able to do other things as well. The four of us would set off in the Chevy often stopping at the Mall for a little window shopping and maybe an ice cream cone. The freedom to have a car and being able to go somewhere without asking a parent for a ride was intoxicating. After the mall, like zombies, we would likely join the caravan of cars following the path through town commencing once again at the McDonald's on the lake.

All of this riding around with friends was tons of fun. Some of the best memories were derived from driving through our hometown after piling into Rodents red 1964 Dodge Van. Whenever possible a group of us would jump into the back of the van, find a cozy spot on the floor and off Rodent would drive. Part of the fun of riding in the van had to do with it fitting at least 10 or more people inside. We were naturally happiest when we could locate a few girls willing to risk riding along with us as we circled around the McDonald's driveway.

We occasionally left the city traveling the region looking for things to do. One of our favorite trips was searching for an old orphanage west of the city. The old orphanage, Gore Orphanage, supposedly burned to the ground with kids dying inside. At least that was the story that circulated around and the one we chose to believe. As a result of the decades old fire and especially the associated deaths, was naturally rumored to be haunted and this made it an even more enticing destination. We must have driven through the countryside for hours on weekend evenings never really locating the burned out remains of the site where children supposedly perished. Before our search, friends told us they had seen ghosts walking around in the fields surrounding the foundation of what used to be the orphanage. They also swore they heard screams from the burning children when they visited the site. Some even mentioned that they smelled what they considered to be burning bodies of the orphans who were all looking for the security of their old home.

We searched for the orphanage many times in the dark without any luck finding it. Finally, one night as we drove we believed we finally came upon the correct site. As the group of us exited the van and slowly moved through the darkness, there before us was what we believed were figures moving in the distance. We saw white puffs moving yards ahead of us in the field. We were sure they were ghosts of the orphans floating over the farmer's field. As we began to explore the site, Rodent kept the van idling on the side of the pavement just in case we needed to get moving in a flash. As we moved near the white puffs we began to hear noises resembling what we considered were the cries of orphan children lost in the fire. Almost at the same time, someone stepped in something squishy that we imagined must have been a child's decomposing body. Soon we began to hear other noises too but reality finally set in when it was finally discovered that the noises we heard were really just the bleating of sheep. After cleaning off our shoes caked with sheep dung, instead of what we imagined were orphan guts, we got back in the red van and quickly drove to town stopping off first to spray out the interior of Rodent's now smelly vehicle.

We never did find the spot where the orphanage was originally situated. There were many attempts designed to find it but without a GPS we likely never came close to its exact location. We sure had great times trying, over and over, to find it while spinning crazy tales about children walking around looking for their heads and other body parts. As it can easily be found now on the internet, the correct name of the orphanage is historically, Swift Mansion or the Light of Hope Orphanage. It was located on Gore Orphanage Road but the word "gore," has nothing to do with death or the burned, bloody body parts of children. Gore is actually a wedge-shaped piece of land surveyors use to make corrections to their errors. In addition, there was in fact a fire on the location of the original orphanage but only an auxiliary building burned down. This occurred around 1917 but no one was hurt or died as a result of the small fire. Dying or burning children developed into an urban legend many decades after the orphanage no longer existed and the tale continues even today. Searching for the site of Gore Orphanage has been undertaken by many generations of teens, adults too. Some searchers are fortunate enough to locate the site marker of the original building site while others swear they were serenaded by the screams of children who perhaps continue to haunt the hillside. Who knows for sure?

When we were not searching for burnt out orphanages, Rodent simply drove us around our hometown looking for fun and entertainment. Each night that we cruised around town in Rodent's red Dodge van was different and we never grew tired of our travels. On nights when it seemed no one of importance was around for us to impress we could always find great fun harassing the prostitutes downtown. We would make a quick stop, roll down our windows, flash some play money, and when their faces lit up we would quickly drive away. We must have been pretty bored on those nights. But usually our trips through the city in Rodent's van were an adventure of their own kind since we never knew who we would pick up or where the evening would lead us. Admittedly, packing nine or ten kids in the back of the vehicle was not very safe but we loved it anyway. Adventure and invincibility are the name plates of the teenage years. While all the guys and girls agree that we had great times in the back of Rodent's Dodge van, we remain unanimous that none of us would knowingly allow our kids to do the same. We were lucky to remain safe and Rodent must have been a good driver since we never got a traffic ticket or got into a wreck. The closest we ever came to a ticket was when a spot light from a car shined on us and we heard the loud speaker tell us to pull over. As we pulled to the side of the road we found out it was not the cops after all. Instead it was our friend, Chase, who had borrowed a used police car recently purchased privately by a family friend. The car had the police insignia removed but continued to sport its standard driver's side spot light. After a big laugh we were back in the van driving to nowhere. Maybe it was Karma that watched over us. After all, Rodent and I were certified heroes who saved the woman's car from being squashed by a locomotive, almost supermen we were, Rodent and I?

No one has seen much of Rodent since graduation. I only recall running into him once since those days and that was at a high school reunion. Rodent indicated that he had moved out of state after marrying. We all recall his big smile and positive personality but especially remember all of the good times we had with his family and especially riding in the back of his dad's red Dodge van. Aside from the late paychecks, Rodent's family was kind to us and treated us as adults. They made us feel like our thoughts and opinions were important and that we had something to offer the world. We shared many great times in their home during those crazy days and it was good remembering all the miles we logged riding along together through the streets of our little hometown. In fact, not long ago, I was walking with friends on our way to a local museum on Pittsburgh's North Side. As we turned a corner into an alleyway, seemingly sitting there waiting for me to find it, there it was. Yes, a red, 1964, Dodge van, just like Rodent's only this one was up on blocks. I had not seen one in years. While it was not exactly in pristine condition, being speckled with rust and with only one wheel remaining attached, it brought a pleasant tear to my eye. I rubbed my hand across its fender as we passed, wishing I could release it from its blocks and drive it away. I briefly dreamed of locating Rodent and picking up the old crew and then making one last spin through the MacDonalds before cruising down the circuit that we had loved so much. It seemed like kin, that old van, as if it we were a relative, reuniting with it after being apart for so many years. What a find, returning me home.

What A Drive: The College Visit

In fact there were many "car" stories in our past involving various makes and models of automobiles. Some have already been described. Most of the old stories have me silently asking myself, "What were you thinking when you did that?" For example, Chase and I, without our parents knowledge, bought an old, army green, 1960 Rambler station wagon for around $250. We were slightly over seventeen at the time with me being the ever-present money man, paying for the majority of the car and Chase storing it at his house. Chase made up a line about how there was not enough parking on my street and asked his parents if it would be okay to keep the car in their unused parking space. Chase's mother was suspicious of what was going on but she had so many other issues to deal with that she just let our story stand. Besides, they did not own a car and were told they could use the old Rambler any time they wanted. This would be the first of three cars I would own without my parents' knowledge.

The best story involving the army green Rambler was a road trip Chase, Rudy, and I took to a nearby college approximately an hour south of town. Rudy and I cut school one Friday to accompany Chase as he was scheduled to interview with the college's wrestling coach. The coach was interested in Chase and Chase hoped to perhaps earn a sports scholarship to the school. Chase was a talented wrestler and his skills were obviously noticed by a scout from the college. So off we headed in our army green Rambler station wagon skipping school that Friday morning informing no one of our hair brained scheme. We were heading for what would be another memorable adventure and one that topped many on the stupid list of dumb things guys can scheme up together. I think we were so giddy driving south to the college that we sang a couple of choruses' of, *We're Off To See The Wizard.*

We had no idea what to expect when we arrived at the college but we hoped it included having a good time and impressing coaches of our athletic ability. We knew nothing about colleges in those days as none of our parents were fortunate enough to have ever attended. It was our senior year and we three wanted to have fun together as graduation and life decisions would soon creep up on us. We were three screwballs, but attendance was not tracked reliably in those days therefore no one would be checking our whereabouts since our high school was quite large. So we figured why not skip school and just go? After all it was an educational outing.

Neither Rudy nor I received an invitation to check out the small college but justified attending by convincing ourselves that maybe the coaches somehow overlooked our football prowess and after meeting us would realize that we were superb prospects who should be considered. We figured the coaches would, after hearing our story, offer Rudy and I a full ride to their institution perhaps even begging us to play football for their school. We three had the crazy notion that it would be fun to go off to college together. The best thing we ever did was, we realized later, not to go off to college together. Nonetheless, we envisioned that after receiving their offer to play ball at their institution that we would simply inform them, quite cavalierly, of course, that some serious thought would have to be given before we could accept their offer. What egos we must have had.

If there was a chance that any one of us would be positively assessed by a coach at that college we likely blew the idea within the first five minutes of meeting the school's head wrestling coach. See, not only were we coming unannounced and without an invitation, but we were also arriving without our parents. Topping things off we showed up together in a dilapidated army green Rambler Station Wagon. These variables alone would have added up to be an unhealthy first impression but they did not constitute our dumbest decision of all. Best and craziest idea of all was we had also decided to pop a handful of what we believed were "Speckled Dexi's" in our mouths a few miles before reaching the campus. The pills were stolen from someone's medicine cabinet but I do not remember exactly whose. In those days Dexedrine was a popular drug readily prescribed by physicians as a means of promoting weight loss. People soon found that the pills were more often used to get high rather than for losing fat so the pills eventually began to be difficult to obtain. The bottle indicated that the patient should take no more than one pill per 12-hour period so we figured that two a piece would be plenty. Besides, this was the second time we took the drug and we had a fairly good idea of what to expect. Why we would take pills on the way to a college interview is plain asinine but the notion somehow justified our action. I guess we were just sticking up our middle fingers at life yet again and also at authority even though we really did not have that much to complain about. Sure, we all had our problems with family so I guess we concluded that the world was not fair. We convinced ourselves long before that trip that the world was against us. Therefore, the way to cure our problems, we concluded, was to reap personal mayhem wherever we went even if it was probable that the mayhem would backfire mainly against us. Maybe it was a self-fulfilling prophecy or something equally ridiculous. Who knows? We were determined to show the world we were somebody and the three of us decided to prove our silly point by making fools of ourselves at the college du jour.

By the time we arrived on campus, around 9:00 a.m., the Dexi's had begun to take effect. We were starting to feel the expected result including excessive self-assurance and feelings of superiority. The pills were providing us with something we had not developed on our own, that is, self-confidence, or so our internal psyches transmitted. The Speckled Dexi's, we believed, were making the world appear much clearer than reality thus allowing us to possess great powers of introspection. Yes, we surmised that we could now analyze and assess any broad situation placed before us with pinpoint accuracy. Being already suspicious of adults, for instance, the Dexi's intensified those feelings by highlighting the slightest indignity or perceived phony promise. College visits, especially with coaches, can be filled with semi-truths and that is accepted as a given by most normal people. Right? Well, we thought worse at the time and the Dexi's substantiated our beliefs. Since we were less normal than usual, any unsavory expression or suspicious change in body language by the coach would be immediately considered a direct insult and would register high on our built in "phony boloni-meters."

The coach greeted us with a handshake and from the look on his face it was obvious that he did not expect to see two extra guys tagging along with Chase. "AHHHHH," we made note. The coach's expression of surprise caused him to fail the initial test. His glance earned him his first negative mark on our "Phony-Boloni Meter." Right away our built-in radar, bolstered by the Dexedrine, registered a blip on the meter. Next he indicated that it would be unlikely that any interviews for Rudy and me with the football coaching staff could be arranged but that he would try. Worst of all, he did not provide the necessary amount of praise for our football conference, nor be sufficiently impressed by our team's win/loss record. This error earned him one of our lowest ratings, the last straw award score of, "Phony Squared." Later on the coach indicated that he was sorry but no one was available to interview Rudy or me so we placed the coach in our three strikes and you are out subcategory, that is "Phony strike one, phony strike two, and phony strike three you are OUT." From there we saw what we wanted to see and what we saw was a middle-aged White guy who did not take us seriously, was obviously judgmental in the wrong direction, and was unable to satisfactorily gauge our inherent athletic qualities. We were used to meeting his type or so we thought. Regarding his treatment of Chase, well the guy appeared, given our sharp pinpoint clairvoyance, as more concerned with how much Chase could help his team rather than someone who appreciated Chase for his skills. It appeared for certain that he could have cared less about Rudy and me but we were too stupid to foresee that possibility before the trip. See, we had recently read, *The Catcher In The Rye*, by J.D. Salinger in English class so we felt fully aware of life's hypocrisies. We knew all about adult phoniness but were willing to give older people one last chance to illustrate their innocence. We, along with our internal phony boloni checklist, felt, by the end of our college visit that we had uncovered just one more adult who underestimated us. The college coach was just like all the others and we congratulated ourselves for uncovering another hypocrite. Congratulations to us for a job well done.

Still, Rudy and I were a little unhappy afterwards, disappointed, that the coach was not drooling all over the place for having two such fine football specimens like us standing before him. We figured that all we had to do was inform the coach about where we played football and he would want to sign us up right on the spot. Did he not know that we grew up and sort of succeeded in a cultural melting pot having to deal with all sorts of tough guys? Did he not know that we appeared small in stature yet were much better than our physiques otherwise indicated? Did he not know we had successfully negotiated screwed-up families to become local athletic heroes, or so we thought too? Did he not appreciate that we played, without injury, for one of the premier football leagues in all of Ohio? Somehow none of that seemed to register with the coach so we might have been upset but we had predicted as much beforehand. It was to us just another mid-level shocker. We had achieved our very own self-fulfilling prophecy so maybe it was good we took those pills in the first place.

About midway through our campus visit the Dexi's began to really kick in making it difficult to remain serious and hold back our laughter. For the remainder of the tour we needed to refrain from eye contact with each other or else risk flying into uncontrolled giggling. We somehow made it through the interview and subsequent tour without making total jerks of ourselves. Perhaps the coach noticed we were inappropriate but we did not know it for sure. The drug helped blind us from our own behavior. All we knew was we had another nutty adventure under our belts and laughed nonstop all the way back home. We had proven, I guess, what we set out to prove and that was that the world looked down on us, we were under-appreciated, and this was just as we had always surmised. There we were three clever guys, self-proclaimed athletic prodigies who had just unearthed another phony adult. Somehow we felt superior for flushing out the guy but in the long run, it did us no good.

We got back into the army green Rambler and headed north. As we arrived back home the first place we headed was McDonald's, naturally, our local mecca, not only to see our friends but also because the Dexi's were wearing off and our appetites were raging. We probably laughed more that day than any other day of our lives. As we repeated the tale to all our friends they laughed along with us thus justifying for us our trip and establishing the three of us as the temporary occupants, that is, the ultimate monarchs of the local ding-a-ling thrown.

We did not care that we probably ruined any chance that Chase would have had to earn a scholarship to the college. Chase eventually, as expected, got a form letter from the coach thanking him for checking out the college but as figured, there was no scholarship offer. Rudy and I never heard anything from the coach either but we guessed as much. Now, as adults the three of us simply marvel at our nutty behavior each time we recall the event. We admit that our adventure to the college, all things considered, was irresponsible and one of the most pea-brained things we had ever done. At least we did not bring Donald with us who perhaps would have slugged the college coach before we returned home. Chase admitted during one of our reunions that he knew from the start before we ever stepped foot on the campus, that the college would have been unable to offer him enough money to attend no matter what had transpired during the interview. Even if Chase's whole tuition was paid by the college, he concluded that he still would not have had the money for books, room and board, or maybe even the application fee. If the college planned to offer him a full ride, which we now know small colleges cannot offer to athletes, showing up with two lunatic friends was a sure way to toss that idea into the toilet. We had fun that day adding another foolish tale to our list of chowderheaded experiences. The trip truly illustrates the nutty desperate things guys will do if given half the chance. The army green Rambler did not last long after that trip. When it broke down a few weeks later we got it running long enough to drive it slowly to a local junk yard, a well-known local business recognizable due to a compact car parked on its roof. I remember always wanting to go into that junk yard to do business or just to check it out as it represented an unofficial city landmark as it was the first thing that a visitor saw when entering the city. The small car parked on the roof was not very classy but it made my hometown appear noteworthy.

Strangely, it may seem improbable, as if I am making it up, but Chase and I soon bought a second Rambler, exactly like the first one only the second car was painted pink. We, of course, named it the *Pink Panther* and we drove that car everywhere during the early part of 1968. The Pink Panther in short order became well known around town as it turned heads wherever we drove it. The car was so ugly that Chase and I were given significant credit for being brave enough to simply drive it around the city. Most people concluded that we purposefully painted it pink for laughs. We never researched the reason behind its color but some concluded the car was once used to sell Mary Kay cosmetics. What we did know was the Rambler got laughs and it strangely became a chick magnet. After all, who would not want to be seen driving up and down the avenue in a 1960 pink Rambler station wagon? The car seemed to scream, "Notice Us!" I even got a girlfriend, two years my senior named Carolina out of the deal, and I think the car, rather than my looks, had much to do with it. Carolina and a host of others were driven all around the city in the Pink Panther having much fun driving it up and down the avenue and all through the town .

Chase and I co-owned that car for six months or so and kept it until the truth behind its ownership was about to be uncovered. That is, our parents were going to find out that Chase and I secretly owned the car. So before we got caught he and I sold the auto for a few dollars more than we paid for it and got out of the mutual car ownership business for good.

That did not curtail my secretive car ownership. There was one last automobile that I should mention and I bought it on my own during the summer right after high school graduation. I purchased a 1957 Buick Special, already 12 years old, for $50 from one of Rudy's cousins. The car was gray and most of the paint was worn off as if it had been parked for years in a sand storm. If it had had a swastika painted on its side and a red flag waving from the antenna the car would have looked much like a staff car belonging to the Third Reich. The car was a certified wreck but it started every time and it got me where I wanted to go for a few months. It was the kind of car that first-time owners should own so that their incorrect mechanical decisions do not mess up a quality vehicle.

For example, there was a time when the Buick ran low on transmission fluid so I added more fluid to top it off. However, when I checked the level it was still low so I added another quart. I checked the level one more time and even though it continued to register low I drove the car anyhow. It did not take long to determine why the transmission fluid level registered low even after adding two quarts. Instead of adding the fluid to the transmission, I was pouring it down the engine oil spout. Soon after making this error I was driving the car and had to quickly pull over to the curb because thick smoke began billowing out of the engine compartment. Apparently, like an upset stomach, the car projectile vomited the transmission fluid all over the interior of the engine compartment. The only mystery after that was why, after regurgitating all that fluid onto the hot engine, the car continued to function. Again I was lucky escaping the close call.

The Buick continued to run through the following week, long enough to allow Deanna, a girl who I was dating at the time, and I to get ourselves in a small but memorable fender bender. We were driving down Oberlin Avenue one sunny afternoon when we made a quick stop in front of a local creamery due to noticing railroad flashers flashing a few cars ahead of us. We had no sooner stopped when, "Bang!" Both our heads snapped back and due to the impact we were immediately sprayed by all the knobs and gizmos from the radio, heater, and whatever else could become dislodged. I remember distinctly being smacked in the kisser by the magnetized St. Anthony figure that flew from the dashboard into my face as the car jerked forward. When we composed ourselves and realized that neither one of us was injured, I quickly exited the car to see what happened and also to survey the damage.

Behind us, already out of his car, was a well-dressed man in a suit apologizing for not stopping on time. He seemed pleased that neither one of us was injured. As he spoke it was obvious that his breath strongly smelled of alcohol. He may have been a little looped but he was sober enough to very wisely ask if "we could settle this thing without calling the police." As I gazed at my car, built like an armored war vehicle, I noticed that the bumper was slightly dented but the car was still drivable while his car sustained quite a bit of damage We agreed to leave the police out of the situation since I did not want my parents to find out about the car and Deanna and I wanted to get going to make the most out of our date. I, therefore, agreed to meet him the next day at his downtown office to settle the matter. The fellow gave me his card and as I took it I could see from the look on his face that he was both relieved and thankful.

As I sat back in the driver's seat next to Deanna, in those days it was customary for girls to sit right next to the guy since cars still had bench seats, I began to read his business card. I immediately recognized the fellow's name. The man dressed in the spiffy suit with alcohol on his breath was a prominent lawyer in town. I recalled seeing his political signs posted on lawns throughout the city during recent elections as well. I knew why he was so relieved when I opted to leave the police out of the situation. Before putting the car in gear, Deanna and I replaced all the blown-out knobs as well as the religious magnet back into their respective spots. We put the minor accident out of our minds and ended up having a pleasant afternoon on the beach.

The next day, as scheduled, I visited the previously inebriated counselor at his downtown office. When I met with him privately this time there were no smiles or pleasantries. Right after crashing his car into mine he was sheepishly apologetic while standing in the middle of the street with the smell of booze seeping out of his pores. He was ever so pleasant when I agreed to leave the cops out of it, however, now his demeanor had changed, it was quite different. Mr. Lawyer was now acting high-handedly as he began accusing me of "trying to rip him off since," according to him, I knew my car was "a cheap pile of crap which shouldn't even be allowed on the road." While I silently agreed with him about the status of my vehicle, in theory, I still felt I deserved some compensation for the inconvenience as well as the damages he caused. I also did not appreciate his accusations or the way he was treating me. Being eighteen and in a lawyer's office I was admittedly intimidated but while I remained cautiously assertive I informed him that I was not leaving empty handed. He may have been an adult but he had begun to anger me just as other guys had, for instance, like Kenny did at the gang fight and Rusty did inside the church narthex. Fortunately I was controlled enough this time to not challenge the guy to a fight or blurt out anything stupid like, "Big daddy," at the Ishkabibble-like lawyer. Finally, after the creep lectured me some more about cheating him, he relented and offered me $100 in cash. I could have been a creep myself by demanding more but felt the $100 was satisfactory compensation particularly since I originally bought the car for $50. The councilman cum lawyer made me sign a waiver admitting that the matter was settled to our satisfaction and that I "would not demand any further redress." Many fancy words were on the waiver but I signed it anyway and felt pleased to have my $100 in cash as I hightailed it out of his office.

I hated the guy's attitude but learned a lesson about the world that day. Call the police when people smash into your car. After one leaves the scene of a wreck attitudes change, promises are forgotten and gratitude erodes. Nonetheless, at a minimum, I now had a car bought for $50 and a profit of $100 from a drunken barrister. The money would come in handy as I would be entering college in a few weeks.

When a guy is young and in a car there always seems to be stories. For instance another quick adventure involves Mac and I driving down the road with our friend, Johnny Boy at the wheel and driving us around in one of his old cars. While driving, as usual to nowhere special, we suddenly began to smell smoke. One of us turned around and saw a ton of smoke coming out from under the back seat. We quickly pulled to the side of the street as thick fumes began swirling out of the windows. As we jumped out of the car, we quickly opened all the doors wondering what to do next. Luckily, an idea quickly came to Johnny Boy as he seemed to automatically grab a thought from somewhere and pulled the backseat out of the car with one big tug. We three began to stomp on the seat and the fire was eventually extinguished. Apparently, Johnny Boy's discarded cigarette butt landed in the back seat rather than on the highway thus lighting up the faux leather seat and its stuffing. After a few laughs and a few four-letter words directed at Johnny Boy's poor aim, we snuggly replaced the backseat into its bracket and continued down the road. We had once again escaped a collision with danger notching an ever-increasing number of comical events to our growing automobile script.

All this car business was going on secretively without either my grandparents or my friend's parents knowing anything about it. When I think about all the problems attached to owning my three vehicles I am thankful I made it through that period relatively unscathed. With no insurance, I could have wrecked the car and caused my family significant financial loss. Instead, Marietta and Giuseppe were following their prescribed life style which included cooking, gardening, catering to their boarders and bragging about what a wonderful guy I was. My grandparents continued thinking that I was the greatest and their unconditional love was building something inside of me that would get me safely through this nutty phase of life.

College Is Coming

Many of the guys planned to attend college or some other form of higher education right after high school graduation. In addition, none of us ever gave much thought to which institution we would eventually wish to attend. Since our parents did not enroll in college nor had they any experience with the whole college application process we were on our own when it came to higher education decisions. Rudy eventually was accepted and was accepted into a small college a couple of hours from home as he had earned a full football scholarship and thus his situation was well taken care of. Mac decided on his own to attend a seminary to become a catholic brother and Luke and Chase did not seem to have any immediate plans. Most of the rest of the crew simply applied to the state college of their choice, Ohio State, Kent State, Ohio U., etc. I chose Bowling Green State University. BGSU was chosen on the spot when I registered for the American College Test (ACT) as one of the demographic questions included in the registration asked, "Where would you like test results mailed?" BGSU was as good as any college as it was close enough from home, reasonably priced, and besides it was the first school that came to my mind. My father wanted me to attend Oberlin College but I knew enough about colleges to realize that it was beyond my GPA as well as our family's income level. My grandparents liked the idea of Oberlin too since it was only 20 minutes away from home thus allowing them to regularly deliver leftover pasta and maybe loaves of Italian bread to my dorm room. When you are a teen the last thing a guy wants is his grandparents showing up at his dorm room with leftovers. As an adult my opinion is quite different. I think about how I passed up a golden opportunity back then. Had the family crew shown up with a picnic basket filled with sausage, ziti, and cannolis, I would have been a big hit in the dorm. College food was terrible back in the 60s so a basket full of Italian leftovers would have had both guys and girls beating down my door wishing to be included in the feast. I could have been quite the popular guy.

Attending Bowling Green, two hours from my hometown, turned out to be one of the best decisions I ever made in my life. My grandmother, while proud of my attending college shed a few tears as I headed off to school. I smiled all the way to BGSU as I could hardly wait to get out of town. I headed off on my own without any of the old gang planning to attend the same school with me. The unintentional decision made independently by the guys, my pals, about splitting up and not choosing to go to the same university was a very wise choice as I have already said. Going to the same school would likely have been a total disaster, probably a recipe for failure. One small incident sums it up for Rudy and I.

Perhaps I should set the scene. Unlike Rudy, I was tired of playing football by the end of our senior season. I had been playing organized ball basically since grade four. I was encouraged by coaches to apply to the same school and play ball alongside Rudy but I had no desire to continue playing the sport. Eight years on a football team was enough for me. My body could not endure any more pain which is a constant when playing football. I would soon find that attending a different college than Rudy was a smart choice for us both.

Rudy and I did not see much of each other throughout college. We did spend one or two memorable weekends together which only reinforced the notion that it was better that we studied apart rather than together. I first visited Rudy midway through the winter term of our freshman year. The first night we drank our share of these small pony bottles of Rolling Rock Beer. As a result I did not recall much in the morning but realized I was very hungry. Rudy had no food in his dorm room and it was too late for a college breakfast so he said, "Come on, let's go down to the diner." So that is what we did, just he and I.

We easily found two seats at the counter and Rudy informed me that I should eat all that I wanted since he was going to take care of everything. The diner was crowded with locals and it was obvious, even to me, that there were few non-White patrons in the place. I eventually learned that most cities out in the country were demographically nothing like our melting-pot hometown.

We were hungry as we placed our large orders. We ate our fill of omelets, hash browns, pancakes and orange juice. When we had eaten all we could fit into our hungover bodies Rudy grabbed the check. I offered to split it with him but he said, "Don't worry about it. I will take care of everything." A few seconds later he drank his last gulp of OJ and as he got up he told me to follow him and not ask any questions. We walked toward the cash register using our familiar hometown pimping gate that was, incidentally, way out of place in a fully Caucasian farm town in western, Ohio. Rudy led the way all right but instead of heading toward the cash register he continued walking directly out the front door. There was no hesitation or even a glance toward the cashier, he just kept pimping right on through and out the door. As he turned right outside and headed toward the college he began to run as only a guy from our hometown had learned to run away from something. My legs, conditioned from my years of following Rudy around town, also went automatically into high gear. We ran laughing crazily all the way until we felt we were safe. I can still feel that familiar rush of adrenaline flowing through my being as we got away with committing another dirty trick. What we did was wrong but I guess we remained immature screwballs continuing to seek out adventure even after high school graduation, as well as, now in a strange environment. We roared all the way back to campus just as we laughed at the naive guys at Harrison School after we fooled them and cleaned their clock playing football.

One thing was certain, Rudy provided his college teammates, while he was a member of the team, with an excitement that they had never known before attending college. For me, I was used to his antics, our antics. Rudy often lit up an evening with crazy merriment and today his personality remains the same. Whenever he enters a room heads still turn as his boisterous talk and good looks capture the attention of the whole crowd.

Characters like Rudy filled my early life. That is why my, our, adolescence might have seemed, at least to us, longer and more exciting than everyone else's. Adolescence seemed figuratively lengthened for us due to jamming so many crazy experiences into such a short period of time. The experiences, we believed, were not common in the lives of most young people and they remain ever dear to us today. We agreed that our group was truly fortunate to weave such a long list of wacky hijinks and relationships together. We are pleased to be able to relive them with friends, old and new any chance that we get.

By the way, years later Rudy and I sent cash back to that diner near his college in an attempt to pay for our previously stolen breakfast. Equipped with a brief letter of apology we hoped our letter reached its destination and that the diner was managed by the same people or at a minimum their relatives. Our anonymous letter explained our immature behavior and we thanked them for the wonderful breakfast we enjoyed many years earlier. While not proud of ourselves for leaving that diner without paying, the act spoke volumes about who we were as kids. Sending payment, we hoped, represented who we had become as adults. We did not sign our real names remaining a little too ashamed for what we had done so we remained anonymous. Instead we identified ourselves as, "A Couple of maturing, old Gents." In more ways than one that is exactly what we had become.

Without ever directly stating it, all of us, somehow silently knew that we stood a better chance of success upon graduating by following different paths away from each other after high school. We were to become friends from afar as we decided to go to different colleges or training programs. If we had lived closer to each other, we agreed, our luck may not have lasted. As adults, we remain secure in our memories and happily recall each of them whenever possible.

The Exciting Eggplant

One of the food traditions that reminds me most of my grandparents has to do with their yearly marinating of vegetables. Marinating, to them, was a way to lengthen the growing season and continue to enjoy vegetables through the winter. One of the ways they marinated vegetables was through using rather large wide-mouthed jars that they had accumulated over the years. On Grandma's floor, staring at me that one day before the auction were a few of those jars that I associated with growing up in Giuseppe and Maria's household. The large jars were pulled out and sanitized each fall in preparation for marinating vegetables, such eggplants, "melanzana," and banana peppers that they religiously pickled each year. After the tomatoes were canned and stored neatly on the overflowing fruit cellar shelves it was time, a yearly tradition, to marinate eggplant and peppers. I really loved the taste of those vegetables that were flavored with tons of garlic, salt, olive oil and vinegar. Marinating melanzana represented one more big food day on our yearly calendar and required much planning and preparation. For example, just finding enough eggplants to marinate was a chore. Eggplant in the 60s were an obscure vegetable ranking low on the list of America's most treasured foods. I never recall seeing an eggplant dish grace the table of any of my American friend's dinner tables. Imagining Wally asking the Beaver to please pass the melanzana was too foreign a concept to even consider. Eggplants were to vegetables as octopus was to seafood back then, that is, scoffed at and rejected by most upstanding citizens of the new world. Many people were confused by the vegetable anyhow. While not so confusing as the artichoke, which we also regularly consumed, most people had no idea how to prepare the purple orb for consumption. That is, of course, even if they realized it could be eaten at all. Why fiddle with an eggplant when there were corn, lettuce, and green beans available to consume? Who would eat something purple anyway? But Italians did, they ate everything consumable. They were culinary pioneers ready to turn anything edible and obscure into a regular delicacy.

When eggplant marination day arrived at our house at least three bushels of fresh vegetables were needed to fill the empty jars. In addition, at least one overflowing bushel of banana peppers was also mysteriously obtained from some nearby farm. That is when at least a half dozen largemouth jars, accumulated over the years, were called into action. The vats would be readied serving as the final resting place for the soon to become marinated "melanzana." My grandfather was usually in charge of cleaning the husks from two to three dozen or so garlic bulbs after making sure that each jar was boiled and sanitized. Grandma and others were readying for the process of skinning the melanzana. When the skins were removed and the eggplants readied, they were sliced maybe a quarter inch thick and salted to get them to bleed out their sour juices. Someone was then assigned the task of cutting the banana peppers and removing their seeds. After the juices from the eggplants had begun to flow, my grandfather grabbed a handful of the slices while squeezing and twisting them in a wringing motion that was intended to remove all the excess sour water. Next the eggplant pieces were towel dried and a layer of them were placed at the bottom of the first jar above a thin layer of olive oil and a few sliced pieces of garlic. Next, on top of the first layer, more garlic was added followed by a layer of peppers placed on before a mixture of olive oil, vinegar, and oregano was poured over the top. This layering process continued until each of the jars were filled.

Finally, a clean cloth followed by a heavy rock to keep the mixture immersed in the protective oil, was placed on top before the lid was screwed on to the jar. The concoction was then stored for a few weeks in the fruit cellar while the vegetables completed marination. When the pepper and eggplant was ready to eat it was placed in salads, sandwiches (paninis) or on top of meat dishes. I have not had any marinated melanzana like the ones my grandparents prepared since their last jar was consumed, that is, decades ago. One day I will make my own marinated eggplant and hope it tastes at least close to the flavor I recall from those jars produced down the basement at the hands of Joseph and Mary. I use their names because the foods those two produced were considered almost sacred, godly.

Being personally attached to the wide-rimmed glass jars sounds strange but knowing how they were employed each year, part of our family's tradition, was personal to me. The jars were history. What used to hold a delicacy was now being readied for anonymous sale. Grandma continued to believe in the importance of those jars feeling their value and utility would somehow be recognized by someone in the auction crowd. Perhaps someone at the sale would see the jars and be reminded that they needed to marinate some eggplants and banana peppers down their basement. My grandmother and I both found the jars important but only one of us realized that their eggplant marinating days were over. Who would really want old wide rimmed jars and for what? Certainly no one would want them to marinate an eggplant. The days of marinating or even recognizing the vegetable was vanishing back then. For example, "What is this," said a teen checkout girls during one of our grocery shopping trips to a local grocery store. "Is it a turnip," she asked? Bah! Fortunately there has been a renaissance in the vegetable world with many people not only recognizing but also consuming eggplant. I am unaware, however, of anyone who marinates the purple veggie in the way my grandparents did.

Deep down I realized that no one would really care to buy the jars, objects that could easily be purchased at a yard sale for perhaps 50 cents for the whole group of them? The jars, almost members of our family, dating back to the days, the 1940s when my grandparents owned their Italian meat market, held sentimental value for us but no value at all to anyone else. Grandma and I both silently wished otherwise as it was tough seeing them end up perhaps trashed or recycled but what else was there to do with them. Recycling the jars was almost like taking your old sick dog to be euthanized. At least trying to sell the jars seemed more humane, perhaps giving them a second life, a new home. We kept our fingers crossed. Jars anyone?

Belly Flops At River View Swim Club

Each day was different as we grew up as many of us were engaged in our individual ethnicity while also trying to be "American" kids. As teens we spent most of our time chasing girls, trying to be cool, as well as, driving around town on the circuit with anyone who had room in their vehicle. While it was not foremost in our minds, our ethnic backgrounds helped build who we were becoming. For example, Anton and Guido, arrived from Italy, and had one foot in the American dream but were constantly reminded that they had an Italian culture to deal with when they arrived home. Rudy and Rafael might be driving in the green 59 Chevy but being Mexican-American guys they would be reminded of their ethnicity in certain situations, such as when it came to dating non-Latina girls. I never heard any of the guys complain much about racial or cultural issues and their resilience likely originated from the parental support and care they received. The rest of us may have complained about our cultural situations but without realizing it, our personal backgrounds were shaping our personality. For example, Luke often complained that his parents required him to attend weekly religious classes as well as Sunday worship at their orthodox church. Even though he disliked the Sunday obligation, steeped in his ethnic traditions, it must have had an effect on him. We were all surprised after graduation when he ultimately became an evangelical minister building a large church serving an even larger congregation. Decades later we would all be mesmerized while watching him, a guy who once carried a chain and a knife, deliver hypnotic weekly sermons on Cleveland TV. Surprise!

While there were negative issues related to race and ethnicity all around us most were outweighed by the positive experiences we all learned both from our relatives and also from each other. Perhaps most important was learning that people are more the same than different and that it really does not take that much to get along. Interacting cuts through the stereotypes relegating race as secondary or even a non-issue. We were all really lucky in the long run to be so immersed in ethnicity. Sometimes, however, those lessons were most difficult to understand as our teenage egocentrism got in the way. Thinking only of our own needs made it difficult to understand the feelings of others. For instance, while I wasted time bellyaching about life at home, I was learning valuable lessons that would positively shape my future. Due to my dissatisfaction with Dad and Hanna, for example, I continued to spend much of my time with my grandparents especially after engaging in some kind of argument or another with Hanna. While I complained, I benefitted immensely from all of my experiences, good and bad, even those from Hanna. For example, after dad's remarriage, even though Hanna and I often did not get along, I learned to appreciate the difficulties she faced growing up in WWII Germany. Hanna was lucky to be alive as fighting neared her home and her family often wondered where it would get their next meal. Her many stories highlighted the plight of the average German trying to lead a normal life as the government made horrific decisions. Hanna and her family endured many hardships and after her father died, she made the difficult decision, with her mother's encouragement to move away from Germany to the United States leaving family behind. Hanna joined her aunt and uncle who had already settled in our hometown. I enjoyed many good German meals cooked by Tante Erna who from the start seemed to accept me unconditionally into her family. I recall that she and my new uncle did not seem to care about my reputation for being a rather spoiled and out of control kid. In addition, as newly arrived citizens, Germans, after the war, Tante, Onki, Hanna and Jean had to endure much ethnic stereotyping and prejudice. They were sometimes taunted and criticized just for being Germans. Germany's past history of wars could sometimes haunt them in social and emotional ways. The bigotry they endured was something that I was not aware of as they never complained openly about their treatment. Instead they worked hard to prove that they were worthy to be Americans and assimilated into our multi-ethnic city.

Given my immersion in a multi-cultural environment it was no surprise that I would eventually marry a Japanese-American woman. It was as if it was destined from the start, Italian, German and then rounding it out, Japanese. When my wife and I married it seemed like a reunion of the Axis Powers since throughout the reception hall one could easily hear German, Italian, and Japanese languages spoken alongside English. However, instead of a WWII reunion party, all guests interacted peacefully and were happy as they celebrated our marriage. My wife and I were likely not the only ones who recognized the rather strange union of cultures that only a few decades earlier were united in fighting a horrendous war against our country and many countries thought Europe. Deb and I secretively kidded that the CIA and FBI, perhaps even J. Edgar Hoover himself, had strategically placed operatives in the bushes to monitor our wedding in case there were any international espionage issues that required their attention. Happily an enjoyable and harmonious time was had by all.

In my hometown, ethnicity was always a factor to celebrate. We were enveloped by it by both ethnicity and race. Growing up we thought everyone grew up surrounded by various cultures and that one's heritage was an important piece of life. However, as people generally got along in town there were inevitable instances when racism and bigotry got in the way of peace and harmony and that was considered unfortunate. There was, for instance, one time that our multi-cultural friendships hit a snag as racism reared its ugly head around us.

As teens, we did not harp on race other than to joke with one another over one thing or another. We tended to use old stereotypes of one sort or another kiddingly against each other just to joke around. We obviously had never heard of political correctness back then. Surely, we were aware that racism existed all around us, especially in the 60's, since demonstrations and riots over inequality were regular front-page stories. We mainly engaged in ethnic jokes poking fun of each other's nationality, Mexican, Italian, Puerto Rican, Hungarian, Black, Romanian, Polish, and others. Each of us likely knew of or experienced directly the negative effect of a racial or ethnic slur but they seemed to be infrequent. Among each other there was never a time when I remember that either race or ethnicity was used to enrage or settle an argument. It was never even considered as a variable.

There was, however, one memorable instance of racism that we all recall that could not be overlooked by any of us. The situation occurred at a local swimming club a few of us joined during the summer of 1967. Being young and egocentric our group paid little attention to political and/or current events. We knew everything about Diana Ross and the Supremes but very little about why guys were being sent to Vietnam. We were instead focused on fun and adventure. Americans may have been protesting the war, women were fighting for equal rights, and Blacks continued marching against racism, but we were mostly oblivious to national news caring mainly about music, sports, and females.

With that in mind, one summer, the summer we were matriculating into eleventh grade Mac, Luke, Corto, and I decided to join the River

View Swim Club. I still remember that it was only $75 per person to join for the whole summer. The summer we joined turned out to be much hotter and more humid than most Ohio summers so we got our money's worth by joining that year. River View, we surmised, would not only cool us off but hopefully also give us a beautiful tan, a healthy dose of fun, as well as, we hoped, exposure to girls.

The four of us spent as much of our free time as possible at the pool swimming, diving, and trying to impress the young women. We spent hours attempting to perfect the jackknife dive from the low board and complete a respectable double flip from the high board. When we were not trying to be a young Greg Louganis we were busy making the girls laugh by absorbing the pain from hotdogging belly flops and making everyone wet from our creative cannonballs. Luke, due to his height, was the master of the cannonball and usually soaked unsuspecting bystanders with each of his dives. This was also the summer of the Tommy Roe hit song, *Sweet Pea,* and Mac, being true to his sense of humor, developed a whole *Sweet Pea* dance routine that we would immediately jump into, almost like an early flash dance, when the song was played over the loudspeaker. Mac was always ahead of his time.

We messed around at the club and had a blast for much of the summer spending numerous hours out in the sun. We had a great time all through the hottest months of July and August and somehow managed to behave well enough to never be tossed out. We hung around with many of the same girls and guys we knew from school and also the bunch from Central Park. As summer was ending, a group of us composed an idea. We devised a plan to have a small pool party and invite some of our other friends who were not members of the swim club. Rudy, Galen, Rafael, and many others were invited and planned to attend. Our plan included gathering at the pool at around 4:00 in the afternoon for some swimming and general screwing around as we figured to pack some food and hang out until closing time, about 9:00 p.m. Our plans covered everything necessary for a good time, we believed, except one major issue was not imagined. Unfortunately, being mainly Caucasians doing the planning, we were oblivious to the one issue that should have been considered. That is, we did not contemplate and include the effect of racism and bigotry into our plans. We were therefore at first surprised when the plan began to unravel right before the party was to begin. Once we recognized the problem it was not at all foreign to us but there was no time for blaming ourselves. That is, we White kids were confronted firsthand with racism in a way that we had not experienced it before. We wagered it was the type of racism faced on a regular basis by many of our minority friends. Never contemplating how the management would perceive Latinos and Blacks entering the mainly Caucasian membership, we thought nothing of inviting our non-White friends to the party as our guests, and that soon became an issue that needed to be addressed.

While we were all standing in line ready to sign in our guests, and before they paid the entrance fee, the manager, all flustered, closed the gate and made a lame excuse for why our friends could not be admitted. I think he said something like there were already too many guests admitted that afternoon, their quota was reached, or some other ridiculous lie. All of us, but especially Rudy, clearly figured out right away what was happening especially as we looked around seeing the pool area only slightly populated. Rudy, usually quick tempered, was adept at moving from pleasant to infuriated before heading toward almost violent in just a few seconds. His Race-O-Meter was now beginning to move with the speed of light into the red zone after hearing the manager's fishy excuse and his seeming unwillingness to change his mind. We could almost see the steam coming from Rudy's ears. It was obvious that Rudy had experienced something like this type of excuse from White adults before and was super sensitive to how his ethnic background was devalued by select others. We all had to calm him down while we figured a plan or else we knew that real trouble would occur and then the focus would change from the manager's racism to our tempers.

Mac, Luke and I quickly had to come up with a solution before the afternoon was totally ruined. Furthermore, we were getting angry over the flagrant racism shown toward our friends and knew that our fuses were almost as limited as was Rudy's. We were uncharacteristically calm and diplomatic as we developed a plan which included pulling the manager aside and attempting to reason with him. Defusing the situation and continuing with the party as planned was our goal. We began by informing the fellow that these were our friends and that they should be allowed to enter just as all the "White" guests had before them. For extra measure, we also slipped in that we would call not only our parents, who knew important city officials but also the local newspaper that had recently been reporting on racial tensions within the city. It was pointed out that standing in line were guys and girls from all sections of the city therefore any sign of a snub due to race would surely be advertised throughout the entire town. After all this was the first summer after Dr. Martin Luther King, Jr., had been assassinated and racial tempers were still high. We were sure to mention that a story about a bigoted club manager in the all-White section of town could be just the headline the local press would latch on to as a means of accentuating its point. Our story was really a stretch of the truth because our parents did not know anyone in power nor did we know whether or not the newspaper cared about another racial inequality story, one that involved a group of teenagers. The manager being a hick from another city luckily did not know that we were simply bluffing.

In the end we were fortunate. The manager reconsidered his dictum and eventually let our friends enter, "But just this once" we remembered him saying. "Any sign of trouble and you will all be kicked out of here," he threatened. He was also quick to point out that there had better not be any monkey business or he would call the cops. That is when Mac told him sarcastically, that, "Oh don't worry, our parents only let us hang around with nonviolent Blacks and Latinos who follow all the White man's rules." I could tell the manager wanted to smash Mac but simply said he would keep an eye on all of us. The manager accentuated that he would be specifically watchful of the "hot-headed 'Puerto Rican' kid" who he already mistrusted. We ended up having a fantastic time that afternoon in spite of the manger keeping a watchful eye on Rudy, referred to as "the hot-headed Puerto Rican kid," who was really a hot-headed "Mexican-American kid." The manager did not know it but we saved him from getting his head ripped off by Rudy that afternoon. Our pals, unfortunately, would experience more racism over the years and due to that day at the club, the rest of our antennae were better tuned into racism's existence and how it negatively affected our friends.

Growing up in a multiracial and multicultural city provided us all with a living laboratory from which to learn about discrimination and bigotry. We were offered numerous opportunities while gaining valuable insight into how differing groups are stereotyped and how it effects social interactions. These were skills that may not have been so easily learned elsewhere. Without knowing it we were receiving a first-hand education concerning the inequalities that existed in our society and how those inequities hurt people. Growing up in a melting pot was a good thing for me, for us, something cherished and I will benefit from that life lesson until I die.

Marco Polo and Gene Carroll

Certainly, Italian culture and history were always forefront of our home. It is difficult to count the number of times that I heard my grandfather speak about famous Italians such as, Marconi, Leonardo da Vinci, Michelangelo, Marco Polo, and Enrico Fermi. Grandpa's list went on and on as he pounded the names of famous historical Italians into my head. My grandmother, on the other hand was more contemporary with her focus. She tended to be more interested in famous modern-day Italians especially those that were TV and movie entertainers. She and her friends enjoyed watching television and identifying people that they believed were Italian. For them it was almost a game as they wagered whether a particular entertainer was Italian or not. Marietta and her gang would sometimes compete with one another oftentimes getting into heated discussions over who was and was not Italian.

Grandma: "She's-a Italiano, no. See itsa Connie Stevens-za. Italiana, I'ma know dat for shoo (sure)."

Aunt Celina: "She's not Italian. Look at her blond hair."

Biagina: "Oh, she-Italiana all-a right. Dye'sa the hair, like-all da movie
stars-za. Muddyetta she'sa right dis-a time."

Aunt Celina: "No I think she's Swedish or maybe Polish. Can't be Italian. Her skin is white as snow."

Grandma: "You tink Italiana only dark-a skin. You see mine. Like-a mine, come la neva (like the snow). Whatsa matta yoo?"

Aunt Celina: "Maybe you are right. But maybe some Swedish blood too."

There was no Internet back then nor did the group pour over magazine gossip columns. They depended on the testimony of others, grapevine stuff, to get their information. It turned out that Granny was somewhat correct about Connie Stevens. She was one-half Italian/Sicilian, that is, Concetta Rosalie Ann Ingoglia, on her father's side and one quarter Irish and one quarter Jewish on her mother's side. Grandma and her friends would have loved knowing Ms. Stevens' true heritage. Italian, Irish, Jewish, Sicilian-that combination would have given them months of identity issues to discuss. I would have enjoyed knowing that Connie, like me, was also reared by her grandparents after her parents were divorced. Small world. Information acquisition was not so easy during the 50s and 60s being dependent on visits to the library, newspapers, from rumors, or from the TV itself. *The Lawrence Welk Show*, for instance accentuated ethnicity by openly identifying a person's heritage just before they either sang, danced or played an ethnic tune on their instrument.

Certainly, some entertainers were easy to identify, like Dean Martin, Frank Sinatra, and Tony Bennett. Those guys emphasized their Italian heritage plus they looked Italian. Others were not so easy, such as Jerry Vale, Connie Francis, and Frankie Laine because they did not say much about their background and their name did not end in a vowel. Grandma and her friends could only guess whether or not a star was a paisano and they enjoyed a good time arguing over their ability to scope out someone as being Italian or not. The women enjoyed the identification game. Aunt Celina, being Polish mainly listened while Grandma and her friends conjectured about who might be Italian. Sometimes, however, Celina fruitlessly chimed in if she disagreed or felt someone was perhaps Polish-American like her. Since she was outnumbered by the Italian matriarchs in the room, her comments were at best given a slight nod but usually she was simply ignored. The Italian women could not care less about who was Polish. They only wanted to know about Italians. There were other performers too, such as Madonna, "Weird Al" Yankovic or Frank Zappa who may have had Italian blood in their veins but they and their ilk were not appreciated by the friends of Ms. Marietta. People who they did not like or who they felt embarrassed their culture were usually considered non-Italian and their Italian heritage was either ignored or denied. "She-a no Italiano, no way. She-a just show off hur bosom-a, thatsa all," someone once remarked about the singer, Madonna. All the women thought it blasphemous that a woman flaunting her derriere would even consider calling herself Madonna in the first place. The ladies especially enjoyed Italian crooners and their numbers seemed to skyrocket back in the 50s and 60s. Singers, such as, Julius La Rossa or Sergio Franchi were family favorites. I suffered through endless debates regarding who they believed was Italian and who was clearly not. I cannot count the times I heard the story of how Perry Como worked as a barber in my hometown just before he hit it big on Broadway. The stories likely continue to this day.

Grandpa: "Jovy, Perry Como, he's Italiano. 'Taglia i capelli' (cut the hair) in-a da south part o town."

That is the story people, particularly Grandpa, would tell me each time Como was on TV as if I was being informed for the very first time. They would then mention someone they knew who got his hair cut by the crooner before Como became famous. Unfortunately, history was not on their side since the singer never cut hair in my hometown. Instead, he once sang before a crowd at a local downtown theatre the same place where my friends and I habitually flattened and subsequently threw our popcorn boxes through the air during matinees.

Another thing I heard each week was a result of a local Cleveland area variety show that aired each Sunday afternoon. The program was called *The Gene Carroll Show.* My grandparents and their friends enjoyed reminding me each week, when I was in junior high school, that if I practiced my trumpet enough, I too could be as famous as one of the kid stars who appeared regularly on the show. The teen's name was, Ray Sapishio, and, of course, he was Italian-American. Each Sunday young Ray, approximately my age, was highlighted as he played a classic Italian tune or two on his trumpet or maybe also sang some snappy ballad like, *You're Nobody Til Somebody Loves You.* I think every guy in town hated Ray because their parents compared us all to him. Every young Italian-American male in the viewing audience was considered a failure if he did not measure up to good old Ray. Once Ray made the scene the rest of us young guys were chopped liver. The elderly Italian women drooled over young Ray whom they considered a local prodigy. I was informed repeatedly by my grandparents, whose opinions were reinforced by their friends Biagina and even Polish Aunt Celina, that had I continued playing my trumpet just a little more I could have been right up on stage next to Ray. Without ever meeting the fellow I grew to dislike the guy. He, to me, was considered a traitor to boyhood as I and most of my friends defined it. Instead of throwing rocks through windows, stealing baseball cards from Goldberg's corner store, or ringing doorbells before running off like bandits, young Ray was singing, dancing, and trumpeting all over the TV screen. What was wrong with him, my friends and I repeated. Why can't he just be a regular kid like us? We hated everything about Ray, even his last name. Translated into English his last name meant, "tasty," and we all knew what taste he put in our mouths, "merda," or shit.

I learned to brush off the comparisons to Ray Sapishio and years went by without me giving him much thought. After marrying and beginning a life in upstate New York, my wife and I became friends with a new couple in town who like us moved out of Ohio and into the Finger Lakes region of New York State. Right from the start of our friendship, we enjoyed comparing notes about living in northern Ohio and as we talked we found out that they, like me, were both from an Italian heritage. One story led to another and we found many common experiences to laugh over. They smiled widely when I eventually brought up my memories surrounding *The Gene Carroll Show* zeroing in on my hatred for the smiling trumpet boy, Ray Sapishio. The couple could hardly contain themselves as they finally revealed what they were smiling about. They blurted out that my pain was nowhere near their pain. They further explained that I had nothing on them since Ray happened to our male friend's cousin. What a coincidence as I thought I suffered but could only imagine the family comparisons resulting from being related to the miniature Frank Sinatra wannabe.

We roared over the many likenesses between our families but especially the relationship with Ray the young Italian troubadour. What were the chances? Best of all, our new friends soon surprised me with a small gift on my first birthday after we discussed Ray S. The gift turned out to be one of the funniest and best gifts I ever received. I opened the present and was surprised. There I was, face-to-face with Ray when he was maybe 14-15 years old. The couple obtained a framed 8 X 10 glossy of their cousin and he signed and dedicated the print to me. It turned out that Ray still had a box full of his glossy's that he regularly mailed out to long-time fans. Old

Ray Sapishio was not such a bad guy after all as I was informed that he too had a good sense of humor over the whole situation. Turns out Ray was always aware of his reputation around the Cleveland TV viewing area and was not afraid of laughing a little at his former self. Serendipity, happenstance, fate? Funny, Ray was a good guy all along.

Rock and Roll

****

Hippie: “I just love Ed Sheeran. I just discovered him. Not sure where I have been. Seems like everyone else has heard of him too. I saw him on YouTube the other day. You know in that Carpool Karaoke thing with James Corden; I loved it.”

Stripes: “Right, know what you mean. I wish they would put a hologram of Elvis next to Corden, i n t ha t c a r i t wou ld r e a lly b e m y w i s ...”

By now I had lost track of my stroke speed on the rowing machine and when I gazed at the monitor in front of me I was surprisingly rowing at twice my usual rate. My trip down memory lane was having a positive effect on my exercise routine. I was on my way to burning twice the number of calories as usual and my heart rate was maxing out at above 120. Perhaps I should thank the two circling magpies for the day’s improved workout. I had to admit that their mention of Corden’s Carpool Karaoke with Ed Sheeran was a favorite of mine too.

Thinking that day about singers, Sinatra, Martin, and Elvis too, surely pushed my rowing rate above average. Those crooners from days gone by conjured up so many recollections, especially of my family. My grandparents enjoyed entertainment especially if the old tunes were sung by Italians. My grandfather, although, went nuts when the Beatles generation hit. Entertainers like Elvis made him crazy too and as if he was not upset enough with rock music in general, then the Beatles with their long hair came along. Gramps flipped out as the world as he knew it seemed on the brink of unraveling. Beatlemania began to surge and it almost sent him back to Tussio. Not only did they have long hair and play rock n roll but they were English, that is, a culture that he concluded was not European at all, not even its culture. Maybe if the Beatles were Italian or Greek Grandpa would have eased off the criticism and his doomsday attitude would have been somewhat blunted. Being from Great Britain as well was simply too much for Giuseppe to accept. Each time the likes of the Beatles, The Jackson 5, forget about Mick Jagger, were featured on *The Ed Sullivan Show,* Signore Pepine would scoff and restate his prediction that rock and roll would never last.

"You see, Jovy, they no gonna last this-a rock and a roll, bull-a shit you gonna see what I mean?"

Rock music to Zio Pepine marked the end, an apocalypse. Grandpa would get so worked up that his face would turn bright red as he rose from his black faux leather lounge chair and pretended to dance like the teens on Dick Clark's, *American Bandstand.* Joe began mimicking the gyrations of Elvis and others while raising his arms in disgust. My grandmother and her friends would get a kick out of my grandfather's attempt to copy the rock and rollers. Soon his complaining would be shouted down when some artist appeared whom the women enjoyed seeing on the 28-inch screen of our RCA TV. As stated, the women, like my grandfather, had little use for most rock singers unless they were Italian and not too controversial. Grandma and her buddies even waited for the likes of Frankie Avalon and Annette Funicello who were among their favorites despite my grandfather's negative opinion of them too, Italian or not. I could always count on my grandmother finally yelling at my grandfather's criticisms and incessant protests by loudly proclaiming:

"Pepino, siediti e state zitta, silenzio, shutuppa yu mozth," basically, sit down and shut up.

Grandpa would simply return to his black Lazy-Boy recliner, lean back, and snicker, self-confidently predicting and proclaiming the eventual collapse of the "Rock and Roll Era." "Shit, the rock an a roll itsa no gonna last," he would fret as Giuseppe would proclaim one last time. Self-confident and now reseated on his thrown, silenced temporarily by the queen and her court, Pepino felt he had safely reassured himself and society that soon his prognostication, that is, the death of the Rock Movement, would soon come to fruition. His prophecy would, as it turned out, never happen during his lifetime. His prediction was only a pipe dream and it would never vanish or disappear, unlike Chubby Checker's twist disappeared months earlier. Grandpa remained confident, until his last day on earth, that all he had to do was simply wait for the day that singers like Luciano Pavarotti and Tony Bennett reclaimed their rightful perch at the top of the music charts. Rock and roll scoundrels be damned, Grandpa Giuseppe had spoken and predicted their downfall. I think that if he had lived long enough to witness the rise of Hip Hop and the likes of The Notorious B.I.G., Tupac Shakur and god forbid, Eminem, their style of music would have sent him immediately into cardiac arrest and to an early grave. Giuseppe mostly was a quiet man but there were a few things that pulled his chain, such as rock music and republicans, for instance, and both did the trick. Otherwise, he was a peaceful guy who never hurt a fly and worked hard each day of his life.

The Parking Lot

Now poised on the other end of the music spectrum was my friend Anton who as I described was thrilled with Elvis from the very first time that he viewed him on TV. One of my last trips back to my hometown was to celebrate and witness firsthand one of Anton's performances as an Elvis Impersonator. For years Rudy, Mac, and others raved about Anton's part-time gig and we promised ourselves to someday attend one of his concerts together. While we shook our collective heads in amazement over his life's path, we were very much familiar with the origins of his choice. We were all right there, together as friends, from the very beginning when Anton was bitten by the Elvis bug. Therefore, when Mac organized a visit for all of us to attend one of Anton's performances we jumped at the opportunity. Due to Mac's persistence we somehow found ourselves, Mac, Rudy, Chase, and I together one more time in a car driving through our hometown on our way to an Anton performance. We had not been together in decades and were excited to have a good time planned ahead of us looking forward to finally viewing Anton impersonating Elvis. How many times can old friends claim a nostalgic trip back home to party together with other old pals? Making the trip to witness a friend impersonate Elvis, well that is simply special and almost too good to be true. So one day in October, around 2010 or so Mac kissed his lovely wife goodbye and we headed north to finally be in the audience of Anton the Elvis impersonator.

Anton was slated to perform at a local Knights of Columbus hall one evening in October 2014 so Mac called the guys and we all agreed to meet in our hometown. After picking up the boys, the four of us, Mac, Rudy, Chase, and I decided to drive around the city to catch up and wolf to each other about who we once were and who we had become. We did not want to be the first ones to arrive at the scheduled party as we used to enjoy the attention that we received in the good old days for being fashionably late. Why change things now? Besides, Mac telegraphed ahead informing the boys from the class of 1969 that the party was planned. Everyone from the old gang was invited. Word must have circulated quite well because as we entered the hall's parking lot there were only a few spaces left. As we turned into the lot and searched for a spot to park, Rudy soon recognized a familiar face and yelled out the window to the fellow walking toward the car. "Hey, buddies," the guy responded to Rudy's greeting and this automatically signaled me to stop. It did not take long for Rudy to begin shucking and jiving while asking the fellow all kinds of questions in the hometown vernacular I recalled using many decades earlier. I was now in the beginning stages of being transported back to my former self, that different person, who was not necessarily in shape for using the cool talking style from days gone by. The sound of the familiar chatter brought back memories of life from long ago. Rudy and this guy went on and on thumbing through their jobs and family and as they were talking I struggled to determine just who this familiar face was. Who was this guy that Rudy was speaking with in such an animated fashion?

While they conversed in the typical hometown form, I immediately recognized the jive as it had not changed much in decades. As they spoke, the fellow kept gazing back and forth from Rudy to me then back to Rudy. Rudy was carrying on as if this fellow and I were good friends but I had moved away after high school and none of us looked all as much as we did back then. As they spoke, this guy and I kept studying one another and while he seemed to recognize me I was busy searching his face for clues to his identity. Because Mac had notified the hometown crew that we would be attending the event this apparent old friend had the advantage of knowing that we were showing up but I was not as prepared as the face looking back at me through the window.

As Rudy kept talking I shook my head as if I understood what they were gabbing about, when suddenly Rudy mentioned something about wrestling in high school. That is when the alarm went off in my head and the face outside the car window was immediately recognized. It was G-Z who was the captain of the wrestling team and later the leader of a mock club we formed known as *The Gang*. He and I had not seen each other in over 45 years or so but once I knew who it was outside the car bells began ringing through my head and a big smile enveloped my face. G-Z was a guy we got to know quite well near the end of high school and he was one of the chief architects involved in the creation of one of the screwier things that we did as a group. That is, we started a second club that became known as, The Gang, and its sole purpose was to poke fun at our old club the Gents, as well as all the other clubs historically formed in the city, especially since those old organizations were fading away. The Gang was formed as a joke, sort of turning a sarcastic eye inward at ourselves. It was created during our senior year of high school about two years after we disbanded the Gents As I analyze it now, forming The Gang fit our script at the time as it also dovetailed well with our theme as friends. Creating The Gang, was simply another form of rebellion, our lifeblood while growing up, but at least this time it was meant to be humorous and would not get us into any trouble, or so we thought.

G-Z and I finally shook hands and I admitted not instantly recognizing him as we both laughed while silently reminiscing about our experiences together decades before. Meeting up with G-Z was like returning home to family. Just knowing we were kids together who shared so many common experiences brought forth feelings of satisfaction and contentment. The recognition between old friends was in a sense calming, and peaceful.

G-Z was a couple of years older than the group of us from the class of 1969. I got to know him initially when I joined the school's wrestling team as a sophomore. Where G-Z was an excellent wrestler I never won a match. More importantly, Mac became good friends with G-Z and another guy named Rico as they and Anton formed a band followed by the creation of the farcical club by the same name, *The Gang*. Somehow, someone, probably G-Z, and Rico, both possessing great senses of humor, came up with the lamebrain notion of forming the quasi-club and also naming it, *The Gang* as another way to have fun as well as to just screw around.

Eventually, the club began to develop stupid behaviors rather than steadfast rules with the behaviors mainly designed to set us apart by attempting to make everyone laugh. For instance, it became routine that each time a member of *The Gang* met up with another club member, especially in our high school hallway or places such as Yaya's Pizzeria, the members would loudly shout out in unison, THE GANG! At the same time, we would simultaneously make a fist while pumping our right arms high in the air. Sounds fairly infantile now but we had a chuckle each time we did it and we tended to yell it out every chance we got. The greeting likely elicited much disdain from adults within earshot of the ridiculous chant, especially teachers, but our friends realized we were just goofing off and had as much fun with it as we did.

Where the club was designed as a mockery, the band by the same name was meant to be serious. I recall that the members seemed to practice much more than performing in public but it gave the band a goal. The band probably helped launch Anton's career as an Elvis impersonator as well. Band practices were held in a member's basement, usually Rico's, often on weekends followed by everyone playing football. After the game drinking beer and getting loaded was the next order of business. I guess that there were times when football and beer drinking occurred simultaneously but then that was something else altogether.

The memory that holds members of *The Gang* the closest involves a sham hazing, a quasi-initiation for new members, that took place only one time. The pretend hazing was considered another farce and simply a means of having a good time. The night of the first and only initiation ceremony was memorable and was supposed to be for a good time rather than to ridicule and degrade members wishing to enter the club. A few new guys, Rudy, Dirk, and Chase, were to be initiated and become real "artificial" club members. We planned to gather at the home of a nerdy guy, Woiyme, who made the mistake of letting out the news that his parents were on vacation. After crashing the party at Woiyme's and drinking all his parents' alcohol, *The Gang* planned to meet on a hill behind a local nursing home for a formal, (informal) initiation.

Members of *The Gang* left the party at different times as they planned to meet later for the initiation. We found out the next day that Woiyme's house was left in shambles and that his parents were pretty angry when they arrived back home. Someone said a couple of guys drank too much at Woiyme's and for some reason went on a rampage destroying the living room but identifying the culprits is still open for debate. Someone mentioned that they thought one of the *Gang* members went a little nuts and decided to run through the living room wall but this has never been verified. I knew I had nothing to do with it, and no one in our group admitted to the damage, so we left it to Woiyme to figure it all out for himself.

All *Gang* members knew the fake initiation would begin on the hill at 10:00 p.m. that night. G-Z, Rico, and Anton had organized the ceremony and the only thing the rest of us knew was that it was going to be entertaining. Another situation we were not privy to until the next day occurred in the interim between leaving Woiyme's and showing up on the hill at 10:00 PM. A couple of our crew had gotten themselves so thoroughly plastered at Woiyme's that they decided to try to take a neighbor's car out for a joyride. It may have been the same duo that messed up Woiyme's but again no one knows for sure. While one of our messed-up pals pushed the car, the other, sitting in the driver's seat, attempted to get the car to start by popping the clutch. Due to their lack of car-stealing experience, as well as, their foggy coordination both succeeded only in ramming the car into a telephone pole before scurrying off.

Our two buddies, sober enough to flee the scene, soon joined the rest of us as planned on the hill overlooking a nursing home. Once all the guys had gathered, G-Z, dressed in a black hood and cape, with candles burning, began the ceremony. He and Anton also decked out in black and began behaving like silly and mysterious mystics while the bunch of us cracked jokes and prepared the new members for initiation.

We had only begun to laugh at some of the mock proceedings when suddenly, from out of nowhere, searchlights began to shine on us from seemingly every direction. It was like being in a prison break movie. At first, it appeared that the lights were part of the ceremony but we soon recognized that they were not a joke. These were real lights attached to real police cars. All I could envision was the old actor, Broderick Crawford from the 60s TV show, *Highway Patrol*, sitting in a nearby law enforcement vehicle waiting to snare the bunch of us while contemplating sending each guy off to Sing Sing

Penitentiary. More than likely either our noise or the neighbor whose car was smashed against the pole telephoned the police. Our mock hazing, designed to be a farce, had now gotten us into real trouble once again. Here we were up on a hill surrounded by the law while engaging in a stupid activity that no police officer would ever believe was occurring all in fun. Facing another run from the cops at this point seemed to be part of our DNA.

Our years of escape experience was called into action once again. We would need real luck extracting ourselves from this tight situation. Fortunately most of us knew just what to do. That is, nothing needed to be announced as we immediately scattered in every direction running like gazelles on the Serengeti. Getting away was the sole responsibility of each participant just as it was when we were Gents running from our ill-fated gang fight. Teamwork was not frowned upon but was usually considered impractical. Little did the police know it but they were trying to apprehend the high school quarterback, a couple of all-conference linebackers, two future principals, two future members of the clergy, a businessman, two wrestling champions, a future drug and alcohol counselor, and a guy destined to become an Elvis Presley impersonator. The police did not stand a chance, not with guys the likes of us who had many years of experience running away from the law. Our numerous close calls, honed smooth during our formative years, provided practice which was once again paying dividends. Dividends, yes, because not one of us was caught that evening. Luckily we all escaped capture one more time.

The chase by the police did have its costs. After hiding under a car in someone's garage for about 15 minutes, I began to run again when the police saw me walking home in front of the Catholic Church. As I ran I was soon clotheslined by a rope cordoning off some parking spaces behind the church. My neck was aching as I then neatly hid in a church dumpster before finding it safe enough to make the final trek home. Rudy ended up getting his butt bitten by a dog as he careened through backyards on his way to his home on 19th Street. Chase met up with Mac who got home only after crawling 50 yards through thick mud. Other guys had similar tales but we were all pleased that the cops came up empty-handed on that starry night of the now-famous, "Gang Bang 69--The Fake Initiation."

The next day, as each of us ran into one another, a much heartier, "THE GANG," chant erupted from our lungs. We had beaten Goliath, the law, and we were now somehow supercharged. Another mockery of a totally insane situation had been achieved. We were guys, young men now bonded more closely together having beaten the system once again. Yelling, "THE GANG," was our way of raising our middle fingers at those who would try to best us.

As I gazed out of that car window at G-Z that evening, in a matter of seconds the entire tale of our *Gang* initiation night lit up my synapses. Not only was I able to negotiate around my hometown in a car after more than 40 years of being away, but I was also able to re-visualize that night of the initiation. I was transported back seeing us as we were, just teens, slimmer and more vibrant. I could see the faces of who we once were standing under those intersecting spotlights as the police scanned the group of us on that godforsaken hill behind a rest home during the spring of 1969. G-Z and I did not really have to say anything more to one another once recognition was established. We did not need to say it aloud, the words were already ringing in our ears, "The Gang," those words from that wonderful night so many decades earlier. Those two words silently repeated between us said it all.

More Thoughts-Losses Begin

I was now back in my hometown with old friends and soon to be reunited with people I had not seen since I left in the 1970s. We were there to witness Anton's performance. Memories of past experiences buzzed through my head. There also existed a renewed closeness in my mind regarding my grandparents that I had not felt in years. Before I entered the car with the guys that night and drove toward the Knights of Columbus, I was also aware of all the people whom I would never see again. My grandparents, for example, who began to lose friends and relatives starting in the 70s. Prior to that, people's lives seemed to be stable and I thought people would live forever. But things like age and health creep along, unstoppable, and begin to take their toll. Sure Orlando had passed away but he likely experienced significant stress from being incarcerated. My uncle, Grandma's brother, Rudolpho, was one of the first to go. One day he was healthy and the next a diagnosis of lung cancer seemed to appear from nowhere. Smoking those Pall Mall cigarettes were judged as a contributor to his death. He was relatively young being only in his fifties when he died. Just a few weeks seemed to pass from the time he was diagnosed to his eventual death. The next one to go was Domenic Spolano, a heart attack got him but he was at least in his 60s when he died. Next was his wife Biagina about 7 years later. One by one people got older and no amount of red wine, olive oil, garlic or anything else associated with their Mediterranean diet was going to save them.

I think Feliciana Cappello was next. Before she died her husband, Joe, became legally blind, at least that is what was said. I remember that Joe kept in fairly good spirits during the years after his wife passed away and as his sight began to worsen, he handled it in stride.

Joe was a survivor making the best of both his loss of sight and life partner. Instead of complaining, Joe used his blindness to help cover for his sneaking peaks at women's behinds and the pocketing of small trinkets whenever he could safely snatch them. If caught Joe found a way to blame his poor eye sight for causing him to mistakenly put the item into his pocket. Who was going to challenge the judgement of a short, old, blinding guy? Joe's regular visits began to lessen after Feliciana died. Either my dad or a family member needed to pick him up and then deliver him back home in order for Joe to visit. When Joe spent time at our house he still packed along a bottle of his famous rot-gut wine, brought his hearty appetite, and continued to laugh at my grandfather's tales. That was not the case for some others, however. Tony Pisano, for example, went into a depression when his car keys were eventually taken from him as his ability to safely drive through the city became a problem. We never saw much of Tony once he lost his independence and could not drive. We missed his morning visits over coffee even though they seldom lasted for more than 10 minutes each day.

My grandparents did not say much about the loss of their friends but they were not foolish. They knew that they too were aging, especially my grandfather, a full decade older than his wife, Maria. They knew his time was limited and could only hope that the end would be quick without suffering. Health did become a concern for my grandfather starting in the early 1970s. His stories, the ones he continually repeated, were becoming an issue that could no longer be ignored or blamed on the ramblings of an old man. When his right hand began to shake and his repetition of stories seemed to increase we knew things were not right. The situation began to seem part of a syndrome. People pleaded for him to see a doctor but grandpa, like many old-world Italian men, was opposed to wasting good money on doctors. As the pressure to seek medical advice mounted, along with his symptoms, he finally relented. Unfortunately, Grandpa chose a doctor who would eventually be prosecuted for unethical behavior as he tended to prescribe whatever a patient wanted rather than what their health needs indicated. No one, however, disputed the conclusion that Grandpa was at a minimum suffering from Parkinson's Disease which was eventually diagnosed by a competent physician. When Pepino's strength began to fade and further medical problems arose, some type of cancer was suggested as an additional cause of his problems. The doc did not recommend anything except returning home to die rather than perish in the sterility of a hospital. Correct or not, that is how the family dealt with Grandpa's situation.

We received the call that Signore Giuseppe, Si Pepine, Grandpa, Joe, had died on November 22, 1976 at age 84. My wife and I were by then living in Morgantown, West Virginia. Grandpa lived a good life as he took a risk leaving his family back in Italy and setting out for what he hoped would be a better life in America. His risk paid off. Grandpa was so pleased to live long enough to see his dream for me come true. After graduating from, "the collegial school," as he always wished for me, I not only graduated once but twice earning a master's degree from the same institution. I was also pleased that Gramps lived long enough to see Deb and I married in 1975. I may have been a pain in the ass Italian prince growing up under his care but I at least did not squander his excellent advice. That is, I earned a good education and married a wonderful woman just as he always wanted for me to do. People were slipping away as I entered college, they continue to be missed today. I credit my family, my grandparents along with their colorful friends for heading me in the right direction.

Collegi-A School

Seeking a degree beyond high school was one of the best pieces of advice anyone ever gave me. Following my family's wishes I not only received an education but I also met the person who would become my wife during my first year at BGSU. That was in January 1970, a few years before my grandfather's death she and I began dating during the height of the Vietnam war. A friend of mine, Kathy, from where else, my hometown, made the introduction as we all gathered at what was called a beer blast, a big party designed to get first years students to interact and make friends. For me this tidy little social situation achieved its goal with dividends. Dee and I had both indulged quite heavily on the low-alcohol, 3.2% beer that Ohio allowed 18-year-olds to drink at the time. I was quite the gentleman walking Dee and her friend, Tracy, back to their dorm and asked if she would like to go out with me the following weekend. Dee accepted my invitation to go see a movie in Toledo even though admittedly the beer erased any memory of who I was and what I looked like. She was not desperate for a date but was the type of person then as well as now who fulfilled her promises. A friend of mine, Jim, owned a car so I arranged a date for him with Tracy and the four of us drove north to Toledo to see the movie, *Paint Your Wagon*. That was in mid-January, 1970 and our relationship continued into the spring.

During that spring term, Deb and I along with a bevy of friends sat out on the lawn under the sun between classes facing the administration building at BGSU while listening to speakers educate us about the immorality of the Vietnam War. It was the beginning of a new decade and we were out there along with hundreds of other hippy types as well as our opponents, the pro-war fraternity brothers, listening to numerous speakers convince us that the war needed to end as soon as possible. Each speaker was sporting the very latest and longest hair styles of the period. In addition to the long hair, I remember thinking that never was there gathered so much buckskin in Ohio or anywhere else except perhaps on the popular TV program of the day starring Fess Parker as Daniel Boone. We, my friends and I, felt that the war was wrong too and people, especially young men, many guys that we knew were fighting and dying needlessly in a small country in Southeast Asia. We did not start the anti-war protests, they had been going on for years, but protesting helped many of us feel as if we were doing something to end the bloodshed. As a result, my friends and I were out there that ill-fated day in May when our tidy little worlds met up with reality. We were out there on the lawn with all those other baby boomers, when a prediction was made.

I was walking with my hometown pal, a guy from my Harrison School days named, Kerry, when the news was blasted over the loudspeakers as we walked across the commons. I had totally forgot my cynical but accurate prognostication made during our short walk but Kerry reminded me years later that my prediction that day was unfortunately on point. When we heard through the loud speakers that the Ohio National Guard had shot four students dead at Kent State University I apparently blurted out, "I bet one of the kids is from our hometown." I was regrettably correct. We knew the guy too. A basketball player from the other side of the city, the other high school. We saw the fellow play basketball games against Bubbles, our high school's star player of the day. Now he was shot dead because he stopped to look at the hubbub down below. He was with another old friend who we also knew from elementary school. What a memory to add to your first-year college experience. How many experiences can a guy have coming from our little-known hometown? It was a sad day for all no matter where one hailed from but the war continued on for a few more years in spite of the tragedy. Many colleges hastily closed early that spring after Kent State and the students, protesters and all headed back to their hometowns, to the respective safe places. We left too along with the rest as a means to protect colleges from being burned down and maybe to protect more kids from being shot dead.

My future wife and I managed to travel safely home that spring. While still at BGSU, however, we marched a little more in protest of the Kent State deaths but that was about it. We were totally against the war but we had college to focus on. I was safe, protected from the war. My draft number was 244, too high to expect to be drafted into the army. So I could continue to study without worrying about fighting across the world. I had it easy mostly tending to hang with Dee and her roommates until graduation. Rudy, Anton, Mac, and my old pals were all scattered creating new lives and they were never drafted into the army either. At BGSU we, my new friends and I, socialized and successfully honed our psychology skills as we were mostly psychology majors. Our skills were placed into practice early by helping to keep one of Dee's roommates alive in spite of her numerous suicide attempts as she listened continuously to Joni Mitchell's albums. Joni's music, we found was good but sorrowful, not always upbeat, and thus not so good for depressives. We also studied together and soon realized that in order to get a job in psychology we would all have to go on to graduate school and some of us did. My wife and I, therefore, began looking at different graduate schools in different fields of psychology. Right from the start I thought that I would like to practice psychology in the schools. I had no knowledge that such a job existed until one of my psychology instructors suggested I see a professor in the education department who was believed to run a program that blended education with the practice of psychology. He indicated that the professor I should see was a fellow by the name of Ned Chalmers. At the time school psychology was a newer branch of psychology and was anchored inside of the university's education department.

I made an appointment to see Professor Chalmers and it was set for us to meet in his office. The education building was a contemporary building on campus at the time and was composed of a series of 6 square floors that all looked the same. Offices were honeycombed rooms of equal size and similar appearance arranged both on the interior and exterior walls of the building. I recall that after some searching I finally found Ned's office on the fourth floor.

When I arrived at the designated office I noticed that the door was slightly ajar. As I looked in I noticed a slightly built fellow bent over a desk while shoving papers here and there. The person I saw had a rather long pony tail and a pitiful looking scraggly beard, the kind that leaves open blotches of skin on the face where no hair seems to grow. It appeared that his beard was the result of attempting to shave in the dark while drunk. The little man I was observing also wore a tattered green army jacket that was all the rage in those days, especially among the non-combative hippy types. The wearing of army coats, I suppose, was designed to symbolize opposition to the war. As I gazed into the room I felt like the parents in, *The Night Before Christmas,* as they peered into the living room and attempted to describe Santa Claus.

As I continued looking into the office, I thought this must be a graduate student or perhaps a burglar rummaging through the professor's possessions. Not knowing what to do, I knocked and asked the long-haired gentleman if he could tell me where I could find Professor Chalmers. His response was, "Come on in, I'm Ned,

Ned Chalmers." At this point, I noted to myself, "This program could prove to be super interesting."

After some small talk Ned began to explain the school psychology program to me in a calm straight forward way using all the appropriate slang of the day, such as, "Far out," or "Right on," and "Dudes," and everyone's favorite, "Out Of Sight." Disregarding the slang, I became immediately struck by the points he communicated about public schools, psychology, children and how the professions of education and psychology intersected to not only help educate youngsters but also to help all kids feel included. He emphasized the need for children with disabilities to receive an improved education something that was just beginning to emerge in the 1970s. After speaking with Ned I knew that the school psychology program was the course of study for me. I quickly concluded that I needed to do everything, find a way to make sure that I was somehow admitted into Ned's program.

During our discussion, Ned asked about my grades and course work but was most interested in my experience volunteering at a 24-hour drug drop-in center, complete with a phone-in hotline that was located close to campus. The phone drop-in center was called Karma. From his appearance, it was not difficult to conclude that anything having to do with drugs would interest this fellow.

Again, I was at the right place at the right time. Karma was created my sophomore year at BGSU by one of the college's psychology professors who advertised the program's need for volunteer counselors during one of our classes. The hotline, he said, was looking for volunteers to answer the phone and help assist with drug-related walk-ins. Fortunately, I volunteered, received training, and worked there for two years. I worked alongside hippies and local freaks many of whom had first-hand experience with every drug that circulated during the era. My little foray with Dexi's on the way to the college with Rudy and Chase was child's play compared to the experiences of the clientele and my colleagues at Karma.

Shifts at Karma varied. Mostly my job was to answer hotline questions and make walk-ins feel comfortable. Working during daylight was usually uneventful but the all-night shifts, especially on weekends, were filled with excitement. They often included walking overdosed characters up and down the sidewalk in front of the house making sure to keep them lucid enough so they would not expire. Using this particular maneuver has been replaced nowadays with hospitalization of overdosed, drugged out, and unconscious drunk students. In the early 70's doing crazy stunts like handling the situation ourselves was common at the local neighborhood 24-hour drug help center. We did not know it but our do-it-yourself approach made us early pioneers in keeping health costs low. Who knew or even considered that our efforts were sacrificing the safety of our clients and setting ourselves up for potential liability suits? In those days we felt we knew it all and had control over every situation. Karma volunteers were certainly taking huge risks, however, liability suits must have been a lesser consideration in those days. Besides, we were college students who had all the answers. Lawsuits and lawyers would not have scared us from completing our mission. We at Karma were probably fortunate since our decisions were never challenged and to my knowledge, no one died under our supervision.

While at Karma, I met most members of the area's drug aristocracy. For instance, I became friends with a local guy who lost his leg in Vietnam. Before Vietnam, he was a hometown athletic legend. Losing a leg in Vietnam left him with only the legend as he returned home with few options. After using drugs and feeling sorry for himself for a couple of years, Zero, as he liked to be called, decided to focus his attention on assisting those who abused substances or used them naively. In the early 70s, this population, experienced ex-drug abusers, was in great supply not only in Bowling Green but on most college campuses.

I will never forget one experience I had with Zero. Zero's car was in the shop for repairs and he needed a ride to pick it up so I volunteered to drive him. Zero was a rather large overweight guy with long stringy hair and a well-developed curly brown beard. His appearance represented how every countercultural guy of the times wanted to appear, except for the prothesis, of course. In addition to wearing a large brimmed hat and well-worn African Dashiki shirt, he often wore heavy black boots designed to help stabilize his metal leg. To situate himself in the front seat of a car Zero needed to swing his heavy metal left leg over as he entered and sat down. His practice was to first sit on the seat then swing his missing leg over and into position as he maneuvered himself into place.

On this day I was borrowing my friend Johnny Boy's Dodge Duster complete with a white racing stripe across the hood. As Zero swung into the passenger seat, something unfamiliar to him as he usually was driving, a little mistake was made. While swinging left into place his huge metal leg accidentally came down heavily on the glove box, making a huge bang as he finally sat down. As I looked over at Zero to see what caused the bang I noticed that his heavy prosthesis crushed the glove box denting it sufficiently enough that it no longer could be opened. "Oops," was all Zero had to say as I placed Johnny Boy's souped-up metallic green Duster into reverse and drove Zero to the service station. Johnny Boy was not at all pleased with the way I returned the car but I figured he was not going to bill a guy for repair money who had been shot up in the war and possessed a steel leg. The dent did make a good story to tell when Johnny Boy went out on an occasional date in his otherwise pristine 1970 Dodge Duster.

At Karma, I also became familiar with the college's local antiwar icon who enjoyed great fame, although fleetingly, while still a student on campus. Sal Teleferio was credited with organizing numerous marches, protests, and occasional college shutdowns. When he was not leading marchers during "sit-ins," designed to obstruct foot traffic into the university's administration building, one could usually find Sal burning flags or draft cards while surrounded by a bevy of similarly minded braless and rebellious hipster women.

Sal often frequented Karma, mostly showing up in the middle of the night after he had toked a little too much of some illegal substance and needed a place to crash before he carried out his next antiwar rebellion. We were all so proud when Salvatore, known locally as The Floater, turned up at Karma. He usually arrived at Karma with an entourage of starry-eyed female followers looking for some R & R after one of his lengthy substance-abusing forays. We were kookie for worshiping such a rebel but we were young and naive ourselves and similarly hated the war. By honoring Sal, many followers felt they were contributing at least something toward the antiwar movement without having to risk being sprayed with tear gas, billy clubbed, or hauled off to jail. We also enjoyed the antics of his female friends who were never shy about displaying too much of their bodies as they sat or laid way too casually while making themselves at home on the dusty *Karma* furniture.

At Karma, time during day shifts moved slowly and was most often boring. Out of this boredom, I began spending the majority of my time doing homework while listening to Cat Stevens who I had newly discovered. Listening to Cat Stevens music was an epiphany for me. His lyrics woke me up to the revolution that was happening all around our country. In high school our thoughts were on other less political things. Now in college, during the Vietnam War era, I was becoming, like so many of my peers, cynical politically about the world and American culture including many of its inequalities. We tried but deluded ourselves into thinking that we would change the country making all people safe, free, and equal.

As I lounged on the second-hand furniture, newly donated to the center, I listened, over and over, to Cat's album, *Teaser and the Firecat*, while contemplating where our world was heading. Karma helped me become the typical college student of the sixties. I daydreamed about the social rebellions going on around me and whether wars would ever cease occurring. Like many other college students I began to believe that the youth movement of the sixties could not only stop wars but also cure most of the world's other social problems such as racism and sexism. These were the early days of the "isms" and we were ever so optimistic about the prospects for change. Being part of Karma was going to be my contribution to world peace and equality and I intended to adopt the music from *Teaser and the Firecat* as my anthem. If anyone walked through the doors at Karma while I was on duty they were immediately greeted by *Morning Has Broken*, *The Wind*, *Peace Train* and all the other wonderful songs on that now classic album. Cat Stevens did not know it but he was becoming my secret mentor and like so many of my generation I was searching for the meaning of life through his music.

Karma was a magnet for all types of loonies and maybe I was one of them too but working there turned out to be a wise decision. In September 1973, thanks partially to Karma, Ned Chalmers welcomed me into his school psychology program at BGSU. Certainly, my grades and interview alone would not have qualified me for entrance into Ned's program, I concluded, so it must have been my quasi-hippy appearance and my volunteering at Karma that served as the deciding factors.

My future wife decided on a somewhat different route to further her education. Deb applied and was subsequently admitted to West Virginia University hoping to earn a Ph.D. in developmental psychology. I still vividly remember the day her parents and I dropped her off, all by herself in Morgantown. As we headed back to Ohio, neither her parent nor I said the obvious, that we were worried about leaving her to fend for herself miles away from home. Not yet married, Deb and I were hoping it would all work out, that our relationship would survive given the miles that separated us. We did not know it at the time but things would turn out just fine.

Meanwhile, I remained at Bowling Green, six hours from Morgantown. My friend Johnny Boy, who decided to return to college, and I found an apartment right next to the railroad tracks and for four academic quarters we roomed together. A requirement for certification as a school psychologist included a one-year internship after successfully completing the classroom curriculum. So another fellow, a member of our school psychology class, Geoff and I were the first, sort of pioneers, to accept an internship placement in Richland County, Ohio the county schools surrounding Mansfield. Geoff had recently returned from Vietnam earning the rank of captain after just two years of duty. Geoff and I had become good friends our first year of grad school while taking classes designed to prepare us for the internship.

We began our internship in August 1974 and simply by chance we were assigned a supervisor who hailed from guess where, yes, my hometown? It seemed that no matter where I ended up my hometown somehow followed along with me. Coincidentally, when I was a high school sophomore my new supervisor's younger brother, Robbie, two years older than me, played quarterback on our high school team. Robbie was the same guy who years earlier threw the pass that indirectly broke Rudy's collar bone. If I had cut through the backyards of our home on 21st Street, I would have been right at his house. Small world I thought at the time because my hometown was situated approximately two hours away from Mansfield, Ohio.

Cal, our new supervisor was about 32 years old and Geoff was 30 with me being just 24 at the time. Both of these guys were married and for the year I spent in Mansfield we had great times working and hanging out together. Geoff was a good mentor to me, often better than Cal. This was especially true because Geoff had natural leadership and social skills perhaps fine-tuned from his rank as captain in Vietnam.

We were happy with our internship in Mansfield especially since Cal pretty much left us alone. He did expect us to eat dinner at his house once a week and play touch football in his back yard and we had no problem with those requirements. Cal was a good guy and he and his wife helped us assimilate into the community and our new positions. One of the ways this was accomplished was to also require us to watch Ohio State football games on select Saturday afternoons at his place. These were the days of Archie Griffin and Coach Woody Hayes so viewing the games together was something we really enjoyed.

My year in Mansfield is a distant memory but one I look back on with fondness. Becoming a school psychologist was a dream for me and without realizing it the role put me, once again, in the right place at the right time. I had lucked into a profession that would be in high demand and allow me to easily find future work wherever I moved. Geoff and his wife especially took good care of me during my time in Mansfield and I often silently thank them both for their generosity. In addition, Geoff remains a good friend today but unfortunately his wife passed away just a short while back. He lives across the country so we unfortunately seldom get together while Cal died about 15 years ago from a heart attack.

During my time in graduate school Deb and I made sure we saw each other once or twice per month with her driving to see me followed by me driving to stay with her in Morgantown. On free weekends, I was close enough to my family that very often I would drive the two hours back home. By this time my relationship with Hanna had deteriorated to the point whereby I stayed with my grandparents when I drove to visit family. I visited with Dad and Hanna and we were cordial, but it was simply easier on everyone if she and I spent less time interacting. We were basically in peace treaty mode during those years.

Those frequent family visits enabled me to keep up with my grandparents' schedule, basically the same one that they had been following for years. Both remained busy gardening, canning, and cooking. I was able to help out every so often as they were visibly growing older and I was becoming less of an Italian prince. I helped them a little as well with things such as turning the mattresses and changing the linens for their boarders. There were even a few times that they trusted me enough to paint or fix a broken window, tasks they never would have asked me to perform when my grandfather was healthy. While they trusted me to perform a few menial tasks I was continually reminded that my work quality was still not up to their standards. For instance, I clearly recall a time I was trusted to paint two rocks white. The rocks were placed on the side of the driveway so people did not run over the grass. I thought my painting was satisfactorily completed so I cleaned the brushes and put away the paint. A few hours afterwards, however, I saw my grandfather out touching up my work. Marietta had assessed my work quality while I was cleaning up and decided that there were spots on the rocks that did not receive enough white paint so Giuseppe was sent out to finish the job I started. My grandparents prepared me for college but obviously my blue-collar skills were still considered substandard, even faulty. Now each time I see one of those white painted rocks serving as barriers on the side of someone's driveway I am reminded of my grandparents and I simply break out into a smile.

By this time, Grand-pop's health was beginning to really deteriorate as his hand shaking was visibly increasing (it should be noted that even with a shaking hand he could paint the rock better than me). He never complained much over the hand shaking except when it came to feeding himself. So while my home maintenance skills were not that good I sometimes helped in other ways, sometimes in silent ways. For example, most of my old friends went off to college, seminary, or the armed services and they additionally managed to pull themselves out of the trouble making business after high school. There were, of course, some exceptions. One of them was a guy named Butch who was an old friend. Butch turned to abusing drugs after the rest of us scattered as he continued down a negative path. Butch apparently traded our group for a really messed up bunch of addicts, guys that were really going nowhere. The last time I saw him was when I was working at a local department store during my undergraduate years. Butch and a couple of his sketchy friends entered the store, Economy Sales, together all wearing their coats draped over one shoulder. Apparently they must have believed no one would find their shady appearance unusual. Our manager figured immediately that something was up and asked me if I knew the group of vagabonds snooping all through the store. Responding affirmatively I then excused myself so I could go talk with Butch and his group of stooges.

I confronted old Butch by the electric blenders, not much high tech in those days, and told him that he and his friendly knuckleheads needed to leave, pronto sans the stolen merchandise they had already tucked under their coats. Butch said he forgot I worked in the store and apologized. He and his cronies, fortunately, complied with my request. That was the last time I saw old Butch. I informed the boss that if they came in again to call the police.

The next time I heard about Butch was a couple of years later after beginning graduate school. My father called me and said that my grandmother had rented a room to a guy who informed her that he was an old friend of mine. Sure enough, it was Butch. Without elaborating I calmly asked my dad to tell Butch that we spoke and I would consider it a personal favor if he respected my grandparents while he lived under their roof. This was code for "better not mess up or someone's ass would be whooped." Butch knew I had a temper since he was with us the day I lifted the Yaya's Pizzeria employee up against the wall. He knew I meant business and I did. Fortunately, Butch moved from my grandmother's house a couple weeks later without paying his rent but I considered that nothing in comparison to what could have happened. A guy never knows how he can be of assistance but small towns lend themselves to things of this sort of personal stuff.

Another time that I assisted my grandmother was simply through asking Rudy to check in on them when they had a little plumbing emergency. Rudy easily fixed the problem and they subsequently hired him to paint their entire basement. Rudy was not only paid for the painting but each evening he was sent home with enough food to feed his growing family. Grandma, in her broken English, always referred to Rudy as "Ruby." My pal laughingly told me that the only person in the world he would ever allow to call him Ruby was Grandma Mary.

That was life immediately after high school. Friends entered and some friends left as new friends were made. I was among the lucky ones and as I matured the effects my family had on my life became much clearer.

The Grand Entrance

****

"I remember so much about my childhood as if it were yesterday," remarked Stripes as the women were about to invade my consciousness once again.

"Me too," responded Hipster. "No worries just fun, carefree. If we only knew t h e n w h a t w e k n o w n...,"

Save your memories, dialing them up later in life can provide great joy. Fifty years later they are still mine.

With the car safely parked in the crowded lot, having said to G-Z we would see him inside, the four of us got out and walked into the Knights of Columbus. We would soon be enjoying a night of nostalgia and storytelling with old friends. Here I was, only a few blocks from where I played football, not very far from the church where my grandfather prayed and right next door to a bowling alley where Johnny Boy, Mac, and I often headed to play pool on Saturday nights. For me, walking through the door of the Knights of Columbus, it felt as if I had entered a time warp. Leaning against the bar and standing about with drinks in their hands, were the faces of many people that I knew decades earlier. Only now, however, my old schoolmates were shaped in appearance more like our parents than us. Who had we become I asked myself?

The first person we stopped to converse with was a guy who was a star football player at our high school when we were still in junior high school. Rudy introduced me to the fellow and I mentioned that

I recognized his name from school and was glad to finally meet him. I barely got the words out of my mouth before I began being pulled aside by countless others who I had not seen in years. I found myself smiling and sometimes waiting for the chance to whisper a question to Dirk, who arrived before us, asking him who I was speaking with since the face was not the same as in high school. Dirk even got the chance to get something off his chest that he had kept a secret since our days as Gents That is, one of the first things Dirk asked me, seeing him for the first time in years, was whether I recalled that he, Rudy and I secretively split the club treasury after the Gents disbanded. I had to admit that I had forgotten all about this little sneaky transgression. What I did not know, until Dirk confessed, was that he kept even more money from the treasury for himself never informing either Rudy or me of its existence. He kept over a hundred dollars that the rest of us had forgotten about. I guess Dirk figured the statute of limitations had run out thus allowing him to confess his crime. We had a big laugh over the confession and I thanked Dirk for reminding me of yet another crafty situation to be ashamed of now that I spent my career as an educator preaching to children about the values of honesty and fairness. I did a quick calculation and told Dirk he owed us, maybe, $495 compounding interest at 4% for forty years or more. He just smiled. Here was something I had forgotten and even though I was not proud of my part in the scheme I still treasured its memory. I was beginning to get dizzy from shaking my head in disbelief over all the crazy and dishonest things we had done as kids. It seemed as if I was doing a post mortem of my life while still living.

At one point during my conversations with Dirk I looked across the room and immediately saw someone who had not changed very much at all. It was Rafael's older brother, Paz, who was there with his wife who I had never met. I had not seen Paz since 1969 and could easily picture him driving us around in his white Ford convertible with the red faux leather seats. Just as Paz introduced me to his wife, Rudy came up from behind and grabbed him. Rudy found it easy to segue into the story regarding the night he fell off the back of Paz's car and ended up in the emergency room with, luckily, only a concussion. Rudy reminded all within earshot how the hospital called the police and how difficult it was to convince them that Rudy's injuries were only due to an accident, no foul play was involved as the cops likely surmised.

I immediately remembered that cool spring night. We had just finished a little partying and showing off in front of our female friends and the group was disbanding for the evening. As we walked outside, there was Paz driving by looking for us and looking for something to do. He stopped the car in the middle of the deserted street while we all ran up to the car asking him to drive us around town to find something to eat and another spot to hang out. Paz indicated that he could only take a few guys with him since he was with another friend, named Cheech, leaving room in the car for only four of us.

One thing led to another and as was customary Paz decided to be cute while we jockeyed for who would get to ride. His cuteness consisted of stepping on the gas each time a guy tried to open the door and get in. This went on a few times before Rudy got the wise idea of jumping on the car's trunk to make the rest of us laugh and to force Paz to stop playing and let some of us get in. It must have been that Paz did not notice Rudy sitting on the trunk because he decided suddenly to floor the gas pedal laying down rubber before squealing away.

Unfortunately, Rudy held on for about 25 feet before he came tumbling off the trunk of the car landing on his head as he rolled to the middle of the road. Rudy hit his head hard on the pavement and was laying on the concrete shaking as if he was convulsing. After a few minutes he fortunately regained consciousness so we placed him in the backseat of Paz's car and off we sped to the hospital.

Rudy's parents were immediately called, and the hospital must have reported the mishap to the police as we had to explain another one of our nutty situations to the authorities. It is mind blowing the number of stories some parents have to endure about their kids. Rudy's father and mother withstood a lot as did the parents of most of our crowd.

Rudy ended up with a mild concussion that night and it took all of us pitching in to convince the police that the whole matter was just an accident. We agreed to allow Rudy to take the blame for his mistake leaving Paz out of it as best we could so he did not face some traffic violation. The police eventually believed our story making this event, like many others, an experience, another one that represented a narrow escape. The rest is history. We were really scared for Rudy but luckily he had a hard head and things eventually turned out all right. We dodged another disaster with only a resulting concussion while adding one wackier story to tell our grandchildren.

Almost on cue an old girlfriend of mine, Katie, wandered up to join in on the story. Her appearance could not have been timelier since Rudy's mishap on the trunk of Paz' car occurred right on the street in front of her house. It was her basement where we had holed up that evening before venturing out only to meet up with Paz and Cheech. Katie and I were an item in high school breaking up and going back together seemingly all the time. She and her friends and the group of us hung out an awful lot down her basement flirting and showing off. As we spoke, Katie reminded me that she recently met my stepsister at a baby shower. The two of them enjoyed comparing notes on me with my stepsister admitting, "I always wondered who my brother was visiting back then as he cut through the yards over to the next street. Now that mystery has finally been solved," she said.

Katie, it turns out, remained good friends with Rudy's spouse Mary Lynn all these years and like so many at the party was now a grandparent. She was just as beautiful that night as I remembered her to be many years earlier. Katie indicated she had no regrets about how her life had turned out as she remained married all these years raising two successful children in our hometown. That did not stop me from kidding her by saying, "Who knows what would have happened had I not decided to go off to BGSU." We laughed and it was just good to have the chance to fill in the blanks and catch up on our lives.

Seeing Katie and all the others was wonderful. Stories about the Gents. football, old relationships and life after high school dominated the conversations. Missing were pretenses replaced now by genuine caring, renewal, and just real happiness. All were interested in honest listening to the life stories shared among former school chums. I could feel the nostalgia filling the room among so many old pals who had one more moment of time to share with one another. It was proving to be a spectacular night and the party had just begun.

Then, all of a sudden, Mac grabbed me breaking us free from the group of high school pals. He maneuvered us into an outside courtyard and there seated with a group of friends was Anton. I had not seen him since high school and the first thought that came to my mind was that he had not physically changed a bit since we were kids. He remained as I remembered him, tall, slender, full head of black hair and, as I would soon witness, as hyperactive as the first time we met. The only thing missing was his checkered pants. He was still wearing pointed Italian shoes, that part had not changed, but they were unlikely the same pair he wore when he entered my second-grade classroom many years before.

We embraced and after a few uncomfortable cliches we were right back to being pals, just kids hanging around 18th Street throwing rocks while trying to dislodge ripe buckeyes from their branches. We then repeated some of Anton's now famous phrases, such as, "Two bucks a fifty," and a few others. We often kidded Anton in good fun about the way he pronounced words and phrases as he learned English as a kid and some of his phrases became legends. He then tied one of his statements to the phrase, "Should we help im?" This sentence, only meaningful to Anton and me, were words that were etched in our minds many years earlier.

It was a hot Saturday morning in the summer, maybe 1960 or 61 and we were on Anton's front porch wondering how to spend the day. Suddenly the quiet of the morning was interrupted when a little boy across the street lost control of his bike and crashed into a telephone pole. He quickly fell over and got tangled in the bike's spokes and handlebars. As the first traces of a bloody nose became evident and it appeared that his anguished cries would not summon his parents, Anton turned to me and asked the now famous question, "Should we help im?" Almost fifty years later we still remembered the ridiculous question. Of course we were going to help the little boy but something about the way Anton had to ask, in his Italian accent, if we would perform the obvious, was an experience we would never forget. It made us laugh then and we laughed again that night at the party.

We recalled a few more memories before Anton suddenly excused himself. In perfect Anton style, while in mid-sentence, he simply jumped up and vanished. It only took a minute before I realized that Anton had to go back stage and morph into Elvis. Soon the lights dimmed and the curtains opened and as I gazed toward the familiar voice coming from the stage there he was, Anton, up at the microphone looking more like Elvis than Elvis. Standing nearby were a few of our other buddies, Jaime, the guy with the only remaining Gents jacket, and a guy named Mikey, both serving as bodyguards since it turns out that even Elvis impersonators need protection from overzealous female admirers.

Seeing Mikey seemed so strange too having not seen him since we were teens. Mikey, when we were kids had one of the finest powder blue 1964 Mercury Comets. He was a few years older than us, good looking and a regular babe magnet. Riding along in his souped-up auto was a cherished event making us always feel like such big deals. Upon seeing Mikey that night, Mac was quick to recall how Mikey would introduce himself to attractive girls. Mikey would walk up with a smoke hanging from his lips, as if he were Humphrey Bogart or something, and say something like, "Hello, I'm Mikey and who might you be?" We laughed and a chill went up my spine as if it was 1969 and I was witnessing his flirtatious introduction for the very first time.

As Anton, or should I say, Elvis began to play, the first song sung was apt, "Jailhouse Rock." It took 50 years or so but here I was full circle watching Anton performing in the role of the musician he loved so much as we grew up watching the real Elvis perform on,

The Ed Sullivan Show. I was certainly pleased to not only finally see Anton perform but was quite impressed with both his style and showmanship. It was easy to see why his Elvis "career" was so successful

Anton sang a few more pieces before the night was over and I could not help thinking back to that night sitting on his living room floor with all the family and friends gathered around anticipating Elvis' TV performance. Sadly, most of those folks sitting in that room were no longer alive including "The King" himself. I also had an immediate vision of my grandfather rising from his La-Z-Boy chair and angrily emulating Elvis making all of Grandma's friends break out in laughter. Elvis may have been hated by my grandfather but he remained loved and alive in Anton that night at the Knights of Columbus Hall and that was priceless. Some things change while others remain the same as friendship and Elvis somehow merged in the past as two guys became amigos many decades earlier. Who knew it would last so long?

As the group of us greeted more old buddies and Anton completed his act, we all got a chance to reminisce over old times together. We kept digging up memory after memory as we spoke about our youth. Anton and I could not help ourselves from recalling the way we were welcomed at each other's homes and especially the way he was fed by my grandmother. We enjoyed recalling stories about all the food he could consume as my grandmother was in heaven shoveling more and more pasta on to his plate. I remembered wondering at the time who would tire first, Anton from eating or my grandmother from serving. We, of course, also spoke about the many games and dirty tricks we played on each other joined in by his younger brother, Guido. He asked if I "revembered," all the times we played hide-and-go-seek down his darkened basement and how Guido and I would whack him with his mother's polenta paddle. I use the word, "Revembered," because it is another one of the many mispronunciations Anton regularly produced due to his Italian accent as we continually busted him over his diction. Anton got used to our joke as guys like Mac would surely mention each messed up word or phrase almost every time that we met up both then and now.

Here we were, Anton and almost the whole group of us together in the same space again after years of being apart. Finally, we witnessed Anton on stage appearing as Elvis and sharing our stories from long ago. It was almost too emotional to handle. We had all changed physically but the stories remained the same. The group of us, old Gents, old Gang members or simply old friends were continuing to age and with each year the tales had a way of becoming more precious. What could be more fun?

Full Speed in Reverse

Book pages are littered with the recollections of those who attend their high school reunions or any major event with old friends. Why not? When emotions are high everyone feels like a poet. From meeting up with Anton and watching him impersonate Elvis to reconnecting with Dirk and listening to his confession about pocketing the remainder of the *Gent's* treasury, it was easy to see why so many writers feel compelled to write about their reunions.

The stories continued to flow at the Knights Hall for the remainder of the evening. Nothing was more wonderful than knowing that the stories, our memoirs survived. It soon got late and people began hugging as pictures of family members were wagged about and promises to remain in touch surfaced. "If ever in Boston," or "Nashville," or "Phoenix," to name just a few of the places that some of us replaced for our hometown. People were excited wishing to extend the good time by inviting each other over for a visit. Anton even invited me over to his house sometime for a polenta dinner and a nostalgic game of Scopa. He forcefully indicated, however, that he was not going to withstand any more whacks from the polenta paddle. He kiddingly claimed to still have scares leftover from our punishment and like a football player could have lingering effects from CTE.

Things were wrapping up and it appeared that the night was coming to a mellow end. But then suddenly, just as we were readying to leave the hall, Mac came racing in and said that Rudy was at the bar and had too much to drink. According to Mac, just like in the old days, Rudy was ready to fight some big guy who appeared to have a large group of his friends ready to help take him down. I told Mac to go find Chase and the others and meet me at the bar.

As I reached the bar, I could see that Rudy was crazed about something and was ready to fight. Somehow he had gotten himself into a fix with these oversized fellows I had never seen before and the whole scene was somehow familiar being reminiscent of the old days. Would we have to fight our way out of the Knights of Columbus just as Rudy had to fight his way out of The Hotel Horner or as we fought our way out of Yaya's Pizza in 1966? As I stood there trying to determine what to do, Mac arrived with Chase, Anton, and Dirk followed by Rafael and G-Z. All we could see was Rudy encircled by a group of guys none of us recognized, continuing to talk jive, while a big tough looking screwball was rolling up his sleeves readying to pounce on Rudy.

Mac said for us all to just wait. Miraculously, out of nowhere, he formed an idea of how to extract Rudy and the rest of us from the messy situation. Mac first whispered into each of our ears and motioned for us to follow his lead. The first thing that happened was that Anton stood on a chair with the microphone. He began talking like Elvis, "Now listen up ladies and gentlemen," Anton, or should I say, Elvis, snorted into the mic. "I've got a last song, a request, to sing this evening and it goes out to all you nice people out there circling the bar," he went on. Next Anton began crooning Elvis' hit song, *Don't Be Cruel.* Soon after Anton began singing, Rafael entered the circle and began dancing with Katie directly between Rudy and the toughs just like in our old dance competitions from many years back. As the tough guys began to look confused, the crowd slowly started to pay more attention to the singing and dancing than the impending altercation.

Mac's turn was next. He looked straight into Rudy's face and using a beer bottle as a microphone began to loudly sing, *Baby I'm Yours,* by Barbara Lewis. The group of tough guys did not know what exactly to make of all these shenanigans but the humor sunk in long enough for Rudy's wife, Mary Lynn, to grab him by the collar and rush them both out of the place. Soon the rest of us joined Rudy on the way to the parking lot and we ran as if we were running from the cops during that mock "Gang" initiation. It began to feel like the old days only about 50 years later. We might have been in our sixties but our legs could still get us where we wanted to go. Furthermore, we were smarter than in 1969, smart enough to find a way around a fight rather than risk everything including injury for very little reason.

On The Road Again

As we simultaneously reached the car, Mary Lynn wisely tossed Rudy into the back seat and left the four of us out in the parking lot. As we sped out of the lot we nearly ran over G-Z and somehow slowed down long enough to lower the windows and raise our arms to yell, "The GANG," one last time. G-Z returned our farewell. We soon turned left passing the flashing lights of a police cruiser heading toward the Knights of Columbus Hall as we began cruising up the Avenue. Soon we would drive past that hill where the mock hazing took place, three blocks from the church where some of us played football and where I was clotheslined while running from the cops decades earlier. In approximately 50 more yards we would pass Yaya's Pizzeria on the left where we were tossed, like pizza dough, so many times. Next, immediately to the right and across the street was the former site where Sandy's Hamburgers used to be, the same spot where Luke got punched in the mouth leading us into our ill-fated Gents gang fight. Here we were, adults, escaping from the law one more time. As relief replaced excitement and as we began to feel safe, there was the realization that we had evaded another catastrophe, something the four of us learned many years before. That is when we spontaneously began to laugh hysterically. I had to admit that I had not felt so exhilarated since Rudy and I ran out of that diner without paying our bill when we were college students.

One by one the boys were delivered home safely. On the way, we made some empty plans to have breakfast together the next morning but each of us secretly knew that would be unlikely. Besides, from our conversations, I figured each of us had family obligations and plans to get back to our respective lives. Our night together was truly extraordinary. It is hard to describe the feeling of nostalgia the party imparted to me and from looking around at my old pals it left a joyous feeling in them too. With one brief phone call Mac did it, he brought us all together for one last fling.

Since that evening a few of us have met for dinner, funerals, or short visits. Each meeting can only be described as a gift. When we sit together, besides the joking there is a calm and an understanding between us that can only be gotten from old buddies. Somehow these feelings are not the same between friends acquired since those early days.

I know I am fortunate to have grown up where, when, and how I did. Times were not always easy but then I realize that perhaps my stories would not have been so memorable had things gone differently. What would life have been like had my parents not divorced? Would I have ever sat in front of Rudy at Harrison School? Would I have played football and had the opportunity to meet up with all those interesting guys on the team? Would Anton represent just one more Elvis impersonator? Would I have befriended Mac off the football field and worked with Rafael and Rudy delivering all the cheap furniture all over town? How about the opportunity to serve Chase the poop burger? Who knows for sure? Certainly, I am thankful for my old friends and for meeting people along the way who helped nudge me in the correct direction. Each of them, Mac, Chase, Luke, Rudy, Anton, Rafael, and most of the others fortunately also found someone who helped them make something of themselves as well. I also realize that by hanging together we served as each other's closest mentors. That is a little scary but it helped build some resiliency in each one of us.

But the real heroes for me, the ones who had the greatest influence on my character, were my grandparents, Giuseppe and Maria. I kiddingly say that thanks to my grandparents, I have trouble pounding a nail into a board, or even painting a rock but my homemade gnocchi is second only to Maryetti's. My grandmother, "mia nonna," protected me from physical labor while she taught me to be Italian, "Mangia." Hopefully, I do not push too much food on guests who eat at our table. I am known to make, as did Marrietta, enough food for there to be leftovers for guests to take home with them and I think that feeding the world is a good thing. Maybe I dabble in the kitchen to honor her, my grandmother, who knows? My grandparents were devoted to me, serving as my surrogate parents when they were most needed. Fortunately, even though I was a spoiled Italian prince they somehow imparted values that have stuck assisting me to hopefully treat other people right.

Last Lap

****

Stripes: “This is going to have to be my last lap. I have so much to do today.”

Hipster: “Know what you mean. So much stress, with ballet lessons and dinner to prepare. My in-laws are visiting. No idea what to cook but something like past...”

My grandmother never fully recovered from her old self after my wife and I spent that one day with her in her own home. Selling her possessions was simply too much for her to bare especially for someone whose mind was beginning to vanish. She was faced with a bad situation as she faded away but understood there was no better choice for her than to move. Her health and mind were beginning to fail and she disliked others making decisions for her. Proud, Muttietta hated feeling trapped into moving in with Dad and Hanna but where else could she live? While this was her best option, Grandma disliked losing all control over the few things that meant so much to her. She fought it. From cooking to cleaning to sharing her food with the world these would all soon become things of the past. She would only last two years with Dad and Hanna. Slowly, Grandma would wither both physically and mentally eventually needing to move one last time. Her last home would be a nursing home. Marietta would not realize it but I saw the irony in her placement as if it occurred through divine decree. Of all the senior care facilities dotting the city, she was placed in the home located right in front of the hill where our comical *Gang* hazing took place decades earlier. Was this place chosen by happenstance, certainly, but it seemed to complete a storyline providing an ending with an almost comical sort of meaning? When I recall that night on the hill I now pretend my grandmother was also watching our antics from her room in the home. "Jovy, watcha dah machine," I can imagine hearing her saying. I see her wearing the torn dress, and signature apron along with those black rubber boots still unzipped. In her hand is a large platter of pasta waiting for us to come inside and eat after the initiation. She would even invite the police in for a meal. "THE GANG," we would all yell. In a way, at least for me, she was always an honorary member of the club.

Grandma was lost when she entered the nursing home and perhaps this was best. The less she realized the better since understanding where she ended up would have been pure torture. While she died about four years after being admitted, on January 5, 1992, at age 90, she had given up on life the first day she entered. Her funeral was a blur but I vividly remember a couple of important things. I remember the endless flow of guests who came to pay their last respects to the one known as, Comare, Cooma, Zia, Aunt, Mrs., Mary, Muttietta, Maryetti, Muddyetta, Aunt Mary, Mee-etta, and so many other names. I recall most of those who attended especially my old pals and many of the recipients of Granny's generosity, like Jackie and Mr. Zucchero. I recall being surprised that so many people came even though Grandma had outlived all of her contemporaries. The biggest surprise of all was the attendance of a fellow named, Johnny Poltroni. Johnny was one of my father's best friends as he grew up. We had not seen much of Johnny in the last few years as he and his wife Anna used to be regulars around the house throughout the early days. John was a lively man and full of energy when he was young. He was also known for being full of boloni much of the time but that is what made him so interesting and fun. What I remembered most about Johnny was his focus on boxing as he was a Golden Gloves boxer as a teenager. After my mom and dad divorced he took a personal interest in teaching me the art of self-defense. I remembered John's exuberance while demonstrating for me, over and over, how to jab and throw a meaningful uppercut. As soon as I saw John poke his head around the corner at the funeral home saying, "Joey, is that you," I could almost hear the voice of my grandmother also chiming in,

"Ma tu sei pozzo, mio nipote non boxerà mai.," (Are you crazy, no grandson of mine will ever box?). John's praise of my jab was infectious when I was eight or maybe nine years old repeating many times over how he was sure I would be a great golden glove boxer one day. He made it a point each time he visited to put me through my paces volunteering to be my coach when I was old enough to enter the ring. While I enjoyed the attention I always knew Johnny was full of it and that day as an adult standing in the funeral home I silently thanked my grandmother for putting her foot down against any Golden Gloves involvement. Back then, John and my dad built up my ego leading me to believe that my punch was above average and that I could be the next Rocky Marciano. Grandma ended that notion just as she intervened against working with Orlando or owning the motorcycle. I may have been a fast puncher but standing no taller than 5'7" I would have been knocked around pretty well once I entered the ring. Johnny knew better than to push back against my grandmother's dictate since he was used to losing many similar arguments not only with Zia Muttietta but also with a host of other Italian matriarchs including his mother. I am sure his mother, one of my grandmother's closest friends, put an end to many of Johnny's crazy notions. Mrs. Poltroni died when I was perhaps four years old so I never got to know her very well but her memory was spoken of frequently around our house. She was spoken of so often as I grew up that it was as if she had never died. There was always a picture of Christ in our house and next to it was a picture of Mrs. Poltroni rather than The Virgin Mary. John was also wise enough to back off of the boxing preparation or suffer the "Maloik," that is, the "malocchio," or evil eye from Granny. Even people who were not superstitious did not want one of those curses laid on them by my grandmother. She did not get crazed often but when she did Grandma's reputation preceded her.

The other thing I remembered about Johnny was his wife, Anna. They did not have kids, and I never knew why, but I did know that Anna was especially fond of me, especially after my mom left town. Even as a kid, I sensed that her kindness toward me had something to do with not having a child of her own. Whenever possible she volunteered to read me a story before bed and see to it that I was securely tucked in. I always appreciated both her warmth and Johnny's praise. Seeing Johnny turn up at the wake was special, a welcomed surprise that brought back so many warm memories. He was a bright spot during a difficult time.

The other memory I cherish from Grandma's wake was seeing how our kids behaved, Jean's and mine. I enjoyed seeing the four of them getting along so well together because Jean and I failed miserably while growing up. I already confessed that I fault myself for that ill-fated contribution to our family's history. A smile still fills my face as I remember how our four children sat and played so nicely during the wake while the rest of us greeted well-wishers. Sitting there interacting so innocently, the four of them did not understand the reason for the sadness filling the room. Our children would not know how much they missed not knowing their great-grandmother. They would have to depend on stories to learn how much she affected their lives. They would have no notion of the history, good or bad, between Grandma and Hanna or Grandma and my mother. They would likely never hear the phrase, "Goodbye Jack," when a stray cup fell onto the floor and shattered. It was also unlikely that they would ever experience the same level of freedom allotted to me as I grew up. Regrettably, they would also not taste Grandma's pasta or experience her generosity either. We would, however, make sure that they learned the many tales associated with my grandparents' generosity and her love for family. Instead, it was our job to make sure the children sitting so nicely in that funeral home would indirectly reap the benefits of my grandparents' love. The world would miss Marietta and it would take years for our kids to understand why. My grandparents now lay side by side in a large cemetery on the outskirts of my hometown. If there is a heaven I hope there is a gas stove and an iron skillet where Grandma can fry a steak next to a large pasta pot necessary to boil her noodle while using up some of her canned tomatoes made from those grown in my grandfather's garden.

Life has been good for me, no regrets. From meeting up with the guys like Rudy, Paulie, Skeeter, and Mac to watching Elvis on Ed Sullivan with Anton, to the formation of the Gents and finally The Gang my life as a kid was super. More than one person has asked me how it is that I remember so many details from my early days growing up. I tell them how could I not. I also inform them that it helps to have an archivist like my old pal Mac and relive those days occasionally with my other old buddies as well. When life is so exciting memories flow and they simply stick. Now is there anything better than that?

Epilogue

Wandering around that living room gazing upon all the memorable items strewn about the floor was a melancholy experience. Nostalgia was at its peak for me. Most items were sold at auction and as predicted very little money was made. A few possessions were left over, not sold, and those that were left behind and considered unimportant were donated to charity. All was not lost, however. I was able to salvage a few things that to most people would mean nothing but to me they meant everything. I salvaged three things for myself. The first is a brick, buff in color, one that was left over from the construction of my grandparents' house built on the lake. My wife and I have moved the "silly brick" as she calls it from Ohio to New York, to Massachusetts and it now sits in our garage in Pennsylvania. Recently while researching this book I came across the second item, one that I had forgotten I possess. Looking through an old cedar chest I found my grandfather's pocket knife. It is a simple knife with a black plastic handle complete with scales or indentations on its side for decoration. As I looked more closely at the knife I realized for the first time that it still had dirt embedded in its scales. I could not help but touch the handle knowing that my grandfather transferred that dirt from his hands onto those decorative indentations. This occurred decades ago but there it was, dirt from way back still embedded in the knife's handle. That knife was in his pocket daily as he dug the earth behind their duplex on Lake Erie, behind the garage on 21st Street, and likely many of the other properties he owned through the years. Lastly and strangest of all I have a pair of my grandmother's boots. I have the last known pair of her boots, the ones she always wore around the house. The boots helped keep her feet warm but more importantly, they ended up defining her. Anyone who knew my Grandmother can visualize her wearing those ugly old floppy black boots as she tromped up and down her basement steps. I imagine that if I looked close enough that I could find particles of tomatoes and pieces of parsley lodged in the lining of those cheap black rubber soles. Seeing those crummy old boots transports me back to another time. Together those three items represent so many memories and are all I could grab on my way out of her house that one day. It has to be just enough for me. Oh by the way, I'll be back one d...

The end.

"Together at the birthday party, we were a group of old friends getting their picture taken standing out under the stars. We were not as fit as we were as teens but we were still trying to look so cool. We felt special again for sure as our group relived those old times together when we were just kids. Yet soon we would go back to our present lives, stash our memories, and return to acting our age. We would have had the chance to be, just for a few moments, young people again."

"Sedersi, mangiare, bere, è la tua casa,"

About me: Living in Sewickley, Pennsylvania by way of Ohio; Morgantown, West Virginia; Geneva, New York; and Wellesley, Massachusetts. Living in retirement up a steep road among the trees and the hills after a career serving as a school psychologist, an elementary school principal, and later as an academic coach. The best jobs, still paying wonderful dividends, are husband, father, and now grandfather.

CPSIA information can be obtained
at www.ICGtesting.com
Printed in the USA
LVHW041037140623
749653LV00005B/78

9 781958 889381